15 Summers Later

Books by RaeAnne Thayne

15 Summers Later
The Cafe at Beach End
All Is Bright
Summer at the Cape
Sleigh Bells Ring
The Path to Sunshine Cove
Christmas at Holiday House
The Sea Glass Cottage
Coming Home for Christmas
The Cliff House
Season of Wonder

Haven Point

Snow Angel Cove
Redemption Bay
Evergreen Springs
Riverbend Road
Snowfall on Haven Point
Serenity Harbor
Sugar Pine Trail
The Cottages on Silver Beach
Summer at Lake Haven

Hope's Crossing

Blackberry Summer
Woodrose Mountain
Sweet Laurel Falls
Currant Creek Valley
Willowleaf Lane
Christmas in Snowflake Canyon
Wild Iris Ridge

Look for RaeAnne Thayne's next novel
The December Market
available soon from Canary Street Press.

For a complete list of books by RaeAnne Thayne,
please visit raeannethayne.com.

15 Summers Later

RaeAnne Thayne

CANARY STREET PRESS

**CANARY
STREET
PRESS™**

Recycling programs
for this product may
not exist in your area.

ISBN-13: 978-1-335-14765-3

15 Summers Later

Canary Street Press
22 Adelaide St. West, 41st Floor
Toronto, Ontario M5H 4E3, Canada
CanaryStPress.com

Printed in U.S.A.

My deepest thanks to the staff
at Cache Employment and Training Center for their dedication and passion
toward improving the lives of people with disabilities.

1

The present is a delicate tightrope walk between liberation and the haunting memories that cling to us. The scent of freedom is both intoxicating and terrifying, and each step away from the compound feels like a small victory against the darkness that threatened to consume us.

—*Ghost Lake* by Ava Howell Brooks

Madison

"HERE, LET ME GET THAT FOR YOU. YOU SHOULDN'T be grabbing heavy bags of food off the shelf without help. You might hurt yourself, honey."

At the well-meaning but misguided efforts of her seventy-year-old neighbor, Madison Howell tried not to grind her teeth.

Under other circumstances, she might have thought the old rancher was being misogynistic, assuming any young woman was too fragile and frail to heft a fifty-pound bag of dog food onto her cart.

Unfortunately, she knew that wasn't the case. Calvin Warner simply thought *she* couldn't do it.

How could she blame him, when the majority of her neighbors shared his sentiments, believing she was forever damaged?

"It's fine. I've got it," she insisted, taking a firm hold of the bag.

"Now, don't be stubborn. Let me help you."

He set his cane aside—yes, he actually had a cane!—and all but shoved her out of the way.

Short of engaging in a no-holds-barred, Greco-Roman wrestling match right there in the farm supply store with a curmudgeon who had arthritis and bad knees, Madi didn't know what else to do but watch in frustration while he lifted the bag onto her large platform cart.

"Thank you," she said as graciously as she could manage. "Now I need five more bags."

"Five?" Calvin looked aghast.

"Yes. We have twenty-two dogs right now at the rescue. You don't need a new Aussie, do you? We have four from an abandoned litter."

"No. I'm afraid not. I'm a border collie man myself and I have three of them. Twenty-two dogs. My word. That must be a lot of work."

Yes, the work required to care for the animals at the Emerald Creek Animal Rescue was endless. All twenty-two dogs, ten cats, two llamas, three potbellied pigs, four goats, two miniature horses and a donkey required food, attention, medical care, exercise and, unfortunately, waste cleanup.

Madi didn't care. She loved the work and adored every one of their animals. After years of dreaming, planning, struggling, she considered it something of a miracle that the animal shelter was fully operational now.

For the past three months, Madi had been running full tilt, juggling her job as a veterinary tech as well as the hours and hours required to organize her team of volunteers, hire a full-time office assistant and do her part caring for the animals.

She was finally ready to take a huge leap of faith. In only a few more weeks, she would be quitting her job as a veterinary technician at the local clinic so that she could work full-time as the director of the animal rescue.

She tried to ignore the panic that always flickered through her when she thought of leaping into the unknown.

"The dogs are easy," she answered Calvin now. "Don't get me started on the goats and the potbellied pigs."

"I heard you were doing something over there at Gene Pruitt's old place. I had no idea you were up to your eyeballs in animals."

"Yes. We've started the first no-kill animal sanctuary in this area. Our goal is to take in any abandoned, injured or ill-treated animal in need, help rehabilitate them and place them in new homes."

He blinked in surprise, his bushy eyebrows meeting in the middle. "Is that right? Are there really that many animals in need of help in these parts?"

"Yes. Without question. We have no other no-kill shelters serving this area of Idaho. I'm grateful we have been able to fill that need."

For years, since finishing college and returning to Emerald Creek, Madi had been struggling to start the shelter. She had modest success applying for grants and seeking donations from various national and local donors, but it still seemed out of reach.

A year ago, the sanctuary had come closer than ever to reality when a crusty old local bachelor with no remaining family had left his twenty-acre farm, as well as a small house on the property, to the Emerald Creek Animal Rescue Foundation.

She was still overwhelmed at Eugene Pruitt's generosity.

Even so, it had taken an additional incredibly generous gift from an anonymous donor to truly allow them to be able to take care of the start-up operating expenses for the sanctuary without having to heavily mortgage the property.

As hard as she had worked to make her dream a reality, there were still plenty of people in town who would never see her as anything other than that poor Howell girl with the leg brace and the permanent half smile.

"Thank you for your help, Mr. Warner," she said, after the two of them managed to load up the platform cart.

He appeared slightly out of breath and his hand trembled as he reached for his cane. She shouldn't have let him help her. The strong, confident woman she wanted to be would have politely told him to move on. Thanks but no thanks. She could handle it, as she had been handling all the challenges that had come her way since her mother's death when she was twelve.

She had a fair distance to go before she truly was that strong, confident woman.

"Glad I could be here." Calvin gripped his cane. "You know, they have staff here that can give you a hand next time. They can probably help you take this out to your car. That's why they're here."

She forced a smile. "I'll keep that in mind. Thanks. And if you decide you need an Aussie, let me know. They're smart as can be and are all caught up on their shots. Dr. Gentry takes very good care of all of our animals at the sanctuary."

"He's a good man. Not quite the vet his father was, but he's getting there."

Before she could object on Luke's behalf and express that he was an excellent veterinarian in his own right, the rancher's eyes went wide and he suddenly looked horrified at his own words.

"I'm sorry. I wasn't thinking. Shouldn't have brought up old Doc Gentry with you."

Madi could feel each muscle along her spine tighten. "Why not?" she managed.

Calvin gave her a significant look. "You know. Because of… because of the book."

The book. That blasted book.

"The wife bought a copy the day it came out, after she saw all the buzz about it online. She's a good reader. Me, not so much. I like audiobooks, but we've been reading it together of an evening. It's awful, everything that happened to you."

Madi tightened her hands on the handle of the platform cart, fighting the urge to push it quickly toward the checkout stand.

The last thing she wanted to talk about was her sister's memoir, which had hit bookstores two weeks earlier and had become the runaway success of the summer, already going back for a third printing.

Madi didn't want to talk about *Ghost Lake*, to hear *other people* talk about it or to even *think* about it.

"Right. Well, thank you again for your help, Mr. Warner. I should get on with my sh-shopping."

Now she did tighten her hands on the cart, jaw tight.

She hated her stammer that sometimes came out of nowhere. She hated the way her mouth was frozen into a half smile all the time, how she only had partial use of her left hand and the way her leg sometimes completely gave out if she didn't wear the brace.

And she especially hated the way her sister had exposed their history, their past, their pain to the entire world.

"Take care," Calvin said, a gentleness in his gruff tone that made her somehow want to scream and weep at the same time.

"Thank you," she said, as graciously as she could manage, and then pushed the unwieldy cart toward the checkout stand.

She reached it as the woman seated on a high stool at the cash register slid a book with a familiar white-and-bloodred cover beneath the counter.

That blasted book was everywhere. She couldn't escape it.

"Hi there, Madi." Jewel Littlebear, whose family owned the feed store, gave her a nervous-looking smile, her gaze shifting in the direction of the book.

Jewel had been in Ava's grade at school. The two of them

had been friends once, before Madi's sister walked away from everything she once cared about here in Emerald Creek.

"Hi, Jewel. How are things? How are the boys?"

Jewell had three hellion sons. She and her family lived on the same street as Madi's grandmother, in a small ranch-style home where the front yard was covered in toys and bikes and basketballs.

"They're good. All three of them are playing baseball this summer. I swear, I spend more time over at the park watching their games than I do in my own house."

She smiled, rose from her stool and carried the handheld scanner around the counter so she could capture the codes on the large bags of food without Madi having to lift them onto the counter.

"Um. That will be a hundred sixty-five dollars and fifteen cents. I'm sorry."

What exactly was she sorry about? That the price of quality dog food was so high? Or that Madi had caught her reading That Book?

Madi decided not to ask. She swiped the rescue's credit card and felt a burst of pride when it went through easily.

A moment later, the register spit out her receipt, which Jewel handed over with a smile.

"There you go," she said, handing it to Madi.

"Thanks. I'll see you later."

She hadn't even walked away from the checkout counter before Jewell pulled the book back out and picked up where she had left off.

Was she reading about their mother's car accident and the raw, visceral pain their family went through afterward?

Or their father's steady but inexorable downward spiral into obsession, depression, mental illness?

Or those final horrible days when she and Ava, fourteen and sixteen respectively, had escaped a grim situation that had become impossible, only to find themselves in even worse circumstances?

She didn't want to know.

Madi hurried out to her pickup, the classic, if dilapidated, teal 1961 Chevrolet Stepside pickup she called Frank that she had inherited from her maternal grandfather.

A few months ago, she had ordered a vinyl-lettered sign for Frank's side, with the stylized teal-and-yellow logo for the animal sanctuary. Now she only used Frank for sanctuary errands and for social media purposes. It photographed wonderfully and helped raise awareness for their mission.

She had considered driving the pickup in the town's Fourth of July parade in a month, maybe with a few of the animals in crates in the bed, but now the idea made her slightly ill. She could imagine how everyone would point and talk about her now.

There goes poor Madi Howell. Did you read about what happened to her?

I knew she was odd, with her perma-smile and that limp and her curled-up hand. I guess now we know why.

Renewed fury at her sister broiled under her skin. She did her best to push it away as she maneuvered the big cart to her pickup and opened the tailgate.

Though there were several vehicles in the parking lot, none of them was occupied. At least she didn't have to fend off more offers of help.

She loaded the bags by herself into the back of the truck, then paused a moment to breathe away her stress, trying to focus instead on the glorious early June day, with the mountains green and verdant and still capped with contrasting white snow that had yet to melt at the higher elevations.

She dearly loved living in Emerald Creek. This small community a half hour from Sun Valley was home. She could never forget how warm and supportive everyone had been when she and Ava moved back to live with their grandmother Leona after everything that happened.

She had wonderful friends here, a job at the vet clinic that she had loved for eight years and now her passion project, the animal sanctuary.

She had never seriously considered living anywhere else.

But sometimes she had to wonder what it would be like to make her home in a place where she could be a little more... anonymous.

Did that place even exist, now that her sister had spilled their secret trauma to the whole blasted world?

She climbed into the cab of the pickup, fighting a headache, then drove away from the farm supply store, heading through town on her way toward the sanctuary.

It was a beautiful summer afternoon. A couple of older men sat on a bench, shooting the breeze outside the Rustic Pine Trading Post, and she saw a healthy line of tourists waiting for the always-busy Fern & Fir Restaurant to open.

As she turned onto Mountain View Road, she slowed down when she spotted a trio of girls on bicycles ahead of her. Four, she realized. One bike held two girls. She was aware of a quick, sharp ache. How often had she and Ava ridden together through the streets of their own town in eastern Oregon like that? Too many to count, but that was in the days before their mother died and everything changed.

She waved at the girls as she passed, recognizing Mariko and Yuki Tanaka as well as Zoe Sullivan and Sierra Gentry. Sierra and Zoe both volunteered at the animal rescue a few hours a week.

She pulled the truck over ahead of them, and the girls rode up beside her. "Hey, girls. What are you up to on this beautiful day?"

Sierra leaned into the open passenger window, her brown hair streaked with sunlight. "We were hanging out at my place and thought maybe we would ride to the Dixon's farm stand and grab some fresh strawberries."

"We really love strawberries," Zoe said with a giggle.

Madi strongly suspected the real draw wasn't so much the strawberries but Ash Dixon, the heartthrob fifteen-year-old whose family ran a popular farm stand and also had a stall at the Emerald Thumbs Farmers Market on Saturday mornings.

"Sounds like fun. Enjoy a crepe for me."

"I will. Bye, Mad. See you later."

She waved and put the truck in gear again, though before she drove away she thought she heard the words *book* and *Ghost Lake* from the girls, through her open window.

No. She was imagining things. That damn book seemed to be popping up everywhere…but only a narcissist would think everyone in town was talking about her, right?

2

I am a coward. It is a grim, humbling realization for someone who has always considered herself strong.

—*Ghost Lake* by Ava Howell Brooks

Ava

EVERYONE IN TOWN SEEMED TO BE STARING AT HER.

As she drove down Main Street in Emerald Creek, Idaho, Ava told herself she was being ridiculous. Why would they possibly be staring at her?

She had only lived in Emerald Creek with her grandmother for a few years, between the ages of sixteen and eighteen, and had been away for more than a decade, with only the occasional visit home. She probably didn't know all that many people who still lived here and those who *did* know her likely wouldn't recognize her anymore.

When she drove past the new-and-used bookstore, Meadowside Book Nook, she almost drove into the back of a big black dually pickup truck ahead of her.

Out of the corner of her gaze, Ava's attention had been caught by the window display at the bookstore. The entire front window featured the red-and-white cover of *Ghost Lake*, with that moody line drawing of a mountain lake.

Oh, this was bad. Really bad.

Madi must be so furious with her.

What did her sister think when she drove past this display every day?

Maybe she hadn't noticed it.

Ava knew that was a ridiculous hope. Of course Madi would have noticed it. And she was probably angry every single time she saw it.

Ava knew from her grandmother Leona in one of their frequent Zoom calls that Madi was furious about the book.

She didn't quite understand why. It wasn't as if Madi hadn't known it was coming. Ava had tried to give her sister plenty of warning the book was releasing in late May.

When she first began to realize herself that her book's journey toward publication was actually happening—and much faster than she'd ever imagined—Ava had been upfront with her sister.

Six months earlier, Ava had sent her an advanced reading copy of the manuscript, then she waited for a response. And waited. And waited.

When she nervously called a few weeks later, her stomach tangled with nerves, Madi had been nonchalant, even blasé. She had made excuses about how busy she was, still working at the vet clinic while trying to organize all the details to open the Emerald Creek Animal Rescue.

"Anyway, I lived it," Madi had finally said as their awkward conversation drew to a close. "I'm sorry, but once was enough. I don't really need to go over everything again."

Ava should have pushed her to read the book. She should have made sure Madi wouldn't be blindsided when the book started to receive prepublication buzz.

How could Ava have known everything would explode as it

had? Everyone involved with the book had high hopes it would succeed, but even her publisher had to rush back to print more copies in order to keep up with demand.

Ava's hands were tight on the steering wheel as she drove through town and finally pulled into the driveway of her grandmother's two-story house, with its extravagant, colorful garden in full bloom.

She was relieved when she didn't see Madi's small SUV or their grandfather's ancient pickup truck her sister drove occasionally.

Ava would have to face her sister at some point. Not yet, though. She was far too exhausted to deal with Madi right now. After she had rested, maybe. She was tired enough to sleep for a week, though she wasn't sure even that would be enough to ease her bone-deep fatigue.

When she climbed out of the vehicle, her bones ached and nausea roiled through her.

She swallowed it down as she spied her grandmother working in one of the gardens near the house, wearing a floppy straw hat and a pair of overalls.

Her grandmother wore earbuds, her back to Ava, humming along as she clipped back her bleeding hearts. She probably hadn't even noticed the car pull in, Ava realized when her grandmother didn't come to greet her.

She moved in that direction and a German shepherd mix suddenly rose from the porch and gave a single bark. Ava froze, instant panic washing over her, icy and raw. After a few seconds, she forced herself to relax. That was only Oscar. He wouldn't hurt her.

She hoped.

The dog's greeting must have alerted Leona to her company. Her grandmother turned around, and Ava saw the shock in her eyes before Leona dropped her pruning scissors with a shriek and rushed toward her, arms outstretched.

"Ava! Darling! What are you doing here? Why didn't you call to tell me you were coming? Oh, my dear. It's so wonderful to see you, even though you're far too thin."

Leona reached her and wrapped those arms around her tightly, and Ava wanted to sink into the comfort of her embrace.

What would her grandmother do if Ava simply rested her head on her shoulder and wept and wept and wept?

Leona seemed to sense something was wrong. She pushed Ava away from her and studied her closely, blue eyes behind her thick glasses missing nothing. Ava faced her, aware of the deep circles under her eyes, the lines of fatigue she knew must be sharply etched on her features.

"What is it? What's wrong?"

So much. Everything.

She couldn't tell her grandmother yet. She would, but she needed time to figure out the words.

"I need somewhere to stay for a few weeks. Maybe even all summer. Would that be all right?"

Concern and alarm flashed over Leona's wrinkled features. "You know you're always welcome, my dear. And Cullen as well. Is he joining you?"

The sound of her husband's name was like a stiletto to her heart and it was all she could do to remain standing.

"No," she managed. "He won't be joining me. Cullen is working on a dig up in the mountains near here this summer. Some fossilized bones were found on national forest land and Cullen and his team think it might be an entirely new dinosaur species."

She tried to be casual with the words and not spill them all out in a rush. "He's ecstatic to be leading the team. It's a dream come true for him. You know what a dinosaur nerd he is."

"Indeed." Leona smiled, though that worry lingered in her gaze. "It's a good thing he likes them. It would be odd if he didn't, since he teaches paleontology. What a wonderful opportunity."

"Yes. I'm thrilled for him. We're both hoping this might help him make full professor, with tenure."

"How exciting!"

"Yes. But he'll be mostly out of reach for the summer and I... I didn't want to stay by myself at our apartment in Portland. After only a few days, I couldn't stand it, so I packed up everything and headed here. I hope that's okay."

She couldn't find the words to tell her grandmother that her marriage might be as dead as those fossils.

"Oscar and I would be delighted to have you stay with us. Won't we, Oscar?"

The dog's tongue lolled out as he studied her. Oscar. Why hadn't she remembered her grandmother and the dog were a package deal?

Every time she visited, she felt as if he were watching her out of eyes as sharp as Leona's, waiting for his moment to swoop in and attack.

The dogs are growing closer. I can hear them baying from the next ridgeline. Could our scent carry that far? I have no idea, nor do I think I can ask Madi to go through the river again to try disguising our path. We have crossed it dozens of times already. Each time, more of her minuscule energy seems to burn away.

They bark again and my heart pounds so loudly, remembering sharp teeth, slavering tongues, wild eyes. Surely the dogs can hear each pulse of my blood, each ragged breath.

She quickly pushed away the memory, the words.

"Thanks, Grandma Leelee."

Her grandmother's features softened at the nickname Ava had come up with for her as a toddler.

"You're welcome, darling. You can stay in your old room upstairs. I'll have to move a few storage boxes out. I've been clearing out closets of all my old crap and have put everything in your room so I only have to make one trip to Goodwill eventually."

"You don't have to move anything. I can work around some boxes."

"It's no problem. I'll put them in your sister's room for now, since she's living full-time at the farmhouse on the animal rescue property these days."

Ava tensed at her sister's name, though Madi hadn't left her thoughts since she rolled into town. "How is she doing?" she asked, her voice low.

Leona brushed dirt off her overalls. "Well, you're not exactly her favorite person right now. Let's put it that way."

She swallowed hard. "I told her about the book. I sent her an advanced copy. She had plenty of warning."

"Yes. She knew it was coming. But you know Madi. She tends to focus on what's directly in front of her. She's been so busy trying to get the animal rescue off the ground, I think it was easier for her to put your book out of her head and pretend it wasn't really happening. Now that it's out, she can't escape it."

She had known the publication of her memoir detailing their months in the mountains and all the events leading up to it would be a pivotal event in her life. She hadn't realized how every single one of her relationships would be impacted, from her casual friendships to the guy who used to fill up her car with gas to her fellow faculty members at the middle school where she taught English.

She wasn't sure her marriage could ever recover.

You never told me half of the things you went through.

Cullen's voice seemed to echo through her memory, stunned and upset and...hurt as he looked down at his copy of *Ghost Lake* as if it were a viper that had suddenly invaded their bed.

I feel like I've been married to a stranger for the past three years.

He had been the one to suggest they use their separation

while he was working in the remote mountains near here to figure out what sort of future they could salvage.

I love you, Ava. That hasn't changed. But I think we both need time to figure out where we go from here.

Her entire world was falling apart because of the words she had written. The same stark, painful honesty that seemed to resonate with the rest of the world now threatened to destroy the two things she held most dear, her relationship with her sister and her marriage to Cullen Brooks.

"Come on. Let's get you settled before you fall over," Leona said with a warm smile that made Ava again want to weep.

Her grandmother carried her laptop case into the house while Ava followed behind with her suitcase.

The house smelled of vanilla and strawberry pie, scents that made her stomach rumble with the reminder that she hadn't had anything but a few crackers since dinner the evening before.

This trip had been completely impulsive. Reckless, even. After spending three nights alone in their apartment in Portland, she decided she couldn't take the echoing silence another moment. That very morning she had awoken gritty-eyed from a night of tossing and turning. One moment, she had been brushing her teeth, the next, she'd grabbed her suitcase out from under the bed and started throwing in everything she thought she might need.

After talking to her neighbor about keeping an eye on things and picking up their mail, Ava headed out, stopping only twice during the entire nine-hour drive for gas.

What else could she do? She couldn't go ahead with the book tour, pretending everything was fine when her entire world felt...broken.

She should have told Cullen everything. She supposed she had hidden the truth because some part of her wanted, like Madison, to pretend none of it had happened. To pretend they were two average girls with an average childhood whose average parents each had died tragically, a few years apart.

That last part was certainly true, though only a small measure of the whole, complicated, messed-up story.

One could make the argument that the first part, about two average girls living an average childhood, was true as well… until the summer she turned fourteen and Madi turned twelve, when their mother died and everything changed.

Being here, in her mother's childhood home, only made her miss Beth all the more. Her mother had exemplified quiet strength and grace. She had been kind to everyone, the kind of person who drew others to her, eager to warm themselves in the bright light of joy that burned within her.

Ava missed her every single day.

Her phone rang as she carried her suitcase to the room that had been hers for the final two years of high school.

After sharing a room with her sister all her life, this room had been the first one Ava could claim as exclusively her own, and that was only because Madi's room downstairs had to be outfitted for all the things she needed to help her rehabilitation.

She pushed the memories away and pulled out her phone. Her literary agent, she saw when she checked the display.

Sylvia Wittman was a lovely woman who absolutely wanted the best for Ava. At this particular moment, they couldn't quite agree on what that was.

She sighed and let the call go to voicemail, as she had all the others that day.

Sylvia was no doubt calling with news about the various film and TV offers that had already come their way or to let her know some other book club wanted to feature *Ghost Lake*.

Most writers would consider it a dream come true to see their work go viral and generate so much interest on the national and international stage.

Ava supposed she wasn't most writers.

She only wanted to pull her old comforter off the bed, carry it to the closet and hide in the corner until all of this went away.

Tomorrow. She would deal with everything tomorrow, after she had the chance to sleep away this exhaustion that had seeped into her bones, her sinews.

Then she would have to figure out if there was anything she could do to fix her marriage or the rift with her sister...or if the wounds she had inflicted on the people she loved through her words could ever heal.

3

Blood stains the earth beneath us as the reality of our escape becomes painfully tangible. The pursuit of freedom comes at a terrible cost.

—Ghost Lake by Ava Howell Brooks

Luke

IF HE WASN'T CAREFUL, HE WAS IN DANGER OF BEING kicked in the groin by a goat.

Luke Gentry shifted positions as he tried to hold tight to the annoyed animal. "I'm not going to hurt you," he murmured. "I'm trying to help so you can walk better and without pain. I promise, you'll be happier when I'm done."

He continued talking nonsense to the goat as he trimmed her hooves carefully.

For a long time, he hadn't been sure this was the career choice for him. While he had always loved animals and never minded helping out at his father's veterinary clinic, he had resented everyone's automatic assumption that he would naturally want to follow in Dan Gentry's footsteps.

Luke once had other dreams. He had wanted to become an

adventurer, to rock climb all the highest peaks in the world and ski the steepest slopes.

He hadn't really cared where, he had only known he hadn't wanted to be tied down here in Emerald Creek, Idaho.

Em-C, as the locals called it, was a pretty little town with plenty of recreational activities, but it had always felt too small to hold all his dreams. The world was so much bigger than this community of genuine ranchers and farmers as well as outdoor lovers and weekend cowboys near Sun Valley.

Over the years, his perspective had changed. He loved being the town's only veterinarian, building his home and his career here with his daughter, and couldn't imagine his life any other way—as long as this goat didn't manage to emasculate him, anyway.

He finally finished the last hoof and released Martha. "There you go. All done. See? That wasn't so bad."

The goat bleated at him and retreated to the other side of the pen. He opened the pen door to the outside and she escaped with a high-spirited leap into the Idaho sunshine.

He was heading to the office inside the Emerald Creek Animal Rescue barn when the double doors burst open and Madison Howell burst through, almost staggering under a large bag of dog food that probably weighed half as much as she did.

Luke had to fight down his instinctive urge to take it from her. He knew Madi well enough to know that probably wasn't a good idea.

She dropped the bag inside the barn and straightened, arching her back. Her features brightened when she spotted him. "Luke! Hey! I didn't expect you to drop by this evening, after you've already had a long day."

"So have you," he pointed out. He knew that all too well, since she was a veterinary technician in his clinic when she wasn't hauling dog food around here at the animal rescue. "I had a free few hours, so I swung in to check on Barnabas's injury and take care of Martha's hooves. He's doing fine and Martha should be good now and ready to rock and roll."

She gave her half smile, the one that always managed to brighten his entire day.

"Thanks. I could tell they were bothering her."

"She was a trouper, for the most part." He nodded toward the bag she set down against the wall. "Do you have a lot to unload?"

"Four more bags. That was all they had at the feed store."

"I can help you bring it in. Might as well at least save you a few trips."

Predictably, Madi looked as if she wanted to argue. Stubborn thing. She could be as obstinate as that goat, though he would never dare verbalize such a thing to her.

Finally, she bit her lip, the side that didn't lift. "Thanks," she said instead.

Her vintage pickup looked cheerful in the fading sunlight, all teal and yellow. Looking at the truck made him smile almost as much as looking at Madison did.

Luke hefted a bag over each shoulder and carried them back into the barn and set them against the wall, where she added the one she had carried.

"I'll grab the last bags."

He thought she would argue, but she only nodded. "Leave one in the truck, if you would. It's for Leona's dog. I'll run it over later tonight or in the morning."

When he returned to the barn, he discovered she was cradling a small calico kitten. He was familiar with all the sanctuary animals as he usually gave them a health exam when they first arrived. He didn't recognize the kitten.

"Where did you find this one?"

"On my way back from the feed store, I got a call from Charla Pope. She found a stray kitten mewling in her flower bed, with no sign of the mama cat anywhere. It's been there since last night. I stopped on my way home and the poor thing looks half-starved."

Madi had an uncanny knack for locating stray creatures. He suspected they were drawn to her, sensing a friend and savior.

She hadn't changed. She still tried to bring home every stray animal she could find, only now she did it officially, through the auspices of the Emerald Creek Animal Rescue.

"Want me to take a look at it?"

She gave him her unique smile, her eyes bright with gratitude. "Do you mind?"

"Not at all. I've got time. Let's take her into the exam room."

Still cradling the tiny kitten, Madi picked up her laptop from the office before following him into the small treatment room at the center.

She opened her laptop and created a treatment file for the kitten. "Want to name her?" she asked him.

He was lousy at picking animal names. "You rescued her. Go ahead."

She studied the kitten. "How about we call her Callie for now?"

"Sounds good."

She typed a few things onto the screen, with so much efficiency it was easy to miss how her left hand had a slight contracture and didn't work the same as her right did. It was nerve damage from injuries sustained fifteen years ago, but Madi didn't let it bother her.

He handled the animal with gentleness as he weighed it first and measured its size, reporting all those numbers for Madison to record.

"I don't see any sign of obvious disease or injury," he said after his initial exam. "She appears healthy, if a little malnourished."

"How old do you think she is?"

"Pure guesswork, but I would estimate her to be about five or six weeks old."

"That's what I was thinking. So no vaccinations for a few weeks and she's also old enough to be weaned."

"Yes, but I would still feed her kitten milk replacement along with some soft kitty chow."

"I've got some at the house. That sounds like a good plan."

"I'm going to guess she's part of a feral litter somewhere. Doesn't Charla's neighbor down the road have barn cats? Maybe this one wandered away. Or maybe something happened to the mother."

"You're probably right. I'll put the word out to Charla and others in her neighborhood to keep an eye out for any more strays. Thank you for taking a look."

"I'm happy to, but you didn't really need me."

She shrugged. "You're the professional."

"So are you."

For him, veterinary medicine was his vocation. For Madi, caring for animals was her calling. She adored them, with a depth of compassion that never failed to astonish him.

"On paper, I'm the vet, maybe," he went on. "But you know exactly what to do. You can handle anything, whether I'm here or not."

She made a face. "Tell that to everyone in town who doesn't think I am capable of even carrying a bag of dog food. Cal Warner insisted on loading my cart today. I'm not sure he even felt like I was capable of holding his cane, what with my fragile condition. And Ava has not helped matters at all with her stupid book."

Frustration shimmered off her in waves. "She has made everything so much worse. Why did she have to go and open up all those old wounds? We were doing fine."

He wasn't entirely certain that was true. Madi presented a

calm, happy front to the world, but Luke knew she had deep scars she hid from nearly everyone.

He felt fortunate to be one of the few people able to know the real Madison.

"Who did you catch reading it this time?"

"Calvin told me he and his wife were reading it together. And Jewel Littlebear at the feed store hid a copy below the counter when I checked out. I don't know why she bothered. I could still see it. Isn't everyone in town reading it?"

"Not quite everyone."

His phone rang and he glanced at the display. "That's Sierra. She's not reading it."

"No. But I think her friends are," Madi said darkly. "Or at least her friends' family members."

His phone rang again and she gestured to it. "You should get that. I saw her on my way here with her friends. They looked like they were having fun."

While she returned to the office and set down the kitten to explore her surroundings, he answered his daughter's call.

"Hey, Sierra. What's up?"

"Can I stay over at Zoe's house tonight?"

He frowned. "I thought we talked about heading into town and grabbing takeout sandwiches and then hiking up to Hidden Falls for a picnic."

"I know and I still really want to do that. But Zoe has to leave tomorrow to stay with her dad in Utah for six whole weeks. She'll be gone forever. This is, like, our last chance to hang out all summer. We wanted to do a slumber party with Mari and Yuki. Her mom says it's okay and she'll be home with us the whole night and so will Zoe's grandma."

Zoe's parents' divorce had not been amicable, he knew. Her mom currently lived with Zoe's grandmother across town.

"Sure. That's fine. I can give you a ride."

"No need. I have my bike. I'm going to grab a few things at

the house and put them in my backpack and head over now. Thanks, Dad. Love you. Bye."

"Love you back," he answered.

The click of the phone told him she had already hung up. He felt fortunate she had remembered to say goodbye as she was usually heading off in a dozen different directions.

He felt again that little tug at his heart. His baby girl was growing up. For the past four years, since her mother's death, they had been a pretty self-contained unit. He couldn't say it was them against the world, as he would have been lost without all the help from his mother and sister, as well as dear friends like Madi.

He and Sierra had a tight bond, though, and he always looked forward to the rare times they were able to hang out, only the two of them.

Apparently that wasn't going to happen that evening as he had hoped.

His sigh did not go unnoticed by Madi. "Sounds like you got stood up. Does Sierra have hot plans?"

"She wants to spend the night over at Zoe's place with Mariko and Yuki. Why not? That's much more fun than hanging out with her boring old man."

"I don't think she would agree. You know she adores you. Sounds like she got a better offer, though."

"Right. I can't really compete with a night of watching You-Tube videos and practicing TikTok dances."

"Sorry about that." She gave her half smile. "You can always come to the Burning Tree with me and Nic tonight. The Rusty Spurs are playing. Should be a wild time. If you want to play the boring-old-man card, you can be our designated driver."

He snorted. "I don't think you and my sister really want a chaperone, do you?"

"No. Absolutely not," she said, so quickly he had to smile. "But you can still come with us, have a drink, listen to the music. You deserve some fun in your life, Luke. Consider it self-care."

"I'll think about it, Dr. Howell," he said, though he expected *thinking about it* was all he would do. He would probably spend the night popping some popcorn and enjoying a beer and a baseball game.

Not a bad Friday night, in his opinion. Did that make him sound pathetic?

"Thanks again for your help," Madi said as they both headed out of the barn. The kitten was once more tucked into her bag.

"You're welcome."

Outside, the shadows of the late afternoon were long, with golden light that gleamed in the treetops and danced in her hair.

"Seriously," she said when they reached his truck. "You should come out tonight. The band starts playing at eight. If you don't want to drive us, you can meet us there. That way if you want to leave early, you won't feel trapped."

He shook his head, hand on the door frame of his blue pickup truck. "When did this become a done deal?"

"Admit it, Luke. You could use a night out. You work too hard. When you're not working, you're taking care of Sierra or helping out here at the animal rescue. Tell me the truth. When was the last time you did something simply because you wanted to?"

He snorted. "Who said I want to go hang out at a noisy bar with a bunch of half-drunk cowboys?"

"Plus your sister and me," she pointed out. "We'll be there, too. Don't you want to hang out with us, outside of work?"

"You're not going to let this go, are you?"

She grinned. "You'll have fun, I promise. It's better than sitting home on your own, watching some kind of lame sports ball."

"I happen to enjoy watching lame sports ball."

"I know, but how often do you get to watch live music surrounded by two hundred neighbors and strangers?"

"You're not exactly selling this."

"Your first drink is on me."

His mouth quirked. "Oh, why don't you say so? If free booze is involved, how can I say no?"

She laughed. "We'll save a spot for you at our table. See you there. Wear your dancing boots."

He didn't happen to own dancing boots. Or any other kind, except hiking boots, which probably wouldn't be too helpful on a dance floor.

"I'll see," he said, but she was already walking up the graveled pathway that led to the farmhouse where she lived with his sister.

4

One harrowing night, we find ourselves scrambling up a rocky scree, loose stones cascading beneath our feet. The jagged terrain threatens to betray us, and I feel my sister's hand slip from mine as we stumble and slide down the unforgiving slope. Bruised and battered, we rise again, our determination unbroken.

—*Ghost Lake* by Ava Howell Brooks

Madison

AFTER GREETING HER DOGS, MABEL AND MO, WHO were both eager to see her at the end of a long day, Madi settled the kitten into a small crate in her bedroom, still smiling about her encounter with Luke.

She had no idea if he would actually come that night to the Burning Tree. She hoped so. He really did need to let go.

The man was fiercely dedicated to his patients, his family and his community. She wasn't sure he had even dated anybody since his wife, Johanna, died four years earlier. If so, he had kept it quiet from everyone, even his family. Madi was quite certain his sister would have told her, if Nicki had known.

What would she have done without him in her life? It was a question she often thought about.

For one thing, she never would have been able to open the rescue. Luke and his semiretired partner, Ray Gonzales, both insisted on providing care free of charge to the animals who wound up at the sanctuary. Whenever she encountered something unusual or out of her comfort zone, Luke was always willing to drop everything and come to the rescue.

Luke sat on the board of the Emerald Creek Animal Rescue Foundation and had also been instrumental in convincing Eugene Pruitt, a huge animal lover and conservationist, to donate his property for the animal rescue.

She owed Dr. Gentry a gigantic debt.

Her smile faded as memories pushed in. Her debt to Luke and the rest of his family was mammoth, so enormous she knew she would never be able to repay it.

She was continually amazed that his entire family—Luke, Nicki, their brother, Owen, their mother, Tilly, even Sierra—was so willing to accept and embrace her. By all rights, the Gentrys should hate her. Because of her, their family had suffered a loss so profound, they were still bereft, fifteen years later.

Why didn't they hate her?

She had wondered that often over the past fifteen years. No one could blame them, especially after reading Ava's stupid book, which painted the whole story in bitter, painful detail.

The reminder of *Ghost Lake* soured her mood all over again.

She had been foolish to think everything would blow over. When Ava first told her about the book, originally written as her master's thesis, Madi had stupidly assumed it would be one of those dusty academic tomes nobody ever bothered to read.

Yet one more thing she had been wrong about.

Instead, the world had embraced the story about two lost girls trying to survive amid people, groups and circumstances beyond their control.

Madi glanced at her watch. She still had two hours before she needed to be ready to go out that night with Nicole. That would give her plenty of time to stop by and drop off the dog food for her grandmother and maybe squeeze in a quick visit.

After making sure the kitten was now sleeping in her crate, she grabbed her truck keys from the wooden bowl on the counter.

While she typically used her own small SUV as it had better gas mileage, she loved every chance to climb behind the wheel of her grandfather's old pickup truck. Driving it provided plenty of exercise, working the clutch and the gearshift, plus it was a moving advertisement for the sanctuary, keeping it fresh on the minds of townspeople and tourists alike. Only a few weeks ago, she had received a lovely Venmo donation given by a tourist couple from Virginia who had seen her out and about in the truck and subsequently researched the mission of the organization.

The evening was mild, with a light breeze blowing down out of the Sawtooths. The old truck did not have air-conditioning, so she drove with the windows down and the wind blowing through her hair. By the time she reached her grandmother's house on Elkridge Drive, she felt almost sanguine about the world.

Her grandmother had a visitor. A small sporty SUV she didn't recognize, with Oregon plates, was parked in the driveway behind Leona's old four-door sedan. Madi parked in front of the house so she didn't block the other car from leaving if the visitor needed to go.

She hefted the bag of dog food in both hands, ignoring the pain in her weak leg at the weight, then carried it up the long sidewalk to the house.

Madi propped the bag next to the door and walked in without knocking. Leona would have been offended, especially as this had been Madi's de facto home since that summer fifteen years ago.

After college in Boise, she had returned to live with her

grandmother for a few years, until she and Nicki rented a basement apartment together from a friend of Tilly's about three years ago. They'd both been happy to move out of the basement to Gene Pruitt's old farmhouse, despite all the work they still needed to do at the place.

To her surprise, Leona was not in the living room chatting with a friend, as Madi expected, or in the kitchen, sitting over a cup of coffee and a piece of huckleberry pie, though she did find Oscar, Leona's German shepherd mix. She petted the dog, her concern growing.

Had she missed her grandmother out in the lush garden somewhere? She didn't think so. And if she were in the garden, she would have had Oscar with her, since the dog loved being out in the yard.

Leona wasn't in the living room, either, Madi found. As she stood trying to figure out the mystery, she suddenly heard muted voices from upstairs. It sounded as if they were coming from the bedroom Ava had used for the two years they had lived here together, before her sister left for college in Oregon.

With a vague sense of foreboding that seemed to spring up out of nowhere, Madi walked up the stairs, trying to identify the other female voice speaking with her grandmother.

As she reached the top of the staircase, her unease ratcheted up as the voice became clearer.

"I really am sorry about the mess," Leona was saying. "Once we clear out these boxes, you'll be able to find the bed."

"I told you, we don't have to move anything," a second voice, now familiar, said. "Especially not tonight. I'm fine working around them. I only need a bed and a desk and maybe a few drawers for my things."

A hot wave of fury mingled with disbelief washed over Madi.
No.
It couldn't be.
Not here.

She should have known when she saw the Oregon plates.

Catching her breath, she moved to the doorway of Ava's old room, where she found her beloved grandmother, usually a source of unending support and love, consorting with the enemy.

Leona was poking through boxes while Ava sat on the bed, blonde and lovely and traitorous.

They both must have sensed her presence. They looked up simultaneously, and if she hadn't been so stunned, Madi might have been amused at their reaction.

Leona looked apprehensive, her eyes widening and her gaze flitting between the two sisters, as if she expected them to start pulling hair any minute.

For one brief instant, Madi almost thought Ava looked terrified before she blinked away any emotion, returning to the cool, composed stranger she had become over the years, at least to her.

"What is she doing here?" she demanded of her grandmother, her voice harsh. She didn't trust herself to say a word to Ava yet.

"Good news." Leona's voice took on a chipper edge, though her expression remained wary. "Your sister has come back to Emerald Creek for an extended stay. Isn't that wonderful?"

Wonderful? Madi could think of a dozen words that fit the situation far better than that particular one.

"Why?"

Her voice sounded gruff, ragged, as if she had scooped up a handful of pebbles from the garden walkway and swallowed them all on her way inside.

Leona appeared at a loss for a long time, as if words had escaped her.

Finally, Ava spoke up. "Cullen is working on an excavation in the Sawtooth Mountains about an hour from here. Rather than stay by myself at our apartment in Portland over my summer break, I…thought it would be nice to spend some time with Grandma. Plus this way, I'll be closer to him."

She was lying. While in many ways, her sister was a complete stranger these days, Madi still knew her well enough to sense when she was skirting around the whole truth.

Ava's tells hadn't changed. When she lied, she shifted her gaze away and blinked about twice as often as usual.

After everything the two of them had survived together, Madi once thought they would always have an unbreakable bond, forged through fear and loss.

She could not have been more wrong.

"You don't b-belong here anym-more."

Madi screwed her eyes closed, hating that whenever she was upset, the connection between her brain and her words seemed slippery and undependable.

Communication skills had never been her strong suit. Surviving a bullet to the brain certainly hadn't helped matters.

Ava ignored her stammer, giving her a cool look in return. "I don't believe that is your decision to make. This is our grandmother's house and she welcomed me into her home."

"Grandma, seriously?" Madi exclaimed, filled with frustration and helplessness, feelings that were only too familiar. "How c-can you even let her in the house after everything she has d-done!?"

"Madison Howell. That's enough. This is your sister. She will always be your sister, just as she will always be my daughter's oldest child and welcome in my home."

Leona didn't take that firm tone with Madi very often. It made her feel like a child being scolded, not a fully capable adult with eminently reasonable objections.

"I know she's your granddaughter. But she certainly was n-not thinking about you, Mom or me when she decided to spill our family's story to the entire world."

Once more, she thought she saw a flicker of raw emotion in

her sister's green eyes, one of the few physical traits they shared. It disappeared so quickly, she couldn't be sure.

"Don't tell me what I was or was not thinking about when I wrote *Ghost Lake*," Ava said quietly, her voice expressionless.

Who was this cool, composed stranger in her sister's body? She knew Ava could be passionate, fierce, when the situation demanded it. Madi was grimly aware she wouldn't be alive right now if not for her sister's determination and pluck.

She missed that sister.

"I hear your book is a runaway *New York Times* bestseller. Congratulations."

She did not bother to mask the bitterness in her tone.

"Thank you," Ava said. "I'm thrilled."

She sounded far from it, though Madi wasn't quite sure why.

"I'm sure you are. You're our town celebrity now, aren't you? Have you seen the d-display at the bookstore? It's quite impressive. Too bad I'm the one who has to live here and deal with the fallout from your runaway b-bestseller."

Ava said nothing, though her jaw tightened.

"I can't walk through the grocery store without people wanting to s-stop and talk to me about the book. Did you know that? And every single volunteer at the animal rescue seems to be reading it. How thrilling it all must be for you."

"Stop." Leona's voice held a warning that Madi couldn't ignore. "I know you are upset with your sister right now. I understand. But she is still your sister and I have invited her to stay with me as long as she would like. When you're here, within the walls of my house, I expect you to be civil to each other."

She glowered. "I can't believe you're choosing her s-side!"

"I'm not choosing anyone's side." Leona's voice was soft but firm. "I love you both and I hate seeing this book come between you."

"I'll remind you that I am n-not the one who chose fame and fortune over family loyalty."

"Would you like to stay for dinner, Madison?" Leona asked, a slightly desperate edge to her voice. "I'm making that chicken pasta bake you like so much."

Her stomach growled suddenly, reminding her she hadn't eaten nearly enough that day.

She did love her grandmother's cooking, but the thought of eating in the same kitchen as her sister took away any hunger pangs. She found a petty satisfaction in seeing her sister's features turn slightly green at the mention of food.

Maybe Ava's guilty conscience was making her queasy. It was exactly what she deserved.

"I don't think so. I'm suddenly not very hungry," she said, her tone flat. "Anyway, I need to go. Nicki and I have plans."

"I meant to remind you that Sunday is our monthly get-together with the Gentrys. Six o'clock. Don't forget."

Leona and Tilly Gentry Walker, Luke's mother, had been friends for years, long before the events of that August fifteen years ago linked their families together forever.

Usually Madi looked forward to their monthly dinner, when the people she loved most were all gathered in one place.

Would Ava ruin even that?

She wouldn't let her, Madi vowed. Her sister had taken enough from her by publishing the memoir. Madi wasn't going to let her take that, too.

5

In this abyss of shadows, the cold granite walls press against my back, and the stale, oppressive air suffocates any hope of escape. I can feel the dampness seeping through the thin fabric of my clothes, clinging to my skin like an unseen adversary.

—*Ghost Lake* by Ava Howell Brooks

Ava

AS SOON AS HER SISTER LEFT THE HOUSE, AVA LET OUT a long, ragged breath.

She felt pummeled, bruised, with that greasy nausea curling around in the pit of her stomach again.

"I truly don't have to stay here," she said to her grandmother. "I don't want it to be a problem for you with Madi. I could always look into booking a vacation rental somewhere in town or over the pass in Sun Valley. I'm sure I can find something with decent summer rates around one of the ski resorts."

"I doubt it. Nothing is cheap around here anymore. We're starting to have as many tourists in these parts during the summer as we do during the winter these days."

She had noticed during her occasional visits home to see

Leona that the crowds spilling over from Sun Valley to the protected community had increased year-round.

"I'm sure I can find something. Or I can always go back to Portland. This visit was a whim anyway, because I didn't like being alone at our apartment without Cullen."

Leona's stern look beetled her brows. "Don't be silly. You're staying right here. You need to work things out with your sister."

"Work things out? Seriously?" Bile rose in her throat, the nausea that had been ever present since her husband had packed his things and left. She swallowed, trying to will it away. "I'm not sure that is going to happen. I don't think she will ever forgive me."

"She might, if you told her the truth."

Ava caught her breath, suddenly on guard. "What truth?"

"About why you really published the book."

She shifted her gaze away and blinked hard, not trusting herself to meet her grandmother's gaze. Ava was lousy at lying and Leona was eagle-eyed about that kind of thing.

"Isn't it obvious? I wanted fame and fortune. That's what Madi thinks. Isn't it what you think, too?"

"No. I think there might have been a deeper issue."

"I don't know what you're talking about."

"Don't you?"

Ava chose silence rather than try to lie further to Leona.

After a long pause, her grandmother picked up a couple of boxes and headed for the door. "Fine. Keep your secrets. I'll remind you that I raised two children of my own. I have been lied to by far better than you, my dear."

She didn't want to lie to her grandmother, but she couldn't bring herself to tell her the truth, either.

She had too many secrets. Sometimes her entire soul ached from the weight of carrying them all.

"I don't have any secrets left," she lied to Leona. "I threw everything out there in *Ghost Lake*."

"Not everything."

"Not everything," she finally agreed. "Still more than I should have, according to Madi."

"You are dealing with your past the best way you know how. Your sister is doing the same."

Her grandmother studied her closely, her eyes filled with so much sympathy Ava had to fight the urge to rest her head against her shoulder and cry.

"Now," Leona said gently. "Why don't you have a rest and unpack your things while I work on dinner for us? Later, you can catch me up on everything that has been going on since your book came out."

Where to start with that? The past few months before and after the book release had been a whirlwind of media requests, interviews, social media buzz.

In the midst of all the chaos, like water inexorably dripping away at sandstone, had been the steady, heartbreaking erosion of her marriage, the one stable thing she thought she would always be able to hold on to.

I feel like I've spent the past three years married to a stranger. Why didn't you tell me any of this?

The memory of her husband's voice, low with suppressed pain, scraped along her nerve endings with painful clarity.

After the fact, she could think of a dozen things she might have said in response. Instead, she had withdrawn inside herself, all of her porcupine quills aquiver as she became defensive and self-protective.

Because it is part of my past. It's not who I am now.

Cullen's voice had been more sad than angry. *Don't you see, Ava? What happened to you during those six months at Ghost Lake made you who you are. Now that I've read the book, I can see so many things more clearly. I would have understood. You had to know*

I would have understood. Instead, I feel as if you have spent every moment we've been together hiding your true self from me. You never completely trusted me. Us. Did you?

The memory of the hurt and betrayal in his warm brown eyes knocked into her like a wrecking ball. She felt lightheaded suddenly, a mixture of exhaustion, regret and fear.

"Take a rest." Leona touched a cool hand to Ava's face. "Everything feels better after a little nap."

"It's close enough to bedtime. If I nap now, I'll never go back to sleep."

"I'm the same way. I get it. Well, unpack your things and then come down and you can help me in the kitchen."

Her grandmother bustled away and Ava sagged onto the bed, eyes closed as she tried to push away more memories that crowded in. Cullen's silence as he packed his things for his summer fieldwork. The thick tension in their apartment as she tried to think of some way to fix everything that had been rent apart by her words in *Ghost Lake*.

Her phone rang. Sylvia again, she saw on the display. She let it go to voicemail, but it immediately rang again.

With a sigh, she answered. She couldn't avoid the woman forever. "Hello."

"There you are! I was beginning to worry, darling. I thought maybe the Coalition might have come looking for you."

She shivered, even as she knew that was highly unlikely. The Ghost Lake Survival Coalition had completely cracked apart after that final shootout fifteen summers ago. The thirty-odd core members of the prepper cult that had temporarily taken up residence deep in the Sawtooth Mountains had been arrested or fled long ago.

The leaders, including the man she had been forced to marry when she was only sixteen years old, were still serving prison sentences for shooting and wounding two federal officers and for killing an innocent man who simply had been trying to help her and Madi.

"I'm sorry. It's been a hectic few days."

Oh, and my life is falling apart. So there's that.

"Where are you, Ava? You sound like you're a million miles away."

"I'm in Idaho. I came to visit my grandmother for a...for a few weeks."

"Oh. How far are you from...you know. Where everything happened?"

She closed her eyes. She was never very far away, at least in her memories. "About an hour."

"I wonder if you could go there and take some pictures of you holding the book there. It would look great on your socials."

That was absolutely the last thing she wanted to do. She would be happy never going into those mountains again, though how she expected to reconnect with her husband when he was in roughly the same area remained a mystery.

To her relief, Sylvia didn't wait for an answer, quickly moving on to the reason for her call.

"Your publicity team is so upset about having to cancel the tour. They're wondering when they could reschedule."

"I can't answer that."

"Next month? Two months?"

How about *never*?

She couldn't say that, unfortunately, as much as she might want to. Part of her deal with her publisher entailed her agreement to participate in promotional events, including the ten-city book tour she had ditched.

"What about early August?" she suggested. "I only need to wrap up in time to return to my classes around the twenty-second."

"That might work. It's only six or seven weeks after you were originally scheduled. I'll talk to them and get back to you. If the book tour conflicts with the start of the school year, maybe you could get a substitute for a few weeks. Or better yet, take a sabbatical or something."

Ava hated the idea of someone else starting the school year with her students and of missing those important first few weeks of the school year.

She didn't feel as if she had many options, though.

"How are you feeling?" Sylvia's brusque, down-to-business New York accent softened.

"Better," she said. She didn't want to lie to yet one more person in her life. Fortunately, Sylvia couldn't see her over the phone.

"Oh, I'm glad. Maybe a few weeks of rest are exactly what you need."

"Yes. Maybe."

"I have more fun news. Looks like *Ghost Lake* is on the short list for several of the big book-club picks. My prediction is that, at this rate, you're going to stay on the bestseller lists all summer long and into the fall. So maybe August is good timing for a tour after all."

"Great news," Ava said, even as her stomach protested.

"It's so exciting. There's nothing I love more than when one of my clients writes a phenomenal book that the world adores as much as I do."

They spoke for a few more moments about print runs and sell-throughs, before Ava was able to end the call with more vague promises.

She turned her phone to silent, moved a few more boxes off the bed and lay down for a moment, staring at the ceiling and wondering how she would endure the summer when she felt so physically and emotionally wretched.

6

The scars on our bodies may have faded, but the wounds on our hearts remain tender, a constant reminder of the price we paid for freedom.

—*Ghost Lake* by Ava Howell Brooks

Madison

SHE LOVED THE BURNING TREE ON A JUNE FRIDAY night, especially when a band she loved was playing.

Live music, good friends, cold drinks and a new crop of summer guys.

What more did she need?

She adjusted her skirt—a tad shorter than she was comfortable in—and shifted in the booth she and Nicki favored. It gave them a great view of the small stage inside the tavern as well as of the front door, so they could check out any new arrivals.

Jamie Keller, a friend who went to school with them, brought over their drink order.

"Sorry that took so long," she said, brushing away a strand of auburn hair that had slipped out of her ponytail. "We are hopping tonight."

"Looks like it." Across from Madi, Nicki took a healthy sip

from her rum and Diet Coke, the same drink she always ordered.

"Good for business, though," Madi said. Jamie's husband, Mark, had taken over running the place from his father. Mark and Jamie owned it now and over the past few years had turned it from a rather disreputable roadhouse to a happening night spot that drew people from several neighboring towns.

Jamie blew out a breath. "A bit too good. I wish I could sit down with you and catch up, but we're down two servers tonight, so that's not happening. Grab me if you need another round."

"We will," Nicki said.

Nicki usually had two drinks, but Madi's guilty secret was that she didn't particularly care for alcohol or any other substances that could impair her thinking. Since that long-ago summer when she was injured, she had spent entirely too much time feeling a vague disconnect between her brain and the rest of her body. Why voluntarily sign up for something else that might impair her cognitive abilities when she already had a brain injury that sometimes did that all on its own?

So on the nights when she and Nicki came to the Burning Tree, she would order one drink and nurse it all night, mixing it up with sparkling water or a Dirty Diet Coke if she needed a little caffeine jolt.

She was glad she had come. For weeks, she had been pouring every ounce of her energy into her final days at the vet clinic and going through all the necessary steps to make the animal rescue operational.

She loved what she did, but sometimes a girl only needed to kick back with her friends and enjoy being young, relatively healthy and completely unattached.

"What about those two over there?" Nicole gestured to two athletically built blond guys a few years younger than they were, with the tanned faces and raccoon eyes that proclaimed to the world that they spent most of their days outside wearing sunglasses or ski goggles.

"I don't know. They seem kind of self-absorbed. The shorter one keeps checking himself out in the mirror above the bar."

"I'll take that one. You can go for the taller one who looks like Austin Butler."

"Eh. I don't know."

Nicole frowned and sipped at her drink. "It's already the second Friday in June. Before you know it, the season will be over."

She rolled her eyes. "It's barely even summer. We still have snow in some of the higher elevations."

"I know, but you know how short the season is."

Since returning to Emerald Creek after she finished school as a veterinary technician and Nicole earned her nursing degree, she and Nic had fallen into a comfortable pattern. In the winter, they each tended to date ski instructors or ski patrol guys, who were only there for a few months until the weather warmed again. In the summer, they went for the guys who spent those warm months guiding fishing excursions or river rafting expeditions in the area.

Neither of them was interested in anything serious at this stage in their lives. The guys certainly didn't seem to mind. At the end of each season, it was easy for them to say goodbye when they inevitably moved away again, on to their next adrenaline fix.

Madi hadn't dated anybody for nearly a year. Over the winter, she had been too busy working through all the details of the animal rescue to devote much energy to anything else, much to Nic's frustration.

Madi had promised her friend she would put in more effort during the summer. She didn't want to admit it to Nic, but casual dating sometimes seemed like so much work, trying to be bright and funny and attractive all the time. These days she was finding she would much rather expend her energy toward working on the sanctuary's social media presence or writing another grant.

"I'm going to go talk to them." Nic smoothed a hand over her hair, checked out her own reflection in the mirror above the bar and headed in the direction of the two guys.

They looked pleased to talk to her. Why wouldn't they be? Nicole was gorgeous. She was tall, slender, with the same wavy dark hair and blue eyes as her brother. She certainly didn't have a mouth that only smiled halfway or a curled hand or a stammer that sometimes came out of nowhere.

"What are you doing here by yourself?"

She turned her attention away from the stage, ready to rebuff some overeager cowboy, and was shocked to find Luke sliding across from her, a froth-topped beer in his hand.

"Enjoying the music." She raised her voice slightly to be heard. "I have to say, I'm surprised to see you. I never expected you to really come out with us."

He shrugged. "I enjoy live music as much as the next guy. Also, I believe I was ordered to come so I can be your designated driver."

"I was teasing. I usually only have one drink over three hours. I doubt that will leave me too impaired to drive."

"You never know. You're small enough that even a tiny amount of alcohol probably hits you harder than two or three would for me."

"Possibly."

She never considered herself small in stature, but she supposed compared to the tall Gentry siblings, she was a shrimp.

The band switched to one of her favorites, a ballad that had been their first single release and had gone on to hit the local charts.

The song always struck a chord with her, about lost innocence and misplaced trust. While the song was about a romantic relationship, for some reason it made her think of her father, which always made her throat feel tight and her eyes burn.

"Want to dance?" Luke asked.

The question came completely out of the blue. To her startled dismay, she felt her cheeks heat and was grateful for the dim lighting inside the Burning Tree.

Why would she have such a reaction? Luke was her friend. She had known him for more than a decade and was close to everyone in his family, including his daughter.

Yes, he was technically her boss but only for a few more weeks. Luke had never really felt like her boss anyway, more like a friend she was lucky enough to work with. Even at the clinic, theirs had always been more of a brother-sister relationship.

Maybe that was why the idea of dancing with him seemed... odd.

That was silly. They could certainly dance to one song together without things getting weird. Right?

"Sure," she said, rising before she could overthink things. "I would love to dance."

He looked surprised, as if he hadn't expected her to agree, but rose as well and held out his hand to her. After a moment's hesitation, she took it.

His skin was warm, his hand strong in hers. He smelled of leather and rain-drenched pine needles.

Had she ever danced with him? Yes, she remembered. Three years earlier at his brother Owen's wedding. It had been one of those organic things, everyone dancing with everyone else, though, and he had only been a year out from losing Johanna, so she hadn't thought anything of it.

The band's slow, sweet notes swirled around the dance floor, where a dozen other couples already moved together, including Nicki and her clearly besotted river guide, who looked as if a genie had popped out of his beer bottle and granted him his fondest desire in the form of a tall, dark-haired nurse with vivid blue eyes.

This was not a good idea, Madi thought. For one wild instant, she wasn't sure where to put her hands. Around his neck, like Nic was doing? That seemed far too intimate under the circumstances.

He solved her quandary by placing one hand at her back and using the other one to grip her fingers.

He was a good dancer. She wasn't sure why she was so surprised. Luke was athletic and strong. She had worked with him for years and had seen him outmuscle even the most obstinate of patients.

Still, the graceful way he moved across the dance floor left her feeling awkward and ungainly in contrast.

"So," he said, gesturing toward his sister. "Looks like Nic has picked her summer guy. What about you?"

She looked over at her friend, who was now resting her head on the guy's considerable chest.

"Not yet."

"What's stopping you?"

She frowned, not liking that she was so predictable to him. Maybe she had fallen into a lazy pattern. "I've been so busy, I barely had time to come to the Burning Tree tonight. I don't know if I have the energy right now to put into a relationship, even a casual one."

"You can't devote your entire life to the sanctuary. That's not healthy."

"So says the man who has done nothing but work since the day he returned home to practice veterinary medicine in Emerald Creek."

"That's different."

"Why is it different?" she asked, genuinely confused.

"Maybe it's not that different," he conceded. "We're both

passionate about what we do. But I have the added complication of Sierra, trying to fill the role of both parents for her."

"That's true. Lucky for you, she's a good kid."

"Fingers crossed that continues. She's only thirteen. Or she will be next week, anyway. I'm afraid I'm not out of the woods yet."

"You don't have to worry about Sierra. She's amazing."

"She misses her mom so much sometimes," he admitted. "It breaks my heart."

She had always liked Johanna, though they had never been precisely friends. The other woman had been a professional as well, a physical therapist with a busy career working out of the regional hospital and in her own practice.

It had been through her work that she caught COVID-19 in the early days of the pandemic, before much information was known about the virus. Johanna's underlying medical diagnoses of both asthma and type 1 diabetes had led to complications and she had spent two horrible weeks in an intensive care unit in Boise before succumbing to the disease.

That had been such a horrible time for all of the Gentry family. Luke had seemed…numb for a long time and Madi's heart ached when she remembered how devastated Sierra had been at her mother's death.

As Madi had lost her own mother when she was twelve, that shared experience had helped cement her close relationship with his daughter.

Did he still grieve his wife? she wondered. Most of the time, he seemed fine. Kind, generous, well-adjusted. Maybe he was hiding his pain on the inside.

Was that why Luke never dated, at least as far as she could tell? Maybe his heart was too scarred to ever think about letting another woman in.

The idea left her depressed, somehow.

"Sierra is fine," she said to him. "She's turning thirteen. In a few years, she'll be driving, and a few more after that, she'll be heading off to college."

"Don't remind me."

"I'm only saying you should think about getting out there."

His shoulder suddenly felt tight beneath her hand.

"If by *out there*, you mean the dating scene, I'm not interested in something meaningless."

"That's your word, not mine. Why does it have to be meaningless?"

He gave her a long look she didn't quite understand. "It just would be."

Before she could answer, the song ended and the band moved into a more up-tempo song. She thought Luke would lead her back to their table. Instead, he seemed content to continue their conversation on the dance floor.

He had moves, she had to admit. How long had it been since he really let loose?

"We should work on finding you someone this summer. What about that nice new nurse from Colorado who works at the hospital with Nicki? Vanessa something."

"Vanessa Perkins. I'm afraid she's not available."

"Did you already try to ask her out?"

"No."

"Then, how do you know she's not available?"

He gave her an amused look. "Because last Friday on your afternoon off, I treated her little Yorkie for an ear infection. Vanessa brought him in along with her girlfriend, Courtney, who works at the Topaz Trail Hotel. They are recently engaged, brimming over with wedding plans."

"Oh. Well, that's too bad. But still. I'm sure there's someone out there for you. What about Janie Carlton?"

As the music ended, she angled her head toward a woman with short, streaky blond hair sitting with a couple of girlfriends in a corner booth. "You two have a lot in common.

She's a single mom, too. I guess her son must be with her mom or her ex."

"Janie is very nice and so is her French bulldog, Alexander. But I'm not in the market, Mad. For either a relationship or for a French bulldog," he said as they returned to their table.

"If I had to choose, I would pick the French bulldog," his sister offered with a grin, reaching the table at the same time.

"Would you? You seem to be getting along well with the muscled raccoon over there."

She didn't seem offended. "He does have the look, doesn't he? It's all those hours spent in the hot sun. It's hard to get a good tan when you're hiding behind sunglasses all the time."

She slid into her chair across from them and reached for a healthy sip of her drink. "I have to say, I'm surprised and happy you decided to leave your cave and join us. Where's my favorite niece?"

"Sleepover. Her friend Zoe Sullivan is going to stay with her dad for the summer, so the girls wanted to have one last blast before the big separation. As if they won't be FaceTiming and texting all day, every day, anyway."

"Does the muscled raccoon have a name?" Madi asked. "You two seemed to be hitting it off."

"We were. We are. His name is Austin Yates and he's super cute. He and his buddy Ryan O'Connor are both grad students in the Seattle area. He's from Canada. Vancouver. This is their second year as river guides. Last year, they both worked over in Jackson Hole, but this year, they wanted a change and wanted to go somewhere less touristy. I told him my friend thinks his friend is cute."

"Do I?" Madi asked with a laugh. Luke, she noticed, didn't seem to find the conversation amusing.

"Ryan ordered another round at their table, so I told them to join us as soon as they have their drinks."

Again, she saw Luke didn't look particularly thrilled at this.

They were at a large table with room for six, but she could see where he might feel like the third wheel. Or fifth, in this case.

She didn't want him to feel awkward, especially after she had basically dragged him out of his house to join them.

"Sorry," she murmured.

He shrugged. "I expected it. I know how you two operate. Would you rather I get lost?"

"Don't be silly," his sister said. "It's a big table. We want you to stay, don't we, Mad?"

"Sure," she answered. A moment later, the two came over, with Austin carrying a pitcher of beer.

Nicole quickly made introductions and Madi held her breath, waiting for either of the guys to grimace or otherwise react negatively to her half-frozen smile. Meeting new people always made her anxious until they became used to seeing her features that were a little...off.

Neither Ryan nor Austin seemed to blink as Nicole quickly made introductions. Before Madi knew it, she was chatting with the taller of the guys. Ryan.

He seemed smart and funny, a native Washingtonian and a journalism grad student, with aspirations of being the next Norman Maclean. He was only a few years younger than she was, Madi learned, and was deeply inquisitive about the area.

"There's so much history here," he said, after they had spoken at length about the community and some of their suggestions for points of interest to see while he was in town.

"I find it so fascinating, especially since I'm reading a book set in this area. Or at least in the mountains near here."

Madi instantly tensed. "Are you?"

"Yes. Are you a reader?"

"I listen to audiobooks more than read," she admitted. She did not tell this perfect physical specimen that reading for too long gave her a headache. "Right now I'm listening to a suspense novel about a bunch of people trapped on a cruise with a killer."

"Oh, I think I've seen that one advertised. It looks great."

"It is so far," she said. "I'm about halfway through and it was hard to come out to the Burning Tree tonight instead of staying home to listen to my book."

She purposely didn't ask what he was reading, because she didn't want to know. He answered the unspoken question, anyway. "I just started that book everyone has been talking about. *Ghost Lake.* That book is intense! Have you heard about it?"

Madi didn't dare risk a look around the table at Luke and Nicki.

"I've heard of it," she said, desperately searching for a change in topic.

"What do you like about it?" Luke asked, deliberately prolonging the conversation. She wanted to smack him.

Ryan's features lit up as if he were a teenage boy talking about the latest Marvel movie. "The suspense. I mean, you know the girls must have survived. At least one of them did so she could write the book. But man. What they went through was straight-up brutal. And it all happened not far from here, right? Amazing that there was a whole survivalist cult living in the mountains for months and nobody knew about it."

"People knew," she said, before she could stop herself. Even she could hear the bitterness in her voice.

"Then, why didn't people do anything about it? Why didn't anybody help them?"

She had no answer to that. After a brief, awkward silence, Luke spoke up. "People in town knew they were up there. It's hard to miss a pop-up community of that size. They were living on private land but certainly within sight of several groomed snowmobile trails that were used as fire roads in the warmer months."

Madi shivered, despite the overheated bar. Luke noticed. His eyes sharpened and he placed a hand on hers, beneath the table, for only an instant, providing comfort and support. Warmth seeped back through her and she picked up her drink and took a bigger gulp than she usually might.

"According to the book, they were heavily armed and practicing commando maneuvers," Ryan said, his features incredulous. "Didn't that raise red flags?"

"This is Idaho," Luke said quietly. "Like other states in the West, many people are heavily armed. They were survivalists, but that's not unusual here, either. The few people from the Ghost Lake Survival Coalition who had contact with the local community seemed harmless, on the rare occasions someone would come to town for supplies. Polite, well-spoken. No one knew exactly what they were doing or that children were in jeopardy, or I can promise they would have been stopped earlier."

"Can we talk about something else, please?" Madi said abruptly. She was here to let off steam, not to be thrown back into the hellscape of her memories.

Unfortunately, something in her voice drew Ryan's attention and he gave her a long, intense perusal. "Madi. Nicole said your name is Madi but she didn't say your last name. That wouldn't be Howell, would it?"

She said nothing, wanting him and his raccoon friend to simply go away now.

His eyes widened. "You're the girl from the book. The younger sister. So you survived!"

"Spoiler alert," Nicki said, her voice dry.

That damn book. She couldn't get away from it, no matter where she went, not even a night hanging out with friends listening to a live band at the local night spot.

If she were interested in a summer fling, Ryan O'Connor would have had potential. He was cute, smart, fun. What more did she want?

Not now. She could imagine few things worse than a summer filled with curious questions about her experience up in the mountains with the Coalition.

She didn't even want to endure the rest of the evening with him now.

Fortunately, the band started playing again, one of their most popular tunes, and the rowdy crowd in the bar stomped its collective boots and whooped in delight. Soon the small dance floor started to fill.

"Come on, Austin. Let's go." Nicole saved the day, as best friends do, by grabbing the other guy's hand and tugging him out of the booth. "Madi, you and Ryan should dance, too. This song is great."

Glad of the distraction, Madi jumped up. Ryan basically had no choice but to follow her as she hurried toward the front of the stage and the speakers, where the music was so loud there was little possibility of a conversation.

They danced through that song and the next two, all of them raucous party songs, until she was breathless and damp. When the band started up a slower number, Madi headed to the bar, where she asked Mark Keller for an ice water that she carried back to their table.

Luke was still there, she saw. He was sipping at a beer and tapping his toe.

Ryan grabbed a seat across from him. Madi sipped at her ice water, then set it back down on the table. "Thanks for the dances, Ryan, but I need to run."

"You can't leave! The band said they have another hour to play."

"It's been a long day and I've got to work tomorrow, I'm afraid. Sorry. My boss is a bit of a tyrant."

Luke, the most easygoing employer she could possibly want, merely rolled his eyes, but Ryan didn't appear to notice. His features filled with disappointment.

"That's too bad. I would have loved the chance to talk to you more about Ghost Lake."

Which was exactly why she was leaving, Madi thought. "Maybe another time," she said, though she meant *never*.

He frowned. "I thought Nicole said you worked at a vet's office. They're open on Saturday?"

Caught in the lie, her gaze met Luke's. To her vast relief, he swept in to save her.

"Not usually, but we do have to work tomorrow morning. I've got to go vaccinate some new lambs on a local sheep farm. I'm afraid I can't possibly do it without Madi's help."

Ryan looked between her and Luke. "He's your boss? The tyrant? But you were dancing with him."

"I guess we caught him on a good night," she said.

"Right. Get a beer in me and I'm almost human," Luke said.

Madi wanted to hug him for rescuing her. "It was really great to meet you, Ryan," she lied.

"I'll be around all summer. I'd love to get together again. You're a great dancer, plus I would love to hear more details about Ghost Lake!"

Yeah. Right. That was absolutely the last thing she wanted to do. In fact, she would now do her best to avoid Ryan O'Connor for the rest of the summer. Too bad, too. Not only was he great-looking but he was a good dancer and he liked to read. That normally would have been a huge mark in his favor.

That stupid book.

"I'm sure I'll see you around. Nic is my roommate and best friend, and it looks like she and your pal Austin are getting along great."

The two of them, she saw, were dancing close together and seemed extremely chummy. She had a feeling she would be seeing plenty of Austin over the next few months, until the leaves started to change.

"Are you sure I can't give you a ride home?" Ryan asked.

She held up her keys. "I've got my own car. I'm good. You stay and have fun."

"I feel like I should at least walk you to your car."

"I'm leaving, too." Luke slid his chair back. "I can walk her out. I think we're parked next to each other."

Oh hurray. She owed her tyrant of a boss big-time. She could imagine Ryan following her out to the parking lot. Something told her he was not the kind of guy who would let go of a topic of conversation, especially when it interested him.

Nicole and Austin returned to their table, their hands entwined. Her friend looked at Madi, holding her clutch that was only big enough for her phone, her keys, a couple of mints and maybe a tube of lipstick.

"You're taking off?"

"Yes. Headache. Plus, work tomorrow. Good thing we drove separately tonight, isn't it?"

Nicole looked as if she wanted to argue but something in Madi's expression must have told her it was futile. She finally shrugged. "I'll cover your one measly drink."

Luke shook his head. "We can settle up with Jamie on our way out."

After they paid for their drinks, she and Luke walked together out to the parking lot. The June evening air smelled of pine and sagebrush. A cool wind blew out of Emerald Canyon and Madi shivered, wishing she had thought to bring a jacket. She should have. She certainly knew evenings here in the mountains turned cold once the sun went down.

"Thanks for the save," she said as they neared her SUV. "Multiple saves, actually. Do I really have to go vaccinate sheep with you tomorrow? I've got a full day planned at the rescue."

"You don't have to. But I could use the help. It's easier with two people. Tomas will be out of town and Carly has a bridal shower for her cousin. I was planning on Sierra's help. Maybe

I can drag her away from her sleepover early enough to come with me."

She sighed. She owed him, even if he hadn't come to her rescue that evening. "I'll do it, if we can get it out of the way early in the morning. I've got new volunteers coming in the afternoon for training."

"Fine with me. Should we say seven?"

She did a quick mental calculation. "Let's make it eight so I can feed the hordes."

"Okay."

She opened her SUV door. Before she could slide inside, Luke leaned down.

His scent, masculine and clean, brushed against her again at this close proximity. He must have shaved before going out on the town, she realized, as his late-afternoon shadow was gone. Was it his aftershave that smelled so good?

Whatever the cause, Madi inhaled deeply, hoping he didn't notice.

"So. Ryan O'Connor. He seems pretty smitten. Will he be your summer guy?"

She released her breath. "Highly doubtful, unless I want to spend all summer trying to avoid the subject of Ava's stupid book."

He raised an eyebrow. "It's not a stupid book. You know that, right? It's beautifully written and very gripping."

She stared at him, feeling as if the car door had somehow slammed into her gut. Beautiful? Gripping?

"How would you know that?" she demanded. "Surely you haven't read *Ghost Lake*, have you?"

She suddenly wasn't sure she wanted to know the answer to that question.

7

In our pursuit of help, we find allies who listen to our harrowing tale, their eyes mirroring a mixture of disbelief and compassion.

—*Ghost Lake* by Ava Howell Brooks

Luke

HE WAS TREADING ON DANGEROUSLY THIN ICE HERE.

He studied Madison in the streetlight, skin glowing and hair still slightly damp from dancing.

She looked lovely and fragile, with her mouth permanently frozen on one side, and he fought the sudden fierce urge to tuck her against him and protect her.

It was a battle he fought often, whether that was in the office when a wounded dog tried to lash out or sitting in a town hall meeting with her as she tried to persuade local politicians that a no-kill shelter would only benefit the community over the long haul.

He had learned a long time ago that Madison Howell didn't want him—or *anyone*—to protect her. She wielded her independence like a Valkyrie with a sword.

He had seen her wounded, so pale he wasn't sure she was still alive. He had seen her bandaged and hooked up to machines. He had seen her crying in pain and frustration from the physical and occupational therapy necessary for her to come back from a serious brain injury.

He wondered if she had ever been as vulnerable and exposed as she was now, since her sister had written about their experience in the mountains fifteen years ago.

He wanted to protect her, which was why he struggled for a long moment with how best to answer her heated question about whether he had read Ava's book.

If he told the truth, that he had read every single word more than once, Madi would be furious and see it as one more betrayal.

If he lied, she would immediately know he wasn't being honest with her. She had an unerring radar about those kinds of things. They had been friends long enough that she knew him well. He could never successfully deceive her.

He finally decided the truth was his only option.

"She sent me, Mom and Nicki each an advanced copy of the book."

"I know that. We talked about it. She sent you the...last few chapters so you could read about what happened with you and...and your d-dad."

Her words tangled, as they sometimes did when she battled fatigue or emotional turmoil.

Still, he could feel the pain spasming through him, the flash of memory of his good, honorable father lying in the dirt, his features pale, blood seeping through his shirt where he had been shot.

"She didn't only send us the final chapters," he said, his voice as gentle as he could make it. Clouds shifted over the moon and he could see her clearly, her green eyes murky and her mouth twisted into a frown. "She sent us the entire thing. I don't think Nicki has read it yet. Mom has. She read it right away."

"Why...why didn't Nicki tell me? Or your mom? They should have t-told me. *You* should have told me."

He couldn't blame her for feeling betrayed. He would feel the same, in her shoes.

"It took me a while to bring myself to read it from the beginning, especially because I know the ending all too well. I finally read it right before it was released. I have to say, Ava is one hell of a storyteller."

He knew he was only adding kindling to the fire of her temper but he couldn't continue keeping the truth from her.

She glared at him. "How could you? Especially when you know how I feel about it."

"I did not know how you felt until the book came out and started gaining traction," he pointed out. "For most of the past six months, you've been ignoring the topic of Ava's book, if you'll recall. You were quick to change the subject every time anybody brought it up. I'm sure you were hoping it would all go away."

"Okay, yes. I'll admit to some degree of magical thinking. Can you blame me?"

"No," he said, his voice soft. "I can't blame you."

"Most of the time, I don't even think about it. I can go days without remembering. But now that Ava has written her book, I can't go an hour without being reminded. I hate it."

"Oh, Madi." His heart ached for the pain in her voice.

"I don't only hate being forced to relive it, over and over. I hate that now everyone else knows what happened to us. I see them judging me. Seeing me as only that poor girl whose dad dragged her and her sister into a survivalist cult and tried to marry them off to men three times their age."

He hated that part, too, thinking about how desperate and frightened she and Ava must have been through their whole ordeal.

Reading *Ghost Lake* had been a torturous exercise for that alone, for the simmering fury that made him want to punch a hole through his drywall, even as he found the words and the story profoundly moving, even humorous at times.

He took her hands in his, feeling the weakness in her left hand compared to the other one. "No one who knows you sees you as anything other than a strong, capable woman who did everything she could to escape her circumstances."

After a moment, she pulled her hands away. "That book is ruining everything. Now it's even wrecking my love life. Ryan would have been perfect for a summer fling."

In the past, he had found her and Nicki's penchant for choosing guys in town only for the short term rather amusing. When had it started to bother him so much?

"Maybe that's not such a bad thing."

She made a face. "How can it be anything other than lousy?"

He chose his words carefully, aware he was on shaky ground here. He certainly couldn't tell her the idea of her picking another seasonal guy this summer had started to make him feel slightly rabid.

He had absolutely no right to comment on her dating patterns, he reminded himself. He was her employer and her friend. That was all.

"You said yourself how busy you are right now with getting the animal rescue off the ground. You've got plenty on your plate. A new guy might be too much of a distraction."

She blew out a breath that ruffled her hair. "I know. You're right. That's what I've been telling myself, t-too. That doesn't mean I have to like it."

She slid into her car before he could answer.

"On that note," she said, "I should go home and check on the new kitten. What time are you picking me up in the morning to take care of Paul Lancaster's sheep?"

She sounded less than enthused at the prospect, which didn't surprise him. Paul was a crotchety son of a gun who exhibited little patience and even less gratitude.

"You really don't have to go with me. I can drag Sierra into helping out."

"I'll go. What time?"

"We said eight. That way we can be done by ten or ten thirty, which would still give us time to grab an omelet at the Fern & Fir, if you want."

"I don't think I have time for that. My day is packed. But I'll help you with the sheep. I'll see you in the morning. Have a good night."

She closed her door and started up her small SUV. He watched until she drove out of the parking lot before climbing into his own pickup truck.

He couldn't stop thinking about her as he drove toward the house he and Johanna had bought when they first moved back to Emerald Creek, a few blocks from the veterinary clinic.

He shouldn't have danced with Madi. Even as he asked her, he had known it was a mistake, as if he were crossing some invisible barrier he had carefully maintained between them for the past few years. His own personal Maginot Line.

They were friends. That was all. Or so he told himself, anyway.

Their families were close, almost tighter than the Gentrys were with actual relatives. His mother adored her and she was his sister's best friend and his daughter's close confidante.

Since the moment she and her sister had stumbled onto their camp fifteen years earlier, theirs had been an unbreakable bond, forged through shared trauma from the events of that day that others could never understand.

If lately he had begun to wonder if perhaps his feelings toward Madi had begun to grow into something else, something far more than he ever expected, that was his problem to handle.

He would never risk damaging that bond between them by expecting more than she wanted to give.

8

I sag into our grandmother's arms, her kindness and understanding the balm that soothes the wounds of the past, offering a glimpse of the love and acceptance we so desperately need.

—*Ghost Lake* by Ava Howell Brooks

Ava

"THANK YOU AGAIN FOR HELPING ME TODAY. I CAN always use another set of hands."

"I don't mind," Ava lied to her grandmother, giving her a practiced smile. In truth, she had absolutely zero desire to sit all morning at the Emerald Thumbs Farmers Market at the town park that took up an entire city block in the center of downtown.

Less than zero.

Too many people knew her in this town—friends of her grandmother and of her sister as well as Ava's own friends from the two years she had lived here while she finished high school.

She wasn't even sure which of her friends were still in town, as she hadn't done a great job of keeping up with people.

She had never been particularly great at small talk. She did not expect she would suddenly find she was any better at it now, after spilling everything raw and real in her memoir. What could she say to people, now that everyone knew?

If she had her way, she would spend the entire summer hiding away here at Leona's house, tucked away on Elkridge Drive.

She couldn't do that, unfortunately. She owed her grandmother far more than the sacrifice of a few hours selling bouquets of flowers at the weekly summer market, as well as early strawberries, new potatoes, peas in the pod and baked goods prepared by Leona's tight circle of friends she affectionately called the Esmeraldas.

Her grandmother had opened her life and her heart to the two of them after the events of that summer. Not for an instant had she wavered from her willingness to take on two orphaned teenage girls suffering emotional and physical trauma.

Leona had provided love and care, a roof over their heads, endless trips out of town to doctors and rehab specialists for Madi, hours spent helping Ava's sister with exercises and physical therapy.

And love. Especially love.

Leona had offered them the sweetest gift of all, her unconditional love and support. That alone had done more to help them begin to heal than anything physical therapy or counseling ever could.

Ava knew she could never repay her grandmother. Spending a Saturday morning at the local farmers market couldn't even begin to reconcile the ledger.

"I don't mind," she said again as she carried the final bucket of bundled flowers toward her grandmother's stall at the farmers market, covered with a large flowered patio umbrella. "You might have to help me figure out what I'm doing, though."

"Nothing to it. You only have to stay there until everything is gone, which usually won't take longer than two or three hours. Then we pack up the table and our umbrella and go."

"Sounds easy enough."

What her grandmother did not mention were all the people Ava would have to talk with. High school friends. Neighbors. Church acquaintances.

With any luck, the farmers market would mostly be frequented by tourists staying in town to enjoy the mountain setting, the hiking and biking trails, and the many recreational opportunities from the actual Emerald Creek the town was named for and the mighty rivers that curved their way through the landscape outside town.

If not, she would simply smile and be polite and try to deflect any questions or comments about her book.

"Sometimes your sister helps me out at the market, but she was busy today. Something to do with helping Luke this morning with some sheep."

At least Ava wouldn't have to deal with another Madi confrontation.

Her sister was so angry with her. Ava had no idea how to defend herself, or if she should even attempt it.

"We should have ordered some copies of your book for you to sign," Leona grinned at her, her lipstick bright and her silver hair with its blue highlights gleaming in the sunlight. "We would have had a line all around the park! Maybe we can do that another week this summer."

Right. That was never happening. Ava shuddered at the very idea.

"I don't know if that would be fair to Meadowside Book Nook. I saw they had a big display."

"We can order them through the store so they get a cut. I'm all about saving our local independent bookstore. Ingrid Jenson has worked so hard to make that place a success."

Ava had gone to high school with Ingrid. Right after *Ghost Lake* came out, the other woman had reached out to Ava through their graduating-class Facebook group, begging her to come to town and do a signing. Ava had refused politely, explaining she didn't get back to town often.

This had all been before her impulsive decision this week to escape to her grandmother's house.

"I'll try to stop in and sign some of her inventory," she said now to her grandmother.

"You should! What a great idea, though, of doing a signing at the market. It's called the Emerald Thumbs Farmers Market, but why not celebrate our local authors? Planting seeds through words is as important to the mind and the heart as growing vegetables can be to the body."

Ava couldn't disagree. That still didn't mean she was in a big rush to do a book signing while she was in town. Signing inventory was one thing, where she could do it on her own time and didn't have to interact with readers. A formal book signing was something completely different.

"Oh, I am loving this idea. Meet the author at the farmers market. I'll talk to Joe Hernandez. He runs the market."

Joe was another friend from high school, a year ahead of her in school. Ava had always had a bit of a crush on him, with his dark eyes and high cheekbones.

That girl who used to blush every time she saw him in the hallways of their high school seemed another person, so very far away.

"How long have you had a table at the farmers market?" she asked, quickly changing the subject.

"I started last summer. My flowers are so gorgeous, I love the chance to share them with the community. And then I have always grown far too much produce than I could use. I've been giving it to the food bank but even they couldn't use it all. I had the idea of selling the leftovers to help your sister. So now any of my friends who have extra produce donate theirs, and I have other friends who always make baked goods to sell every week. It's one small way we can help Madi with her efforts to run the no-kill shelter."

Ava greatly admired her sister's efforts to save animals—and her grandmother's efforts to help *Madi*.

"What a good idea. Like a PTA bake sale except for animals."

Leona chuckled. "Exactly. Except we're all in our seventies and haven't had to go to a boring PTA meeting in years. I'm not sure the PTA would have us now. The Esmeraldas are considered the town troublemakers. We picketed the grocery store last fall because they stopped selling organic, locally sourced beef and chicken. Too expensive, they said."

"Did your protest make a difference?"

"Yes! We picketed and also led a boycott until they decided they couldn't afford to make us mad. Now they offer both. Yes, it's more expensive to go with organic producers, but there are plenty of us who are willing to pay that price to help the environment as well as our local community."

"I would have to agree," Ava said with a small smile of approval for her rabble-rousing grandmother.

Ava's mother had inherited Leona's activism. She could remember Beth marching in a protest against the school board's book censorship in their eastern Oregon hometown.

Her father, she remembered, had fully supported her. That was before Beth died, before grief and loneliness had somehow twisted him into someone unrecognizable.

The air was still cool at Emerald Park, but the square buzzed with activity as people unloaded vehicles and set up tables and shade canopies.

They were situated directly across the street from the historic courthouse, with its pillars and sweeping stone staircase. She had often thought the building would make a lovely backdrop for wedding pictures.

Her own wedding pictures had been rushed. She and Cullen hadn't wanted a huge wedding. They had married in the leafy backyard of his mother's house in Portland in a ceremony officiated by his grandfather, who was an ordained pastor.

Those in attendance had consisted mostly of his friends and family and their shared group from the university in attendance. On her side, only Leona and Madi had been there, she remembered, along with her best friend, Jada.

Jada had texted her five times over the past two days, asking how she was doing. She was the only one who knew the truth about the rocky road her marriage currently faced, and while Ava appreciated her concern, she really didn't want to talk about it. As a result, she had ignored each of the messages.

She was going to have to get back to her friend at some point but right now she had no idea what to say.

As soon as the Emerald Thumbs market went live, Ava quickly realized why her grandmother wanted her assistance. Yes, she had been helpful carrying items from Leona's car, setting up the stall and putting up the umbrella. But Leona really needed her to handle the cash register and the tablet for online transactions so that her grandmother could spend the morning chatting with every single person who walked past.

Leona seemed to know everyone, from the older people around her own demographic to young mothers pushing strollers to middle-aged couples loading their bags with produce.

If Leona didn't know the shoppers, she chatted with them anyway, asking where they were from and how long they planned to visit the area.

Ava didn't mind. Though their table was shaded by trees and the large patio umbrella did the rest, she kept her sunglasses firmly on and pulled down the sun hat she had borrowed from Leona.

With any luck, no one would recognize her and she could make it through the morning without having to talk to anyone about anything but Leona's vibrant flowers and whether they had any gluten-free offerings among their baked goods.

After the first hour or so, she started to relax. She might have even begun to enjoy the simple hustle and bustle of the market, if not for the vague nausea she couldn't seem to shake and the ever-present worry that she wouldn't be able to fix her marriage or her relationship with her sister.

She was busy helping a woman with pink-dyed hair choose between a dozen chocolate chip cookies or a dozen sugar cookies—why not get six of each?—when she sensed some strange shift in the atmosphere.

A disturbance in the Force, her Star Wars–loving nerdy husband might have said.

A scent drifted to her above the baked goods and the sweetness of the flowers. Something earthy, rugged, masculine, with notes of black pepper, sandalwood and leather.

Cullen used that same kind of soap. She bought it for him at a trendy boutique in Portland's Nob Hill area.

She scanned the area, trying to pinpoint whatever man might be using the same kind of scent. She spotted a couple of guys in the next stall over and stared at them.

It wasn't some other man using Cullen's scent.

It was Cullen himself.

The air seemed to squeeze out of her lungs and she felt light-headed, shaky. The mild nausea bloomed into something more and she fought down the dry heaves.

She really should have tried to eat something.

Ava gripped the edge of the table to keep her balance. What on earth were Cullen and his fellow researcher doing here, at the Emerald Creek farmers market?

Buying produce, apparently. From the neighboring stall, they bought early cucumbers and tomatoes that had to have come from a greenhouse, as naturally grown tomatoes were still weeks away from being ripe.

As the men finished the transaction and paid, Ava couldn't seem to figure out what to do. Should she make some excuse to her grandmother and escape into the crowd or should she stay and try to talk to him?

She was still trying to decide when he took the choice out of her hands. He and Luis Reyes left the neighboring booth and headed toward theirs. She quickly averted her face, shrinking farther into the shadows under the umbrella as she heard him recognize her grandmother.

"Leona!" he exclaimed. "How good to see you."

Out of the corner of her gaze, Ava saw Leona send her a surprised look, then her grandmother reached out and hugged him.

Cullen and her grandmother had always shared a good relationship. Why wouldn't they? Cullen was smart, interesting, dynamic. For all his nerd tendencies and his passion for all things dinosaur, he could carry on a conversation with anyone and was genuinely interested in other people's stories.

What had he ever seen in her in the first place? It was a question she had asked herself often over the past four years, since they started dating seriously after meeting at a party thrown by a mutual friend.

And he was gorgeous. She couldn't forget that part.

She hadn't seen him in nearly a week and the sight of his handsome features—already tanned and stubbled from living in primitive conditions in the mountains—seemed to steal her breath.

Something sharp and hard lodged under her breastbone and she fought the urge to rub at the spot.

"Why, Cullen. Darling!" her grandmother exclaimed. "What a wonderful surprise! What brings you to town today?"

Ava shrank farther into the shadows, wondering if anyone would notice if she sank to the ground and commando-crawled to hide under the table.

He stepped away, still not noticing Ava. "I'm working a fossil dig site in the area, up in the backcountry. I'll be around all summer."

"I know that part. Ava told me. I wondered what you were doing *here*."

"Oh. Right. We had to resupply our provisions and this is the closest town with a large grocery store. Our alternative is heading ten miles farther into Hailey. We were trying to make it a quick trip. I didn't realize today was the farmers market. To be honest, I didn't realize Emerald Creek even *had* a farmers market."

"That's because you haven't been back to visit often enough in the summertime. We've had it for several years now. It's a great place to pick up all your fresh produce needs, especially in a few more weeks when more vegetables and fruits will be in season. Can I interest you in anything?"

He and her grandmother stood outside the circle of the umbrella, on the other side of the tables displaying Leona's offerings. Ava stayed firmly on the opposite side of the stall, her back turned to him.

He still hadn't noticed her. She told herself she was relieved, even as she felt a pang that apparently he hadn't sensed her presence like she had his.

On the other hand, she had full knowledge that her husband was working in the area, while he had absolutely no idea she had packed up her suitcase and headed to Idaho after him.

"I don't think I really need flowers right now. Not sure where I would put them. But thanks."

"We have a lovely assortment of baked goods. The proceeds all go to help feed Madi's animals at the sanctuary."

"Oh, that's nice. How's that going?"

"It's great. She is officially open now and will be quitting her job to start giving all her energy full time to it in a few weeks."

"That will be great for her."

"Everything looks delicious," Luis said. "We can grab some cookies. You know how much the team loves treats."

"Choose what you'd like. I'll cover you," Leona said.

"Don't be silly," Cullen said. "It's for a good cause. We can pay for our own cookies."

"Fine, if you insist. Ava will be happy to help you check out."

A shocked silence greeted Leona's words, words Ava knew had not been uttered by accident.

Left with no choice, she turned around slowly to face the man she loved with all her heart. The same man she had wounded deeply, possibly irreparably.

"Ava!" he exclaimed, looking staggered to see her. "What are you doing here? You're supposed to be in Portland."

She forced a smile. "Surprise."

She waved to Luis, who had worked with Cullen for years in the same university department and was a good friend to both of them. He had attended their wedding.

He, at least, looked happy to see her. "Hi, kiddo. Good to see you. Congrats on the *New York Times* bestseller list. You are officially a Big Deal. Capital *B*, Capital *D*."

She hugged him. "Thanks."

After she stepped away, she wasn't sure what to do. Should she embrace her own husband? He stood looking down at her, his features still shocked to find her here, as if she were one of his dinosaurs come to life.

She took another step away from both men, a move that apparently didn't go unnoticed by Luis, who looked between the two of them with a concerned expression.

"Um. I'm going to keep shopping, Cul. Text me when you're ready to take off. No hurry."

Another customer had moved up to the stall and was considering which bouquet of flowers to buy. Leona started talking with the woman, which left Ava to face her husband alone.

He continued gazing at her with stunned disbelief. "Why didn't you tell me you were coming to visit your grandmother?"

"It was…a last-minute decision."

She immediately felt stupid. Of course it was a last-minute decision. That had to be obvious to him, considering he had only left their apartment earlier that week and she had said nothing to him about coming to Emerald Creek.

"What about the book tour? I thought you were supposed to be going to New York to kick things off."

"I… It's been postponed indefinitely."

She didn't tell him she had backed out after realizing she would completely collapse under the pressure of trying to be engaging and articulate to readers and booksellers when she felt so wrecked, physically and emotionally.

Her publisher was not thrilled with her about it.

We need to ride the wave right now, Andrew Liu, her in-house publicist had said, looking almost in tears at a virtual meeting Sylvia had arranged to explain to her team that they needed to pause plans for the tour. *You're hot right now and everybody wants to meet you in person. We've had interest from indie bookstores all around the country. I hate to tell everyone no. In another month, someone else might have the book du jour.*

The book du jour. The phrase made her cringe. She didn't want to have penned the book du jour. While some tiny part of her couldn't help being thrilled that others apparently found her words worth reading, on the whole, she found the entire fuss mortifying.

At the same time, she knew she was in no state to show up in public and talk about being a survivor, when right now, she felt anything but resilient, when she was failing at the one thing she valued above anything else. Her marriage.

"What does Sylvia have to say about that?" Cullen's expression was veiled and she wished she could read what he was thinking.

"Everyone agrees it's for the best right now," she lied. "Maybe before school starts again, we can do a tour. The timing isn't right."

"That's good."

They acted like polite acquaintances, like dozens of other people who had visited their stall and chatted with her grandmother about the weather and the price of hay and the volunteer fire department's pancake breakfast, coming in a few weeks.

Her chest felt heavy, each breath scouring her lungs.

They weren't polite acquaintances. Cullen was the love of her life, her rock, the one person on the earth who made her feel cherished and valued and...safe.

From the first time they met, he had seemed like an old and dear friend. She remembered talking with him for hours at that party, and then, when he offered to give her a ride home, they had sat for hours more in his car on a rainy Portland night, enclosed in an intimate bubble as they shared hopes and dreams and life experiences.

She knew about his first kiss in second grade, delivered by a girl who had caught him under the art table when he had rolled the persimmon crayon there and they both crawled after it.

She knew about his older sister's problem pregnancy and his father's death when he was seven, and his mother's successful career as a pediatrician and her remarriage.

She had told him many of the details of her own life, too. Growing up in eastern Oregon, the small hobby farm where her father had grown corn and tomatoes by the bushel and about her beloved sister, Madi, who was studying to be a veterinary technician.

And the car accident that had killed their mother when Ava was fourteen and Madi was twelve.

She had glossed over so many things. The long, hard months after their mother's death they had all spent in eastern Oregon on the farm. Her father's descent into conspiracy theories and survivalist dogma as a way of coping with his grief. His association with others who were like-minded, an association that had somehow morphed into Clint Howell's absolute conviction that he needed to protect his daughters by selling their farm and moving with them to the mountains of Idaho, to a compound ruled by a pair of heavily armed brothers she now considered sociopaths, at the very least.

She also hadn't shared with Cullen other details of that time. The constant gnawing hunger, bitter cold, cruel punishments meted out for any small infraction of the Coalition's ever-fluid rules.

Or her "marriage" that had lasted less than a day, to a man she abhorred.

She had loved Cullen Brooks with her entire heart, from that very first night. That he had fallen for her as well, Ava had considered nothing short of a miracle, a rare and priceless gift from a capricious God she thought had abandoned her a long time ago.

You should have told me everything, Ava. How do you think I felt reading about all these things that happened to my own wife? Things I had no idea about, things I should have known from that first night? It is a huge part of what makes you who you are and you never told me anything. I have to wonder if the woman I thought I married ever even existed.

"Would you…want to grab a coffee?" she asked, hoping he couldn't hear the desperation in her voice. "Leona tells me the food truck over there sells a good blend. The scent has been drifting over us all morning and it does smell delicious."

He shifted his gaze to the group of food trucks selling everything from homemade empanadas to freshly pressed lemonade.

"I don't have time. Luis will be looking for me. We still have to finish our grocery shopping and head back to the site.

We have a new crew of student volunteers showing up this evening."

"Okay. Um. Will you be coming through town again soon? We could…meet for lunch or something."

"I'm not sure. I really don't have a set schedule yet. I can't commit to anything."

At least that wasn't an outright no. He had suggested they take a break while he was working at the dig. Her following him to Idaho and hounding him to meet up the first chance he had probably didn't exactly qualify as a break.

"How's the excavation going?" she asked, desperate to keep talking to him.

His features lit up and a smile even played at his mouth. "Amazing. Better than we expected. It's a nest of some kind but the fossilized bones don't really fit the pattern of the usual dinosaurs found in this area. We might be on to something big."

She was happy for him. He had worked so hard and so long for this opportunity. "I'm so glad it's working out. You must be thrilled."

"Yes," he said, his features still bright. As he looked down at her, her mind filled with memories of all the evenings they would sit together at their small kitchen table with their laptops. She would grade papers or work on her thesis, the work that eventually became *Ghost Lake*, and he would prep lesson plans or go over research documents.

Sometimes she would look up from the screen to find him watching her with the expression of a man who had been given everything he could ever want.

She wanted to cry, suddenly, and had to fight back the tears.

"How long will you be staying with Leona?" he asked.

She debated how to answer him. Should she tell him how much she had hated even a few nights by herself in the apartment, how the rooms echoed with emptiness?

"Right now my plans are open-ended," she finally said. "My

summer break seemed like a good opportunity to spend some time with Grandma and Madi."

Of course, Madi currently wasn't speaking to Ava but she decided not to mention that small detail to Cullen.

"I've talked to the Fosters next door about collecting any packages and forwarding mail," she went on.

He nodded, looking as if he had much more to say. Instead, he looked at his watch.

"I should go."

"Right. Okay."

He gazed at her. "Maybe while you're here in Idaho so close, you could come up to mountains sometime and check out the site. It's pretty rugged in parts. You'll need a Jeep or an all-terrain vehicle to get all the way there. You could park down below and I could come get you in the side-by-side."

Panic fluttered through her. She knew exactly where the site was. About a mile away from the actual Ghost Lake.

She hadn't been back there since the night she had drugged James Boyle with valerian root and mountain deathcamas Madi had found, on the rare occasions they were allowed out of the camp to bathe in the creek.

That had been the same night she and Madi had crept away through the darkness, braced for the instant when the dogs that had been cruelly trained to attack would be let loose on them.

She forced a smile, trying not to shudder. "Maybe," she said, hoping her expression didn't betray her deep reluctance.

"I need to go," he said again. He hugged her, the gesture awkward and stilted, then he was gone and her heart cracked apart a little more.

There was a time not very long ago when they couldn't keep their hands off each other.

They used to try to coordinate their return from their respective campuses.

She usually arrived only moments ahead of him. She eagerly

waited until she would hear his key in the lock, for that moment when Cullen would open the door, set down his battered messenger bag beside the comfortably battered armchair and pull her into his arms with a deep, heartfelt sigh.

As if she were his moon, his stars, his everything.

Cullen had been hers.

And she had been his.

All day as she tried to teach sentence structure and literature to largely disinterested middle school students, she would anticipate the seconds until they would be together again, when she would feel his strength around her and smell that masculine soap on his skin and the cinnamon mints on his breath as his mouth covered hers.

Her breath caught and more tears rose in her throat.

"Are you all right, darling?"

She looked up to find Leona watching her, eyes brimming with concern.

"Yes," she lied. "Fine. I just…wasn't expecting to see Cullen this morning. I didn't realize he would have to stop in town for supplies periodically."

"You never know what will happen at the farmers market. That's one reason I love having a stall here so much. Embrace the unexpected. That's what I always say."

Ava had never once heard Leona say that. Her grandmother had plenty of other pithy adages.

Don't be afraid of an honest day's work.

Live in the moment.

Say you're sorry, but only if you mean it.

Embrace the unexpected was a new one. She appreciated the sentiment, though in reality, facing the chaos of change had never been easy for her.

Ava had always struggled with new things, even before that year when their world had been completely upended.

She was a long way from embracing the unexpected.

"You look wilted, dear. Like a daisy in a rainstorm. Do you need to sit down?"

"Yes. That's probably a good idea," she said. The busy scene around them spun as Ava sank into one of the blue canvas lawn chairs she had helped carry to the booth.

Again, she thought that she should have tried to eat something for breakfast, even if the thought of food right now made her stomach twist.

"Can I get you something? We've got a couple of scones left." Leona's voice was soft, tender. Ava suddenly wanted nothing more than to rest her head against her grandmother's ample breast, close her eyes and weep.

"I'm okay," she lied. "I only need a moment to catch my breath."

"At least have something to drink," her grandmother ordered.

That adage hadn't changed. *Drink more water* had been another of her grandmother's mantras.

Leona handed over Ava's insulated water bottle, ice clinking. She wanted to gulp it down but forced herself to sip, knowing too much cold water on her empty stomach probably wasn't the greatest idea.

He wanted her to come visit him.

Near Ghost Lake.

She sipped at her water, wondering how she would ever find the courage to go back there.

"Here. Eat a scone," Leona pressed. "It's cranberry lemon, my favorite. My friend Agnes makes them and they're so delicious."

Ava still wasn't hungry but she forced herself to take a bite. The pastry melted in her mouth and helped settle her stomach a bit, she had to admit.

"There. You look better. Not so pale, anyway. I thought you were going to pass out."

"I didn't eat anything this morning. I'm sure that was to blame."

"Is that so?" Leona looked doubtful.

"Yes. My blood sugar probably dipped."

"Right. Well, finish that and you can go back to the house and make yourself an omelet or something. I can handle the rest of the market."

She was slightly ashamed at how tempted she was by the suggestion. Her grandmother's house offered a calm and peace that always seemed to embrace her when she walked inside.

She wouldn't. What good would come from trying to hide away from the world so she could grieve for the marriage she might have destroyed?

"I'm fine. I feel much better now. The scone helped. Thank you."

"You're welcome, dear. Though taking a rest and putting your feet up would probably be even more helpful."

Ava shook her head. "You're almost sold out of everything. We shouldn't be here much longer. I'll stay to help you carry everything back to your car."

Her grandmother looked as if she wanted to argue but she only shook her head, eyes worried, as she turned back to greet another customer.

9

The world beyond the compound is a kaleidoscope of over-whelming sensations, vibrant colors of a world we had al-most forgotten.

—*Ghost Lake* by Ava Howell Brooks

Madison

THE DRIVE OUT TO THE LANCASTER SHEEP FARM THE next morning was quiet and lovely, with bucolic views and few other cars on the road.

The sun was beginning to crest the mountains when Luke picked her up in the vet clinic pickup truck. She handed him a go-cup of coffee, which he accepted gratefully.

"Thanks. How do you always seem to know when I forget coffee?"

"Maybe I'm psychic." She smiled, though it really didn't take any sort of extrasensory perception. He was always forgetting to turn on the coffee machine at his place the night before. He usually slept in and didn't have time to brew it in the morning.

"You must be."

"Lucky guess. Even if you already had coffee, I figured you

might need extra this morning. You're not used to partying late into the night."

"Right. I'm such a stodgy old man these days."

"I didn't say that." She sipped to hide her smile. "I meant you don't spend a lot of time hanging out at the Burning Tree. You're out of practice."

"I'm not *that* out of practice. And it's not like I partied until 3 a.m. anyway. I was home by eleven and sound asleep by midnight."

She had *not* been asleep by midnight. Instead, she had spent a restless night. Somehow she couldn't seem to get the memory of dancing with him out of her mind.

He turned on a gravel road that led to the Lancaster farm. Morning dew gleamed on the fields around them, glistening in the sunlight like scattered gems. Some of the neighboring farmers had already cut their first crop of hay and it still lay in geometric rows, waiting for the balers.

Madi knew if she rolled down the window, the air would smell of cut alfalfa, new leaves and earth, fresh and clean and dearly familiar.

"What time did Nicole wander home from the bar last night?" Luke asked.

"Shortly after one."

She didn't think it appropriate to inform Nic's brother that when Madi had been awake to let out her dogs around that time, she had seen her roommate making out in the front seat of a Jeep that had a roof but no doors.

"She seems to be getting along well with the new river rat. What's his name again? Houston? Dallas?"

"Right state, wrong city. I believe his name is Austin."

He sighed. "Right. Dallas was a few years ago, right?"

She didn't remember all the names, but it wouldn't surprise her.

While they both dated widely, the main difference between

them was that Nicole was hoping to find lasting love with one of them while Madi only wanted a nice, temporary guy who was fun and charming and, most important, didn't treat her like all the local guys did. Like she was some kind of fragile figurine who would crumble into dust if someone touched her.

"Are you coming to my mom's place for dinner tomorrow?" he asked. "I was supposed to ask you yesterday and I forgot."

"It's on my calendar. I was planning on it."

The big Sunday dinner was one of the highlights of her month. Tilly was an amazing cook and the meal was always wonderful. The company was even better. She and Leona weren't the only strays Tilly invited. There was usually a revolving door of friends or relatives, both local and from out of town.

"I don't know Leona's plans for sure, though," Madi said. "Ava is with her now, so who knows?"

He sent her a sideways look across the cab of the pickup truck. "Ava has an open invitation from my mom. Your grandmother can bring her along if she wants to."

She gave him a polite smile, fighting the urge to cross her arms across her chest and sulk like his young niece did if the marshmallow she was roasting fell into the fire.

"That's fine. Tilly can certainly invite anyone she wants to. Just as I can choose with whom I want to spend my Sunday afternoon."

"Are you saying that if Ava goes, you won't?"

She remained stubbornly silent and he gave her another sideways look.

"Don't ask my mom to choose between you and your sister. That's not fair. She loves you both."

She glowered at him, annoyed that he once more seemed to treat her like a pesky little sister.

"Tilly doesn't have to choose between us. If Ava is going, I will choose for everyone by skipping it."

He frowned. "You're being unreasonable, Mad. If your sister plans to enjoy an extended visit with Leona here in Emerald Creek, chances are good you will have to spend time in the same room with her at some point. You can't avoid her all summer."

"I can sure as hell try," she muttered.

He opened his mouth to respond but closed it again as they pulled into the driveway of Lancaster Sheep Farms, a low-slung house surrounded by barns and silos.

Paul Lancaster trotted out to greet them, wearing his traditional denim overalls and plaid shirt, rolled up at the sleeves. In his late seventies, Paul was a hardworking farmer, who along with one of his sons, ran a herd of around five hundred sheep.

He was meticulous and fussy and preferred to have vaccines administered by the veterinarian rather than do it himself or have his workers handle it, like most producers did.

He greeted Luke with a handshake but only gave Madi a stiff, rather cool nod, something dark crossing his expression so quickly, she wondered if she had imagined it.

Odd. She and Paul usually had a cordial relationship. He was friendly with her grandmother and always seemed comfortable enough with her as well.

"We're ready for you, Doc. Glad you could make time for us. We're about to take the herd up to our summer grazing allotment. We've got our herders in place and the trucks are coming this afternoon."

She knew he moved his sheep to the mountains during the summer and that transporting them was always a big production.

"Good thing you remembered your lambs need vaccinating before they take off for the hills," Luke said mildly.

"In the old days, your dad used to call me when it was time for the boosters."

Luke's jaw tightened for a brief instant. How difficult it must be for him to constantly be compared to his father. Yes, the previous Dr. Gentry had been a wonderful veterinarian, from all she had heard of the man, but Luke was amazing, too. He shouldn't have to constantly prove himself to the people of Emerald Creek.

"Yes, I checked on that after you called yesterday. According to our records, we mailed a reminder postcard three weeks ago that it was time to schedule, but they can be easy to miss. I'll make a note in your chart to have the office staff give you a call next year."

"Thank you. Appreciate that."

Without further ado, he led them around the barn to a large pen where around a hundred ewe-lamb pairs milled.

She loved seeing the lambs, so gangly and adorable.

With the herders and Paul's help, over the next hour, they were able to separate the lambs and drive them through a chute to where Luke could quickly check them each out for disease or injury, vaccinate them, then return them to the pen where the ewes bleated in confusion and concern.

Madi's job was mainly to hand him the next vaccine and discard the used one. Nothing too demanding, which gave her time to watch Luke's gentle competence with the animals as well as the drama playing out as the lambs were returned to the pen.

She was invariably amazed at how the ewes were able to effortlessly find their own lambs in the crowded pen. She saw a few stray lambs who weren't immediately reunited with their mothers, but things were soon sorted.

Paul Lancaster joined them as Luke was putting away his medical bag and removing his surgical gloves.

"There you go. That should cover you for now."

"Thanks."

They chatted about the herd's upcoming trip to the mountains as Paul walked them back to Luke's truck.

Only when they reached the pickup did the old farmer turn to Madi.

"I hear your sister is back in town," he said bluntly, without a segue, as if he had been stockpiling the topic and now realized he had almost missed his chance to bring it up.

Madi could feel herself tense. "Yes. That's right."

"That book of hers. Why'd she have to go and stir up all that ugliness again? She ought to have let sleeping dogs lie."

Madi couldn't disagree with the man, though she knew they had very different reasons. It must be hitting very close to home for him, she suddenly realized, annoyed with herself for not connecting the dots earlier.

His daughter Mariah and her husband, Benjamin Woodley, had been active members of the Ghost Lake Survival Coalition fifteen years ago. For all she knew, Paul had as well. She knew there were other followers of the Boyle brothers who had never been caught, others who had bought into their combination of conspiracy theories wrapped up in mystical prophecies and pure hogwash.

Both of the Woodleys had served prison time, though they had cooperated with authorities and testified against the leaders of the group. Last she heard, they had moved to Nevada somewhere.

She was able to give them more grace than some who had been there, as Mariah Woodley had always been kind to her and Ava and used to sneak them food when she could. Madi had the impression Mariah and her husband had been trying to extricate themselves from the group prior to the events of that summer.

"I d-don't know why Ava wrote the book now. That's a g-good question. One you'll have to ask her. I can't answer for my sister."

"When you see her, tell her she should have left well enough alone. Nothing good comes from raking up the past, digging up old bones," he muttered.

Madi found herself in the uncomfortable position of feeling as if she had to defend her sister against something she agreed with one hundred percent.

Before she could find the words, Luke spoke up.

"Ava has every right to publish her story."

While his words were said in an even tone, Madi could see heat kindle in his eyes.

"Not when it doesn't only affect her. There are people involved like my daughter and son-in-law who have paid their debts to society, changed their ways. They don't need everybody pointing fingers at them and whispering. My son-in-law is worried about losing his job. How's he supposed to support his family if that happens?"

Maybe he should have thought of that before becoming tangled up with men who twisted logic and reason into something hideous and evil, she thought.

"I'm sorry that's happening to Benjamin," Luke said, his voice careful and without expression. "That's nothing to do with Ava or her book."

"He and Mariah have spent years trying to put everything behind them only to have that woman go and dredge it all up again."

"*That woman* was a child when she and her sister were dragged into a situation they didn't choose. When they refused to go along with abhorrent plans for them conceived by twisted, evil men, they were locked up, tortured, starved. When these *young girls* finally found the courage to escape, they were pursued by heavily armed men with vicious dogs. I'm sorry your son-in-law and daughter are upset about the book. But Ava had every right to tell her story, to let people know about what happened in the mountains near here while others did nothing to help them."

Madi caught her breath at his vehemence, the harsh tone she never heard from Luke.

Paul said nothing, his features dark with anger. When he spoke, his voice was low. "I'm sorry to hear you say that. I hear there's a new vet up Hailey way. I always liked and respected your father and was sorry as could be that he was killed. But maybe it's time I look elsewhere for my next round of vaccines."

"That's certainly your choice," Luke said, his voice even. "Let my office know whatever you decide so someone else can handle your next round of vaccinations."

He nodded to the man and climbed into the truck. Madi, still stunned from the argument, climbed into the passenger seat. She had barely closed her door before Luke drove away, leaving Paul Lancaster to watch after them with a dark expression on his weather-beaten face.

10

Our journey takes an unexpected turn as we reach the edge of a fast-flowing river. The water roars with a deafening intensity, a turbulent barrier standing between us and freedom. With no other choice, we wade into the icy stream, the current pulling at our legs like invisible hands trying to drag us under. The frigid water numbs our limbs, but we press on, the urgency of our escape drowning out the discomfort.

—*Ghost Lake* by Ava Howell Brooks

Luke

MADI FUMED BESIDE HIM FOR THE ENTIRE DRIVE BACK to her house on the old Pruitt farm.

"How nervy," she finally burst out as he approached the farmhouse. "The man drags you out on a Saturday to v-vaccinate his lambs at the last minute because *he* forgot to schedule an appointment. And then he actually threatens to take his business elsewhere over something completely out of your c-control. Now do you see how that st-stupid b-book is ruining everything?"

"He has every right to take his business elsewhere. That's his choice. I don't have the monopoly on veterinary medicine in the area. There are several other excellent vets within a sixty-mile radius."

"None of them are as good as you," she said with a loyalty that touched him. "Can't he see that you're a completely innocent victim in this whole thing? Your family had absolutely nothing to do with the Ghost L-Lake C-Coalition, but you all paid a terrible price because of them. B-because of us."

Her words tangled more than usual, a certain sign of how upset she was. He glanced across the cab of his truck briefly before returning his gaze to the road. That quick look was enough to show him she was almost vibrating with anger.

"Not because of you," he corrected. "You and Ava were the most innocent victims."

"Innocent victims who…who dragged you and your family into a nightmare you had nothing to do with. Your father is d-dead because of us. Sierra and your niece and nephew never had the chance to meet their…g-grandfather."

Her voice hitched on that last word, and Luke felt the familiar ache of sorrow, missing his father keenly. He pulled the truck to the side of the road into a clearing overlooking the vast peaks of the Sawtooths.

A mountain bluebird flitted through the red twig dogwoods along the creek and he could see a couple of magpies watching them warily.

"You can't think you're to blame for what happened to my dad."

Had she truly held this inside her all these years, blaming herself for the choices of others?

"Can't I?" she looked out the window at the still-snowcapped mountains, green and rugged and beautiful.

"You shouldn't. You were an innocent child. You could not have known what would happen."

"We never should have approached your camp," she said. Her words flowed more fluently, which told him she had thought this many times. "We had spent days avoiding people after our escape, trying to work our own way out of the mountains without being seen, without being scented by the dogs. We had stayed away from the few people we caught glimpses of from a distance. That was partly because we did not know who to trust, but also because we did not want to drag anyone else into the situation. But I was starving and sick and Ava... Ava knew I wouldn't have lasted much longer. I wish to God we had stuck to our original plan and skirted around your camp on our way down the mountain to our grandmother's house here in Emerald Creek. We had no idea they were so close b– behind us."

What he remembered most about that day was the argument he and his father had been having. Luke had been nineteen, home for the summer after his first year of college.

He had announced only the week before that he didn't want to return to school. A friend of his had taken a job on a fishing trawler in Alaska and wanted Luke to come join him.

The money was amazing. He could work a few seasons and save up enough to finish school without having to take out student loans.

What he hadn't told his father was his own self-doubt, the anxiety that he wasn't cut out for even undergrad work, forget about the rigorous requirements to earn a doctor of veterinary medicine. Luke had feared he was a failure who could never measure up to the amazing Dr. Dan Gentry, so what was the point in trying?

They had agreed to a cease-fire so they could both enjoy a long-planned fishing trip to their favorite lake deep in the Sawtooth wilderness.

This had been an annual tradition for them, when his father would close the practice for a few days and take him, Nicole and Owen on the seven-mile hike into the backcountry to Three Peaks Lake, which teemed with native trout and Arctic grayling. They would camp beside the lake and fish and eat and talk and fish some more.

It was a tradition they loved and looked forward to all year.

The first night had been good, with everyone getting along. But the second afternoon, angry words had seethed between him and his father, until Owen had stalked off to the lake to fish on his own and Nicki had retreated into her tent with a book.

He and his father were sitting in angry silence when two sunburned, bedraggled girls wearing ripped, filthy, old-style prairie dresses had burst into their camp.

He could remember it like it had happened that morning. The girls were half-starved, covered in insect bites, Ava sobbing as she begged for their help.

The two girls had poured out an unbelievable story of imprisonment, beatings, abuse.

He and his father had easily set aside their argument, both of them aghast at what they were hearing. Dan Gentry had a satellite phone that he always carried with him into the backcountry. He quickly called for help, and Luke could remember how his father had tried to explain what was happening to a confused dispatcher. His father had finally snapped out that they had found two kidnapped girls and needed an immediate rescue.

Luke had provided their GPS location and they had been pulling down their provisions from the bear-safe food bags hung in the trees when they first heard the dogs and the shouting of men on the hunt.

He pushed the memory away now. He had enough nightmares about what came next. He didn't need to focus on it.

"You and Ava could not have known what would happen," he said now to Madi.

"We should have," she argued. "We had been running for our own lives for d-days. We had traveled through miles of wilderness to try to get them off our trail. Up and down mountains, crossing rivers again and again, knowing they couldn't be far behind us. That they would never stop until they found us. We knew what they would do to us and anybody who helped us. We should never have stopped at your camp."

He took her hand, the one that curled slightly and could never straighten completely because of all that had happened to her. His heart broke a little as it trembled in his.

"Madi. Stop. My dad would not have done a single thing differently. You have to know that. He never would have turned his back on the two of you, even if he had known that it would ultimately cost him his life."

That was yet another way Luke could never measure up to his father, yet he had spent every day since then trying his best. He failed most of the time, but that would only spur him to try harder the next day.

"I wish none of it had ever happened," she mumbled, her mouth twisted.

"I know, honey. I'm sorry." He hated that she had paid such a bitter price, and would for the rest of her life.

She sniffled but didn't cry. She was tough, even in this. Still, he handed her a tissue from the box he kept in the door of his pickup. She wiped at her nose. He studied her, fierce and brave and lovely, and couldn't help himself. He pulled her across the bench seat and into a hug.

She sagged into him, resting her cheek against his chest. They sat in silence for a long time, both of them lost in the past. This wasn't the first time he had held her in an embrace. They were friends, almost like family, and she was always generous with her hugs.

They had danced the night before, and he had been caught by the softness of her skin and the strawberries-and-cream smell of her shampoo, wondering why he had never noticed how perfectly she fit against him before.

Something felt...different between them. A deeper connection tugging them together.

He wanted to kiss her.

The desire blossomed in his chest like her grandmother's big, lush peonies. He wanted to lower his mouth to hers and taste her.

He couldn't do that. Madi was like a sister to him. She had been since she and Ava had burst into their lives. He had no business thinking of her in any other way.

His father would have been furious with him.

A decent man would never even consider taking advantage of a vulnerable woman.

Dan had drilled that advice into his and Owen's heads from the time they were old enough to start thinking about the opposite sex.

He tamped down on his desire and lowered his arms, easing back into his own seat.

"You okay now?"

She gave him a wary look, much like those lambs did when he came at them with the needle. "I... Yes. I think so."

Had she felt that heat shiver to life between them, as if something long-buried had begun to awaken?

She shifted her gaze out the windows, toward the wild, jagged mountains.

"I've kept you much longer than I intended. You told me you had a big to-do list."

"I do. Yes."

"Any concerns with any of your residents?" he asked. "How's the kitten? Do you need me to check her?"

She didn't answer him immediately, as if her mind had been elsewhere and it was taking her time to catch up.

"She's probably fine. I think everyone else is okay for now."

"You know I'm available for you whenever you need me, right?"

She gave her half smile. "I know. Thank you. I never could have made it this far with the sanctuary if not for your help."

"I'm happy it's working out." He paused. "I'll see you tomorrow at dinner, right?"

She made a face. "I still haven't decided if I'll be there or not."

"You have to go. I need you to help me cheer up Sierra. She's going to be moping around like a…"

"Like a girl who's just lost her best friend?"

"Yes. Exactly like that." He smiled. "Surely you wouldn't abandon her in her hour of need. Plus we're celebrating her birthday. You can't miss that."

She sighed. "I don't want to talk to Ava."

"You know how hectic things can be at my mom's Sunday dinners. A few dozen people, filling up the whole house and the yard. If you don't want to speak with someone, it's easy enough to avoid them."

"I don't know. I'll have to see."

He decided to stick his neck out even further.

"You should think about making your peace with Ava. She's your only sister."

"Sure. I'll think about it. As soon as people stop throwing that stupid book in my face, bringing it up again and again."

"You're going to be waiting a long time, I'm afraid. I suspect *Ghost Lake* will only gain more traction as time goes on. Your story is one that resonates with people on many levels."

"Why?" she burst out. "That's the part I don't understand. Who even cares about something that happened fifteen years ago? It barely even made the papers when it happened."

"Because it's a story of survival and courage. We need those kinds of stories as much now as ever."

"We didn't do anything that remarkable," she muttered.

"You were two young girls who endured months of imprisonment at the hands of a violent group of adults who were heavily armed, then somehow found the courage to escape from them. You went on the run into the wilderness with nothing but your own grit. You survived days on your own, living on berries and roots and tree bark and drinking from mountain streams. Then, in that final confrontation, when you were seconds from being rescued by authorities, you were shot in the head."

That was another memory that lived on in his nightmares.

"Yet somehow you survived, again by that sheer force of indomitable will, and have rebuilt your life. People need stories like that."

"Fine. They can get them somewhere else. I never wanted to be the center of attention. I prefer to focus on the animals who need homes, not on something that happened fifteen years ago."

With that, she opened the door and climbed out. "I need to go."

"Okay," he said, sensing she had talked about this all she wanted to. "What about tomorrow?"

She sighed. "Now who is the relentless one? Maybe. If I go, it will be for Sierra's sake. Not to make up with Ava."

He watched her move toward the small farmhouse, which needed paint. *The animals come first*, Madi had said when he suggested she spend some of their recent, generous gift to spruce up the house.

She walked up the steps, her gait slightly uneven from the brace she wore on her left leg, and waved at him when she opened the door.

He knew Madi worried everyone looked at her with pity, that they only saw her weaknesses.

He wanted her to see herself as he did. As the rest of the world was beginning to, thanks to Ava's book—as a remarkable woman, an example of strength and courage and grace.

11

Normalcy is a foreign concept, and every decision feels like a crossroads that could either lead us to healing or trigger the memories we've fought so hard to suppress.

—*Ghost Lake* by Ava Howell Brooks

Madison

FROM INSIDE THE HOUSE, MADI LOOKED THROUGH the gauzy curtains Nicole had hastily sewn after they moved into the farmhouse that hadn't seen a woman's touch in years. She still felt annoyingly breathless as she watched Luke walk away.

What had just happened?

For a minute, she could swear Luke Gentry had looked at her with an expression of...admiration. More than that. *Attraction.*

For the tiniest of moments, he had actually looked as if he wanted to kiss her.

That was impossible. Why would the most gorgeous man in town look at her that way? The man had single-handedly increased the pet adoption rate in the county among the female sector, at least, so they could have an excuse to bring their fur babies into his office.

She had to be imagining things. Luke certainly could not be attracted to her. She was Madison Howell, of the fumbling words and the leg brace and the mouth that couldn't smile completely.

It must have been a trick of the light or maybe her eyes were filled with dust kicked up by Paul Lancaster's lambs.

Eventually, she let the curtain fall and made her way to the kitchen, where she found Nicole sitting at the table, nibbling on a piece of dry toast, a half-empty coffee mug in front of her.

"Morning," she said, her voice a croak. Her eyes had deep shadows and her hair looked like she had lost a fight with a rabid raccoon during the night. Which was probably an accurate description.

"Morning."

"Was that Luke I saw drop you off?"

She nodded, bustling about to make some tea, since she wasn't in the mood for more coffee. "Yes. He needed help giving some lamb vaccines at the Lancaster farm, so I volunteered."

"Did you tell me about it? I don't remember."

"Probably not. It came up last night and we made final arrangements after we left the Burning Tree."

"Oh right. After you ditched me."

"I didn't ditch you! I told you I was leaving. As I recall, you seemed fine with it. But maybe my memories of last night are clearer than yours, for obvious reasons."

Nicole made a face. "You know you should never trust what I say when I'm having fun with a gorgeous guy. What if he had turned out to be an axe murderer instead of a sweet guy from Canada?"

"He still could be. I'm sure they have axe murderers in Canada, too."

"Seriously. You shouldn't have ditched me. What about our buddy system?"

Guilt pinched at her. "You're right. I'm a terrible friend. I should have stayed with you. I was just…tired of people bringing up Ava's damned book."

"I get it," Nicki said, her features soft with sympathy.

Madi was quick to change the subject. "I noticed you didn't bring your car home. I wasn't spying, I was up with the dogs when you rolled in with Austin. He seems nice."

"He is. And smart, too. He's in grad school right now in hydrology."

And advanced make-out sessions in the driveway, apparently.

"Are you seeing him again?"

"Yes. He wanted to go out again tonight but I have to work. We're talking about next week. Also, my mom texted me this morning before I was up. She wants to be sure you're planning on coming to dinner tomorrow."

Oy. Tilly Gentry Walker did *not* give up. Surely Luke hadn't even had time to let her know Madi was conflicted about attending. Apparently the woman wanted to cover all the bases by having Luke *and* Nicole remind her about the meal.

"I'm not sure whether I can make it yet." She sipped her coffee, avoiding her friend's gaze.

"Why not? Do you have plans I don't know about?"

She thought about making something up but that seemed cowardly. Besides, Nic had been her best friend for fifteen years. She always seemed to know when Madi was lying.

"No plans, other than doing my best to avoid my sister, whatever it takes. You know if Leona comes to dinner, she will drag Ava with her and I really don't feel like sitting down at the table with a woman whom I suspect would be remarkably adept at jabbing a steak knife between my ribs."

She frowned. "Ava loves you dearly. You know that."

If her sister loved her, she would have respected her privacy. She never would have capitalized on their shared trauma.

She didn't say any of this to her roommate. In truth, she was heartily sick of talking about Ava.

"Should I tell my mom you can't make it, then? She will be so disappointed not to see you but I have no doubt at all she could find another hungry mouth to feed."

While she knew Nicole didn't mean the words literally, Madi knew they were true. Like many small towns in the West, Emerald Creek was an unfortunate dichotomy, with millionaires snatching up land all over town, especially along the river bottoms and the banks of the Emerald Creek reservoir. Their elaborate Western lodges, gleaming glass and hand-hewn logs, were sometimes planted next door to shell-shocked, long-time locals like Paul Lancaster, who were still trying to figure out what had happened to their cozy rural community.

The workers in these tourism-heavy areas who served in the fancy restaurants and worked at the hotel front desks often couldn't afford to live in the same towns where they were employed because housing prices were completely out of reach.

Madi suspected that some of the animals they had already helped at the Emerald Creek Animal Rescue had been abandoned by owners who could no longer afford their care.

"I'll come, since we'll be celebrating Sierra's birthday next week. If the cost of showing up for that is putting up with my sister for a few hours, I can handle it. Contrary to popular belief, I am capable of acting like an adult occasionally."

"I never said you weren't," Nicki protested.

No one had said it, but Madi felt like a whiny child, anyway.

"I should head over to the barn. I think I need to go hang out with the animals for a few hours. They, at least, probably won't want to talk about Ava's book."

Nicki laughed, then winced at the sound before returning to her toast.

The kitten mewed from her crate in the corner. Madi picked her up, grabbed the kitten milk substitute and headed out for the barn. She would feed her there, she decided.

When she pushed open the door, she was greeted by a cacophony of animals, as well as a wave by Ed Hyer, one of the dozen or so volunteers who helped out.

"Morning, boss."

"Sorry it's taken me so long to get here. I had to work unexpectedly. Thanks for filling in for me. Anything interesting been going on?"

"Everybody has been fed and watered. We had playtime with the senior dogs and I was about to let the young ones into the yard."

"Okay. I can do that as soon as I feed this little girl."

He looked with interest at the kitten. "She's new, isn't she?"

"Yes." She told him the story of Charla Pope finding the kitten in her flower bed and of Luke giving her a preliminary exam.

"He's such a great guy, isn't he?" Ed said.

Madi tried not to remember Luke's arms around her the night before at the tavern or that light in his eyes this morning. "Yes. He really is."

"Oh, we got a phone call from some campers who claimed they saw a couple of stray dogs up in the Sawtooths on the road to Ghost Lake. They looked pretty rough, apparently. One had a collar but the other one didn't. I was thinking about heading up there off-roading this afternoon to see if I can track them down."

This wasn't the first report of stray dogs living in the mountains that she had heard. Sometimes they wandered away from campers, sometimes they escaped their owners in town or sometimes people abandoned them in the mountains, thinking they could fend for themselves.

It usually didn't end well for the dogs in any of those scenarios.

"Sounds good. Can you fit a crate in the back of your side-by-side in case you can find them?"

"Yeah. I have a nice cargo area. I figured I'd take a package of hot dogs and see if that might draw them in."

"Need me to come with you?"

"No. I'll see if my grandson wants to take a ride up in the mountains. Maybe we'll take the fishing rods. Kill two birds."

"Or kill a few fish, anyway."

He smiled. "Never hurts to try. Need me to feed that little thing?"

"That would be helpful. Thanks."

She poured the milk substitute into a bowl and handed him a dropper. Ed was one of her most reliable volunteers, always willing to do whatever was needed.

A retired engineer in his midseventies, he had moved here from the Seattle area with his wife to be closer to his daughter and her family. Sadly, his wife had died of a stroke a few years ago.

She strongly suspected he might have a bit of a thing for another volunteer, Ada Duncan, though he treated her with the same teasing charm he did everyone else.

Sometimes she wondered if Ed was her mysterious benefactor, the donor who had given the seed money for her to take the shelter to the next level. It was possible. He lived in a beautiful log home on some acreage, and she gathered he had a healthy retirement income. She had once heard him talking about investments with another of the volunteers.

Ed had never given her any clue that he was the one responsible for the gift, but she still couldn't help but wonder. Who else would have been so generous?

She spent the next few hours working on paperwork, scheduling social media posts and organizing the volunteer schedule for the coming weeks.

Finally, tired of office work, she decided to take the puppies out to explore the fenced play area. She carried them out in batches of two and was taking the final pair out when she spotted Sierra Gentry pulling up beside the play area on her bike. Her eyes were suspiciously red and she looked upset.

Madi greeted Luke's daughter with a sympathetic smile. "I didn't think I would see you today. I heard about Zoe going to stay with her dad."

"What am I supposed to do all summer without her?"

"She's not your only friend. You have Mariko and Yuki and others."

"I know. And I love my other friends. I do. But Zoe is my *best* friend. My ride or die, like you and Aunt Nicki. I'm going to miss her so much."

Madi felt a wave of gratitude for Nicole, who had befriended her in the early days after her injury, when she was still in rehab and Nic herself had been grieving.

She had come weekly to visit her while she was in the rehabilitation center, then when Madi moved here to Emerald Creek to live permanently with Leona, Nicki would come every day after school to keep her company.

She suspected visiting her had been therapy for Nicki, as well, who was mourning her father and struggling through the trauma of that day.

"And we're going to have to go through all of this again next summer! It sucks," Sierra complained.

"I know it's hard and you'll miss her. But you can video chat all day long if you want. And you have plenty to keep you busy here in town, right? You're helping at the vet clinic and you can volunteer here as often as you want."

"Yeah. That's true." She let herself into the enclosure and sat on the grass. One of the chubby black Labrador-mix puppies plopped in the grass next to her and Sierra smiled, though her eyes remained watery.

The creatures were pretty hard to resist, Madi thought.

One of the puppies came over and tugged at Madi's shoelace and she smiled as she redirected it by throwing a ball.

"I felt so bad after Zoe left for the airport, all I could think about was coming out here and snuggling one of these little guys."

"You're welcome anytime you need doggy hugs."

"Thanks, Mad." Sierra picked up the chubby, cuddly puppy and held him up to her face. "They're all so cute. I don't know how you can ever give them up to a new home."

"They would much rather be in a loving home than here. We have to make sure we find the best placements for them."

"Are you doing an adoption day?"

"I've been talking about it with some of the volunteers. We have to figure out when and where."

"You could really play it up on social media so everybody knows you're doing it."

"Actually," Madi said, "that reminds me. I was going to see if you want to help me out with a special project."

"What kind of special project?" Sierra looked intrigued but wary.

"How would you feel about helping me out with our social media? I know how much fun you have looking at clips on-line. You could take some pictures to document some of the things we're doing and maybe create a couple of short videos every so often with the animals."

Sierra's face lit up, her eyes looking less devastated by the minute. "That could be fun."

"You can be my official deputy social media manager."

"Can I have my own office?"

Madi grinned and gestured around the grassy area. "Sure. How about right here in the play yard?"

"That would be awesome! You can bring me out a desk and everything!"

"A lawn chair, maybe. We could probably swing that."

"Good enough for me," Sierra said, then returned to play-ing with the puppies.

She loved Luke's daughter. She had a generous spirit and a kind soul. When Sierra was younger, she had always been drawn to Madi. Sierra had never seemed to mind when her words didn't come out right or she couldn't smile fully.

Over the past four years since Johanna's death, their relationship had deepened. Madi could relate to losing her mother at around the same age, in a deep, visceral way that others couldn't quite understand.

Sierra would talk to Madi about her mom and how much she missed her. Madi suspected she confided in *her* things she couldn't tell her father, her aunt or her grandmother.

In many ways, she considered Sierra the younger sister she never had.

"Are you feeling better?" she asked, after they had played with the puppies for another half hour.

"It's hard to be sad when you're laughing at these guys."

"I've always found that keeping busy helping someone else is an excellent antidote to feeling sad."

"You sound like my grandma."

"I can only dream of being as wise as Tilly."

Sierra helped her carry the puppies back into their large shared dog run.

She was filling the bowl with food while Sierra refilled the water bowl when the girl spoke out of the blue.

"Do you think my dad would ever date somebody again?"

Madi jerked, startled, and some of the kibble spilled on the floor. The grateful puppies didn't seem to mind.

"Why would you ask that?" she asked, keeping her tone as neutral as she could manage.

Sierra shrugged. "I don't know. Maybe thinking about how weird it is for Zoe, now that her dad has married someone else and moved away. I mean, she likes her stepmom okay but it still seems weird. I don't ever want a stepmom."

Madi did *not* want to have this conversation with the girl

right now, especially when she couldn't seem to stop thinking about how something seemed to have shifted in her relationship with Luke since the other night.

How could she tell Sierra that of all the confidences she and the girl had shared over the years, her father's love life was one subject Madi would prefer to avoid?

None of this was any of her business. But she couldn't shrug off the question. She drew in a deep breath and forced a smile.

"Your mom has been gone for several years. She loved you both very much, but don't you think she would want him to go on with his life eventually? Would you really want him to be alone forever?"

Sierra pursed her lips. "I don't know. That seems pretty selfish, doesn't it?"

"Not selfish. I understand your concerns."

"I mean, he could always wait until I go to college. Then I wouldn't care what he did. That's only five more years."

How could she gently suggest it would be better for Sierra to have this conversation with her father instead of Madi?

"Your dad is still relatively young. It's a lot to ask, for him to put his life on hold."

Sierra grew silent, her brow furrowed in thought as she returned the water hose to the hose bib. Finally, she spoke in a conspiratorial tone.

"I think he might have been with someone last night. I came home to grab my phone charger at about nine and he wasn't there. His room had a bunch of his nicer shirts on the bed, like he had been trying to figure out what to wear, and the bathroom smelled like he had showered and put on aftershave, which he hardly ever uses."

She didn't want to think about Luke getting ready for his night out. It felt far too intimate.

"He went to the Burning Tree with me and your aunt Nicole. We both left about the same time, around eleven.

Unless he met up with someone after that, I don't think you have anything to worry about."

"You'd tell me, though, if he was dating someone, wouldn't you? I don't want to be surprised out of the blue."

"Sure. If I hear anything, I'll definitely tell you about it."

"And if I hear anything, I'll tell you," Sierra said, as if she was doing Madi a huge favor.

Madi didn't have the heart to tell her that if Luke was dating another woman, she suddenly wasn't at all sure she wanted to know.

12

As we heal physically, the emotional wounds run deeper, a reminder that liberation is a process that extends far beyond the physical escape.

—*Ghost Lake* by Ava Howell Brooks

Ava

TILLY GENTRY WALKER'S HOME SAT ON A HILL SUR-rounded by forest land, with a spectacular view of the snow-topped mountains.

Ava had only been here once, several years ago.

When she had lived in Emerald Creek, Tilly had been a widow living in a house much nearer her late husband's veterinary clinic.

Tilly had remarried about five years ago and moved here with her new husband, to this rambling ranch house overlooking town and the mountains beyond.

As much as she admired Tilly, and all of the Gentry family, really, Ava did not want to be here. Her stomach curled with anxiety. If her grandmother were not walking beside her up the front walk to the wide porch, Ava would have turned around, made her way back down that sweep of a driveway and headed back to Leona's house.

The journey was only two miles and downhill most of the way. She could be home in twenty minutes, if she walked fast.

Her muscles quivered as she fought the urge to flee.

She couldn't leave. She had given her word to her grandmother. Ava had hurt enough people lately. She wouldn't add Leona to the list.

Beyond that, she was carrying her grandmother's much-loved frog-eye salad. She certainly couldn't deprive the guests of that.

Over the years, Tilly had become one of Leona's dearest friends. They had always been friendly, her grandmother once had told her. They had belonged to some of the same groups, had served together on the library board and in leadership of a church women's group.

Their friendship had been warm but casual, until the events of that summer had linked their families together forever.

"I believe everyone will be in the back," Leona said now, her arms laden with the marbled brownies she also had made that afternoon. "That's where they usually gather during the summertime. They have a beautiful patio area, with a waterfall and a pond. Have you been back there?"

"Yes, but it's been years. When Tilly remarried, the reception was here, remember?"

"Oh, that's right. I forgot you came home for that. Well, lucky for Tilly, she married a man who loves to garden and he has created a mountain paradise back there."

Ava forced a smile. "Great. I can't wait to see it."

"We'll stop inside first to drop off my salad and brownies and see if Tilly needs help with anything."

"Good idea," Ava lied, when she really wanted to go back to her grandmother's house, climb into her bed and stay there for the next few months.

When had she become such an introvert? She and Cullen

had always loved to throw dinner parties for their friends. They would invite her coworkers at the middle school or other academics from the university where he was an assistant professor.

Ava loved to cook, something she had inherited from her mother and grandmother. She would spend hours coming up with menus and going to the market, then would spend the day prepping the meal and laying out the table, with Cullen popping in and out to help where he could.

Her heart ached as she remembered the long kisses they would always share whenever he came into the kitchen, until she would tell him he had to stop distracting her or nothing would be ready on time.

After the final guest would leave, Cullen always cleaned up. Ava would fall into an exhausted sleep waiting for him, only to awaken with him curled around her.

She fought down the raw yearning. Were those moments gone forever? The day before, Cullen had seemed like a distant, polite stranger instead of a man who had always told her how much he adored her.

She managed not to sob as Leona rang the doorbell. Ten seconds later, a small girl with dark hair and brown eyes answered the doorbell and beamed at them.

"Hi."

"Hello there, Lottie. Remember me? I'm Leona. I'm friends with your grandmother. And this is my granddaughter, Ava."

"Hi. I'm Lottie. I'm three years old."

"Hello. It's lovely to meet you."

"I like to slide."

With that non sequitur, the girl turned around and raced back through the house, a blur of energy.

"Okay. Good to know," Leona said with a smile as she led the way through the house toward the kitchen, clearly well acquainted with the layout.

Inside the huge bright kitchen with its high-end appliances

and gleaming marble countertops, they found Tilly Gentry Walker in the middle of everything, directing an army of helpers as her guests chopped, diced, stirred.

Tilly herself worked at the huge kitchen island, with its contrasting wood to the cabinets, cutting watermelon into triangles while around her the kitchen bustled with activity.

Ava released a breath when she realized her sister, the one person she wanted most to avoid, wasn't here.

Tilly looked up to smile at them, her pretty features lit by the afternoon sun coming in from a skylight in the room. "Ava, my dear. It's been far too long."

She rinsed her hands quickly in the sink, dried them on her pin-striped apron, then rushed toward them to throw her arms around Ava's neck.

"Here's our celebrity author. *New York Times* bestseller, darling. Oh, your mother would have been so proud of you."

Ava swallowed against that ache of emotion that seemed constantly in her throat these days.

Would her mother have been proud? It was a moot question. Circular reasoning. If her mother hadn't died, her father would have stayed grounded in reality, none of the events she had written about would have happened and she wouldn't have needed to write a memoir about any of it.

If said memoir had never been written, she wouldn't have been able to hit any bestseller lists, right?

"Thank you, Tilly." She quickly changed the subject. "I love your kitchen renovation. I especially love the contrasting wood on your island and the waterfall edge."

"Thank you. That's one of my favorite things as well."

"I brought my frog-eye salad and brownies, as ordered," Leona said, holding up her covered tray and gesturing to the salad Ava carried.

"Perfect. I'm leaving the desserts in here for now so they stay cooler. Just find a place."

Leona set them next to two pies and a large platter of cookies.

"How else can I help?" her grandmother asked.

"You don't need to do a thing. Everything is nearly done. Boyd, Luke and Owen are handling the grill and we've got things covered in here. Ava, you remember my sister, Penny. And this is Owen's wife, Valentina. Val, this is Madi's sister, Ava."

"Hello." The woman was small in stature and extraordinarily beautiful. She held a baby bundled against her in a no-hands sling.

"Penny, hello. It's lovely to see you again. Hello, Valentina. I believe we met your daughter. She looks exactly like you."

The woman smiled. "Yes. That would probably be my Carlotta. She loves to answer the doorbell."

"Apparently she was heading out to slide," Leona informed her.

"Good. Her father can watch over her."

"Are you sure we can't help?" Ava asked her hostess. She knew too well what it was like, trying to supervise willing volunteers who sometimes only ended up getting in the way.

"You can go outside and enjoy yourselves! Boyd has cold drinks out there."

"I'll take the salad out."

"Do you need a serving spoon?"

"I can grab it," her grandmother said.

As another example of their close friendship, Leona helped herself, going straight to a drawer in the island and rooting through until she found a large ladle for the salad.

"Come on. Let me show you around the garden."

Leona hadn't exaggerated about the space out here. From Tilly's wedding to Boyd Walker, Ava remembered the garden as a comfortable space with winding paths and random benches for looking out at the town below.

She didn't remember the waterfall cascading over rocks or the small pond with colorful water lilies. She saw Owen Gentry sitting in a chair next to the pond, most likely to keep his busy daughter from wandering in.

The water's song was soothing, comfortable. Ava wanted to sink down onto one of those benches with her journal and write and write until she purged her mind of these twisted ribbons of anxiety.

A low sound of appreciation escaped her. Leona, hearing it, gave a gentle smile. "It's lovely, isn't it?"

"It makes me a little breathless."

"Be sure you tell Boyd. It is his pride and joy."

The man in question was large and barrel-chested, with a full head of white hair and a broad smile.

There was indeed a play area, covered in tire swings and slides and what appeared to be an old-fashioned-playground merry-go-round. She felt something squeeze her chest as she remembered playing on one for hours with her sister at the school near their house in Oregon.

She had been the oldest. The protector.

Watch over your sister.

How many times had she heard her mother say those words as they left the house?

She'd had one job and she had failed abysmally.

"Why don't you take this over to the table?" Leona said, handing the salad bowl to Ava. "I'm suddenly dying of thirst and need to see what Boyd has on offer."

Still looking around warily for any sign of her sister, she carried the bowl to a serving table already heavy with food.

She was thinking she could use a drink as well when she heard a male voice calling her name.

"Ava! Great to see you again."

The voice was dearly familiar and so was the man who said the words, Lucas Gentry. Some of her anxiety seeped away.

There was simply no room for it amid the comfort of a long-standing friendship.

"Hi, Luke. Great to see you, too."

He reached out to hug her and she returned the embrace, heartened at the genuine warmth in his greeting.

"Is Cullen joining you?" he asked when he set her away from him.

She was getting slightly better at ignoring that sharp ache in her chest at the mention of her husband's name. Slightly. "Not right now, I'm afraid. He's working at a job site up near Ghost Lake and it's hard for him to get away."

He sent her a swift look and she knew exactly what was going through his head, the same dark memories she had. Gunfire, screaming, the barking of dogs and the *whoop-whoop* of helicopter blades.

"Is he?" he only said, his tone mild.

"A few campers stumbled onto a fossil bed and further exploration uncovered what might be a new species of dinosaur. He's leading the excavation team."

"Good for him! That's so exciting. What kind of dinosaur?"

"They're not sure. It's different from the Oryctodromeus, which is the most commonly found dinosaur fossil around here. This one is larger and doesn't appear to live in burrows, like the Oryctodromeus. Other than that, they're not sure."

"Fascinating. I'd love the chance to talk with him about it sometime."

"I'll let him know. Maybe you could meet up while he's living in the area."

"Do they let visitors up to the site? Sierra used to love dinosaurs. I mean, she's thirteen, and right now she's more interested in TikTok videos of cute boys dancing, but I have to think maybe there's still some part of her that is fascinated by triceratops and utahraptors."

"I'm not sure what the policy is for visitors. I can ask next time I talk to him."

She looked around the yard. "Where is the birthday girl? I haven't seen her in forever. I imagine she's probably taller than I am by now."

He smiled, eyes bright with love for his daughter. "Not quite. She's still growing into her long legs. She should be here shortly. She spent the afternoon at the animal rescue helping Madi with a few things today."

Ava raised an eyebrow. "I'm shocked my fiercely independent sister lets anyone help her, even a thirteen-year-old girl."

"Madi is definitely independent, but believe it or not, she does let people help her sometimes, when it comes to her animals. She's got a whole team of volunteers on board, now that the animal rescue is fully operational."

Ava hadn't really thought of the work that must go into starting up a no-kill animal shelter in an area that had never had one. "I understand she'll be leaving your vet practice soon."

He made a face. "Unfortunately. She has wanted to do this for a long time."

"Yes. Since she was a girl bringing home every stray cat and dog in the neighborhood."

"She hasn't changed a bit," Luke said with an affectionate smile. "It's so great that everything has come together. First, a local farmer donated his property to the animal rescue foundation in his will, then the foundation received a particularly large gift from an anonymous donor."

Feeling her face heat, Ava carefully kept her gaze away from him, focusing instead on the beautiful, flowing water feature in the garden. Did he know? She didn't want to risk looking at him to search his features, since she was lousy at subterfuge.

"That is fortuitous, isn't it?" she said, her voice deliberately sanguine.

She quickly steered the conversation away from these dangerous waters, asking instead about his veterinary practice. In return, he asked her a few questions about *Ghost Lake* and some of the book's significant milestones.

She knew he had read it. Luke had called her shortly after she sent him the advanced reading copy, prior to publication. He had told her he had been deeply moved by every word. A triumph, he had told her.

Ava hadn't been as touched by any other commentary on the book as she was by his praise, especially as he had actually lived through some of the events she had written about.

They were talking about an interview request with one of the national morning news shows when his daughter burst into the yard, tall, slender, lovely.

She came right over and hugged her father, testament to their strong bond. "Hey, Dad."

Luke returned the hug. "Hey, Si. How were the puppies?"

"So cute! I could have played with them all day."

"Sorry you had to break away for a birthday party in your honor."

"Except my birthday's not until Saturday. Almost a week away."

Before Luke could answer, Madi came out of the house with Tilly, both of them carrying platters of vegetables and fruit.

Her sister looked bright and cheerful and…happy.

Ava caught her breath, yearning for the days when the two of them had been inseparable, before her guilt and shame at her own cowardice, at her own failure to protect her sister, had created a wedge between them that the years had only widened.

And then she had written a memoir that exposed all of the raw pain and dark memories for the entire world.

Yes, she had a multitude of reasons for agreeing to the publishing deal, but she doubted Madi could ever understand any of them.

Her stomach heaved suddenly, her throat burning. She was

going to lose the little she had eaten that day right here in this lovely garden, all over Dr. Luke Gentry and his daughter.

"Excuse me, won't you?"

She rushed into the house, hurrying to the half bath off the mudroom she remembered from Tilly's wedding. After quickly turning on both faucets to hide any sound, she threw up, feeling wretched and sick and wondering how her life could have completely imploded in a few short weeks.

13

Our father's demise, a tragic consequence of our rescue, adds another layer of complexity to my tangled web of emotions. In saving us, we lost him. The dichotomy of relief and grief is a bitter pill to swallow. I grapple with the notion that the man who inflicted so much pain upon us met his end in the chaos he created. It's a paradox that leaves me questioning the nature of justice and the price we pay for deliverance.

—*Ghost Lake* by Ava Howell Brooks

Madison

OKAY. THAT WAS WEIRD.

A few seconds earlier, Ava had hurried past her without a word. She looked through the glass sliding door to see Ava rushing into the half bath off the mudroom.

Madi only had time for a fleeting impression of pinched features and pale skin before the door closed behind Ava.

Her sister seemed genuinely ill. The first time Madi had seen her since she came to town, Ava had seemed more than simply uncomfortable about finding herself in Madi's presence.

Once, in that miserable time they spent in the mountains, Ava had come down with a severe pneumonia, probably from the grim cold and rough conditions. She had hidden it from everyone as best she could, her face turning red in the effort it took her not to cough, until it became impossible to hide.

After her condition continued to worsen, their father—in a rare show of parental concern—had insisted on using some of the Coalition's carefully hoarded supply of antibiotics. They had likely saved her life.

During their escape, Madi remembered, Ava had sprained her wrist falling down a slope in the dark. Madi hadn't known until she was recovering in the hospital and her sister had shown up wearing a sling. She must have been in incredible pain, but she had never said a thing.

What was wrong with her now that left her so pale and shaky?

She didn't care, she told herself. She knew her own words for a lie, especially when she couldn't resist making her way over to Luke, now helping his stepfather, Boyd, and brother, Owen, at the grill.

"Hey," he said with a smile that suddenly left her feeling wobbly inside. "Thanks for bringing Sierra."

"Sorry we took so long. She was a great help to me today."

"I'm glad."

"I saw you were talking to Ava when we arrived," she said, striving for a casual tone. "What happened that made her rush off like that?"

He frowned, looking in the direction Ava had fled. "I'm not exactly sure. She suddenly turned a little green and excused herself."

"Do you think something is wrong with her?"

"I'm a veterinarian, remember? Most of my patients have a few more legs and a lot more fur."

She made a face at him, barely refraining from sticking out her tongue.

He pulled a long, foil-wrapped packet off the grill with long metal tongs and set it on a serving platter, then repeated the process with a second packet. "The salmon is ready. Want to take it over to the table? Owen can carry the chicken over in a minute."

"Or you can," his younger brother said, lifting his beer laconically.

"Or I can," Luke agreed.

She took the platter, grateful as always that Luke never hesitated to ask her to do things. He didn't seem to care that she sometimes struggled with balance issues because of her leg or that her hand didn't work as well as she would like.

He simply assumed she could handle any task he set before her, whether that was crossing the patio with a platter of salmon or handling a reluctant puppy on its way for shots.

There in his mother's backyard, she suddenly realized his unswerving faith in her was one of the single most important things in her life.

As she carried the platter to the serving table, she remembered the day before, when he had looked at her with that expression that made her toes tingle.

She hadn't stopped thinking about that expression, trying to analyze it from every possible angle.

Ultimately, Madi had decided sometime in the wee hours of the night that she must have imagined the whole thing. Luke didn't think about her in that way. To him, she was no different from Nicole. He considered her a younger sister he could tease and provoke.

As she was arranging the platter with a few of the other items, Ava came out of the house, wiping at her mouth with a paper towel and sipping from the water bottle she had brought along.

Her sister did look pale. At least Madi thought so. But what did she know? Prior to her sister's return to Emerald Creek a few days ago, Madi hadn't seen her in person for about a year.

What if she had some incurable disease and didn't want to

share her diagnosis with Madi because of the discord between them?

She was angry with her sister, but she didn't want something
to happen to her. If she lost Ava, she and Leona wouldn't have
much family left.

Leona had one remaining son, who had never married and
lived in California. Her father had two brothers in Massachu-
setts, scions of a highbrow Bostonian family, but Clint hadn't
had a relationship with them since he defied his family's wishes
and enlisted in the Marines.

Madi didn't really know what had caused a rift between him
and his family. Maybe his outspokenness and strong opinions,
his independence and individualism philosophies.

What would *they* be thinking about Ava's book? She couldn't
imagine Clint Howell came out looking very good in the book.
How could he, when he had been the one to drag them into
the whole mess in the first place?

What did the Bostonian Howells think about their family
name being thrown out to the world for public scorn?

Her sister moved to a bench seat in the shade, near the pond,
where she chatted with one of Luke's aunts.

Tilly made a sound to draw everyone's attention.

"The boys are almost done grilling. The salmon and chicken
are ready and I understand the burgers are almost there." She
looked at the table, bulging with dishes. "It looks like we have
all of the side dishes out. Boyd, will you say grace? And then
you can all help yourselves."

As she listened with half an ear to the blessing over the food,
she peeked out from under her lids to see Ava with her eyes
closed and her mouth moving silently.

What did her sister pray for?

Probably more book sales.

Madi frowned darkly, her anger resurfacing. She knew it

wasn't fair, especially during a contemplative moment, but she couldn't seem to help her feelings.

Despite her overwhelming awareness of her sister's presence, a Sunday gathering at the Gentry-Walker home was always fun.

She sat at one of the tables set up under the covered porch and chatted with Nicole and also Boyd's youngest son and daughter-in-law, Brent and Samantha Walker, who lived on a ranch across the valley.

After the meal, some kind of physical contest was always organized in the grass field. One month it might be soccer, another flag football, another baseball. Her favorite was water-balloon volleyball, played with teams of two who held a towel between them to bounce the balloon back across the net.

Sunday dinner was never a sedate affair here. She loved it and would invariably join in the fun.

This time, they were playing soccer and she was designated goalie. She did her best to keep the competitive players on the other team, mainly the children of Boyd's son, as well as Nicole and Owen, from scoring against her.

She managed to successfully avoid her sister until people started to clean up the meal.

Somehow—she wasn't sure exactly what happened or if some interfering busybody had orchestrated it to bring the two sisters together—they both ended up in the kitchen at the same time, with Ava washing the dishes and Madi drying and putting them away.

How many times in their lives had they done exactly this in their house in Oregon?

Fierce longing reached out and smacked her across the face. Before their mother died, when the four of them had been a loving and happy family, she used to love cleaning up with her family after the evening meal.

Her father would turn the radio on and Clint and Beth

would dance around the kitchen while she and Ava giggled and blew bubbles at them from the dish soap.

Her father would in turn dance with each of them, patiently showing the steps as they moved around the kitchen.

The memory made her ache, thinking of his laughing gaze and how safe she always felt with him around.

She tried not to think about the time before Beth had been killed. It was too painful, remembering all those years when their home had been a place filled with love and laughter and peace.

Oh, she and Ava bickered like most other siblings close together in age. Sometimes they would fight about whose turn it was to clean their shared bathroom or who got to be the first one to read the latest book in a series they both loved. Sometimes they fought about who could pick the movie to watch for their weekly family movie nights. They bickered over clothes and toys and friends.

Despite those minor skirmishes, neither of them had ever doubted they were loved.

And then their mother died, a victim of a drunk driver, as she returned home late from a school board meeting.

They had all been devastated, as if the heart and soul had been ripped out of each of them. All three of them had walked around in a fog for months, their world shrinking down to work and school and home.

Without Beth, they were like a canoe caught in a snag on the river, spinning uselessly while the world moved on without them.

After six months, things started to slowly improve. Their father took more interest in life and began to do more than spend every moment in his room or out in his garage.

Neither she nor Ava had any idea that the thing bringing him out of his shell would become so destructive. He started obsessively participating in online forums their mother never would have condoned and spending nearly every weekend at gun shows or emergency preparedness seminars.

Somewhere in all of his fixations, he had connected with Roger and James Boyle and their loosely organized prepper group, the Ghost Lake Survival Coalition.

She had learned many years later from Leona that her father's interest in doomsday prophecies began even before their mother's death, that Beth had been so concerned about the direction his views had been heading that she had been contemplating divorce.

She and Ava had been oblivious to it, she supposed. Two girls more concerned with their favorite boy band breaking up than their father's descent into fanaticism.

She pushed the dark thoughts away as she and Ava worked in silence at the sink, allowing the conversation of the other people cleaning the kitchen to eddy around them like swirls and rivulets on the river.

Finally, they were down to the last dish and Madi brought up the topic that had been bothering her all evening.

"Are you sick or something?" she asked, the question more blunt than she intended.

Ava gave her one quick surprised look, then diverted her gaze back to the sink where the last of the dishwater glugged down the drain.

"Why do you say that?"

"Because you look even more like a pale urchin than usual and you hardly ate anything."

Ava's mouth firmed into a tight line. "Maybe I wasn't hungry. It's hard to work up much of an appetite, knowing you're eating with people who are furious with you."

"You said *people*. Who else is furious with you? It seems to me that everybody else here is fine and dandy with you spilling the tea to the whole world. Tilly invited you to a family dinner, for heaven's sake."

"Okay. When you're eating with your only sister, who hates you now."

Madi sighed, feeling small. "I don't hate you. I'm not very happy with you but I don't hate you. There's a difference."

"At least that's something," Ava muttered.

"So, are you sick?"

Ava swallowed and Madi didn't miss the way she avoided her gaze. "No. I think I must have caught a stomach bug a few weeks ago and I can't seem to shake it. That's all."

Madi knew something else was going on. Ava was a lousy liar. She just didn't know what questions to ask that might persuade her sister to tell her the truth.

"How long are you staying?"

"I still haven't decided. I don't have to be back to school until August."

"What are you going to do while you're here?" she asked.

Ava shrugged. "I don't know. Help Grandma in her garden, I guess. I worked at her stall at the farmers market yesterday, mostly handling the payments. I understand Grandma gives all the proceeds to you for the animal rescue."

She winced. Whenever Leona donated her weekly proceeds, Madi always felt like she was bilking an old lady out of her pocket change. "I keep telling her she doesn't have to do that, that she can use it on herself or the garden, but she insists."

"Every little bit helps, I suppose."

"It does. The whole community has really rallied around the Emerald Creek Animal Rescue."

"You're filling a need."

They lapsed into silence. She could see Ava was about to excuse herself. Later, she wasn't sure exactly what made her speak up. Maybe a yearning for those joy-filled cleanup parties in their Oregon home instead of this stilted awkwardness.

"We're always looking for volunteers to help out at the sanctuary."

"Volunteers?" Ava's eyes widened with shock, but the expression was quickly followed by one of interest.

Madi immediately regretted saying anything. "Right. Our pigpen can always use a good cleaning."

Ava puffed out a breath. "Oh, sign me up for that one."

"For your information, our pigs are adorable and very clean. But if you don't want to do that, you could play with the animals or help us with feedings or work in the office."

"I could maybe do that."

"You can sign up online. You should be prepared, though. We don't let just anybody volunteer. You have to go through our rigorous application process."

"To clean a pigpen."

"That's right."

"Good to know. I'll keep my fingers crossed I can make the cut. Will you excuse me, please?"

Ava set down the dishcloth and turned away from the kitchen, hurrying toward the half bath by the mudroom again. Madi watched her go, frowning. After a pause, she thought she heard the sound of retching, but the water was running loudly and she couldn't be sure.

She didn't really expect Ava to volunteer at the clinic. Her sister was allergic to cats and had a grave fear of dogs.

Cynophobia, it was called.

Madi knew where it came from.

Once at the camp, Ava had been attacked by the poor dogs that had been turned into feral weapons by the Coalition. She had been bitten several times, wounds that had taken weeks to heal.

Her sister had thrown her body over Madi's to keep the dogs away from her. The memory burned.

Ava had done everything she could to protect Madi. She knew her older sister had slipped food to her, had nursed her through illness and fear, had adopted a cheery, optimistic attitude, though Madi knew how much that must have cost her when things looked so grim.

Madi also knew she was the reason Ava had finally agreed to the increasingly harsh demands that she marry a man thirty years her senior.

We need to bring forth the next generation of fighters. You and your children will carry on the battle after we are gone. You believe in the cause, don't you?

She could still hear the swelling tones of Roger Boyle, as if he were standing beside her.

She hated remembering any of it.

She also hated that for the life of her, she couldn't understand the dichotomy of Ava's actions.

The sister willing to endure the horror of being married to a man she both feared and loathed, the beloved sister she had been certain would have died to protect her, seemed so very different from the woman who could spill all that hate and ugliness to the world.

Madi wasn't sure she would ever be able to reconcile the two in her mind.

14

The crisp night air bites at my cheeks as my sister and I steal away from the compound, our hearts pounding in our chests. We've become shadows, slipping through the dense forest under the cover of darkness, our breaths syncing with the rhythmic beat of our frantic footsteps. Behind us, the eerie howls of the cult's guard dogs echo through the mountains, a relentless reminder of the danger that pursues us.

—*Ghost Lake* by Ava Howell Brooks

Luke

"HOW ARE YOU DOING, KIDDO?"

His daughter, looking at her phone with her legs stretched out sideways on the covered swing, lowered her feet to the ground so he could sit beside her.

She shrugged. "I'm okay. The birthday cake was delicious and I loved Grandma and Grandpa Boyd's present. I just miss Zoe so much, you know?"

"I know. I'm sorry."

"I tried not to think about it much until now. Madi had me working with the puppies, giving them some basic training, all day. I was too busy laughing at them to be depressed."

"She's pretty smart, our Madi, isn't she?"

"You should have seen what happened today with that rascal goat. Madi was feeding him and he kept sticking his tongue out at her and blowing raspberries. We were both laughing so hard we almost fell over."

He looked over at the woman in question, sans goat. She was currently chatting with her grandmother in the fading afternoon light as she rocked his nephew in her arms.

Something soft and fragile seemed to unfurl inside his chest, like the new blossoms on the climbing rosebushes near the patio, sending their sweetness into the air.

She was so lovely. He wondered if she had any idea how she suddenly had the power to take his breath away.

What the hell was he supposed to do about this tenderness that seemed to have bloomed out of nowhere?

"Are you okay? Your face looks all funny."

He turned back to his daughter, this girl he loved with his entire heart. Oh, he hoped she couldn't tell what was going on in his head.

"Sorry my face looks funny." He tried for a dad joke. "I'm afraid it's the only one I've got. And I wouldn't be so quick to point out how funny I look, since people are always telling us how much we look alike."

She rolled her eyes. "That's not what I meant. You had a weird expression for a minute when you were looking at Madi. Like you suddenly thought of something you didn't like."

The problem was, he was beginning to realize he liked Madi entirely too much.

"I was thinking that I don't want to go home and do laundry tonight," he lied.

"Ha. Too bad. It's your turn. I did it last week."

"That's right. That means it's your week for the dishes. Maybe I'll decide to make some kind of complicated meal like my five-alarm chili that uses every dish in the house, to keep you from being bored."

She stuck her tongue out and blew a raspberry at him, probably much the way Barnabas had to Madi earlier that day.

He smiled and nudged her with his shoulder. Being a single father was a thousand times harder than he'd thought it would be. It was also one hundred thousand times better.

His life might have been so very different without Sierra.

He and Johanna had only been dating six months when she found out she was pregnant. They hadn't been planning to get married at the time. Neither of them had been ready, both too young with a year left in their undergraduate work.

In those first early days, as they considered all their options, they had talked about adoption. Johanna had been adopted into a loving family herself and had leaned toward that option rather than termination.

Thinking about it now, about not having Sierra in his life, made him vaguely queasy. Luke had been the one to suggest they could marry and try to make a go of it, for the sake of their child.

He had still been reeling from his father's death eighteen months earlier and his own guilt and pain. He knew he hadn't been in a solid place to be a husband, a father. Still, he couldn't help thinking about what his father might have said and at the time felt like he could almost hear Dan's words echoing in his head.

Time to man up and take care of your responsibilities, son.

So they had married and somewhere along the line, he had come to love Johanna and the life they created together.

She had been a wonderful mother to Sierra and had been devastated that she had been unable to have a second child. They had been talking about fostering to adopt and were beginning to work their way through the process when she had caught COVID from a patient and died two weeks later.

Afterward, he had floundered for a long time, not sure he could handle being a single father and running his vet practice at the same time. His mom had helped. So had Nicki and dozens of others in town. Sierra had been surrounded by a loving community.

He wasn't ready for all the challenges her teenage years might bring. But like it or not, his daughter was growing up and his responsibilities as her father were changing right along with her.

Fortunately, he had a good support network to help them both through.

Sierra considered Madi an honorary aunt. That's exactly how Luke needed to think about her. She was part of the family and he had to remember everything that was at stake if he tried to shift the dynamics between them.

His brother Owen's daughter ran over to them, dimples flashing as she reached out for her cousin Sierra to lift her up to the porch swing with them.

"Fast," Lottie said, pumping her little legs with her lips pursed in concentration.

"I'm afraid this swing doesn't go very fast," Luke said with a smile.

She sat with them only a moment or two before she wriggled to be free. "Down," she said.

"Do you want me to push you in the tire swing?" Sierra asked.

Lottie's face lit up. "Yes! I want to swing fast!"

His brother was in for a wild ride with this one, Luke thought with a smile. He couldn't wait to watch the fun.

Sierra hopped off and grabbed the young girl's hand. "Okay. Let's go swing," she said, leading Lottie over to the playset where some of his stepfather's grandchildren already played.

He sat alone for a time, watching the crowd. He was about to get up and head for another beer when Ava walked past.

"Are you leaving?"

She inclined her head toward Madi and Leona. "I came with my grandmother and she is apparently not done yet."

"Have a seat," he offered.

She looked queasy at the easy movement of the swing but finally sank down onto the padded cushion.

"Thanks," she said.

"You made it through dinner with no punches being thrown."

"That's something," she said dryly.

He laughed. "I wouldn't worry about Mad. She'll come around. She never could hold a grudge for very long."

He paused, debating whether he should get involved at all in the tension between the sisters. Then he remembered that ache of longing in Madi's eyes when she talked about her sister and decided to take the chance.

"She misses you," he said, his voice low.

She gave a sound of disbelief. "I don't think so. Right now, I'm her least favorite person on the planet."

"Right now, maybe. She's annoyed with you about the book. She'll get over that eventually. Forgive me if I'm wrong, but I get the feeling there was something of a chasm between you before you ever published *Ghost Lake*. Am I completely off base?"

She looked as if she wanted to argue but she finally sighed. "You're not wrong," she said, her voice low. "I wish things could be different."

"Why can't they be?"

"It's a good question. I don't really have a good answer. Our lives have moved in different directions over the years, I suppose."

He knew that wasn't the full story, but he also sensed Ava wasn't going to open up to him.

"If I can help, let me know. You two need each other."

She studied him in the fading light of the afternoon, her expression much harder to read than her sister's.

"You're a good friend, Luke. Your whole family is always so kind to Madi. I'm very grateful to you."

"We love her," he said gruffly.

Those words rang more true now than he anticipated. She gave him a careful look and he was quick to qualify the statement.

"We love her like she's part of the family. The thing is, while she might feel like part of our family, she *is* your family. Leona is amazing, don't get me wrong, but Madi needs her sister in her life."

"I'm still in her life. We talk on the phone and text quite often and we occasionally have video calls," she said, a note of defensiveness in her voice. "I live nearly six hundred miles away. I can't help that. My husband is there. Our apartment. My life. It's only natural for our worlds to drift apart. We're never going to be as close as we once were when we were... when we were teenagers."

"What about the baby? You're going to need your sister more than ever then," he said, taking another chance. Even as he said the words, he knew his suspicions could be completely off base.

She gaped at him, eyes huge. "B-baby? What baby?"

He gave her a careful look. "Leona mentioned you've been queasy since you came back to town. I wondered if you might be expecting."

"I'm not," she exclaimed, jumping up from the swing. He had to plant his legs to keep it from swinging wildly from the momentum.

"Forgive me," he said. "I suppose I've been working with animals too long, where reproduction is a normal part of life."

She continued to stare at him, her eyes huge. "I'm not a dog about to have puppies! And I'm not pregnant. It's...it's impossible."

What was that sudden desperate look in her gaze?

"My mistake," he said, voice low and even, in contrast to the sudden wild panic in her expression.

"I can't be pregnant," she whispered.

"You're probably not," he assured her, annoyed with himself for putting that panic in her gaze. "Forget I said anything."

She stared at him for several seconds, then shook her head like she was a prizefighter whose clock had been thoroughly cleaned.

"I need to…" She pointed toward the house and rushed inside, leaving him feeling presumptuous and overfamiliar.

He was about to go after her to apologize again when Madi sat down on the swing beside him, her gaze pensive as she looked at her sister's retreating back.

"What was that all about? Is she feeling sick again?"

"I'm not sure. I think she's mostly annoyed with me," he admitted.

Her face lit up with her half smile. "You sometimes do have that effect on women, Dr. Gentry."

He had to laugh, despite his unease over the discussion with Ava. "What can I say? It's a gift. Other men make women go weak at the knees. I seem to have the ability to make them want to punch something."

She sent him a sidelong look. "I would guess you're not all that bad in the weak-at-the-knees department."

What did she mean by that? And why did that rosy blush suddenly climb her cheeks?

"Sierra wants to play cornhole before you leave. She sent me to see if you want to play."

"Sure thing."

He rose from the swing, making the chains bounce and rattle. He reached a hand out to help her up. She wrapped her fingers around his and when he pulled her to her feet, the motion of the swing carried her forward, almost into his arms.

She laughed, trying to regain her balance. The sound enchanted him and he wanted to freeze the moment here on this summer evening and soak it in.

She stepped away, that pink on her cheeks again, and Luke

did his best to push away the inappropriate urge to pull her back, to tug her into the shrubs and kiss her.

He had to stop this or he was going to end up embarrassing both of them, possibly ruining their friendship irrevocably.

15

We plunge into the wilderness, guided only by the dim moonlight filtering through the thick canopy above. The forest floor is uneven, and each step is a silent dance to avoid twigs and fallen branches that threaten to betray our escape. Long nights stretch into an endless procession of uncertainty, the chill settling into our bones as we navigate the labyrinth of trees, desperate to put distance between us and the people who once held us captive.

—*Ghost Lake* by Ava Howell Brooks

Ava

AVA WIPED AT THE CORNER OF HER MOUTH AND STARED at herself in the large mirror in Tilly Gentry Walker's powder room.

She looked haggard.

That was the only way she could describe it. She had deep circles under her eyes, which contrasted vividly with her sallow skin, and her mouth was pinched, tight.

Was it any wonder Cullen wanted nothing to do with her right now?

At least her stomach seemed to be settling.

She took a deep breath, Luke's words bouncing around in her head like an out-of-control Ping-Pong ball.

Pregnant.

She couldn't possibly be. She was vigilant about birth control, taking the little pill on a regimented schedule.

Okay. She might have missed a few pills the week before the book came out, she acknowledged. She had been so busy trying to finish the school year while simultaneously fighting the horrible fear that agreeing to publish her memoir had been a hideous mistake.

She surely couldn't be pregnant after missing three or four pills, could she?

Ava closed her eyes to block out that wretched image of herself in the mirror. Was it possible? Her period was late, but she attributed that to all the stress over the book release, throwing their story out to the world and the instant publicity that had exploded around her.

And after her husband had read the book in its entirety, instead of the small samples she had showed him in the past year during her road to publication, everything had changed.

Panic fluttered on bat wings. If she really was pregnant, what was she going to do?

They had talked about having a child or two in some nebulous future. Of course they had. Any partners who didn't have that discussion were setting themselves up for a potential disaster if one wanted children and the other didn't.

Both of them definitely did. Cullen had talked about taking a baby hiking with him, going on nature walks together, Christmas mornings and birthday dinners and first days of school.

Both of them loved children and somehow had become the honorary babysitters among their friend group when the other young married couples needed a night out.

Cullen was wonderful with children of all ages. He had a knack for teasing a smile out of the crankiest of toddlers, at knowing how to persuade a finicky preschooler to eat, at being able to nap on the sofa with a sleepy baby in his arms.

She wanted to be pregnant. And she wanted his child. A vast yearning opened up somewhere deep inside.

She imagined a baby with his long lashes and that little dimple in its cheek as it gave a toothless smile, chubby arms flailing.

They had decided starting their family should wait until they were more settled, until his assistant professor job was more secure and they could buy a house near campus, something small with a backyard and an office corner for her to use for writing.

One of the many reasons she had agreed to the unexpected publishing offer when it came her way had been for that very goal. With some of the substantial advance she was being offered and perhaps subsequent royalties, they would be able to reach their goal more quickly and could start their family now, instead of waiting a few more years.

As much as she wanted a child, right now seemed the worst possible timing. Would she and Cullen even be able to reconcile after this summer? She had no idea. He had been *rocked* by the autobiography and the vivid reality she had painted of their experiences during those long months with the Coalition.

She pressed a tentative hand to her belly. She didn't want to believe it, but somehow as the seconds ticked by and the pieces slotted into place, the idea didn't seem completely radical.

Even before Cullen left, she had been queasy, much sleepier than normal, with roller-coaster emotions and achy breasts.

She couldn't know yet. In the morning, she would rush to the drugstore for a test so she could have more to base the information on than the suspicions of a veterinarian, however well-meaning Luke might be.

She closed her eyes. If she found out she was pregnant, she would have no choice. She would have to go up to Ghost Lake so she could tell Cullen. If they were going to have an unexpected child, he needed to know as soon as possible.

She couldn't hang around town, waiting to tell him until she bumped into him again at the farmers market.

How would she make it up into the mountains? When she and Madi left, she had never wanted to return.

One step at a time, she told herself. That was the very basic mantra that had helped them find the courage to leave, knowing the risks and dangers ahead of them.

Simply focus on doing the next right thing. That's what her mother had always told her.

With one last shaky breath, she dried her hands on the towel and walked out of the powder room to find Tilly alone in the big kitchen, transferring brownies and cookies from various plates and pans to make an assortment on one tray.

Ava hadn't had the chance to speak alone with the woman since arriving at the house. Now she wished she had stayed in the bathroom longer so she could have avoided her.

She had nothing against Tilly. She was a kind and generous woman, lovely inside and out.

But she also had become a widow because of Ava.

She forced a smile, which Tilly returned with a warmth that made Ava's throat feel tight.

"How are you, my dear?" Tilly asked, her gaze concerned. "You seem under the weather. Are you ill?"

"I'm fine," she lied. "Only tired. It's been a busy few weeks."

"I can only imagine."

She smiled as she set a few more cookies on the platter. "I'm absolutely thrilled your book is doing so well. It's all anyone in town wants to talk about."

"Is it?"

Tilly nodded. After careful scrutiny, her expression slid once more into one of concern. "I hope you'll forgive me saying this, but you don't seem tremendously thrilled by the response. I would have thought you would be over the moon to know your words are having such an impact."

Right. Like a meteor plummeting to earth, causing her marriage to implode along with it. And now she might very well find herself a single mother in eight months or so.

She made a raw sound that seemed to scorch her larynx, but she managed to conceal it with some judicious throat clearing.

"It doesn't seem real, to be honest. I'm still trying to figure out what happened."

"What happened," Tilly said sternly, "is that you wrote a lovely book filled with pain and sadness and truth that still somehow manages to resonate with hope and joy."

The words stunned her into speechlessness. She blinked several times, soaking them in. "You…you can't honestly say that's what you took away from reading *Ghost Lake*," she protested.

"I can and I do."

Ava shook her head, still trying to process her words. "You lost your husband because of the Coalition, simply because Dan and your children happened to be the unlucky campers we stumbled onto in our most desperate hour. He was an innocent victim who did nothing but try to help two terrified girls. And he paid the ultimate price for his kindness."

To her dismay, her voice cracked on the last word. Despite her best efforts at control, a tear slid out, trickling down her cheek, followed by another and another.

Before she quite realized what was happening, Tilly stepped away from the dessert tray and wrapped her arms around Ava, pulling her close.

"Oh, darling," she murmured. "You cannot carry the weight of Dan's death. He chose to help you girls because he *wanted* to help you. That's the man I loved. The very best of men. I'm truly sorry you never had the chance to know him, except for that last horrible day."

"I hate that you lost your husband," she whispered, her voice muffled. "I wish we had never found their campsite."

"If you hadn't, those men would have found you. They

would have beaten you, starved you, forced you to stay married to that horrible man. You would have been raped by him, again and again, and your sister eventually would have faced the same fate, married off to one of the other men, even though she was only fourteen years old."

She closed her eyes, hating the memory of sloppy kisses and fumbling hands after Roger Boyle, the camp leader, had informed her she was to marry his brother, James, though she was barely sixteen.

She would bear him many children, James had said with that disgustingly lascivious light in his pale blue eyes as he confirmed his brother's plan. It was for the good of the Coalition. Their children would be strong and valiant, would be taught correct principles so they could carry on the fight.

She had escaped on her wedding night.

Would she have left, if she hadn't been compelled to protect her younger sister? It was a question that haunted her. She had dreamed of escaping every moment of every day, but she wasn't as courageous as Madi. If not for her sister, Ava wasn't sure she would have found the strength to flee on her own.

She had held on to the hope that someone would save them. Surely someone had noticed they had been missing for the past six months. Leona had to have been looking for them. Their school teachers and administrators in Oregon. Their friends back home, their parents, her mother's friends.

Madi had wanted to flee every single day.

We can go over the mountains and make our way to Grandma's house. It's only twenty miles.

Ava had been the one to urge caution, frozen with indecision whenever she thought about all the risks that awaited them outside the camp.

She had urged that they wait until the time was right to give authorities as much space as possible to launch a rescue.

The only problem was, nobody had been launching any rescues. Their grandmother had gone to the authorities when her son-in-law and granddaughters broke off contact with her but hadn't been able to convince them to listen to her.

The girls were with their father, she had been told. As their sole surviving parent, he had full custody and could move Ava and Madi where he wanted.

Because of Ava's cowardice, she had been married in a ludicrous ceremony in the mountains to a man thirty years her senior, a disgusting human who had been divorced three times, who had long, straggly facial hair and a missing front tooth where a shotgun had misfired and knocked it out. The marriage hadn't been legally valid, of course. It had been legitimate in no one else's mind but James and Roger Boyle's and their acolytes at the camp.

On what would have been her wedding night, she had finally been backed so far into the corner, she had nothing else to do, nowhere else to turn. Only then had she agreed to Madi's outlandish plan to escape.

They had succeeded, but the cost had been so very great.

Ava pushed away the dark memories and found Tilly watching her with an expression of grave concern.

"You look so pale, my dear," she said gently. "Is it your blood sugar? Here. Have some water and maybe a brownie."

The stricture sounded so much like something her mother might have said that Ava had to smile.

"I'm okay. Thank you."

"You should try a brownie, anyway. I don't know anybody who makes brownies as yummy as your grandmother Leona's."

Mainly to appease the other woman, Ava took the small paper plate Tilly offered and selected a small brownie from the platter. She nibbled a corner, letting her tastebuds savor the rich fudge for this brief instant when she didn't feel like hurling everything up.

Tilly handed her a water and Ava dutifully sipped at it.

Maybe she was right. Ava did feel better from both the hydration and the sugar rush.

When the other woman seemed satisfied she wasn't about to topple over in the kitchen, she reached again for Ava's hand.

"I have to tell you this while you're here. *Ghost Lake* is the most extraordinary, emotional book I've read in a long time. Maybe ever. While it's certainly true I have a very personal connection that might be skewing my perspective, thousands of other people who don't have that same personal connection have been forever touched by your words and your story. You should lean into that. Embrace it. Your words have power, Ava. You should never doubt that."

Ava clasped Tilly's hand in hers as the genuine praise seemed to seep through all her self-doubt to reach her heart.

"Thank you," she whispered.

"And that girl who had the courage to do what you did back then is strong enough to face anything," Tilly went on. "Even your own unexpected success."

Tilly smiled warmly at her and cleared her throat, withdrawing her hand. "I need to take these desserts out since it's been all of ten minutes since people have eaten something."

She picked up the brownie tray and headed out the door without giving Ava a chance to respond.

Alone in the lovely kitchen once more, Ava pressed a hand to her abdomen. When she was sixteen, she'd found enough strength to escape with her sister into the wilderness, even knowing they would likely be caught and punished severely for their disobedience.

Together, they had faced hunger, thirst, bug bites, cougar stalkings, even an attack by an unsuspecting porcupine.

If she was indeed pregnant, she would figure out a way to fix her marriage, no matter how hard it might prove to be.

16

Our journey is far from over, but with each word written and every step taken, we reclaim a piece of ourselves and redefine what it means to be survivors of a twisted reality.

—*Ghost Lake* by Ava Howell Brooks

Madison

"ADMIT IT. WE WON FAIR AND SQUARE. HOW DOES IT feel to be whupped by a child, a septuagenarian and a woman with a bum leg?"

Luke grinned down at Madi. "Well, for one thing, one of my teammates walked out in the middle of the cornhole match to have an ice pop. For another, you cheated before my last throw when you faked that stumble and distracted me."

She laughed. "I wasn't faking. I really did stumble. Okay, maybe I exaggerated. It's not my fault you're a sucker for a wounded bird."

"Hey, I think I'm going to stay here tonight."

Madi had been so busy gloating, she hadn't noticed Nicole join them until she spoke.

"Why? Is something wrong?" Madi asked.

"Not at all. I'm off work tomorrow and so is Austin, coincidentally. We talked about taking a couple of the horses on a trail ride in the mountains early in the morning. Since the horses are here, it makes sense to stay so I don't have to drive over so early."

"Oh right." Except how was Madi supposed to get home, since she and Sierra had ridden over with Nicole?

As usual, her best friend seemed to read her mind. "I came over to bring you my car keys. Go ahead and take my car back to the house. I can have Austin drop me back home tomorrow after our ride."

"I don't want to take your car. I can see if Grandma minds going out of her way to take me home."

The idea of being trapped inside Leona's SUV with Ava appealed to her about as much as shaving her eyebrows, but she didn't mention that small detail.

"No need," Luke said quickly. "I can give you a ride. I wanted to swing by the sanctuary anyway tonight to check on Barnabas and see how his leg is healing. I've been meaning to head over there all day and haven't had a chance."

"He is as ornery as ever but you could certainly come check it out for yourself. What about Sierra, though?"

He shrugged. "She and Mom were talking about watching a movie. I'm sure I'll be back before they're done."

"You're not up for movie night?"

"Not this one. It's a tearjerker romance where somebody dies at the end. Not my favorite trope."

Her emotions softened. Of course it wouldn't be, since his own wife had died only four years earlier.

When they returned to the house to say their goodbyes to everyone, she found Ava waiting for Leona in one of the rocking chairs on the porch. She was gazing out at the vast mountain range beyond the ranch, her expression distant and... somehow haunted.

Where earlier in the evening, Madi might have ignored

Ava, she found she couldn't do that when her sister seemed so troubled.

"I'm taking off. I'm sure I'll see you later."

"All right."

Madi paused, then hurried on before she could change her mind.

"I was serious about suggesting you volunteer at the shelter. For what it's worth, I was only teasing about cleaning after the pigs. You wouldn't have to do that."

Ava blinked in surprise. "Thank you. I might do that. You know I'm not really good with animals, right? Not like you are, anyway."

"You'll be fine. We'll put you with the puppies. You can ask Sierra. They're good therapy, guaranteed to put a smile on your face. I'll let the volunteers know you're preapproved. You don't have to go through the vetting process since Luke and I both know you."

Madi didn't know why she was being so generous to her sister, not when she was still furious with Ava. She just couldn't stand by and do nothing when her sister seemed so...shattered.

"I... Thanks," Ava said, as Luke drove his pickup closer to the house and stopped.

"Oh. I didn't realize you came with Luke."

"I didn't. I came with Nic but she's decided to stay the night here. Luke offered to give me a ride home so he can check on one of our animals at the rescue."

Madi also wasn't sure why she felt compelled to explain herself and her choices to her sister.

She gave Ava one last wave and hurried down the steps. As she knew he would, Luke walked around the truck to open the passenger door for her and held his hand out to help her up. She knew she would be wasting her breath to tell him she was perfectly capable of opening a door and that she regularly drove her *own* pickup truck, which was much harder to get into.

She placed her hand in his and let him give her a boost, aware of a strange heat that seemed to jump between them. As soon as she settled into the seat that smelled of leather and pine, she was quick to withdraw her hand, not looking at him as he closed the door and made his way around to the driver's seat.

He pulled away from the house in the direction of the sanctuary on the other side of town, some of Boyd's horses galloping beside them in their paddock, their manes and tails limned by the colorful sunset.

"What a lovely evening," she said, settling into her seat and enjoying the familiar view they passed. Everywhere she looked, she saw people outside enjoying the peaceful Sunday. Families rode bikes on the trail that followed the creek, the large downtown park was busy with informal pickup soccer and baseball games, and they even passed several people horseback riding. "I don't know why anyone would want to live anywhere but here in Emerald Creek."

"It's a pretty great place. Not perfect, of course, but no place is."

"You're right. But in my view, Emerald Creek is closer than most places. It's not only the scenery. I love the farmers market and the Monday-night movies at the park and bumping into friends at the grocery store. I don't know how Ava possibly can be happy living in the city. I visited her once and had a headache the entire time from the noise and the chaos."

"It's good that other people find home in lots of different places or the population of Emerald Creek would explode."

She smiled. "You're right. We wouldn't want that."

They chatted about the upcoming workload for the week at the vet clinic until he pulled into the driveway of the animal shelter. "I can drop you at the house before I head down to the barn," he said.

"You don't have to do that. I would like to go with you to check on Barnabas. I can walk over after."

"You know I'm always glad for your help."

He continued on the driveway and parked in front of the barn.

She didn't wait for his help exiting the pickup but climbed out herself. Her leg wobbled, tired out from the long day, but she managed to catch herself before she stumbled, then she hurried to the door.

She unlocked the facility with her code and let them both into the empty office.

Unless they had a critically ill patient, they didn't keep overnight staff at the shelter. Madi had installed an extensive camera security system that alerted her in case of anything unusual with the animals. Volunteers took turns monitoring the cameras on a schedule, so Madi didn't have to do it herself every single night, worrying about their charges.

Tonight was actually her turn, and throughout the evening, she had been checking the cameras every hour or so.

"Is he in here or out in the field?" Luke asked.

"Probably in here. He usually comes inside at night."

Most of the farm animals at the shelter preferred to sleep inside the facility, where it was warm and dry and safe. She turned on the light over the goat area of the barn and they found Barnabas exactly where she had guessed, stretched out on the hay-strewn floor beside two other goats. The other one, Martha, must be outside.

She smiled. "Hey, Barnabas. Hello. Look who's here. It's your favorite vet. Come say hello to Dr. Gentry."

He gave a grumpy sound, exactly like some of her college roommates used to make when their alarm clocks went off Monday morning after a weekend of partying. Like her roommates at times, the goat made no effort to move, quite deliberately turning on his other side to face the opposite end of the stall from them.

She rolled her eyes. "Barney. Don't be rude. Come on. Dr.

Gentry only wants to check and see how your leg is healing. You should feel special, sir. He doesn't make evening house calls for just anybody."

After a sullen moment, the goat finally lumbered to his feet.

"He seems to be moving on it a little better," Luke observed, putting on his gloves and grabbing the salve from the storage shelf outside the stall.

"Yes. I've noticed that. And it doesn't seem to be as tender when we have to change the dressing."

While she held the goat in place, Luke spoke softly to the animal before gently picking up his left hind leg. Barnabas bleated his annoyance, which stirred up the other goats in the pen.

"Now look," Madi chided. "You've awakened everyone else, dude. Not cool."

The goat clearly didn't care. He blew another of those raspberries that had made Sierra laugh so hard earlier in the day.

Luke applied the salve and reapplied the dressing. "Another few days and you can probably take the bandage off."

"Oh good. That will make him happy. Thank you."

"My pleasure. Is there anyone else I need to check while I'm here?"

She did a quick mental inventory of all their current residents. "Yes, actually," she suddenly remembered. "Chester has been off his feed for a couple of days. Sierra tried to exercise him today and he was having none of it. That's very unlike him. He loves her and is always happy for the chance to hang out and play."

The miniature horse they had rescued from a petting zoo was usually cheerful and energetic, a favorite of all the volunteers.

"I'll take a look."

They made their way together to the stall Chester shared with their Jerusalem donkey, Sabra. The two were happiest when they were together.

Sabra snuffled to greet them, but Chester stayed in the corner of the stall.

"Can you hold him still for me?" he asked her.

Madi wrapped her arms around the gray horse and spoke softly to him while Luke did a cursory physical exam.

Apparently he touched something painful near his abdomen because Chester stomped his hooves and his left front hoof landed square on Madi's right foot.

She gasped as pain seared up her leg, icy and mean. She had worn light canvas sneakers to the party and hadn't changed into her work boots before coming to help him. Big mistake.

"What happened?" Luke asked, his eyes concerned.

"Nothing. I'm f-fine," she lied, embarrassed at the shaky note in her voice.

"Madi. What happened?"

She sighed. Luke wouldn't let it go. "It was totally my fault. He stepped on my foot. I should have put on better shoes."

He looked at her thin sneakers. "Go sit down. I'm about done checking him over and then I'll come take a look at you."

"I'm f-fine, really. I can help you."

"Madi. Go sit down. I've got this."

She glowered at his bossy tone. Some part of her wanted to remind him this was her animal shelter. She was the executive director and didn't take orders from him, no matter how wonderful a vet he might be.

The urge subsided. He was only looking out for her. She couldn't be annoyed at that.

She limped out of the stall and sat on one of the benches in the wide space in the middle of the barn.

"Any insights into why he might not be eating like usual?"

"Looks like he's got sinusitis. He needs an antibiotic and anti-inflammatory."

"Oh no. Poor thing!"

"We should probably get him started on them as soon as

possible. I can run into the clinic and grab meds for you, then you can start him tonight."

"Thank you."

"Enough about Chester. Let's take a look at your foot."

"I'm fine. Don't worry about it."

"Madi."

She sighed, recognizing by his tone that he wouldn't budge. She finally stuck out her sore foot. She had managed to kick off her sneaker but couldn't bring herself to remove her sock. What if her toe was visibly broken or dislocated? No thank you. She would rather not look.

The very thought left her lightheaded.

Madi could help with veterinary care all day, every day, dealing without blinking at all sorts of animal injuries and illnesses that might completely horrify other people. When it came to human physical issues, especially her own, she wasn't nearly as sanguine.

She suspected it was a visceral reaction from the long weeks she'd had to spend in the hospital and rehab center after she was shot, undergoing months of retraining in speech, occupational and physical therapy.

Now she hated going to the doctor and avoided it as long as necessary. Whenever she had to have her blood drawn for a routine test, she had to look away or she would feel shaky, lightheaded.

Luke put on clean gloves from the box on the shelf then sank onto his haunches in front of her. Slowly, gently, he gripped her sock and began rolling it down.

His fingers were warm on her skin and she shivered despite the warm air inside the barn.

He glanced up, his features arrested. Madi could feel herself blush and hoped he didn't notice in the fluorescent lights inside the building.

She was suddenly aware they were alone here. Okay, alone

while surrounded by potbellied pigs, a trio of goats, a miniature horse and a Jerusalem donkey. But there were no other
people around to notice if she wrapped her arms around him
and pulled him toward her...

"Good news," he said after examining her foot. "It's not dislocated and I don't think it's broken."

"You don't *think*? Don't you know?"

"Not without an X-ray," he admitted. "You have many
things here at the Emerald Creek Animal Rescue but as far as
I know, an X-ray machine isn't one of them."

"Maybe I should go to the urgent care clinic. They do have
an X-ray machine, as well as a technician."

She glanced at her watch. "Oh shoot. They closed an hour
ago. I didn't realize it was so late. Should I go to the ER?"

"You could. But if it were broken, I don't think you would
be able to wiggle your toes. If you were my patient, I would
advise waiting a day or two for an X-ray, until the swelling
goes down."

"Good thing I'm not your patient, then."

He smiled, still crouched in front of her. It would be so easy
to lean forward slightly and brush her mouth against his...

"You don't have to take my advice. If you want, I can drive
you to the hospital ER up in Ketchum."

Already the pain had begun to fade to a much more manage-
able level. She sighed, feeling stupid and overdramatic. "You
don't have to do that. I'll be okay. I'm being a big baby."

"You are far from a baby."

Something in his low voice sent shivers rippling down her
spine.

"Want me to put your sock back on?"

Despite the pain receding, Madi suspected it would be best
not to mess with her toes more than strictly necessary. "No.
Just my shoe."

He loosened the laces on her sneaker further, gripped her

heel and slid the shoe on. If someone had told her she could be this stirred up sitting in a barn while a man put a shoe on an injured foot, she would have told them they were making up ridiculous stories.

Yet here she was, holding her breath as if he were taking items of apparel *off* instead of the other way around.

Was it her imagination or did his hand pause on her ankle a little longer than strictly necessary? The heat of his skin seemed to burn through her.

Stop it, she chided herself. This was Luke. Her friend. Her boss. For all intents and purposes, he was her partner in the Emerald Creek Animal Rescue, as he had been behind her every step of the way and gave as many volunteer hours to the sanctuary as she or anyone else.

She couldn't screw things up by letting the tiny crush she had always secretly nurtured grow into something bigger, like a true infatuation, with all the complications that would entail.

What if it was too late? a voice whispered.

She ignored it.

It wasn't. She wouldn't let it be. She only had to forget about this simmering attraction and do her best to keep their relationship in the friend zone. She could do this.

"Come on," he said, rising. "I'll help you back to the house."

He reached a hand out and she let him pull her up.

She gingerly put weight on her foot and was relieved that the pain had eased considerably.

"I'm doing much better. I'll be okay. Thanks for taking a look."

She took a step toward the door, then wobbled, not because of her foot but because she was forced to rely on her weaker leg, now that the other one had been injured.

Luke stepped forward and caught her before she could stumble into something. "Here. I've got you. I won't let you fall. I'll give you a ride back to the house."

"I can walk. It's only a hundred yards."

"But a hundred yards on a sore foot versus five to my pickup and five more up your steps. I think the ride is a much better plan."

He had a point, she had to admit. Luke hooked his arm through hers, his body warm and comforting beside her as he helped her to his truck, then lifted her up into the seat.

She wanted to tell him she was fine, that she could handle this on her own, but it felt nice to lean on his strength.

He drove the short distance she usually walked several times a day. The small farmhouse looked welcoming in the darkness, with the light she left on for her dogs beaming out through the yard.

He pulled up to the porch then helped her out of the truck. She tried not to notice the strength of his arms or the heat of him or his delicious scent of sage and juniper.

She loved evenings here at the farmhouse. Crickets chirped and she could hear the distant call of a coyote somewhere in the surrounding mountains as they made their way up the porch steps.

"Do you have a key?" Luke asked at her door.

She pulled her key ring out of her pocket and unlocked the door. He pushed it open and turned on the foyer light as her old golden retriever, Mo, waddled out, followed close behind by Mabel, her little schnoodle.

"There you are, guys. Do you need to go out? Come on."

She limped to the back door, where she could let the dogs out into the enclosed yard.

"Sorry," she said to Luke. "I have to let them out first, especially Mo. If he gets too excited, he'll have an accident."

"I get it. I've got an old lady of my own."

"Right. How is Ruby?" she asked of his chocolate Lab.

"She's good. Funny as ever. She still loves to cuddle and she's still afraid of the telephone."

She smiled. "How old is she?"

"Eleven now."

"Mo is twelve. That's getting up there for a golden."

"He's still doing okay, though? Anything I need to look at on either of your dogs?"

She shook her head. "I think you've done enough tonight, Dr. Gentry. Put away your stethoscope. A goat, a miniature horse and me with my bruised toe. That's a full evening, especially after a party. Believe it or not, you don't have to take care of the whole world."

His smile. "It's a hard habit to break, one I think I inherited from my dad."

"He was a good man. And so are you."

On impulse, she reached up to kiss his cheek. She couldn't have said why she did it. Maybe it was out of gratitude for his constant generosity of spirit toward her and all the animals she loved or the deep well of gratitude she felt for all his help with the animal shelter.

They had been friends long enough that casual physical affection between them wasn't all that unusual, though perhaps more rare these days.

This brush of her lips against his skin somehow didn't feel casual.

He had a hint of evening stubble on his jaw and he smelled even better this close.

He gazed down at her, eyes wide with surprise. They looked at each other for a long time, the only sound their mingled breathing.

The moment seemed to stretch out, delicate and fragile, then an instant later, Luke shifted his mouth to hers. Her breath caught, tangled with his as his mouth brushed across hers with aching slowness.

What was happening right now?

Madi reeled, dizzy with shock. Luke Gentry was kissing

her—*her*—in her kitchen, his arms holding her close, as if she were infinitely precious to him.

She forgot about the dogs, about her sore toe, about anything else but him and this moment.

She hadn't kissed a man in a long time. Not since her summer fling the previous year, when she had dated a cute cowboy who had come to town to work as a wrangler at one of the dude ranches nearby.

Luke did not kiss like that guy, whose name she couldn't even remember right now.

In fact, she could not remember ever experiencing another kiss like this one, where she felt every heartbeat echo through her, and was certain the world outside this farmhouse had suddenly tilted on its axis.

She didn't want to stop. She wanted to stay forever right here in his arms, where she felt safe and warm and cherished.

They might have stayed there kissing until the morning, if Mo hadn't barked softly to be let in from the other side of the door.

At the sound, Luke froze. His eyes flew open and she could see exactly when the soft, dreamlike state lifted and reality returned.

The expression in his gaze shifted from one of hazy desire to something closer to astonished dismay.

The mouth that had been so delicious on hers sagged open for an instant, before compressing into a tight line.

As he dropped his arms from around her, Madi felt something inside her begin to shrivel, something soft and vulnerable and wonderful that had flared to life during the kiss.

"That was... I shouldn't have... We shouldn't have..."

She should probably say something to ease the extreme awkwardness that has suddenly blossomed between them, but she could not for the life of her, think of any words beyond *wow*, which she didn't think would be quite appropriate.

Why had he kissed her? More to the point, why had she responded as if this was the first kiss she'd ever had that actually *meant* something?

"I don't know what just happened." Luke raked a hand through his hair. "You kissed my cheek and...you always smell so good and I couldn't resist."

She stared at him, feeling as if every single rational thought had completely flown out of her head.

"I... What?"

He grimaced. "I know. It was completely inappropriate. I'm your employer. I should never have taken advantage of you like that."

He was concerned about kissing her because she *worked* for him? That thought had never even crossed her mind. Their relationship was so multilayered, the fact that she was a vet tech in his office seemed a minimal issue.

"Technically I work for you, I guess. But only for another few weeks."

He did not look happy about the reminder. "Still. I shouldn't have kissed you. It was a gross abuse of power."

"You currently pay my salary but it's not as if you hold my entire professional future in your hands. And I'm sorry you find my kisses gross," she muttered.

He gave her an exasperated look. "You know that's not what I meant. I don't know what came over me. I've always been very careful not to...to let myself think about you that way."

She wasn't quite sure how to interpret that admission. "What way? Like a woman?"

"Like a woman at all available for the kind of relationship where we could kiss and...other things. You've always been like a sister to me."

"I'm not your sister."

He gave her a wry, tight smile. "Yes. I'm fully aware. But our lives are deeply intertwined. We work together, both at the clinic and here at the rescue. You're best friends and room-mates with my sister. You come to my mother's house for din-ner every month. For all intents and purposes, you're part of the family."

She couldn't argue with him. They should never have kissed. Everything he said paralleled what she herself had been think-ing.

He gripped her hand in his, his feature set. "You're impor-tant to me, Mad. I care about you. My daughter cares about you. My mom would adopt you if she could. I don't want to do anything to screw that up for everyone."

Had one kiss made things irrevocably awkward between them? She couldn't bear thinking that.

Luke was exactly right. Since the day he and his family had rescued her and Ava, Madi had always been careful to lock away any romantic feelings for him. But how could she help but fall a little in love with a man who had pulled her out of the line of fire and covered her body with his?

He probably didn't think she remembered. They hadn't spoken of those moments and he likely believed the gunshot wound she had sustained had given her short-term memory loss or something.

She remembered everything, though. The smell of gun-powder, the baying of the dogs, the frantic shouts and searing pain as she had been shot.

Luke had been solid and strong, even though scared himself, she knew. He had shoved Ava and Nicki behind a rock, yelled for his brother to take cover and had picked up the family's rifle before covering Madi, who was bleeding copiously from the bullet that had struck her temple and lodged under her skull.

We're going to get you out of this. I promise. Just hang on, kid, he had whispered to her as he fired the rifle in the direction the shots were firing.

She remembered the cries and shouts as his shots and his father's managed to keep their pursuers at bay.

She also knew he had risked his life for her, as his father had. Luke had no way of knowing a helicopter full of federal agents from multiple agencies had been deployed to rescue her and her sister as soon as Dan Gentry had made that first satellite call a half hour earlier, after they stumbled onto their camp.

He had continued protecting them all with single-minded focus.

She drew in a shaky breath. "Okay. Here's what we have to do. We both need to forget the last fifteen minutes ever happened."

He made a rough sound of disbelief, low in his throat. "How do you propose we do that?"

"Easy. We just focus on all the reasons why that kiss should not have happened. You're right. The various strands of our lives are interwoven. You are too important to me. I don't want to lose that. I *can't* lose that."

Something flickered in his gaze, something hot, surprising. She did her best to ignore it.

"We simply have to rewind back to when I unlocked the door. You helped me inside, we put the dogs out, then you went on your merry way for the night. That's how I will choose to remember this evening and I… I suggest you do the same. It's the only way we can go back to…to our regular life. To the way things were."

He sighed. "I wish it were that easy. It's not, especially when I've wanted to kiss you for longer than I care to admit."

She childishly shoved her hands over her ears. "Stop it. I'm not listening. Don't tell me things like that, Luke. Now that's one more thing I'll have to forget."

He released an unsteady breath. "I'm afraid you're right. It's the only option, if we want to maintain the status quo."

She nodded, even as everything inside her ached to step straight back into his arms.

"For the record, it was a pretty unforgettable kiss, but I'll do my best to put it out of my head."

Unforgettable. That seemed a tame word for something she feared would be seared into her memory.

"I should head back. Everyone will be wondering where I am and what animal distracted me this time."

"I am not sure they would believe you if you said the animal was me," Madi said.

He gave a rough laugh, studied her for another few seconds, then shook his head. "Good night. I'll see you tomorrow at the office. Where everything will be professional and comfortable and not weird at all."

"Actually, I'm off tomorrow, remember? Dentist appointment in the morning, then I'm working at the rescue the rest of the day."

"Right. I'll see you Tuesday, then. Good night."

After he left, she let the dogs inside, then headed for the living room.

As soon as she sank onto her favorite spot on the sofa, Mo jumped up on one side and Mabel jumped up on the other.

She hugged them both to her, grateful to have these two in her life and their constant, steady, uncomplicated love.

17

The mountains become both our refuge and our battleground. Scaling steep cliffs, navigating dense forests and surviving on meager rations, we cling to each other like a lifeline. The whispers of the wind carry tales of freedom, and with each step, we etch a path away from the Coalition's suffocating grasp.

—*Ghost Lake* by Ava Howell Brooks

Ava

AVA STARED AT THE RIDICULOUS ARRAY OF PREG-nancy tests spread out in the bathroom.

Morning sun filtered through the gauzy curtains, lighting on all those plus signs.

So this was happening. She couldn't pretend otherwise now, even in her head. Seven—no, eight—positive pregnancy tests couldn't be wrong.

She was pregnant. The word echoed in her mind like a secret she had been keeping from herself for weeks.

She and Cullen would become parents in roughly thirty-five weeks, according to her quick mental calculations.

She could picture a girl with his brown eyes and compassion or a boy with that same sweet smile and quick sense of humor.

"Hi, little one," she murmured, pressing a hand to her abdomen. Already she was linked to the tiny life growing inside her, a life that would depend on her for everything.

What a strange dichotomy, that she felt so connected to Cullen in this moment when they were further apart than they had been since they first met, by both distance and circumstances.

She had to tell him.

She huffed out a breath. She didn't want to. The pregnancy would change everything between them, could become either a lifeline or a wrecking ball.

What would he think when she showed up out of the blue with news like this? Would he be happy? Terrified? Angry?

Maybe she could wait. Couldn't she keep this news to herself a bit longer, at least until she had time to process what it would all mean herself?

He was busy with his dig. That was important to him, an amazing chance, and she didn't want to risk distracting him.

Besides, he had been clear that he needed breathing space, time to figure out whether he could forgive her for keeping huge chunks of her life secret from him.

That alone was exactly the reason she had to tell him now about the pregnancy. If she wanted her marriage to survive, Ava knew she had to be open and honest with him. No matter the consequences.

She studied her hand splayed over her abdomen, where no outward sign gave a clue as to the miraculous changes happening inside her.

She had to tell him now, but how? She didn't want to go up to Ghost Lake by herself. Any mountain terrain would have intimidated her. That one was literally the stuff of her nightmares.

She could ask someone to go with her. Grandma Leona? She quickly discarded that.

What about Madison?

Ava stared at her pale reflection in the bathroom mirror.

Why would her sister help her? She was more likely to laugh in her face if Ava asked.

It was a ridiculous idea, wasn't it?

Maybe, maybe not. Madi had been gracious enough to invite her to be a volunteer at the shelter. Ava knew Madi had a hard time refusing any creature, animal or human, who needed her.

With fresh resolve, she gathered up all the pregnancy tests, threw them in the bathroom trash, then pulled the liner bag out, tying it securely and carrying it out to the bin herself. She didn't want anyone else discovering she was pregnant until she'd found the chance to tell Cullen. This was his child. He deserved to know first.

Keeping that information from Madi might make it difficult for Ava to persuade her to go with her up to Ghost Lake, but she had to try. She was going over to the shelter later that day to fill out the volunteer paperwork. If the opportunity came up for her to ask her sister, she would.

If not, she would simply have to face her fears and figure out a way to make the trip by herself.

Determination stiffened her spine. She and Cullen may not have planned for this baby, but Ava intended to do everything possible to give their child a loving, stable home, no matter what might be required.

"You want me to what?" Madi stared at her, mouth suddenly agape.

Ava wanted to disappear. She should have known better than to ask her sister anything. Yes, they had engaged in an almost civil conversation the night before. That didn't mean Madi was ready to move on from her anger.

"It was a dumb idea. Forget I said anything," she answered quickly.

"Why do you need to go to Ghost Lake?" Her sister's voice

dripped with suspicion. "More research? Don't tell me. You're writing a sequel now."

"No. This has nothing to do with any book. I need... I need to see Cullen. I...have to tell him something and I don't feel good about waiting until the weekend, when he comes to town for supplies."

"It must be important, for you to ask my help."

"It is."

Madi eyed her with an expectant expression. She clearly wanted Ava to give her an explanation about why she suddenly needed to head twenty miles into the mountains, to a place she had always vowed she would never revisit.

"I can't tell you why I need to talk to Cullen. Not yet. I will, though. I promise. After I've seen my husband."

"You want me to go with you back to a place we have both tried to avoid for the past fifteen years, but you can't tell me why."

She twisted her hands together in her lap. "Yes. I'm sorry."

"You seem to be sorry about a lot of things these days."

Oh, her sister didn't know the half of it.

"Will you help me?"

When Madi remained silent, Ava mourned afresh the erosion of their relationship. "You don't have to. It's fine," she said quickly. "But can I borrow Grandpa's pickup truck? And do you know where I could find an all-terrain vehicle?"

"An ATV?" If Madi looked surprised at her request to go with her into the mountains without explanation, now she looked completely thunderstruck. "Why do you need an ATV?"

Ava chewed her bottom lip. "Cullen said the dig site is only accessible by an all-terrain vehicle."

After a long, uncomfortable pause, her sister spoke again. "When did you want to go?"

Was she actually considering it? Ava was afraid to hope. "As soon as possible. Today, if we can do it. This afternoon."

"Today?"

"If we leave before four, we should be able to make it there and back before dark."

"You've thought this out."

She had done very little but think since taking all those tests earlier that day.

"Yes. This is very important to me."

"So important you would really be willing to go up there by yourself? Even though I doubt you've driven an ATV since we lived in Oregon?"

"It's not that tough. I'm sure I'll remember how. And yes. It's that important."

After another long pause, Madi sighed. "We have an older utility vehicle side-by-side that was donated to us for getting around the acreage here. I can load it onto the trailer and pull it with Grandpa's truck to the trailhead. I need to finish a few things here but might be able to leave in a couple of hours."

Madi looked at her watch. "Should we say three? You owe me, though."

Ava was fully aware of how much she owed her sister. This was only one more thing to add to the pile.

She forced a smile. "Thanks. Perfect. Three works. I should be done with orientation by then."

With a vast relief, Ava returned to the tablet Madi had given her for filling out her volunteer information.

She was nearly done completing the forms when an older man she didn't know approached her.

"Are you Ava?"

"Yes."

"I'm Hal Smith. I'm the ECAR official tour guide, here to show you around."

Ava was aware of Madi inside the office, trying to appear as if she wasn't paying attention to them. She suspected her sister was aware of everything that went on here.

"Thank you. I would appreciate that," she said.

He smiled. "Great. While you finish up, I'll grab one of the dogs. We always try to exercise somebody while we're showing around the new recruits."

"Perfect."

She filled in the final line on the form as Hal returned with a huge German shepherd wearing a harness and leash.

"Okay. We're all set. This here is Helga."

Ava stood frozen, unable to breathe or think, thrust instantly back to that summer, to the time when she had been attacked by guard dogs who looked exactly like her.

She still had nightmares about feeling their hot breath on her as they bit her legs, her back.

When Cullen had asked her once how she obtained the scars, she had told him she had been bitten by a dog while they were at the camp. She hadn't told him it had been three dogs, two German shepherds and a bull terrier who had been stirred up into a frenzy.

Her stomach lurched and she felt dizzy enough that she sank back into the chair. She didn't know whether to be relieved or mortified when Madi spoke from the doorway.

"Actually, Hal, I'm at a good place for a break right now. Why don't you take Helga for her walk and I can show Ava around?"

"Are you sure?"

"Yes. Thanks, though."

With a wave to both women, he and the dog made their way outside into the June afternoon.

"I'm sorry," Ava whispered, despising herself for the weakness. She had no problem with some dogs. She could even pet the smaller ones without breaking out into a cold sweat. But anything bigger than a beagle and she freaked out. It had been a point of contention between her and Cullen, who had always had big dogs and would have liked to adopt another one. Fortunately, their current apartment did not allow pets larger than twenty-five pounds. To her great shame, she could admit in her heart of hearts that rule was one of the reasons she had favored their current living space over others when they were apartment hunting.

What would she do when they bought a house together and she could find no more excuses not to accede to his wishes?

If they bought a house together.

She fought the urge to press a hand to her abdomen again, to the tiny, vulnerable, infinitely precious life growing there.

A few more hours and she would tell Cullen and this would no longer be her secret alone.

"You don't have to apologize," Madi said, her tone brisk. "I understand."

She gestured around the space with its comfortable furniture and three desks. "This is the office and reception area, as you can see. All the volunteers check in here first, when they arrive, to receive their assignments for the day."

"How many volunteers do you have?"

"Around twenty-five. We use anywhere from six to seven volunteers a day. They help with feeding the animals, walking them, playing with them. For now, I coordinate all the volunteer hours while my assistant, Elana, and Hal usually handle all the HR and training. I'm currently part-time as I'm still working with Luke at the clinic, but I will be transitioning to full time at the end of the month."

For the next half hour, Madi walked her through the animal rescue facilities, showing her the pastures where farm animals had room to ramble, the large play yard where the dogs were allowed to run at least twice a day and the cat room that featured an assortment of climbing structures and tunnels.

Ava immediately sneezed and Madi closed the door quickly.

"Right now we are limited to about twenty cats. As you can imagine, there are far more than that in the area who need shelter. We do try to adopt them out as soon as we can, but for various reasons, that's not possible for about four of them. They will probably live out their lives here. Same for about five of the dogs and most of the farm animals."

"It's fantastic," Ava said, moved almost to tears by her sister's obvious pride in what she had created here.

Madi looked surprised. "Th-thank you," she said.

"How wonderful, that you have been able to create a safe, comfortable, happy home where they can live out their days."

Madi shifted, clearly uncomfortable with the praise. "We try to do our best with our limited funds. It's not always easy, but through a combination of grants and fundraising, we have a healthy bank balance. We were especially fortunate about six months ago to receive a huge gift from an anonymous donor. We should have enough between all our funding sources to keep us going for at least a few years."

"That's great." Ava gave a polite smile and quickly changed the subject. "You showed me the dog play yard. What about their kennel facilities?"

"Right. Our dogs are split into three groups. Large breeds, small breeds and puppies. We can skip the large-dog area, if you're more comfortable."

"No. I'll be okay." She hoped.

Why wasn't Madi afraid of dogs as well? Ava wondered that as her sister led her into a section of the building that had a row of kennels. Maybe because she had never been attacked by the dogs. Her sister had even tried to befriend the most vicious of the guard dogs.

Each of the kennels was filled with one or two animals, who jumped up to greet Madi with enthusiastic barks.

She opened every door and scratched each dog, no matter how vicious-looking.

"In our small-dog room, most of these rotate out pretty quickly. People are more willing to adopt the smaller dogs and puppies than the big ones, unfortunately."

Everything was clean, comfortable and homey.

"Okay. That's it," Madi said as she led the way back to the office. "In addition to the play areas, we have various trails going through the ranch for our volunteers to walk the dogs. We plan to continue grooming the trails in winter so they can get plenty of safe exercise. Is there anything else you want to see?"

Ava shook her head. "It's wonderful," she said again. "You really love this, don't you?"

Madi shrugged. "What's not to love? We're making a difference. Each of these animals was either abandoned, has come from a home where they were abused or neglected or was given up after the owners either were unwilling or unable to care for them. We're giving them a second chance for a better future."

Madi looked at her watch. "I've got to make a few phone calls before we leave and you probably want to go to Grandma's and grab a jacket. It gets cool up in the mountains in the evenings."

"I remember," Ava said, her voice low.

Madi gave her an unreadable look but said nothing.

"Thanks for the tour. You really have created something amazing here. I'm happy for you."

It was too easy sometimes to think of Madi as fragile, wounded, but she knew that wasn't the full story. Her sister was a survivor, something she had tried hard to portray in *Ghost Lake*.

Madi gave her a wary look, as if not quite sure whether to believe her. "Thanks," she said, as her phone buzzed with a text.

She checked it, then an odd look twisted her features, one Ava couldn't quite interpret. Yet another reason to grieve her relationship with her sister. Once, she could guess everything her sister was thinking.

"I've got to go," Madi said. "That's Luke. I need to call him back."

That was odd. What would cause Madi's face suddenly to turn pink and her eyes to take on that faraway expression?

"I'll heed your advice, then, and head home for a jacket. I'll be back shortly."

"Don't forget a water bottle. I'll bring some extra water if we need it, but you'll want your own bottle."

She nodded and left, already dreading the evening ahead of them.

18

As our escape unfolds, hunger claws at our stomachs, a constant reminder of the price we pay for our freedom. We forage for berries and edible plants, our fingers stained with the juices of the wild. The taste is bitter, but the sustenance is a lifeline in the unforgiving landscape. Each morsel is a testament to our resilience, a reminder that we are survivors, not just of captivity, but of the wilderness that seeks to consume us.

—*Ghost Lake* by Ava Howell Brooks

Madison

AS SHE HURRIED BACK TO THE OFFICE, MADI WAS TORN between being nervous about speaking with Luke for the first time since their stunning kiss or being baffled by her sister's odd behavior.

It was easier to focus on Ava, she decided as she returned to the office. Why did Ava need to talk to her husband so urgently?

Was their marriage in trouble? She wasn't sure what gave her that worry but since Ava had returned to Emerald Creek, she acted so strangely whenever Cullen's name came up.

If it were true, if they were breaking up, Madi would find it beyond tragic. She adored Cullen and had from the first time she met him.

He always treated Madi with kindness and respect and she never saw pity in his gaze when he looked at her.

She understood why Ava couldn't go to Ghost Lake by herself. Madi wasn't thrilled about it, either. She tried to avoid that area when possible. Still, it wasn't as if they would be going to the Coalition camp again. From what she understood, the dinosaur hunters had set up on the opposite side of the lake, at least a mile away from the ruins of the compound.

When she reached her office, Madi sank into her desk chair and took a few deep breaths. She didn't want to sound like she had just raced across the rescue to talk to him, as if he only had to call for her to come running.

Okay, it might be the truth, but Luke didn't need to know that.

Her nervousness annoyed her. Luke was her friend. She had no reason to feel so on edge.

He answered on the second ring. "Hi," he said. "Thanks for calling me back."

She tried not to picture his mouth forming those words—the same mouth that had been flavored with cinnamon and chocolate when he kissed her the night before.

"Hello," she managed. "I got your text. What's up?"

He hesitated. Was it possible he might be as ill at ease to be speaking with her as she was with him?

"You told me Ed went up in the mountains over the weekend, looking for those stray dogs we heard about, but didn't have any luck. I got another report from some sheepherders up there who said they saw a couple of dogs running loose around Elk Flat Road. I thought I might take Sierra up there this evening to look for them. Want to go with us?"

She would much prefer doing that, riding up with Luke and

Sierra looking for dogs, instead of taking Ava on some mysterious errand to see her husband.

"I'm sorry. I can't. I already agreed to take Ava up to Ghost
Lake. She needs to talk to Cullen. We'll be leaving in about
an hour."

"That's a funny coincidence. Okay. Maybe we'll see you up
there, then."

"From what I understand, the dinosaur camp is on the east
side of the lake. We have to travel right through Elk Flats, so
I'll keep an eye out for a couple of strays."

"Sounds good. Be alert, if you see them. It sounds like
they've been wandering the mountains for at least a couple of
weeks, from the reports we've had. If they're starving, who
knows how they'll react to people?"

"I'll be careful."

A silence fell between them but it didn't seem as awkward
as she had feared.

"We missed you around here today," he said, his voice gruff.
"I thought we were going to have to do emergency surgery on
Janet Mitchell's cockapoo again this morning. He had an ob-
struction. Apparently he swallowed a chicken bone he pulled
out of the trash."

This was at least the third time they'd had to retrieve something inappropriate from the little furry vacuum cleaner. "Oh
no. Is he okay?"

"He will be. We gave him some hydrogen peroxide and he
hacked it up about five minutes later. We're keeping him here
overnight for observation."

"I'm sorry I missed that," she said, only half-joking. She
loved when they treated an animal emergency that could be
resolved easily and swiftly.

Those were the things she would miss most about working
at the veterinary clinic, the moments when they were able to

ease a pet owner's mind about their fur baby or help an animal through a frightening health challenge.

Life was a series of trade-offs. She had chosen to start the animal rescue in order to serve a void in the community and had worked hard to make it a reality. In order to devote her whole attention to the Emerald Creek Animal Rescue, she would have to walk away from her work as a veterinary tech at the clinic.

That didn't mean she would never go back, only that she was focusing on something else for now.

They talked about other patients on his schedule that day. Gradually the awkwardness eased and they slipped back into their usual comfortable camaraderie with each other.

Only after they ended the call and she returned to organizing the volunteer schedule for the next month did it occur to her that that was probably the very reason Luke had called her. He must have known that waiting even one more day would only heighten their discomfort with each other.

"This trail can get pretty dusty," Madi said as she climbed into the driver's seat of the side-by-side she had unloaded from the trailer. "Do you have a scarf or a bandanna or something?"

Ava looked startled. "No. Do you really think we'll need one? I thought it was a fairly well-maintained dirt road, at least until we get closer to the lake."

She shrugged. "Hard to know for sure. It will still be dusty. I figured you wouldn't think to bring one and I forgot to mention it, so there's an extra in the side pocket for you."

Ava blinked, clearly surprised. "Thank you. You're right. I didn't think about it."

"I would guess you don't spend a lot of time in the mountains these days."

"Not true," she said defensively. "I go with Cullen sometimes when he needs to explore a possible site. We try to combine work with recreation. We spent some time last summer hiking in both Montana and Utah. It was beautiful."

Madi found it odd to think of her sister going along with her paleontologist husband on a hiking trip into some of the world's most remote places. It was hard to reconcile that with the pale, serene, controlled woman Ava had become.

"I'm assuming you've been in one of these, then."

"Not often. But yes."

"You know what they say. Keep your arms and legs inside the vehicle at all times. We'll be going through some heavy forest. You don't want to lose a hand to a tree limb."

Ava looked concerned. "Would you like me to drive?"

"You can if you'd like. But I'm fine. I quite enjoy it, actually."

With a deep breath, Ava climbed into the passenger seat of the side-by-side and put on her own seat belt.

She gestured to the empty dog crates Madi had tied down in the small bed of the vehicle. "Do you want to explain what those are about? Are you expecting to bring something back?"

"I hope so," Madi said as she started the vehicle. "Apparently there are a couple of stray dogs running through these mountains. I want to be ready in case we see them."

"Ready for what?" Ava asked, clear alarm in her expression.

"To catch them if possible, and take them back to the shelter. Dogs can survive in the summer up here but come fall, they'll be starving."

"So you want to find two half-starved possibly vicious mongrels somehow in the vast mountains, persuade them to jump into the crates and drive them back down the mountain with us?"

Madi couldn't help her laugh. "If we're lucky."

The fire road was fairly well-maintained here, wide enough for two small ATVs to pass each other. Still, the side-by-side didn't exactly offer a smooth ride, jostling over bumps and rocks in the road. Madi glanced at her sister, who looked pale. Was Ava still feeling ill? She couldn't tell and her sister didn't volunteer the information.

The trail cut through beautiful old growth forests, thick with Douglas fir, ponderosa pine, aspen and spruce.

She inhaled deeply. "I love the way the mountains smell."

"Even these mountains?" Ava asked, her hands tightly clasped in her lap.

Madi couldn't see her features because of the bandanna and the sunglasses, but from Ava's posture alone, Madi could tell her sister was nervous.

"These mountains are just mountains," she answered, raising her voice to be heard above the growling engine. "Only a place. Beautiful, remote, wild. What happened to us could have happened in Hawaii or Canada or the Arizona desert."

"I suppose you're right," Ava said.

She grew quiet as the road became rougher. Madi slowed down to avoid some of the worst of the ruts and rocks. As the vehicle bounced through a rocky patch, the sisters jolted against one another.

Once they made it through and the road evened out again, Ava turned to her. "Do you think you could ever forgive Dad for dragging us into it all?"

Her sister's question, completely out of the blue, made Madi stare. In her shock, she took her foot off the gas and the vehicle slowed, then came to a stop, the grumbling engine reverting to a low hum.

"Is that what your book is about?" she asked. "Trying to figure out how to forgive Dad?"

"No. But I have to say, I did learn a lot about him while I was writing it and even more since."

"Like what?" she asked, when Ava didn't elaborate.

"Do you remember that Dad suffered a pretty bad head injury in a motorcycle crash right after you were born, when I was a toddler?"

"I was a baby. How would I know that?"

"I don't remember Mom and Dad talking about it much. I had totally forgotten about it. Apparently he was in the hospital for a week and Mom had to handle us both by herself. Grandma flew out to help her."

Leona hadn't mentioned that to Madi, either. She wondered if everything that had come after overshadowed that singular incident.

"What does that have to do with anything?"

"Maybe nothing," Ava conceded. "But a childhood friend of Dad's emailed me right after the book came out. He said Dad was always the kindest person, always willing to help someone else. Apparently something shifted in him after his injury. He became more... I don't know if *paranoid* is the right term. But willing to see conspiracies and connections in everything. This guy, Larry Hampton, said Mom was always a moderating force on Dad."

"Remember how he used to make us do emergency drills and would sometimes wake us in the middle of the night to go down to the bunker he had made in the basement?"

Ava nodded. "There's a section in the book about that. I guess you haven't read that part yet."

She hadn't read *any* part yet. Madi's hands tightened on the steering wheel and she started up the side-by-side, heading up the trail again.

"I rarely heard Dad and Mom fight," Ava said, barely audible now above the engine, "but I remember them fighting after one of those 3 a.m. emergency drills."

Madi didn't want to remember. She liked pretending everything before her mother died had been perfect in their family and that it had been her mother's death that had sent Clint spiraling. But Ava's words seemed to have turned the key to unlock memories in her subconscious, whether she liked it or not.

"I wouldn't have heard them, except I couldn't go back to sleep like you did, and I had to get up to use the bathroom," Ava went on. "Their door was ajar. I remember hearing Mom pleading with him to get help or she would have to leave. She threatened to take us girls and come back here to Emerald Creek with Grandma Leelee."

"Do you think she would have done that?"

"We'll never know. She was killed only a few months later."

The trail turned rough again, climbing more steeply, and Madi had to concentrate on driving.

She didn't like thinking about their father. It hurt too much. She had adored him all through her childhood, had considered him her hero. He had worked so hard to provide for their family, taking on second jobs to pay the bills when times were tight and his mechanic's salary and the little they made from the farm didn't stretch as far as necessary.

They rode in silence, each lost in her thoughts. It was too hard to carry on a conversation anyway, with the wind in their faces and the engine of the side-by-side throbbing.

The terrain began to grow more familiar. She remembered certain mountains, the winding flow of a creek, that wall of granite rock that curved along a hillside.

They continued climbing, moving deeper and deeper into Forest Service land, around switchback turns and through deep washes.

When they were maybe two miles from Ghost Lake, she pulled off at an overlook, where they could look back at the road they had traveled, so she could grab a drink. She turned off the engine and found her water bottle, drinking thirstily.

Ava, she saw, was shifting uncomfortably in the seat.

"If you need to use the forest, I have a spade and eco-friendly camp toilet paper."

"That might be good," Ava said, her cheeks turning pink.

Madi pulled them out of her pack and handed them over and Ava slid out of the vehicle.

"You won't drive away without me or something, will you?" she asked.

Madi couldn't tell if she was joking or not. "I hadn't planned to. But thanks for the idea. I'm sure you can find your way to Ghost Lake. It's only a few miles farther along the road."

Ava stood next to the vehicle, her hand still on the door handle, her expression alarmed, and Madi rolled her eyes. "I won't leave. I promise."

After another pause, her sister apparently decided her need was greater than her fear, in this particular case. Gripping the spade and the toilet paper, she hurried away from the trail to a thick area of understory.

She returned shortly, handing Madi back the essentials as Madi in return passed her a bottle of hand sanitizer that always came in handy.

"Thanks," Ava said. She gingerly climbed back into the UTV and Madi followed suit.

When they were both settled, she didn't hit the gas immediately. Instead, she asked the question she had been wondering.

"Have *you* forgiven Dad?" she asked.

Ava was quiet. "It's in the book," she finally said.

"Right. I haven't read that part, either," Madi said.

"You haven't read any of it, have you?"

"So give me the short version."

"I read through all the investigative reports and the trial transcripts for the defendants. I found out some things I never knew. Things I wish I could have had the chance to ask him about before…"

Ava didn't need to answer that. Before their dad, the man they once had both loved so much but had grown to fear, had been killed by federal agents in that final firefight.

"Like what?" Madi didn't want to ask but couldn't seem to help the words.

"He wanted to get us out, especially the last two weeks leading up to...up to my marriage. He was making plans but the Boyle brothers had as tight a leash on him as they did us. We escaped ourselves before he could...could help us."

Madi stared out at the forest, the trunks of the aspens blurring together. She wanted to believe their father hadn't abandoned them to their fate, caught up in his own twisted dogma. She couldn't quite get there. The loving, playful father she had adored had warped into someone she didn't recognize by the time they'd managed to creep away from camp into the wild unknown.

"We should get going," she said abruptly. "Otherwise, we won't make it back before dark."

She didn't wait for Ava's response, simply started up the side-by-side and headed up the trail, which grew increasingly narrow and rutted as they drove.

Fifteen minutes later, they crested the final hill to find the beautiful waters of Ghost Lake glimmering through the pines.

Hard to believe something so pristine could once have been home to so much evil.

"From the way Cullen described it, his dig isn't quite to the lake. You need to turn off before we get there on a side trail."

"Can you be more specific? We've seen several side trails."

"No. But I would guess there will be some kind of marker."

She frowned. She had assumed Ava knew right where she was going, not that they were going to have to search out Cullen.

She drove more slowly, keeping an eye out for anything that might indicate a camp.

"There!" Ava said suddenly.

Madi's gaze followed the direction she pointed and she saw

a cairn of stacked rocks with a small pink plastic stegosaurus toy on the top.

Apparently paleontologists had a sense of humor, she thought as she turned onto what could barely be called a trail. Who knew?

The trail led them through thick forest that finally opened out into a clearing where she saw two wall tents and a cluster of smaller ones, some camp chairs and a couple of ATVs.

At first, Madi didn't see any sign of life, then a large black Lab came trotting around the side of one tent, barking loudly as he hurried toward them.

Beside her, Ava stiffened, her knuckles white on the grab bar in front of her.

"Relax. He's not going to hurt us," Madi said.

"How do you know?"

"Because I know dogs and this one is friendly."

She turned to the Lab as he approached their vehicle. "Hi there," she said in calm voice. "We don't mean any harm."

Tongue lolling, the dog came closer. He was almost to the side-by-side when a man walked around the tent after him and came to an abrupt stop, looking as if someone had clobbered him with a tree trunk.

"Madi. Ava. What…what are you doing here?"

At the sight of Cullen, Ava had gone even more pale and pressed her hand to her stomach like she was about to hurl all over the place. She opened her mouth but no words came out, and for a weird moment, the three of them—and the dog— remained in a weird tableau.

Madi finally felt as if she had to speak. "Ava needs to talk to you. Don't you?"

Her sister nodded mutely, that hand still curled over her abdomen. The raw emotion in her eyes as she looked at her husband was almost painful to see—especially when he looked more stunned than happy to see his wife.

"Yes," Ava finally said, her voice ragged. She opened the door and slid out to stand beside the vehicle. The dog moved to greet her, but Madi headed him off by opening her own door and reaching out a hand.

She told herself she wasn't protecting Ava, she just liked dogs.

"I'm sorry to...to bother you," Ava went on. "I wouldn't have come if it wasn't important."

He finally nodded, moving closer to them.

"Okay."

The coolness in his voice raised Madi's hackles. She had never heard her loving brother-in-law speak in that tone of voice.

With more solicitousness than she might have felt if Cullen had been more welcoming, Madi turned toward her sister, who seemed a ghost herself.

"Do you need to sit down? Are you feeling sick again?"

"No." Ava seemed to shake off her strange torpor. "I'm fine. Could we...? Is there somewhere private we could talk?"

Cullen looked undecided, then nodded. "We can walk back into the trees. We've got a bench and a couple of camp chairs there, overlooking the lake."

"That works." Ava moved to follow him.

"I'll just hang out here with your dog," Madi said. "What's his name?"

"Bob. He belongs to one of the grad students but thinks every visitor to the camp is his business."

"Hi, Bob. I'm Madison," she said, adopting a cheery tone, and was happy when the dog wandered closer, his tail beginning a tentative wag.

By the time Ava and her husband walked up the trail, Madi and the dog were the best of friends.

That didn't stop her from watching after the departing figures of the couple and wondering what in the world was going on.

19

Days blur into nights, and our strength is tested in ways we never imagined. The vast expanse of the mountains becomes both a sanctuary and a labyrinth, a place of refuge and a realm of peril. Yet, with every step, we move closer to the distant promise of civilization, leaving behind the haunting echoes of the Coalition and embracing the uncertain path that leads to our newfound freedom.

—*Ghost Lake* by Ava Howell Brooks

Ava

OH, THIS WAS HARD. NOW THAT SHE WAS HERE, FACING her husband, she had no idea where to start.

It didn't help that he seemed like a stranger, with more beard than he'd had even a few days earlier, his hair in need of a cut and a distant expression on his features.

"What's going on? Are you okay?"

Over the years they had been together, she had wondered what it might be like to find out with him that they were expecting a baby. She would imagine it occasionally, usually when friends of theirs would spill their own news that they were pregnant.

This was not at all the way she might have imagined it, sitting in the forest of her nightmares, facing a man who clearly did not want her here.

"I didn't want to come," she admitted. "I know you need space and I'm trying to give you that but… I also think you would want to know. You would be more angry with me if I kept this news from you, and I… I couldn't bear that."

He looked suddenly weary. "I'm not angry with you, Ava. I thought I explained that to you. There's a big difference between being angry and being so deeply hurt that you feel it down to your bones."

She closed her eyes, hating that her fear had brought them to this point. When she opened them, she found him gazing down at her with the same remote expression.

"I…haven't been feeling well for a few weeks now. Since before…everything happened and you left Portland, actually."

He frowned. "I thought you looked pale at the farmers market last week. I assumed maybe it was from being out in the heat."

"That might have been part of it. It doesn't explain everything. The fatigue. The nausea. The…inability to control my emotions."

"It seems to me you have never had a hard time controlling your emotions. You're very good at curating everything you say or do to portray exactly the image you want the world to see."

His words might not have wounded her if he had spoken them in any other tone but that dispassionate, resigned one. As it was, she felt gutted.

"Madi and I learned early after we arrived at the camp to hide our emotions," she admitted, her voice low. "If you stayed quiet, your words could not be used to punish you later for some infraction, intended or accidental."

His eyes softened with compassion before he looked away.

"I don't know how to tell you this, so… I guess I'll come out and say it straight up."

"What's going on?" he asked, wariness in his voice.

She gave a heavy sigh. "I've been suffering for about three weeks with nausea. Someone suggested I might be pregnant. I took about eight pregnancy tests that confirmed it. I know it's the worst possible timing. I didn't plan it and didn't expect this to happen, but...we're going to have a baby."

For one instant, wild joy leaped in his gaze, so raw and real that she wondered if everything would be okay between them after all, if he would sweep her into his arms, kiss her and all the pain would disappear. As quickly as it appeared, it was gone again.

"Are you sure?"

"I haven't been to a doctor yet. But yes. Pretty sure. Again, eight pregnancy tests. I think it's unlikely that all eight of them would give false positives."

Now he looked flummoxed, as if she had shoved the camp chair out from under him.

"How did this...? We weren't planning on a baby right now. I thought we...*you* were taking precautions."

Guilt twisted through her. "The past few months have been so...intense that I haven't been as careful to take the pill every day as I should have been. That's the only explanation I can come up with. I'm sorry."

The last two words slithered out, hovering between them like something ugly and alive.

"Are you apologizing for my sake or for your own?" He looked down at her with burning intensity. "Do you...not want this baby?"

So very much. But not when you are so angry with me that you can't even hug me when I need it desperately.

She couldn't lie to him. "Yes, more than anything. I know the timing is poor but... I don't care. I already love her. Or him. It doesn't matter which. This baby is ours."

He let out a breath and she could see myriad emotions playing out on his features. Shock and joy and anxiety and perhaps even a touch of despair.

"So what happens now?"

We kiss and make up and go back to the blissful future we were planning before I screwed everything up?

"I don't know," she said honestly. "What do you want to see happen?"

"I've hardly had three minutes to process that our lives are about to change forever. I'm still struggling to wrap my head around it."

"I know. I've been the same way. I suspected last night but… I took the tests this morning. I came as soon as I could arrange a ride up with Madi. I wanted you to know right away. I don't want any more secrets between us."

His mouth tightened into a line and he looked haunted again. He said nothing so she continued, "We don't have to make any decisions right now. I am probably only about five or six weeks along. I've only missed one period."

"Are you feeling okay?"

She almost thought she saw his hand lift, as if he wanted to stroke it down her cheek. She ached for the comforting reassurance of his touch with a ferocity that seemed to throb like her heartbeat.

"Not really," she answered. "I've been pretty nauseous. And I've been napping so much, Grandma must think I have some kind of sleep disorder."

His mouth twitched slightly, as if he wanted to smile, but he remained stiff and silent, his emotion-filled eyes the only outward sign that her news had impacted him in the slightest.

She shrugged. "All that will only last another few months, then I'll be fine."

"That's good. Do you…need anything?"

You. Only you.

She shook her head. "No. You should know I plan to keep

the baby. If you…if you decide you can't forgive me for keeping secrets and want to make this separation more permanent, I can raise the baby by myself. Please don't worry about that. I'll make things work somehow."

The very real possibility she might end up a single mother made *her* want to curl up in the fetal position like their child growing inside her, especially when she knew what a wonderful father Cullen would be. But it wouldn't be fair to force parenthood on him when he wasn't even certain their marriage could survive.

He glared at her, suddenly, anger sparking to life in his eyes. "Ava. Do you honestly think I would abandon my responsibilities to you or…to our child?"

He stumbled over the word, as if it still didn't seem quite real to him.

"I know you didn't ask for this, that a baby wasn't something you wanted right now. *Especially* right now. I completely understand. I was the one who messed up and didn't consistently take my birth control. I can't expect you to pay for my mistake."

"If I really hadn't wanted a child, I could have chosen my own ways to prevent conception," he pointed out. "The responsibility was not yours alone."

She twisted her hands together, nails digging into her palms. "I know it's a…a shock to find out we're expecting a baby. But I hope in time, you can be happy about it."

"I'm not unhappy. Only surprised. I'm still processing."

"I understand."

Now that she had told him, she wasn't sure what to say or do next. It didn't feel right to simply drop this bomb and then walk away, like some kind of stealth guerilla. But she had no idea where to go from here.

To her astonishment, after a moment of strained silence, Cullen unexpectedly moved closer and pulled her into an almost desperate embrace.

She stood frozen for only a second before she wrapped her arms around him, hope beating through her with paper-thin wings.

This was home to her, no matter that they were in the Idaho wilderness. His arms. His solid strength. Here, she had always felt cherished and nurtured and…safe.

She pressed her cheek to his chest, feeling the whisper of gentle kisses on her hair. Thick emotion choked her throat. She had missed him so very much.

She wanted this instant to last forever, as if their embrace could heal all the fear, the distrust, the brokenness between them.

"I'm sorry you've been ill," he murmured against her hair.

"I'm all right. At least now I know there's a valid reason for it, that I'm not simply being…weak and depressed."

He eased away to meet her gaze and studied her features. Could he see the loneliness and despair that had consumed her since he left Portland?

She knew nothing had really changed. He still felt betrayed by the secrets she had kept from him and she didn't know how to fix the mess she had created out of self-protectiveness and fear. But at least he hadn't completely pushed her away.

Finally, he lowered his hands and moved away and she tried not to shiver as cool air replaced his warmth.

He sat down again and she did the same. "It wasn't necessary for you to come all the way up here. I was planning to stop by Leona's place on Saturday, when we come down for more supplies. But…thank you."

"You needed to know. It's all I've been able to think about since this morning. I didn't want you to think this was one more thing I was keeping from you."

He nodded. They sat on the camp chairs overlooking the blue waters of Ghost Lake and talked about practicalities. When her due date might be. Whether she would return to Portland now or see an OB-GYN in Sun Valley or Ketchum during the summer. If she had told her family yet.

She shook her head. "I wanted you to know first. I'm sure Madi is wondering what is going on and why I dragged her up here in the first place."

"I'm glad she came with you. Do the two of you want to stay for dinner? It's Luis's turn, which means it will probably be quesadillas or grilled cheese sandwiches. But he makes a pretty good grilled cheese."

If they could maintain this tentative peace between them, she would like to stay all night. She didn't have only herself to think about, though.

"We'd better not. Madi said we should try to be back before dark."

"Probably smart. There are some fairly rough spots on the trail."

She nodded. He rose and reached for her hand. She placed her fingers in his and he pulled her up from the camp chair and into his arms again.

"Thank you again for coming up here. I know it couldn't have been easy for you."

"It was easier, knowing you would be at the end of the trail, though I was terrified about your possible reaction," she admitted.

"I'm still reeling," he admitted. "I think I'll be processing it for some time. But I do know this. If you're happy about it, Ava, I am, too."

He brushed his mouth on her forehead, her cheek, then a soft, gentle kiss on her mouth. She closed her eyes, praying they could make their way through this thorny time to regain the happy ending that had become as vital to her as breathing.

20

In the silence of another moonlit evening, a pair of gleaming
eyes in the darkness catches our attention. A mountain lion
stalks us, a sleek silhouette moving with lethal grace. Fear
seizes our hearts, and we huddle together, our breaths held,
as the predator assesses its potential prey. It circles, a silent
guardian of the mountains, and we inch forward cautiously,
praying it finds no interest in our vulnerable forms.

—*Ghost Lake* by Ava Howell Brooks

Madison

WHEN HER SISTER AND CULLEN CAME DOWN THE
trail after about twenty minutes, Madi could tell something
had shifted between them.

Where they hadn't touched when they walked away, now her
brother-in-law helped Ava over a rock in the trail and touched
her to show her a red-tailed hawk that flitted through the trees
around the camp.

She exhaled deeply, not even aware until that instant how
anxious she had been about the two of them.

"It's good to see you, Mad," Cullen said when they rejoined
her. "Sorry I didn't say that before. I was shocked when you
both suddenly appeared."

Cullen gave her an affectionate hug and Madi returned it. He smelled of dirt and pine and sage and sunshine. It was a smell that reminded her of hugging her father in the *before* days, when they would all go camping together as a family.

She managed her lopsided smile. "Right back at you, Dinosaur Hunter."

"Thanks for coming up here with my wife. I know it's not your favorite place."

"You have a cute dog and a beautiful view. That's enough for me. Anyway, I know from past experience that if not for me, Ava would be hopelessly lost."

It was the very first time in her life she had joked with her sister about anything to do with that time.

In reality, Ava had led them on a circuitous route away from the dogs and the searchers. In the process, they had both become twisted around and had gone for two days in the wrong direction, deeper and deeper into the wilderness, before they realized their error.

After a startled moment now, Ava huffed out a breath that almost might have been a laugh before she moved toward the side-by-side and climbed into the passenger seat.

"You said you wanted to leave before dark. We should probably go, then. You're right. We don't have the best track record up here together."

Madi would have enjoyed having Cullen show her around the dinosaur camp and especially the actual dig site, but she knew it would take them at least an hour to drive back to the trailhead.

With one final pat to Bob, she climbed behind the wheel.

Cullen approached the side-by-side near Ava. "I'll see you both later. I'll try to stop by Leona's this weekend."

There was something meaningful in that, but Madi couldn't work it out. Cullen reached down to kiss his wife and what started as brief, almost casual, quickly transformed into something else. A kiss even Madi could tell seethed with emotion.

"Be well," he said, gazing at Ava intently.

Madi's sister nodded, swallowing hard. Tears glimmered in her eyes as Madi started up the side-by-side and turned out of the camp.

For the first fifteen minutes of the drive, it took all her concentration to maneuver down the narrow, rutted trail toward the larger and better-maintained dirt fire road.

When they were perhaps two miles from camp, she couldn't take all the questions swirling through her head. She pulled off the side of the road to a clearing, cut the engine and faced her sister.

"Okay. Tell me," she demanded. "What was that all about? What was so important that you had to come all this way to a place you hate to talk to Cullen?"

Ava gazed at her, then looked away. Golden hour had transformed the mountainside into a masterpiece of colors, bathing the mountains in amber light. The fading sun filtered through the trees, splotching the road and the undergrowth with columns of light. One lit up a patch of columbine, turning it a brilliant blue.

The soothing sights and smells of the mountains somehow calmed Madi, centered her. She couldn't help thinking that she had come a long way in her journey, if she could find any sort of peace deep in the backcountry.

"Do we have to do this here?" Ava asked, fingers working at a loose thread from her jacket. "I would rather get out of the mountains first so we're not stuck here after dark."

And avoid telling her the truth even longer?

"This thing has headlights. What's going on, Ava. Are you sick? Is it cancer?"

"Why did you immediately jump to that conclusion?"

Icy fear gripped her. She didn't want to lose her sister. Not Ava, as well as everyone else. "Are you sick?"

"I don't have cancer."

"Then, what?"

Ava sighed, looking through the trees. "I'm pregnant."

Madi's heartbeat kicked up and she stared at her sister in disbelief, unable to comprehend how Ava could sit there so self-contained and cool while sharing the staggering news.

"Pregnant? Seriously?"

Ava nodded. At first, Madi couldn't tell how her sister felt about that, then she thought she saw a glint of joy in her eyes.

"That's fabulous. Oh, Ava. I'm going to be an aunt!" Madi instinctively reached out and hugged her, remembering all the times they had talked about the families they might someday have. Ava had always wanted to have children, she remembered, while Madi said she would be happy only having fur babies.

At her hug, Ava was stiff, all thin bones, for only a moment before she hugged her back.

"It's none of my business but…have you guys been trying long?"

Ava shook her head, easing back into her seat. "It was a surprise. A…a happy one but totally unexpected. Before a month ago, we were talking about maybe in a year or two, after we bought a house and felt more settled."

She frowned, picking up immediately on that short disclaimer. "What happened a month ago?"

Ava said nothing, the only sound the breeze rustling the aspen leaves near them and the chitter of a squirrel protesting their intrusion. "What happened a month ago?" she finally answered. "*Ghost Lake* came out and Cullen learned he wasn't married to the woman he thought I was."

Madi stared. "What are you talking about?"

"He didn't read the entire book until after it was released. I didn't…didn't want him to."

"Why not? He knew about what had happened to us at the camp and about Dad, right? About the grooming and the punishments and your sham of a marriage."

Ava didn't answer, gazing at the vast mountains around them. Madi read the answer in her silence.

"You never told him? How is that even possible? You've been married for three years!"

It was such a part of her, even if she didn't want it to be, Madi couldn't imagine concealing that from someone with whom she shared her life.

She might not want to dwell on it or talk about it or, heaven forbid, write a blasted book about it. But she would still want any man she loved to know that part of her.

"He knew bits and pieces. He knew about our rescue and Dad being killed and that you were hurt at the same time. He knew about Dan Gentry."

"Okay. What *didn't* he know?"

"I…might have let him think we were only there a few weeks instead of months. I didn't want him to know about how bad things were."

"Why not? He's your husband! He loves you."

"*Because* of that! Because I didn't want him to pity me or to…to wonder if I was damaged forever because of what happened. We were so happy together and I didn't want that ugliness to cast any kind of shadow on our joy."

"You never told him *any* of it? Did he know about your wedding?"

Ava's denial was in her tightly compressed mouth. "Not until he read the book," she admitted. "It wasn't like it was a legal marriage, anyway. I didn't consider it important."

Not important? Ava's wedding had been the catalyst for everything else that came after.

That had been when Ava finally accepted the grim truth that no one was looking for them, that their situation was untenable and they couldn't remain there.

She'd also had to face the even more painful truth that their father wasn't going to come to his senses and they were going to have to leave him behind. He had been so wholly brainwashed by the warped ideology of the Coalition, by the Boyle brothers, that he had even been willing to give his own daughter to one of them and was planning to hand over the other one.

If Cullen hadn't known about Ava's wedding, at sixteen, to a man thirty years her senior, a man whom she feared and loathed, he couldn't have known about her wedding night. He couldn't have known how Ava had somehow found the courage to drug the man who had just raped her with herbs they had crushed from wildflowers obtained surreptitiously. Or that she had known even as she mixed the dried plants into his tea that they might knock him out, as she hoped, or they might kill him.

At that point, neither she nor Madi had cared which.

"Why?" Madi asked, her voice hoarse. "Why didn't you tell him? I thought you loved him."

Tears welled up in her sister's eyes. "I do love him. I wanted his love in return, not his pity. I wanted him to see me as a strong, capable woman, not as…as a weak, frightened girl, so afraid that she actually went through with an abhorrent marriage rather than fight. A girl who had to be rescued by her younger sister!"

The tears glimmering on her lashes spilled over, gathering in the corner of her eyes before dripping out. The resentment and anger and sense of betrayal Madi had nursed for weeks, since the release of Ghost Lake, didn't seem nearly as important when her sister clearly was suffering so much.

"We rescued each other, Ava."

Her sister scoffed. "Only because you were the one who had the strength to do what I couldn't. While I was torn by indecision, waiting for the impossible, you went ahead and gathered valerian root and deathcamas while you were forced to forage for food with the others. You were the one smart enough to remember what you learned about it from Grandma and Mom, then brave enough to hide it, to dry it, to crush it into tea."

"I couldn't let you stay married to that evil man. Partly for you and partly because I knew I would be next," she admitted.

"I know. Which was one of the reasons I finally agreed to your ridiculous plan."

"My ridiculous plan that worked perfectly, I'll remind you. James fell asleep. He didn't die. I wish you had been able to get him to drink it before he…before he…"

"So do I."

Madi felt the same burning anger she always did when she remembered that dark time. She didn't want to wish anyone dead, but she was glad James had been arrested and that he had died in a prison brawl six months after his conviction.

"It worked. Somehow it worked. For the first night since we arrived at camp, you weren't locked into a room. You were able to sneak out and get me."

She frowned at Ava. "You did nothing wrong. I don't know why you couldn't tell everything to Cullen."

"Believe me, I've asked myself that over and over."

"I also can't understand how you could keep everything from your husband, the man you love more than any other, yet still go ahead and pour every single detail into that damn book."

"It's…complicated."

Ava lapsed into silence. The squirrel had moved away and the mountainside echoed in the quiet.

Then, distantly through the forest, Madi thought she heard something. A faint cry that didn't belong among the hoots and calls and chatter of the mountain's usual inhabitants.

A dog's whine.

"Shhh." She held out a hand to Ava.

"I didn't say anything."

"Be quiet," Madi hissed.

Ava fell silent, her eyes going wide. "What's wrong?"

Madi strained her ears and heard it again. A faint, unmistakable whine.

"Did you hear that?"

"It sounds like a cat or something. Is it a cougar?"

The whispered fear in Ava's voice and her sudden wide eyes and trembling lips were visceral reminders of one of the most terrifying incidents during those days they spent in the wilderness, trying to get to safety. They had been making their way up a slope when they realized they were being stalked by a mountain lion.

They had faced an impossible choice between staying quiet to avoid discovery by their pursuers or making as much noise as possible to scare away an apex predator.

The abject terror in Ava's voice now gave Madi pause, especially when her sister curved an arm over her abdomen.

She touched her sister's hand, trying to reassure her. "I don't think it's a mountain lion. It sounds more like a dog."

She heard it again, that distant yelp, and unbuckled her seat belt. "I have to go check it out."

"You can't leave me here!"

Madi pointed to the keys in the ignition. "If I don't come back in ten minutes, you can go back to Cullen's camp for help. It's straight up the trail, then turn left at the fork."

"No! I won't let you go by yourself. Forget it!"

She thought about arguing with her sister, but that would waste precious moments of their remaining daylight. "Fine. You have to keep up, though."

Ava scrambled out of the side-by-side. "I might be pregnant, but I'm not the one with a bad leg."

"Fair point," Madi admitted.

The undergrowth was sparse at this higher elevation, which made the going easier. They walked over pine needles and around clumps of wildflowers. The barks and yelps continued at random intervals, growing louder as they moved.

"Is it a wolf?" Ava asked, casting a wild eye through the trees.

"I mean, it's possible a wolf might have strayed from the

Yellowstone ecosystem but I don't think so. I've not heard of any sightings up here."

"Coyotes?"

"Again, possible. I suspect it's a dog. Remember, I told you about those strays people have reported? In fact, Luke had planned to come up tonight to look for them."

Ava didn't look any more relieved about the possibility of stray dogs than she might have if Madi had said there were slavering werewolves.

"What kind of dogs?"

"From what I heard, maybe a border collie and a corgi mix that had a collar."

Ava relaxed slightly at that. Madi wanted to tell her any dog could strike out in the right circumstances. If hungry, in pain or scared enough.

"We have to be getting closer," Ava said, her attention fixed on the terrain ahead of them.

"There!" Madi exclaimed. She pointed to a small meadow ahead of them. Perched on the edge of a gaping pit, a small stocky corgi barked ferociously at them.

Ava froze and looked as if she wanted to turn and run back to their vehicle. While she stayed locked in place, Madi moved closer slowly, making her way around boulders and fallen logs scattered through the meadow. She tried to look as unassuming as possible.

"Hey there. Hi," she crooned to the dog, who had stopped barking and was now growling ominously. "It's okay. I'm not going to hurt you. Look what I have."

She stuck her hand in her pocket, grateful that she had had the foresight to bring some treats, just in case. "Look. It's a beef stick. Yum!"

The dog's growling stopped abruptly and it took a step toward her before retreating another step. The dog looked down at the pit and Madi heard it again, a whining yelp coming from the depths.

It was the other dog, she realized. Possibly injured and definitely trapped. Poor thing.

Holding out a piece of the beef stick, Madi took a step closer to the corgi. She needed to see what they were up against, how difficult it might prove to rescue the other dog.

She tossed one small piece to the dog, who almost swallowed it whole in her hunger.

The grasses and weeds growing around the pit were flattened, as if the small dog had spent considerable time crouched here, unwilling to leave the other animal. Her fur was matted, not unlike the grasses, with burrs and other random pieces of debris stuck in it.

Madi tossed her another piece of treat. The dog moved closer this time to retrieve it.

"Good girl. That's right. I'm not going to hurt you or your friend. You're both so hungry, aren't you? Should we see if we can get him out?"

She continued speaking nonsense in the same low, calming voice. Dogs never seemed to mind if she stumbled over words, which was one of the things she loved best about them.

Finally, she managed to move close enough to the edge of the pit so she could look in.

It appeared to be an old mining shaft, about twelve feet deep and seven or eight feet at its widest point. She could barely make out a white blur in the fading daylight until she aimed her flashlight down and saw wary canine features looking back up at her.

"Oh, you poor thing. You must be starving. Here you go. Here's a treat."

She tossed down a large treat for the dog and almost instantly heard lips smacking together as he ate it hungrily.

"What is it?" Ava called.

"It's the other dog. He's stuck down some kind of pit. It looks like an old mine shaft, maybe? I'm guessing he was sniffing around the edge and must have lost his footing. Or maybe the side collapsed or something."

"Oh, that's so sad. How long do you think he's been down there?" She moved closer, though still keeping her distance from the other dog.

"My guess is at least a day or two. See how the grass is tramped down around the opening? I think that was done by his friend here, keeping watch."

Ava's features seemed to soften at that. Madi wondered if she, too, could relate to the trapped dog, feeling as if she had no way out.

"What do we do now? Maybe we should go get Cullen. He and members of his team might know of a way we could get him out."

"It will be full dark by the time we drive back up to the dinosaur camp and then make our way back here. I don't think we'll be able to find him again in the dark."

"We can't leave him here."

"No. We can't," Madi said, feeling closer to her sister than she had in a long time. They shared a purpose now. "I've got a towrope in the side-by-side. I can attach it to a tree and belay into the hole."

"No! No way! What if you get stuck down there, too?"

"Then, you can drive back to Cullen and he can come find me and help me out."

Ava looked horrified at the prospect. "You just said we won't find the dog in the dark. How are we supposed to find *you*?"

"I have a whistle." She pulled it out from the chain around her neck. She never traveled into the backcountry without one now. She had spent enough time being lost in the wilderness. She wasn't keen to ever go through that again. A whistle could be heard over longer distances than shouts, and a person could blow a whistle even after losing her voice calling for help.

"You wait here. I'm going to go back and get the towrope."

Ava's eyes went wide. "No! I'm not staying here by myself. I'll come with you."

"One of us needs to stay here or we won't be able to find our way back. I can stay here if you want to go back to get the rope."

Ava gazed at her, then took a few steps, turned and threw up into the undergrowth.

"Are you okay?"

"Swell," Ava snapped. She wiped her mouth with the corner of her shirt, swished water from the bottle she had brought along and spat it out.

"It will be much faster if I go. Here, take the whistle. You can use my flashlight. I'll use my phone for light if I need it."

"You want me to stay here with the...the dogs?"

"The border collie is trapped and can't hurt you. And the corgi wants to help her friend. Here. You can give her some of these treats. You can toss a few down to the other dog but not too much. I don't know if he has water down there."

After handing over the rest of the treats, she hurried back the way they had come, crossing the space in half the time as before, ever aware of the fading sunlight that cast long shadows through the trees.

She went to the cargo area of the side-by-side. After unhooking the dog crate, she was rooting through the back for the towrope and the headlamp she kept there, as well as extra rope and leather gloves, when she glimpsed the flash of movement coming up the trail and heard the thrum of an engine.

As a woman currently standing alone in the backcountry, with no one else in sight, Madi couldn't help the instinctive spurt of adrenaline and wariness.

She closed her good hand around the heavy winch, in case

she needed a weapon she could swing at someone who might decide to take advantage of the situation.

Her fear instantly eased when she recognized the man driving a side-by-side newer than her own and she relaxed her grip on the winch.

"Oh, am I glad to see you!" she exclaimed to Luke. It was all she could do not to rush to his vehicle and hug him.

He shut off his engine with a concerned look. "What's up? Are you having mechanical difficulties? Where's Ava? Did she stay at camp with her husband?"

She shook her head. "It's a long story, but we found the dogs everyone has been looking for. One of them is caught in some kind of pit about two hundred yards off the trail. Ava stayed with them while I came back here for supplies."

He looked at the array of items in front of her. "Supplies for what? What exactly are you planning to do with your kit here?"

"Get him out," she said simply. "We can't leave him there. I thought I would belay down, have Ava lower the crate down, put the dog into it, then use the pulley and winch to get him back out."

"And how were you planning to get back out?"

"The same way. With the pulley and winch."

He sighed. "Of course. Why not? What could go wrong?"

She decided, in this case, she couldn't do everything on her own. Her customary need for independence seemed pointless when an animal was in need.

"I could really use your help. Ava's not...feeling her best right now."

Without hesitation, he climbed out of the vehicle, grabbed a few supplies of his own out of his vehicle, then picked up the heavy winch in one hand, the crate in the other and followed her into the forest.

21

We find ourselves scrambling across a rocky scree, loose stones cascading beneath our feet. The jagged terrain threatens to betray us, and I feel my sister's hand slip from mine as we stumble and slide down the unforgiving slope. Bruised and battered, we rise again, our determination unbroken, a testament to the strength that has emerged from our shared ordeal.

—*Ghost Lake* by Ava Howell Brooks

Luke

"WHERE'S SIERRA? I THOUGHT YOU WANTED TO BRING her up, looking for the dogs with you," Madi asked as they made their way toward Ava.

"She had a better offer, apparently. My mom scored last-minute tickets to a concert in Sun Valley and invited her along."

"That's fun."

"Yeah. Seems like she is a social butterfly these days. I wonder if I should be feeling left out that she seems to have time for everyone but me."

She gave him a sympathetic smile. "You might want to get used to that."

As he followed Madi through the forest, on no discernable trail, Luke could see she was in pain. She always walked more carefully when her weak leg was giving her trouble, though she would never admit it.

He wanted to tell her to wait back with their vehicles, but he knew that would be like telling the grass not to grow or the snow not to fall in January.

Would she really try to belay down into a mine shift?

Yes. One hundred percent. His Madison was completely fearless.

Not *his*, he reminded himself.

"There they are," she said, pointing through the undergrowth. As they moved into a clearing between Douglas fir and lodgepole pine, he saw a sight he never would have imagined in a hundred years.

Ava Howell Brooks was sitting perched on a fallen tree trunk, crooning softly to a matted corgi with a pink collar.

"Look who I found," Madi called out cheerfully.

Ava looked up and the vast relief on her pale features made him smile.

"Luke! Oh, thank heavens. Maybe you can talk some sense into her. She can't go down into a mine shaft to rescue a dog. It's ridiculous. We have to come up with another way."

Madi glared at the two of them, as if daring him to agree with her sister. The fierce expression on her features made him check his impulse to do exactly that.

She hated people coddling her, treating her as if she were incapable of anything she set her mind to. He knew he was guilty of the same thing, of wanting to protect her. Sometimes he couldn't help treating her like a fragile flower that would bend and break at the first sign of a breeze.

"She's tougher than she looks," he said, a reminder to himself as well.

Madi sent him a swift look of shocked gratitude. "That's right," she said. "I am."

"I know she's tough," Ava said impatiently. "My sister the

superhero, who can leap tall buildings in a single bound, blah blah blah. But now that you're here, she doesn't have to go down there, right? You can do it."

He almost agreed with her, but somehow sensed Madi wanted to do this, if only to prove to herself that she could.

"I should stay up here while she belays down so I can help pull her and the dog back out. I would be too heavy for you to pull up if something went wrong. It should be one of you two. Unless you want to go down, I guess that leaves Madi."

"What about her leg? And her hand?"

"I have full use of both," Madi said sharply.

Ava still looked worried for her sister. Luke didn't blame her. He was worried, too. But he also trusted that she knew what she was doing. He also remembered that she occasionally went to the climbing wall in Sun Valley with Nicki and whatever guys they were currently dating.

If he hadn't been here, how she had intended to climb out of the hole by herself, with only Ava to help, he had no idea.

He attached the pulley and winch to a sturdy tree limb over the opening, then helped her fashion the rope into a makeshift harness, up through her legs and around her waist, trying his best to ignore her softness and her strawberry scent that teased him.

"You sure you're ready for this?"

She nodded, smiling with a confidence in him he found deeply humbling.

"Sure. You're here. You've got my back."

"Always," he murmured.

She blinked, as if not sure whether she heard him or not, then she lowered into the mine shaft. He held on to the rope, giving her enough lead to rappel down into the hole, which he judged to be about a dozen feet deep.

The entire way down, she spoke softly to the dog. "You're almost out. There's a good boy. Almost there."

He felt the tension on the rope ease when she hit solid dirt. "Okay," she called. "I'm down."

He and Ava both aimed flashlights down into the pit. Together with the light from Madi's headlamp, they were able to see her approach the dog with some caution. Smart. A cornered, injured dog could lash out, even at someone trying to help. This one was too tired to do more than wag a tail.

"You're probably thirsty, aren't you? Look. I brought you some water. I don't have a bowl but I can do my best."

He watched her pour some water into her hand. The dog lapped at it and she repeated the process three more times.

She released the rope anchoring her to them. "Can you lower the crate now?" she called softly.

He anchored four corners of the crate with the remaining rope, then slowly lowered it down into the pit. In the beam from the flashlight, he watched as she coaxed the dog into the crate with several treats.

"Okay. He's good," she called back up the hole. "He seems to have injured his back paw, maybe when he fell, but you'll have to take a closer look when you get him out."

The corgi mix, still close to Ava, barked encouragement as Luke used the pulley to haul up the dog.

As soon as the crate was out of the mine shaft and on solid ground, Luke opened the door and the border collie limped out of the crate. The other dog immediately rushed to him, tail wagging a furious greeting.

Luke quickly ran his hands over the dog, even more matted and covered with burrs than the corgi, probably because his fur was longer.

"How is he?" Madi called.

"He'll be okay. We'll take him back to the clinic and clean him up and take a look at his leg. I don't think anything is broken."

"Oh good."

"Are you okay?" Ava called.

"I will be as soon as Luke gets me out."

He remembered suddenly reading in Ava's book about how they hadn't been allowed candles or flashlights at night in the primitive log structure where they had been kept and how the overwhelming darkness had been oppressive and terrifying.

He clipped leashes to both dogs. "Hold on," he told Ava. "After we've gone to all this trouble to rescue them, the last thing we want is for them to slip away into the backcountry again."

Ava looked daunted at the responsibility, but she quickly grabbed the leashes from him and followed her sister's lead, speaking softly to the animals.

He unhooked the crate from the ropes and lowered it back down to Madi. "Will you be able to tie it around yourself again?"

"Yes. I should be able to."

He and Ava both aimed their flashlights down into the hole and she sent up a grateful look. "That helps. Thanks."

She quickly rigged up her own harness again, perching on top of the crate. "I've got it."

"Are you sure you're secure? I'd hate for you to fall."

She tugged at the rope. "Yes. I'm good."

"Okay, steady. I'm going to get you out of there. All you have to do is stay away from the side."

"No problem," she called up.

He used the winch to pull her and the crate out with excruciating slowness, cursing himself for giving in to her stubbornness. He should have gone down instead, no matter how determined she had been to handle the rescue.

He wasn't sure which of them was happier when she finally emerged from the hole and he could pull her to safety.

"There you go. Back on solid ground."

The relief on her features clearly told him how difficult the rescue had been for her, despite her protestations.

"You did it!" Ava exclaimed, her voice filled with wonder. "That was amazing!"

Madi flushed in the last rays of the sun. "Thanks. We're not done. We still have to get them to the UTVs and then back down the mountain."

The border collie did indeed have a tender leg. He made a few limping steps before Luke swept him into his arms. "I'll carry him, if you can bring the crate and the corgi."

"Her name is Gracie, according to her name tag," Ava offered. "I couldn't find a phone number or anything."

"You're a good, brave girl to stay with your friend," Madi said to Gracie.

The border collie didn't have a collar. Had he lost it somewhere during their adventures? Or was he a bad-boy stray who had convinced the other dog to leave the safety of the familiar?

They stopped long enough to let both dogs lap eagerly from a small creek they passed on the way back to the vehicles. When they reached the trail, Madi gave the dogs the sandwich she had packed and Ava handed hers over as well. They were eaten with such alacrity, Luke was certain they must be starving.

"I don't think I could eat anything right now, if you want the truth," Ava said with a grimace.

"Sorry," Madi said, giving her sister's arm a squeeze.

They seemed to have come to some kind of peace, though Luke wasn't sure if it was permanent or only a temporary cease-fire.

After the dogs gulped down the sandwiches, he helped them both settle in the crates he had tied down in the cargo area of his side-by-side.

"Will you be okay driving in the dark?" he asked as Madi slid behind the driver seat in the other vehicle.

"I should be. If I start to drive off the side of the trail, I'm sure Ava will scream loud enough to jerk me back to safety."

Ava didn't look amused. "How about we don't test that hypothesis? Do you want me to drive?"

"No. I've got it. I just need you not to puke on me."

"I can't make any promises," Ava muttered.

"You want to go first?" Madi asked him.

"No. I'm fine following you."

Madi nodded and began driving down the trail. Nights here in the mountains instantly cooled as soon as the sun went down, with an enveloping darkness. As he followed them, Luke wished he had thought to give them the extra blanket he kept under the seat. He considered honking to get their attention so he could hand it over, then discarded the idea. The dogs needed food and water and medical treatment, and he was certain Ava and Madi wanted to get out of these particular mountains as quickly as they could, now that it was full dark.

It took them nearly twice as long to reach the parking lot as it might have during the day, as they had to drive more slowly to avoid rocks and ruts on the trail that were harder to see in the dark.

Finally, she pulled up to her old pickup truck and he drove to his truck and trailer next to hers.

"You two get in and turn on the truck heater. I'll load up your wheeler."

"Ava, you go and warm up. I'll help with the dogs," Madi said, handing her sister the truck keys.

While Ava slipped into the cab of the truck and started the engine, he and Madi transferred the crates to the back of his pickup truck, covered with a shell.

He helped her load the side-by-side onto her trailer and anchored it down.

"I can help you with yours," she said.

"I've got it. You should probably get Ava back home. What did she need to tell Cullen, anyway?"

"It's a long story. And not mine to tell," Madi said. "Do you want to take the dogs to the clinic or to the shelter?" she asked.

"Probably the clinic so I can give them a careful exam."

"I'll drop Ava off at my grandmother's place and meet you there."

"Sounds good," he said. On impulse, he pulled her into a hug. "You're a hero, Mad. You saved them. That collie probably wouldn't have lasted much longer without water, and the corgi didn't seem to want to leave him to get any for herself, either."

She rested her head on his chest. "I'm glad you were here," she admitted, which he knew couldn't be easy for her. "I am fairly confident I could have done it with only Ava's help. But I'm really grateful I didn't have to try. I wouldn't have enjoyed being stuck down there while Ava drove back up to find Cullen."

He tightened his hold, wishing he could kiss her as he wanted to.

After a moment, she stepped away. "I need to take care of Ava. I'll see you at the clinic."

He nodded, climbed into his pickup truck and followed her taillights toward Emerald Creek.

22

As we navigate the terrain of freedom, we carry with us the lessons learned in captivity, using them as compass points to guide us toward a future sculpted by choice, love and the unwavering support we found in each other.

—*Ghost Lake* by Ava Howell Brooks

Ava

SHE WAS SO TIRED, SHE WANTED TO CLOSE HER EYES right here, lean her cheek against the worn seat of her grandfather's old pickup truck and sleep for a week or so.

Even as the truck bounced around on the washboard dirt road, jostling her against the door again and again, she wanted to sleep.

Had it really been that morning when she found out for certain she was expecting? The day felt as if had lasted an eternity.

Now that she knew she was expecting a baby, her mental and physical exhaustion of the past few weeks seemed far more understandable. Growing a baby was tough work. At least she wasn't suffering from some autoimmune condition like chronic fatigue syndrome or Lyme disease.

She remembered again telling Cullen she was pregnant. That

brief, wild moment of joy. Whatever else he might be feeling about her right now, she knew that instinctive response had been genuine. He had truly been happy about the news, until he remembered that while he might want a child, he wasn't as certain he wanted *Ava* along with the baby.

How could she fix things? She did not have the first idea. She couldn't go back and change their history. She had made a decision to bifurcate her past, to, as he put it, curate what she told him into shareable and unshareable information.

She couldn't blame him for feeling as if he had married a stranger, though her initial reaction when she first realized he was upset about all the things she hadn't told him had been hurt and anger.

He loved the woman she was now. Why couldn't that be enough? Why did he have to know every single detail of her life?

As she thought about it, however, his reaction made more sense. How would she feel if he had withheld huge chunks of his life from her, especially if those details had undeniably shaped him?

She couldn't go back and live that time over.

If she had known her decision to stay quiet about their time at Ghost Lake would have such chilling ramifications for her marriage, she still wasn't sure she would have been able to tell him everything.

She did know she would never have finished the book for her master's thesis and certainly never would have allowed her advisor to read it and subsequently to submit it to contacts in the publishing industry.

Every choice had consequences, ripple effects that expanded out to impact others, whether intended or not.

If that drunk driver hadn't killed her mother. If her father had never met the Boyle brothers and been drawn into their twisted ideology. If Clint had only stopped to consider that all their choices had been taken away as soon he moved them to Ghost Lake.

She sighed, shifting on the old truck bench to find a more comfortable position.

"How are you doing?" Madi asked.

"I'm fine." She actually was. Right now, at least, it wasn't a lie. The nausea had faded. Even the bumpy road did not seem to be impacting her dicey stomach.

"I told Luke I would drop you off at Leona's first, before I meet him at the clinic to help him take care of the dogs."

"Don't be silly. It's out of your way. I can walk from the clinic. It's only a few blocks."

"I know, but you've already had a long and stressful day. I can see you're exhausted."

"It's fine. I can make it a little longer. I want to make sure Gracie and her friend are settled for the night."

If Madi was surprised at her concern for the dogs, she didn't show it.

"Luke has turned into a good veterinarian, hasn't he?" Ava said.

"The best. He's an excellent vet."

"And a good man," Ava said.

"Yes. That, too."

Madi kept her gaze on the road but Ava thought she saw an odd expression cross her sister's features.

She narrowed her gaze. Was there something going on between Luke Gentry and Madi? She knew Madi was close with all the Gentrys and that Luke had been a mentor of sorts to her. Leona had told her how much Luke had helped Madi start the shelter and about the many volunteer hours of veterinary care he donated to help the animals.

She knew all that. But was there something else? She had seen them hug after they finished loading up the vehicles. It had seemed more than a hug between friends.

It seemed a departure for her sister. Madi liked to date with the seasons. Living in Portland, Ava didn't see her pattern first-hand but she had heard about it, both from Madi herself and from Leona.

In winter, she tended to date guys in town for the ski or snowmobile seasons. Summer brought trail guides or river rats. From what Ava understood, Madi at least chose nice guys, but none of the relationships were particularly serious, with the kind of guys who would stick around.

She was quite certain that was the idea, at least as far as Madi was concerned.

Luke would be an entirely different level of relationship.

Their lives were so intertwined.

How would all those other relationships—Nicole, Sierra, Tilly—be impacted if Madi and Luke formed a relationship? And what if it didn't work out between them? The awkward-ness and discomfort for both of them would be monumental.

On the other hand, Ava couldn't deny they made an ador-able couple. She thought of Luke's watchful concern for Madi, his careful mentoring, his support of the animal rescue. He re-ally was perfect for her sister, if only Madi could recognize it.

What could she do to push them together? Should she even try, when she wasn't in a particularly good place right now to be optimistic about other people's relationships, given what a mess her own marriage was in?

"Thanks again for your help tonight," Madi said as she pulled up to the clinic. Luke wasn't there yet, as he had been behind them. "A rescue wasn't exactly what we had planned for our evening's entertainment but we couldn't have done it with-out you."

"I'm glad I was there," she said.

There had been something infinitely rewarding about know-ing they had saved two dogs, animals that likely would have suffered an unfortunate fate in conditions for which they were ill-equipped.

She knew how that felt.

"I'm not sure I could have made it down into that dark hole, even if I weren't pregnant," she said quietly to her sister. "You were remarkable. You *are* remarkable."

Madi gazed at her in consternation. "Okay. Are you sure you didn't bump your head out there on the trail? Or maybe you're delirious with dehydration."

Ava frowned. "I'm not concussed or delirious. Only...honored to be your sister."

Madi looked stunned. Before she could reply, Luke pulled up beside them. Madi seemed as grateful for the distraction as Ava was.

With a last baffled look at her, Madi hopped out of the truck and headed over to help Luke unload the animals.

"I can help you carry the crate with the border collie."

"That's probably the safest way to move him. Good idea," Luke said to Madi.

"Ava, can you help with Gracie? She seems to like you. She'll probably need to find a patch of grass after all that water they drank up in the mountains."

Before Ava quite realized what was happening, Madi had attached a leash to the corgi's collar and handed the end to Ava.

"Hi again," she said to the dog.

As Madi and Luke carried the crate into the clinic, the corgi growled after them.

"It's all right. He's not going anywhere. You can stay together," she promised.

As if she understood, the dog licked Ava's hand, then waddled on her short legs to the grass.

Ava found it deeply touching when the corgi returned to her side for reassurance before going out to the grass again.

You don't like dogs, remember?

It was hard to keep that in mind when she was facing this brave, loyal little thing who had stayed by her friend's side under harrowing conditions.

Ava hadn't been as loyal to her sister. After she received a full-ride scholarship offer to attend college in Oregon, Ava had only been too quick to leave Madi behind with their grandmother.

Madi had seemed to settle into the rhythm of life here in Emerald Creek in a way that Ava never had. Ava had been happy to leave Emerald Creek and the nearby mountains that held so many hard memories.

She was even happier when she'd met Cullen as she was finishing her graduate degree.

Gradually her visits back to visit Leona and Madi had trickled to maybe once a year for the holidays.

She knew she had stayed away mostly out of guilt. She hated that Madi hadn't achieved her own dream of becoming a veterinarian. Seeing her sister struggling with words or unable to complete a task because of her physical limitations made Ava want to weep.

She was the older sister and it had been her job to watch out for her sister. Ava had never considered it a burden. She had adored Madi from the day her parents brought her home from the hospital and had always been so very grateful to have her for a sister.

She had failed her sister in so many ways. Watching Madi struggle now only reinforced that.

The dog seemed to be done with her business. She sat at Ava's feet, gazing up at her with an expectant look. Yet one more creature who needed something from her that Ava didn't know how to give.

Gripping the leash, she walked into the veterinary clinic. It smelled of lemons, with an underlying scent she couldn't identify. Maybe it was fear hormones excreted by all the creatures who didn't want to visit the vet, no matter how kind Luke might be.

We're in the back, Madi texted her. You can come back when Gracie is done.

She pushed through a door by the receptionist desk and found herself in a hallway with various small exam rooms leading off it.

Gracie, apparently now scenting her friend, tugged at the leash, leading her toward a door at the end of the hallway. It didn't take great detective work to figure out that was where Madi and Luke must be, since it was the only space in the closed veterinary clinic where a light burned. She followed the dog's waddling steps and pushed open the door, where she found a large, clean exam suite.

Madi looked up from helping Luke, who seemed to be giving a couple of shots to the dog.

"Thanks for taking care of her."

"Where shall I put her?"

"She needs a bath and a good brushing to get out all the burrs and brambles and ticks, but I'm afraid she'll have to wait while we take care of her buddy here," Madi said. "It's a triage thing. The neediest has to go first. There's a crate over there you can put her in until we can get to her."

The dog had been so very valiant, never abandoning her friend even when things seemed dire. Ava scratched her head and was rewarded by Gracie licking her hand.

Already regretting the impulse, she turned and faced her sister. "I could give her a bath and start brushing her out."

Madi stared. "Really?" she said, a world of doubt contained in that single word.

She shrugged. "Sure. Why not?"

"Because you're preg—" Her voice trailed off and she sent a guilty look toward Luke.

"It's okay," she answered. "He already knows. He guessed I was pregnant before I did."

Luke smiled. "I didn't know for sure until now. Congratulations!"

"Thank you."

"Okay. Pregnant or not, you've been wonderful with her so far but I know you're not a big fan of dogs."

"I'm fine with smaller dogs. It's the big, slavering kind I don't like. Gracie wouldn't hurt me. Would you, sweetheart?"

The corgi wagged her tail and Madi looked shocked.

"If you're sure, that would be really helpful," Luke said.

"There's shampoo next to the tub there, as well as towels and scissors for cutting out the burrs. Cutting them out is probably easier and less painful in the long run than trying to pull them out one by one."

She nodded and gripped the dog's leash more tightly. She had no idea why she had volunteered, but it was too late to back down now.

"Come on, Gracie. Let's get you into the tub and then we'll find you some dinner."

The dog followed along, clearly trusting Ava to take care of her.

She could do this, she told herself. How could she be expected to take care of a child if she couldn't even manage bathing a dog?

23

I find solace in the fact that Madi and I have forged a new narrative, one that transcends the confines of our painful past. The scars remain, but they are now badges of resilience, a testament to the strength we discovered within ourselves and the unbreakable bond between two sisters who defied the darkness.

—*Ghost Lake* by Ava Howell Brooks

Madison

MADI FELT AS IF SHE HAD STEPPED OUT OF THE MOUNtains and somehow tumbled into another dimension.

Her sister—prim, composed, elegant Ava—was in the corner of the big treatment room at the clinic, crooning softly to the bedraggled corgi and lathering her fur for a second time.

She never would have expected it. She thought Ava would have been in a hurry to retreat to their grandmother's house so she could recover from their unexpected adventure. Instead, here she was, pitching in to help in an emergency.

Ava had been a rock all evening. Pregnant or not, queasy or not, she had jumped right in to help the two lost dogs as soon as Madi first heard the yelps.

How was she supposed to stay angry with Ava when she was trying so hard to be helpful?

"Looks like he's got a sprained hind-right leg," Luke was saying.

She turned back to focus on the border collie, sleeping now from the light pain reliever Luke had administered when he first carried the dog back. "It's not broken?"

"The X-ray isn't showing a break. Given how hesitant he was to use it, I'm guessing a sprain."

"That's a relief."

"He's still going to have to stay off it as much as possible. He's also going to need a couple of stitches for that cut on his front paw."

"So he'll have to wear the cone."

"Yeah. Looks like it."

"Poor guy. He won't be happy."

"Better to wear the cone of shame than to die of dehydration and starvation in a pit."

"True enough."

While he bandaged the sprain, Madi continued pulling detritus from the dog's coat, similar to what she could see Ava doing right now with the corgi.

"Thanks for helping with him, especially after you've already put in a long day of work."

"I could say the same for you. Anyway, this is my job."

"Mine, too, at least for another few weeks."

His jaw tightened briefly, as if he didn't like the reminder. He didn't say anything. Instead, he angled his head toward where Ava was humming to the corgi while she brushed out her matted fur.

"That's a surprise, isn't it?" he murmured. "I didn't expect her to stick around to help out."

She immediately felt defensive for her sister, even though

she had been every bit as surprised by Ava's behavior. "I think she and the corgi have bonded."

"We should give this one a bath before I do the stitches and wrap his leg."

"Of course."

With the rhythm developed over years of working together, they worked to cut out the burrs and briars stuck in the dog's coat, then waited their turn to put the border collie in the washtub until Ava finished up with Gracie and had moved her to another exam table to brush her out.

She loved watching Luke. He possessed such a calming presence, with those warm blue eyes and his low, steady voice. Whenever things were chaotic or tense at the clinic or the shelter, he inevitably stepped in to calm any humans who might be stressed, as easily as he did the animals.

In this case, as they gave the dog a bath, they worked together easily, each focusing on a different part of the dog. Inevitably, their efforts intersected and her hands would touch his, or her body would brush against his hard strength.

Perhaps because of that kiss they had shared, Madi was aware of Luke on a physical level in a way she never had been before. She couldn't seem to escape it. The heat of him, the leashed strength of him below the surface as he treated the dog with gentle care.

Finally, they were done cleaning up the dog and bandaging his wounds. As Luke carried him to the clean and sterilized dog run for the night, Madi glanced at the clock in the big treatment room. She winced. They had been caring for the border collie for nearly an hour. Ava had left the treatment room at least a half hour earlier.

Her sister must be ready to climb the walls right now.

Madi hurried out to the reception area, where she found Ava stretched out on the leather recliner they kept out there for humans and animals who needed extra snuggles before appointments. The corgi was nestled on her lap, snoring softly. Or maybe that was Ava. It was hard to tell, since they were both fast asleep.

The sight made her smile. In sleep, Ava looked less remote and composed. She looked like the big sister Madi remembered from their childhood. A little rumpled, her cool blond hair hanging around her face and her shirt damp across the front, probably from giving the corgi a bath.

Love twisted in her chest, sharp and bittersweet, like green apples that weren't quite ripe.

She missed Ava. She ached for the time when they used to be able to talk about anything and everything, when they had leaned on each other to struggle through their mother's death and their father's increasingly erratic behavior.

She longed for their relationship to go back to the easy, sisterly love of their childhood, but she did not know how they could ever regain that closeness. It wasn't only Ava's book that had come between them. The chasm had been widening since the day they were rescued.

"They look so peaceful. Maybe we should leave them sleeping." Luke spoke barely above a whisper, head bent toward hers, his breath stirring her hair.

She fought down an instinctive shiver. She really had to cut this out or things were about to get awkward really fast.

"Ava would never forgive me if I left her to sleep all night in a vet clinic with a dog on her lap," she whispered back.

"You're probably right. Too bad. They look really sweet together."

Madi agreed. On impulse, she reached into her pocket for her phone and snapped a quick picture, thinking she might send it to Cullen. Her brother-in-law likely would appreciate the moment for the anomaly it was.

Though Madi's camera phone was muted, Ava must have

sensed them looking at her. Her eyes flickered open and she gazed at them uncomprehendingly until recognition dawned.

"Oh. I must have fallen asleep. Sorry."

"No problem," Luke said. "A good cuddle with you was probably exactly what this brave girl needed."

Ava blinked a few times, still coming out of sleep. She straightened in the recliner and lowered the footrest.

"What's going to happen to them now?" she asked, her tone threaded with worry as she looked at the corgi.

"Our first goal is to try to find their owner or owners," Luke said. "We scanned for a chip on the border collie and didn't find one. Gracie has a collar with her name but no phone number and no tags. Maybe we'll have better luck finding a chip."

He produced the handheld universal chip scanner and ran it around the dog's neck and ears, and then, for good measure, all around her body.

"Well? Does she have one?"

"She doesn't seem to."

"So, what now?" Ava asked.

"We'll have to try more traditional ways of locating their humans," Madi said. "We'll put a notice on the town's social media pages and our classifieds, though I suspect the dogs may have been lost by visitors."

"Or maybe they were abandoned," Luke said, his features hard.

As a devoted animal lover, Madi couldn't imagine simply dropping any domesticated animal into the backcountry, assuming it would be able to fend for itself. They usually didn't have the skills to survive for long and would likely become prey to coyotes or mountain lions.

"After an initial period of observation here at the clinic, probably only a day or two, we will send them to the shelter. As long as Madi has room for them, anyway."

"I'll make room, however long it takes to either find them

a new home or a foster home together," she assured him. "I'm invested in these two now."

"Will they be able to stay together here?" Ava asked.

"I'm sorry," he said, genuine regret in his voice. "Normally I would say Gracie could go to the shelter while we leave the collie here, but I know they want to be together. We have to keep them somewhat separated so Gracie doesn't lick her friend's wounds. But we can put them in runs right next to each other so they can nuzzle each other through the fence."

"That's something, at least."

Madi almost offered to foster the two at the farmhouse but she knew it wasn't the best situation.

The shelter was the best place for them. After the border collie healed sufficiently, the two could share a run and Madi would make sure they spent all their outside playtime together and were always walked at the same time.

"Maybe they could stay with Grandma and me while I'm here, only until we find their owners," Ava suggested, then seemed as surprised by the suggestion as Madi was.

"Really? You would do that?" She almost reminded her sister she didn't like dogs, but that seemed a ridiculous thing to say as she was facing a woman who was sitting in a recliner, cuddling a corgi.

"I would have to talk to Leona first."

Madi considered it. "I don't know. Oscar might not be crazy about having two new canines in his territory, even temporarily. But we can certainly discuss it."

"We don't have to decide anything right now," Luke said with a tired smile that Madi felt to her toes, even if Ava didn't. "It's very nice of you to offer."

After making sure the dogs were all settled for the night, until one of the vet techs would come in around four to check on them, they walked outside. It was late, nearly ten. To her surprise, Ava headed in the opposite direction from the two trucks in the parking lot.

"Where are you going?" Madi called after her, frowning.

Ava turned. "I said I could walk back to Leona's from here."

"Don't be silly. It's late and you're exhausted. I'll give you a ride to Grandma's."

Ava looked as if she wanted to argue but finally shrugged and headed for the passenger door.

"In that case," she said, "why don't you take me back to the sanctuary so I can get my car? That way, I don't have to figure out how to pick it up tomorrow and you don't have to drive out of your way tonight."

"That works."

The night had grown cooler, with dark clouds drifting past the moon. They would have rain within the hour, she guessed, which made her even more grateful they had found the dogs before they had to spend another wet, cold night in the mountains.

Luke walked her to the truck. She wasn't sure whether to find the gesture overprotective or sweet.

"Thanks for your help in there," he said after reaching the door first and opening it for her. "You were wonderful, as always. I'm really going to miss you around here."

"You'll be fine," she said, ignoring the ache in her chest when she thought about not seeing him all the time. "Tomas and Carly are both great vet techs and Marisa will be, too, when she's done with her training."

"They are all excellent. But they're not you."

A shiver rippled down her spine at his low, intense voice.

"We're still going to see each other. You're at the rescue almost as much as I am."

"That's a slight exaggeration," he murmured, "since you live and breathe the rescue, while I only pop in when I'm needed."

She had loved working here at the clinic, Madi thought after they said good-night and she drove out of the parking lot. But perhaps with this new awareness she couldn't seem to shake, some distance would be good for both of them.

"Are you sure the dogs will be okay on their own?" Ava asked, forehead creased with worry.

"Positive. Luke has a great camera system, the same one we have at the rescue. We will both be monitoring the dogs all night. They'll be fine. They're safe and warm and have food and water. I'm sure they'll sleep until the first staff member arrives in the morning."

Ava didn't look completely convinced, but she said nothing.

"You're good at what you do, aren't you?" she said after a pause.

Madi sent her a sidelong look across the cab of the old truck. "I like to think so. I love it. I mean, there are some sad moments, too. Not every situation has a happy ending. But I can't imagine doing anything else."

"Do you ever regret not going all the way and becoming a veterinarian, like Luke?"

Tension crawled through her like a dozen spiders. She and Ava used to argue about this all the time, with her sister pushing her to apply to veterinary schools instead of "settling" for her vet tech training.

Ava didn't understand how hard school had been for Madi, how the words swam sometimes and her thoughts became jumbled if she spent too much time studying.

Ava, a natural student and lover of all things to do with academia, likely would never be able to acknowledge that each day of college had been a struggle for Madi.

That she had managed the very difficult requirements to become a veterinary technician still filled her with a great sense of pride she doubted Ava would ever truly comprehend.

"No," she said, her voice firm. "If I had become a vet, I

would have to juggle the added pressure of running a clinic. I never would have had the freedom to start the sanctuary."

Her words had become hard on the last few words. How did Ava always manage to leave Madi feeling inadequate at handling life?

"Now you're annoyed with me again. I'm sorry I asked."

"Not annoyed," she corrected. "Frustrated, maybe. I thought we had settled this particular argument years ago."

"I have always only wanted the best for you. I hope you know that. I want you to have everything you ever dreamed."

"The core problem is that we have very different definitions about what that is. I am happy with my life. More than happy. I have everything I could ever want. My dream of running a no-kill animal rescue is coming to fruition, and soon I'll be able to devote all my time to it. I am very happy."

Or I was, anyway, until you decided to blab our entire life to the world and now neither of us can escape your book.

Ava looked doubtful and it was all Madi could do not to tell her sister to stay in her own lane, to worry about her own life, which seemed to be falling apart in front of her.

To her relief, her sister let the subject drop and they drove in silence until they were only about a mile from the farmhouse and animal rescue.

She should have known Ava wasn't done making her uncomfortable.

"Luke really watches out for you, doesn't he?" Ava said into the silence.

Madi would have preferred talking about her academic inadequacies. Luke was not a topic she wanted to discuss with her sister right now. Or ever.

Yes, Luke watched over her. And yes, she was grateful for his concern. But how could she tell Ava she wanted the man to stop looking out for her so that he could finally *see* her?

"He's very protective of everyone," she answered, fighting to keep her voice calm.

"But especially of you."

"That seems to be going around," Madi said dryly.

"Lucky you, to have so many people who love you and want the best for you," Ava said.

"Yes. Aren't I lucky?" Madi murmured. Why that left her feeling so bitter, she couldn't exactly define.

24

The day I am forced to marry a man I despise, the ground beneath us crumbles. Desperation becomes the unspoken language between us as we plot our escape, determined to break free from the chains of this twisted reality.

—*Ghost Lake* by Ava Howell Brooks

Ava

AVA WASN'T SURE WHAT SHE HAD SAID TO PUT THAT bleak look in her sister's expression, but Madi pulled her truck next to her SUV before she had the chance to ask.

As she and Madi seemed to have achieved a fragile sort of peace over the course of the afternoon and evening together, she didn't want to ruin it by pushing, either.

She wanted to say so many things, but the words seemed to tangle. She settled on the relatively innocuous. "Thank you again for taking me up to Cullen's camp," she said across the width of the pickup truck cab. "I… I couldn't have made the trip on my own."

She had needed Madi there not only to provide transportation but also for moral support. It was no small admission.

Some of the tension in Madi's stance seemed to seep away.

"In all the excitement of finding and rescuing the dogs, I almost forgot why we drove up into the mountains in the first place."

Ava hadn't. She couldn't stop thinking about Cullen's stunned reaction to her news about the baby.

Again, she breathed a silent prayer that this pregnancy might be the thing to help heal all that was broken between her and her husband.

Even as she thought it, Ava warned herself to be cautious in her optimism. She knew friends who had become pregnant in hopes of healing a troubled relationship. It never worked out as they planned and always only complicated the situation, tangling together two people forever, trapped in their misery.

She hadn't become pregnant on purpose. She hoped Cullen understood that. When they must have conceived the baby, they both had been as deeply in love as ever, with a future that seemed bright and wonderful. Five or six weeks ago, Ava had no inkling how the foundation of their marriage could crumble away like chalk left out in the rain.

"Have you told Grandma about the baby?" Madi asked.

"No. I knew I had to tell Cullen first. And then it only seemed right to tell you next."

"I suspect she won't be too surprised. Leona is pretty wise, with a sixth sense about things like that."

When Ava considered the gentle care with which Leona had treated her since she returned to town, she had to agree with Madi. Perhaps her grandmother had sensed all along.

"I'll tell her soon. Maybe even tonight, if she's still awake when I make it back to the house."

Ava climbed into her car, suddenly more exhausted than she ever remembered being in her life.

Stars spangled the sky, a vast, awe-inspiring display. Living in the city, she forgot how very many of them one could see in more rural areas without all the light pollution.

"I hope everything works out with Cullen," Madi said. "He's

a great guy. No matter how angry he is with you right now, I'm sure he'll want to be involved with the baby."

Yes. She knew that was true. Whether he wanted to be involved with *her* was another story. She sincerely hoped she wouldn't end up having to raise this child by herself.

"After you have the chance to check on the dogs through the camera, will you let me know how they are? You can text me anytime. I want you to, actually. I'll sleep better if I know they're okay."

"We can look now, if you want. I have an app on my phone."

"Do you mind?"

In answer, Madi pulled out her phone, tapped the screen a few times, then held it out for Ava. The two dogs were both asleep, she saw, curled up next to each other on the respective side of the wire fencing that separated them.

"I truly hope we can find their owners."

"So do I. We'll start digging tomorrow. If not, we'll find a good home for them."

Ava could adopt them.

The impulse to offer took her by surprise and it was all she could do not to blurt out the words.

She couldn't. It was impossible. She lived in an apartment that didn't allow anything but tiny pets. Beyond that, she was about to have a baby. She had no idea how she would manage *that*. She certainly couldn't take on two dogs at the same time.

"Can I visit them at the vet clinic tomorrow?"

She saw Madi's eyes widen in surprise. "I'm sure Luke wouldn't mind, but I would guess they'll be coming to the shelter tomorrow or the next day. You'll definitely see them when you come to volunteer."

She supposed that would have to do, though she wasn't sure she could wait that long.

"All right. Well, have a good night. Thanks again. I owe you."

"I'll make sure you pay me back when I put you to work at

the sanctuary. Don't think being pregnant will get you out of walking the dogs."

"Of course not."

She wouldn't have believed it a few hours earlier, but Ava was almost smiling as she started her car and drove away under that vast sky glimmering with stars.

The following days slipped into a pleasant routine for Ava. She worked in the garden with her grandmother in the mornings, when birdsong filled the air and dew clung to the leaves in glimmering droplets.

In the afternoons, she would go to the animal sanctuary, where Madi would indeed put her to work walking the dogs, feeding the potbellied pigs or playing ball with Sabra, the Jerusalem donkey, who loved to bat a beach ball around her corral.

She was still sick first thing every morning, but by midday, she felt fine. The worst of her nausea seemed over, as if her body had been trying to tell her something with the constant queasiness.

The message had been most emphatically received.

She was still tired a great deal of the time and could cry at the drop of a hat. Gradually, though, she had begun to adjust to the idea of being pregnant, the knowledge that another life was growing inside her, created from the best parts of her and the man she loved.

She had been to a doctor in Sun Valley, Dr. Choate, a warm older woman who had assured her all seemed to be fine and prescribed multivitamins and plenty of exercise and fresh air.

She had scheduled an ultrasound in a month, if Ava was still in town.

It might be too early to find out the gender of the baby, Denise Choate had warned. Ava didn't care about the gender. She wasn't even sure she wanted to know ahead of time. She would love the child, no matter what.

Through it all, she continued to get regular emails and phone calls from Sylvia Wittman. Her agent was always brimming over with exciting news. *Ghost Lake* had moved up a slot on the bestseller list that week. Sub rights had been sold for three more translations. Several of the more famous book clubs were considering it for a future monthly pick. A few more movie producers had reached out.

Ava tried to summon adequate enthusiasm, but it was difficult when she couldn't seem to focus on anything but the life growing inside her and her worry over the kind of home she could provide to her child.

Now, nearly two weeks after Luke Gentry had first suggested she might be pregnant, Ava sat once more at the Emerald Thumbs Farmers Market selling flowers and vegetables and baked goods for Leona and her friends. This time, she had both Gracie and Beau at her feet.

Beau, the name Madi had given Gracie's border collie friend, was able to get around better. As his health and strength increased, his personality began to shine through. The dog was smart and curious, quick to learn and eager to show off any new tricks. He loved being in the thick of the action and was completely devoted to Gracie.

When Leona had heard the story about the pair's rescue and about Madi's plan to keep them together at the sanctuary, she insisted that she and Ava should foster them until their owners or a new forever home could be found.

Ava didn't mind. She had come to love the two dogs and was already bracing herself at the impending heartbreak of having to give them up to someone else.

Much to her shock, the dogs seemed fond of her as well—especially Gracie, who loved to snuggle whenever possible. In the evenings, when the shadows were long and the air smelled of flowers and sunshine, Ava would sit out in her grandmother's lovely garden on a bench, with Gracie snoozing beside her while Beau sniffed each flower and vegetable plant, as if they couldn't grow without him.

How would she say goodbye to them when it was time for her to return to Oregon? She didn't want to think about it.

Maybe Ava should stay here and have the baby, in this little cocoon where she felt safe and warm and protected. Where she could hide away from the buzz of interest about *Ghost Lake* that awaited her away from Emerald Creek.

She couldn't escape it completely here, either, she acknowledged. Already that day, she had signed three copies of the book that had been handed to her by market patrons. She cringed each time, wondering if she would ever feel more comfortable with the recognition.

Gracie, who apparently loved her, imposter syndrome notwithstanding, stood and nudged Ava's leg with her cold nose in an expectant kind of gesture.

"What? Do you need to do your business? Now? I'm kind of busy."

Two customers were chatting with her grandmother while they decided which of the flower bundles to purchase. Leona overheard her speaking with the dog and waved her hand.

"Go ahead and take them both for a walk. I'm here. I can handle things. You need the exercise, darling. You have been trapped in our stall all morning. While you're out, you should pick up a treat for yourself. That place on the corner has some wonderful goat-milk lotion. You definitely need to try it."

Their stall had been busy all day, nearly selling out of all the lavender sachets she and Leona had made that week and all but six of their cut flower bouquets.

It had been Ava's idea to add a placard explaining that all proceeds from sales helped provide food for the pets at the Emerald Creek Animal Rescue. She wanted to think that helped them sell out faster.

"Are you sure?"

"Positive. I know how to work the billing thingy on the tablet, now that you've explained it, so I should be fine. It will be good for all of you."

Her grandmother got along most of the time without her, when Ava was living in Oregon. She could handle fifteen minutes of sales on her own without trouble.

As soon as she stood up, the dogs rose to their feet as well, almost as if they had been listening to the conversation and knew what was about to happen.

Ava couldn't help smiling as she hooked on their leashes.

"We'll be at the dog park. Call me if you need me and we can be back in five minutes."

"I won't need you. Go. Have fun."

She quickly made her way through the crowd, as she could tell Gracie's need was becoming urgent. The dog park was at the opposite end of the downtown park from the farmers market, through the trees and past the playground.

Inside the fenced area, two black Labs who looked as if they had energy to burn were chasing each other around while the woman who must have brought them sat on one of the benches looking at her phone.

Ava unhooked Gracie from her leash but kept Beau close for his safety. He still couldn't run and play on his leg, though he was fine to greet the other dogs who stopped to sniff and be sniffed.

She was tossing Beau's favorite ball to him in their short confines of his leash when a voice spoke from behind her, on the other side of the fence.

"Here you are. Leona told me where to find you."

She turned quickly, heart pounding at her husband's voice.

She had seen Cullen briefly the previous week, though not at the farmers market. He had instead stopped at Leona's house on Sunday, in the middle of a grocery run with one of the graduate students, whom he had dropped off at the store while he came to say hello.

Their visit had been too short, without any time to really talk. Her grandmother had invited him to have a quick lunch with them and he and Leona had spent most of the time talking about the dig site.

As she looked at him now in the late morning sun, she saw his beard had grown fuller since the last time she had seen him.

Though it was still neatly trimmed, he looked sexy and disreputable. Would he shave it before his classes started in the fall? She hoped not, though she could predict many of his female students would definitely appreciate the beard.

Beau slapped his tail on the grass and Cullen reached down to pet the dog. The two had clearly bonded during their brief introduction the week before.

"Hi," Ava said, feeling rather breathless. "I was hoping I might see you today, though I know you said last week you weren't sure which day you would be coming down from the mountains to replenish supplies."

"I really thought we had enough to last the rest of the month. It's amazing how much a team of seven researchers can eat."

Their academia friends in Portland had *always* been hungry. Ava had taken it upon herself to feed them whenever she could. She had loved it.

"Is Luis or one of the grad students with you?"

He shook his head. "Not this time. We're in the middle of excavating a pretty complicated area so they all decided to stay back and let me handle the shopping on my own."

"That's got to be a big job, feeding seven people all the time."

"It's not bad. We all decide what to eat for the week and take turns cooking."

"You look thin," she couldn't resist saying, even though she knew she sounded like a nagging wife. "Are you sure you're eating like you should?"

"I'm fine. I eat a lot of PB and J." He gave her a careful look. "What about you? How are *you* feeling?"

"I haven't been as sick this week. Only first thing in the mornings, really. I went to a doctor this week. She says everything seems to be fine so far."

"Good. That's good."

"She gave me a better idea of a due date. I'm about seven weeks along, due sometime mid-January. It will be here before we know it."

Could they mend all that was broken before then? She truly hoped so.

"Can I...give you a hand with the shopping?"

"Aren't you on market duty with your grandmother?"

She glanced at her watch. "Yes. The market goes for another hour and then I have to help her take down everything. I could go with you after that, if you don't mind waiting."

He appeared to consider her offer of help and finally nodded. "I would appreciate that, actually. As you well know, shopping is not my favorite thing. Most of the time, anyway."

She smiled at the memory. Some of their most enjoyable moments involved grocery shopping. When they had been dating, still living apart, they started a regular Saturday morning date where they would go to the store together. After they married, those usually turned into Saturday afternoon trips, since they liked to spend lazy weekend mornings in bed.

Her chest ached at the memory and she tightened her hands on Beau's leash, filled with a fierce yearning that they somehow could manage to regain all they once had.

"What about the dogs?" he asked, jerking her back to the present.

"What about them?"

"We can't take them to the grocery store. Could you leave them at Leona's place?"

"Oh yes. Her dog Oscar does a good job of watching over them."

"Right. Oscar. I can't believe he's still around. He was old when you and I first met."

"Still going strong. I'm sure Grandma can keep an eye on them until she's done here. We can go ask her, to make sure."

He smiled at her. It was tentative but definitely a smile. A little effervescent bubble of joy floated through her.

"While you finish helping Leona, I'll pick up some fresh produce at the market, unless it's all picked over by now."

She made a face. "When it comes to the farmers market, the early bird really does get the worm—or at least the best choice of produce. But I'm sure there will be some good stuff left. Now the trick will be getting Gracie to hold still so I can put her leash on again."

"Gracie. Here, girl," he called.

The corgi immediately waddled over to him as if she had been obeying his commands all her life. He hooked the leash on, held it in one hand and reached the other out to help Ava off the bench.

When he didn't immediately let go of her hand, Ava felt that bubble of joy expand in her chest.

They walked toward her grandmother's stall, each of them walking one of the dogs.

When they arrived, they found one of Leona's friends had taken Ava's place running the charge app on the tablet.

"We're doing fine here," Leona assured them. "Don't worry. Enjoy the market with your husband."

Ava wanted to protest that she had come that day to help her grandmother, but she knew by Leona's firm tone that arguing with her would be pointless.

"Thanks, Grandma." She kissed her wrinkled cheek. While Ava had found this separation from Cullen excruciating, at least she had been able to spend priceless time with her grandmother.

She wished she could say she had been able to renew her relationship with her sister as well. After their trip into the mountains, Ava had nurtured high hopes that she and Madi might be able to slip back into their once-comfortable relationship. Things hadn't quite worked out that way. Her sister seemed determined to maintain a sturdy barrier between them. Granted, her schedule was hectic at best. Madi was still working at both the vet clinic and the animal rescue and seemed to put in long hours at both every day.

"Is he okay to go with us?" Cullen asked, pointing to Beau.

"We are supposed to walk him every day to help stretch his leg. Nothing too strenuous, but I would say walking around the market would be perfect."

They quickly filled up the bags he had brought along, buying fresh peppers, zucchini and cucumbers from one stand and new potatoes and onions from another.

It felt very much like old times to Ava, even if their conversation didn't quite flow as effortlessly as usual.

"I hope you have plenty of room to take all this stuff back to camp," she said, gesturing to the reusable shopping bags he carried.

"That's always the challenge, but we somehow have been able to make it work."

"Are you tired of camp food yet?"

"Not really. To be honest, I don't pay much attention to what I'm eating. The work is too interesting."

He was doing exactly what he always dreamed about, immersing himself in the challenge and joy of scientific discovery.

"Has it been difficult living in the mountains for weeks at a time?" she asked.

"Sometimes," he admitted. "The nights can be long up there. But I have plenty of books to read on my e-reader and I keep reminding myself of all we're accomplishing."

While she had learned to enjoy camping in small portions

since marrying Cullen, spending longer than three or four days in a tent left her edgy and anxious, desperate for a hot shower and a soft bed.

How had she and Madi endured months in the mountains? Ava had hated it. The flies, the cold nights, the lack of privacy and basic sanitation needs.

He husband was there by choice, though. He wasn't a lost and frightened girl, yanked away from everything comfortable and safe. He was in his comfort zone. He was living the dream he'd carried for a long time, of actually working on a research project that could provide significant advancements in the study of dinosaurs that lived in the West.

She used to love listening to him speak with passion and intensity about his work, his eyes sparkling and his words spilling over each other.

She missed that.

She missed a hundred things about him. Curling up against him on a cold, rainy Portland night. His laugh that could come out of nowhere and warm her from the inside out. Their conversations and debates and inside jokes.

And she missed this, she realized. Simply being together. The everyday, mundane things like grocery shopping and washing dishes together that were the mortar filling up the cracks of a marriage, keeping out the bitter cold winds of life.

How could they regain that closeness again? Was it even possible?

She had to protect and nurture that tiny seed of hope.

"Why don't I take these things to the Jeep, then I'll meet you back at your grandmother's stand?"

"Okay."

He held out Beau's leash for her and Ava reached for it, her fingers brushing against his. She had to fight down a shiver at the feel of his skin, callused and rugged from the dig, and it was all she could do not to toss his bags of fruits and vegetables to the ground and sink into his arms.

Ava returned to her grandmother's stall to find her already packing up the few remaining bundles of flowers.

"I sold the last two pints of strawberries a few minutes ago. Pretty good day, overall. I thought I would take these remaining bouquets to the assisted living center. I have a few friends over there who can use a spot of color to cheer them up."

Leona was always doing things like that, trying to reach out to brighten someone else's day. It was one of many things Ava admired about her grandmother.

"I'm sorry I was gone so long."

"You were exactly where you needed to be. Cullen looks good, doesn't he?"

Ava almost shivered again. He looked better than good. He looked rugged and wild and...amazing.

"I offered to help him with the rest of his shopping. Do you mind if I leave Gracie and Beau with you?"

"Not at all. Oscar and I can keep an eye on them this afternoon. As soon as I'm packed up here, I'll drop these flowers off and then I'm going to put my feet up and watch one of my Masterpiece shows."

Her grandmother was passionate about British mysteries and usually convinced Ava to watch them with her in the evenings.

"You take all the time you need," Leona went on. "It will be good for you and Cullen to be together for a few hours."

Ava wanted more than that, especially now with the baby coming. She wanted to figure out how to rebuild what they had before into something even better.

"Thank you." On impulse, she reached up and kissed Leona on her weathered, lined cheek. "I love you, Grandma. I hope you know how much."

"I love you right back, that much and more. And aren't I

lucky to have two wonderful granddaughters who still enjoy spending time with me?"

"We are the lucky ones," Ava said. She meant every word. What would she and Madi have done fifteen years ago without Leona to remind them of goodness and light and love?

25

The scars remain, but they are now badges of resilience, a testament to the strength we discovered within ourselves and the unbreakable bond between two sisters who defied the darkness. Our journey continues, not as survivors defined by our trauma, but as architects of our destiny, reclaiming the stolen years and building a future untethered from the shadows.

—*Ghost Lake* by Ava Howell Brooks

Ava

THE AFTERNOON SHE SPENT WITH CULLEN WAS THE best she'd known in weeks.

He suggested they grab something to eat first before heading to the grocery store, as he would have to leave directly from there to keep the perishables he purchased as cool as possible on the journey back to camp.

Though she wasn't particularly hungry and was keeping her fingers crossed that her morning sickness didn't make an untimely return, Ava suggested the River's Edge, a new brew pub on the outskirts of town she had heard people raving about.

The place was crowded, but they were seated out on the wide, shady balcony overlooking Emerald Creek and the mountains beyond. As they ordered their food and waited for it to be delivered, he sampled some of the brewery's award-winning ale while she had a fresh huckleberry lemonade that was one of the best beverages she'd ever tried.

Somehow, without really trying, they slipped back into their usual comfortable conversations about everything under the sun, from the books he read at night in his tent or under the stars to the shows Leona had persuaded Ava to watch with her.

He seemed fascinated by her volunteer work at the animal rescue and wanted to know all about it. In turn, he told her stories about the dig and what they had found so far and the strong, sometimes combative personalities working there.

He asked her about her doctor's appointment, and while they didn't talk directly about a future together, they seemed easier together than they had in weeks.

Throughout the meal, she noticed a guy with the tan of one of the river guides who took anglers and river rafters onto the local waters. He seemed to be staring at them, though she told herself she was mistaken.

She mostly picked at her salad, but Cullen truly enjoyed his wood-fired pizza featuring smoky red onions, pistachios and freshly made pesto. He was finishing off the last piece when the river guide stopped at their table, giving Ava a searching look.

"I'm really sorry to bother you. I hope this doesn't seem too weird, but would you happen to be Ava Howell Brooks?"

She set down her fork, her stomach suddenly twisting more with nerves than morning sickness. Cullen, she saw, had swallowed the last bite of his pizza and was looking at the guy with wary surprise.

"Um. Yes," she finally answered.

"I thought so. I recognized you from the picture on the book jacket. I met your sister earlier this summer at the Burning Tree tavern. Madison, right?"

"That's right."

"You should have heard me raving to her about *Ghost Lake.*

It's the best book I've read in a long time. I've read it twice already."

She blinked. "Twice? Really?"

"Yeah. I was thinking about getting the audiobook on my library app but there's like a forty-two-week waiting list. Did you narrate it yourself?"

Cullen, she saw, had tensed, a small muscle flexing in his jaw.

"No," she said. "I left that to a voice actor. She's wonderful."

"Well, your writing really moves me."

She never knew what to say when people praised her work. "Thank you," she finally managed, feeling awkward and self-conscious.

"I mean, I can't relate at all to what you went through with your sister, being held prisoner and all, and having to fight your way through the wilderness to survive."

Not surprising. How many people could?

"But I did grow up in a house where my father drank too much and abused drugs. He didn't always treat our mom or me and my sister the greatest. He took off when I was thirteen."

"I'm sorry."

"The way you're still trying to come to peace with the choices your dad made, I could completely relate to that. Lately my dad has been trying to come back into our lives, saying how sorry he is and that he's changed. While my sister has let him, I've kept that door closed and locked tight. But your raw grief about losing your dad, despite everything he had done, really hit me hard. You've given me a lot to think about."

She glanced at Cullen and saw he appeared struck by the man's words.

Her husband had lost his father to cancer when he was young, she knew. One of his best childhood memories had been going with his father in the last weeks of his life to a dinosaur museum.

He had described it to her in vivid detail. The hard parts,

from pushing his dad in a wheelchair after he became too tired to walk to helping him empty his Foley catheter bag in the urinal after it became too full. And the joy they experienced watching paleontologists behind glass as they cleaned off fossils with painstaking care.

He had told her everything, until she felt as if she had lived that day along with him.

And in return, she had completely glossed over all that had made her the woman she was today.

"Thank you for telling me," she said quietly to the river guide, though her words were for the man she loved as well.

"If it isn't too much of an imposition, would you be willing to sign my copy of *Ghost Lake*? I've got it out in my truck. I could run and get it."

She glanced at Cullen and could tell he found the whole conversation disorienting and unexpected.

She didn't want anything to intrude on this rare and precious time she had with her husband or to remind Cullen of the secrets she had spilled to the world and not him. Yet she couldn't ignore the river guide's honesty and his genuine praise.

"Of course. I would be happy to sign it."

"Thanks. Be right back."

After he left, she picked up her water glass and drained it. Cullen watched her, eyes filled with an emotion she couldn't identify.

"Does that kind of thing happen to you often?"

"People around town who know me have stopped me a few times and wanted to talk about the book. I signed a few books at the farmers market today. But I haven't had the chance to speak with many readers, especially since I postponed the book tour."

"About that. Are you planning to reschedule?"

"Possibly. I don't know, especially now that I'm pregnant. We're still discussing timing."

Before he could answer, the river guide came back carrying a copy of the book, with its distinctive cover.

"Thanks again for this," he said, thrusting the book toward her.

"No problem." She pushed aside her unused silverware so she had room to write, then reached into her purse and found the pen she always kept there.

"I'm sorry. I missed your name," she said after opening the book to the front matter and finding the title page.

"I'm not sure I gave it to you. It's Ryan. Ryan O'Connor."

She wrote his name and a brief message with one of her favorite quotes, then signed her full name, as it was on the title. Ava Howell Brooks.

He took it back from her as if she had handed him a box full of precious jewels.

"Thank you. That means a lot to me."

"You're welcome."

"And tell your sister I would still love to go out with her, if her schedule opens up before I leave again for graduate school in late August. I had a lot of fun dancing with her the night we met."

Ava wasn't quite sure how to respond. Her relationship with Madi was still far too precarious for her to risk becoming entangled in her sister's love life.

She finally nodded. "It was nice to meet you, Ryan. Good luck with your father, whatever you decide."

He nodded soberly, gripped his book tightly and walked back the way he had come.

"I'm sorry again for the interruption." She hated anything that intruded on this rare, lovely time with her husband.

Cullen shook his head. "You don't have to apologize, Ava. I knew the book was a bestseller but it's rather different to hear firsthand from a reader who actually has been impacted by it."

To her relief, the intrusion didn't seem to have detracted

from their time together. They resumed the easy conversation as Cullen paid for their meal and drove to the larger grocery store in Sun Valley.

By the time they found all the things on his list, the long day was beginning to wear on her. She fought off the fatigue, not wanting anything to mar her time with him.

"Thank you again for your help. You saved me at least an hour of shopping," Cullen said as they loaded the groceries into the back of his Jeep. Much of the food was dehydrated or nonperishable, as she knew they only had a couple of solar-powered coolers at the camp, but there were a few perishable things they would use up in the next few days.

"I was glad to help. It's good to know you'll have enough to eat this week."

"I'll be fine. Remember, I picked up the jumbo-sized peanut butter jar."

She smiled as she slid into the seat of the Jeep. "You should be covered, then. If you had bought that first, you could have saved a lot of bother and expense. Really, what else do you need?"

He smiled with more genuine amusement than she had seen in weeks. "If I showed up back at camp with only a giant jar of peanut butter for us all to eat throughout the week, there would be mass protests. A few million years from now, scientists would be digging up *my* bones. The team would never send me to do the shopping again."

He drove out of the parking lot and with each passing mile, Ava felt the heavy weight of their impending separation.

Too soon, he pulled into Leona's driveway and moved around the Jeep to let her out.

"Thank you again for your help."

"It truly was my pleasure, Cullen. I'm so glad I was able to spend some time with you. I've… I've missed you so much."

"I've missed you, too," he said, his voice gruff.

Desperate to bridge the gap between them, she took a huge

gamble, moving forward and wrapping her arms around his neck. He returned the embrace, his arms around her waist and his chin resting on her head.

She closed her eyes, cheek pressed against his heartbeat, searing the moment into her memory to help her through the long days without him.

With a soft sigh, he kissed her. The taste of him, the shape of his lips, was wonderfully familiar, like a favorite book she had read hundreds of times. She wanted to sink into his kiss and disappear.

Too soon, he finally eased away from her. "I'm sorry, Ava, but I have to go. I've still got a long drive back up the mountain and I don't want everything we just bought to go bad."

She sighed and nodded, stepping away. She felt the absence of him with a physical ache.

"I understand."

"Be safe this week. Don't overdo things."

She gave a half laugh. "I'm staying with my grandmother, splitting my days between working in her garden and volunteering at an animal shelter. It's not exactly high stress. You're the one who needs to be careful. I wouldn't want any mountain lions to eat you up there."

He seemed reluctant to release her hand. That had to be a good sign, wasn't it?

"Maybe I can slip away one night this week and come down from the mountains so we could go to dinner or something."

"I would like that," she said softly, still afraid to hope.

He kissed her forehead one last time, then slid into the Jeep. He didn't move, though, and she realized he wouldn't drive away until he knew she was safely inside, so she stepped up to the porch and unlocked her grandmother's front door.

As he finally backed out of the driveway, she returned to the porch to watch him drive away through the warm June sunshine.

26

The weight of the past presses on us like an invisible burden and as we stand on the threshold of a new life, the memories of the compound threaten to pull us back into the darkness.

—*Ghost Lake* by Ava Howell Brooks

Madison

AFTER A HECTIC FINAL DAY OF WORK AT THE VETERINARY clinic, Madi gathered the rest of her belongings out of her locker. She walked into the break room for one last goodbye to her coworkers and stopped short.

The entire place was decorated with streamers, Mylar balloons and a big sign with dog and cat paw prints across it that said Good Luck Madison.

All of her coworkers beamed at her, with Luke's smile the biggest of all.

She stood in the doorway, tendrils of sadness curling through her like the strings on those balloons.

As excited as she was to be starting this next chapter of her life, she loved working at the clinic and was sorry to leave her coworkers.

She cleared her throat. "I thought I made it clear I really didn't want a big fuss."

"For the record," Luke said, aiming a pointed look around the crowd, "I tried to express that and was emphatically over-ruled."

"You're a fixture at the Emerald Creek Veterinary Clinic." Luke's semiretired partner, Ray Gonzalez, spoke up. Ray had worked with Luke's father and now handled mostly cattle and horses.

"I remember when you started, more than a decade ago," Ray said, his voice gruff. "You were, what? Sixteen? You were still going through physical and occupational therapy, with plenty of health challenges, but you came into the clinic any-way and applied for a job, willing to do anything. Clean up cages. Comfort scared animals. Scrub the floors of the waiting room. Whatever we needed. You were always such a trouper. We're going to miss you, my dear."

He hugged her and Madi felt her throat tighten with tears. Ray had always been kind to her, from that first day she had come looking for a job. He had been the one to push her into becoming a veterinary technician, promising her a job when she graduated.

Through the years, he, like Luke, had been both a mentor and a friend.

"We wanted to show how much we love you," Evelyn Huff, the office manager, said with a warm smile.

"Thank you," Madi said. "And I love you all in return. Se-riously, though. This really wasn't necessary. It's not a big deal. I'm not going far."

"But you won't be here every day," Luke said gruffly. "This is our way of letting you know how much you'll be missed."

"Thank you," she said. To her dismay, she could feel tears threaten and quickly blinked them back.

Change was hard but it was also an inevitable part of life.

She was leaving a job and people she loved, yes. But she was moving toward something else, a dream she had nurtured most of her life.

For the next hour, she chatted with her coworkers while they enjoyed cake and small chicken-salad croissant sandwiches from the Mountain View Café & Bakery, run by good friends of hers.

"Are you ready for this next stage in your life?" Ray asked her quietly as the farewell party was winding down and people began to head out.

"I think so," she answered. "Ready or not, right?"

His kindly face wrinkled into a smile. "You've worked so hard to make this happen."

She frowned at that. She *had* worked hard, fundraising and writing grant proposals, but it had really been a fortuitous series of events that had led her to this point. First had been Eugene Pruitt leaving his farm and land to the ECAR Foundation. Second had been that generous anonymous donation that would cover the bulk of their operating expenses for the next few years.

She had very little to do with either one of those things.

Luke had been more instrumental than she had in convincing Eugene to leave his property to the animal rescue foundation, and she still had no idea who had given the generous donation.

When there were only a few employees left in the break-room, Madi made her last goodbye and picked up her box of belongings.

"Here. Let me carry that for you."

Oh. She thought Luke had left already, as he had disappeared some time ago. He must have been in his office.

Any other time, she might have given her usual independent answer—that it was a small box and she was perfectly capable of carrying it by herself. But she saw no reason to spoil the lovely goodbye party with unnecessary churlishness.

"Thank you," she said.

Together, they walked out to the parking lot, where the sun was beginning to set above the mountains in streaks of amber and lavender. The glorious sight gave her pause, grateful all over again that she lived in such a beautiful spot.

"I've hardly had time to talk to you the last few weeks, since you've been so busy. How are things?"

He had kissed her a few weeks ago, a kiss she hadn't been able to get out of her head.

Now that she officially no longer worked for him, would he feel more free to kiss her again? She wasn't sure whether she wanted him to or not.

"Really good. Busier than ever at the rescue. We've added four more volunteers—and that's not including Ava, who has been coming in every single day."

"Really?" He looked surprised. "How's that going?"

"Better than I expected," she admitted. "She's still not comfortable with some of the bigger dogs, but she tries really hard. One might even think she is trying to make amends for something."

"For what?"

"Oh, I don't know. Maybe blaring our life story to the entire world."

He sighed. "I thought you might be more comfortable about her book by now, especially after seeing how much everyone seems to love it."

"I'm not constantly angry about it but I don't know how I ever can be completely comfortable that my sister has written a tell-all memoir," she admitted. "The past is the past. It's done. We can't change it. What's the point in dwelling on it?"

"If I thought Ava's memoir was exploitative in any way, I might agree with you. It's not, though. She did a great job of telling your story in a cohesive, fair way, with compassion and grace. Don't you agree?"

Madi opened the rear door of her SUV so he could slide the box inside. She studiously avoided looking at him. "I wouldn't know," she answered.

He stared. "You still haven't read it?"

She thought of the copy of the book Ava had sent her, tucked away in the bottom drawer of her bedside table.

"I endured every second of it," she said quietly. "Why would I willingly choose to relive all the trauma and pain through the pages of Ava's book?"

"You aren't a little curious at what all the fuss has been about?"

She didn't tell him all the times she had pulled the book out, started to read it, made it through a few pages, then had to close it again, hands shaking, as memories poured over her.

"No," she lied. "I'm not."

"Well, when you do get around to it, I think you'll be surprised. It's not as dark and ugly as you might think. There's humor in it and plenty of gentle moments. It mostly shows the amazing resilience and strength of the human spirit."

"Oh, is that what it shows?"

"I don't think people would be responding to *Ghost Lake* as favorably if it only portrayed a grim, hopeless situation. It's the fact that you two battled your way out of it that has touched people so much."

She sighed. "Can we talk about something else?"

"Fair enough. How about I tell you how much the office isn't going to be the same without you? I'll miss seeing you."

That was the dark cloud that prevented her from being wholly excited about the job change. He had been a daily part of her life for years and she wasn't sure how she would adjust to only seeing him a few times a week.

"I'm not exactly moving to Iceland or something. We'll still see each other often."

"I know. But it won't be quite the same." He looked around.

"I'll miss pulling up to the building and seeing your vehicle already in the parking lot. Somehow the day always feels a bit brighter, knowing you're inside."

Their gazes met and she swallowed, immediately captured by the intensity of his words and his expression.

After a few seconds, that expression slid into chagrin. "Sorry. I probably shouldn't have said that."

"Why not?" she asked, her voice barely above a whisper and her heartbeat suddenly loud in her ears. The memory of their kiss glowed through her, sparkly and bright.

I don't work for you anymore. There's no reason you can't kiss me now.

He took a step forward and bent his head. Her breath caught and her pulse quickened. She leaned up for his kiss, but before his arms could wrap around her, they both heard the staff door from the vet clinic open.

She stepped away quickly as Evelyn came into view, carrying a piece of cake on a plate and a couple of the Mylar balloons, bobbing with dog faces on them.

"I didn't want the cake to go to waste so I'm taking a couple pieces home to Jack. I hope that's okay."

"Totally fine," Luke said. "Are the balloons for your husband, too?"

She made a face. "Those are for my grandson. He loves puppies and anything shiny, so these are perfect for him."

She loaded them in her car, parked on the other side of Madi's, then closed the door and faced them.

"Do you need any help at the adoption event tomorrow?" Evelyn asked.

I need you to go back in time and wait inside for about fifteen minutes so Luke will kiss me again. Can you manage that?

"I think we're covered," she said instead. "But thank you."

"Call me if you change your mind. I'm not doing a thing

tomorrow except working in the yard. And I'm always glad for an excuse to get out of that," Evelyn said.

"I will," Madi promised.

"I've got to run. We're babysitting so our son and his wife can have a date night. Hence the balloons. See you both later."

After she climbed into her car and drove out of the parking lot with one last wave, Luke turned back to Madi. "I didn't know you were planning an adoption event tomorrow," Luke said.

"Yes, at the farmers market. We've reserved a booth and are hoping to find new homes for all the kittens and puppies and a couple of the older dogs."

"That should be great. You'll likely find more foot traffic there than anywhere else in town on a Saturday."

"It was Ava's idea," Madi said. "She's been going with Leona on Saturday mornings to sell flowers and produce."

"I know," he said. "I bought a bouquet of flowers from her last week. My mom was thrilled with them."

"We thought people might want to take home a new puppy, along with their zucchini."

"Why not?" He smiled.

"I'm surprised Sierra didn't tell you what we're doing tomorrow. She signed up to volunteer for a couple of hours."

"She didn't mention it, but between my schedule and hers, I haven't seen much of her the past few weeks."

Madi winced. "Sorry about that. She's been hanging out at the shelter a lot."

"No need to apologize. I'm glad she has found something she loves. It helps her not miss Zoe as much."

"We have three or four other volunteers around her age. She seems to be enjoying their company a lot."

She didn't mention that Ash Dixon, whose parents ran a farm stand in town, had just started volunteering at the rescue and she suspected Sierra had a thing for him.

"If you don't have anything else planned, you're welcome to come help us tomorrow. People would probably love to talk to a veterinarian about what they could expect if they adopted some of our older or special needs animals."

"You might not have the DVM behind your name, but you know as much about veterinary medicine as I do," he said, his voice gruff. "But I can try to make it. That might be my only chance to hang out with my daughter for a few minutes."

"Sounds good. I'll see you tomorrow, then."

She didn't add that she would probably see him that night in her dreams, too, if the past few weeks were any indication.

27

As Madison and I navigate the uncharted territory of our new lives, we are determined to rewrite the narrative that once confined us.

—*Ghost Lake* by Ava Howell Brooks

Luke

LUKE WALKED INTO THE LARGE DOWNTOWN PARK under a painted sign reading Emerald Thumbs Farmers Market.

It smelled delicious, a mix of kettle corn and roast coffee and empanadas from the various food trucks parked along one side of the park.

He waved at a couple of people he knew standing in line at a crepe stand and stopped to chat with a neighbor buying a flat of glossy red strawberries.

As he passed Leona Evans's stall, he stopped again, this time to speak with Simon Walford, who stood admiring the lush and colorful peonies.

Luke strongly suspected the man was admiring Leona as well. He had seen them together at a few community events and Simon's usual taciturn features seemed brighter somehow around Madi's grandmother.

"Dr. Gentry. Hello there."

"Hello, Simon. Hi, Betsy."

He waved to Ava and Leona as he reached down to rub the regal head of Simon's Westmoreland terrier. "She's looking well."

"Thanks to you," Simon said gruffly. "You saved her life. I'll never forget it."

"I'm glad we were able to find the problem and fix it."

A few months earlier, Simon had reached out to him in a panic, with Betsy in extreme distress. Luke and Madi, his tech on call at the time, had met him at the clinic in the early hours of the morning, where he quickly rushed Betsy into surgery. The dog had a blocked digestive tract.

"I'm so happy to see her looking so perky," he said, scratching the dog's throat.

"Our Lucas is a miracle worker." Leona beamed at him. "Look how well Beau is doing after he sewed him up. That dog was a sorry-looking creature when he was first rescued in the mountains, I'll tell you that."

"He's a handsome lad now." With a look of approval that was mostly aimed at Leona, Simon nodded toward the dog lying in the shade of the display table.

"Still no leads as to the owners of him or Gracie?" Luke asked Leona.

"Not a one." Leona's lips pursed, plainly giving her opinion about someone who would abandon their domestic animals in the dangerous backcountry. "Nobody has called the animal rescue or the county animal control officer looking for them, and we haven't heard of anyone who has lost a dog matching either of their descriptions."

"Darn shame," Simon said.

"It is," Leona agreed. "They're both the sweetest dogs. No trouble at all, either one."

"Any plans to make them permanent members of your household?" Luke had to ask.

She glanced pointedly at Ava, who was petting Gracie, the corgi. "We'll have to see. I've been telling Ava here that she could use a couple of dogs when she goes home to Oregon."

Madi's sister raised an eyebrow. "And Ava has been reminding you that she lives in a two-bedroom apartment that doesn't allow dogs over twenty-five pounds. Gracie might qualify, but not Beau."

"I don't think they should be separated. What's your professional opinion, Dr. Gentry?" Leona asked him.

"I have to admit, I don't think they will thrive well if they're separated," he answered honestly. "They obviously have a well-established bond."

"Well, my Madi will figure something out. Have you been by to see the adoption event?"

Luke shook his head. "That's why I'm here."

"She set up on the other side of the market," Ava offered. "They're close to the dog park so prospective adopters have the chance to play with the dogs in a contained area."

"Great idea."

"That's our Madi. She's always thinking about what's best for her animals."

"She is, indeed."

"I wish she would focus once in a while on what's best for herself," Leona said. To Luke's surprise, she gave him a pointed look, as if he had any say in Madi taking better care of herself or any brilliant insight into how she should accomplish that.

"Don't we all?" Ava muttered.

"Since you're headed that way, can you do me a favor and take her one of these banana muffins I baked this morning? If I don't nag her, she forgets to eat sometimes. And take one for yourself, too."

"I wouldn't mind a muffin," Simon said.

"They're two dollars apiece for everyone else," Leona said primly.

Harsh.

Luke had to hide a smile. Did Leona have any idea she was dangling poor Simon on the hook?

"They look delicious," Simon said, undeterred. "In fact, I'll buy a half dozen and freeze them. I don't get home-baked goods very often since my Mary passed."

"That's very good of you," she said, her tone more gentle now. She donned a plastic food glove and added a half-dozen muffins into an eco-friendly box, then sealed the lid.

"Would you like me to keep them for you here until you're done shopping? I can set them aside."

"Excellent idea," Simon said, his tone more cheerful, probably because he now had a ready excuse to stop back here and chat with Leona again.

Luke studied the remaining muffins. "What flavors do you have?"

"Banana nut and blueberry."

"I'll take a half dozen of each. And yes. I know they're two dollars apiece." He handed over a twenty and a five. "I'm sure Madi has plenty of volunteers who would appreciate a delicious home-baked muffin made by the legendary Leona Evans."

She beamed at him as she transferred nearly all of the remaining muffins into two more of the cardboard containers.

With offerings in hand, he waved goodbye to Madi's grandmother and sister as well as Simon and Betsy, then headed across the crowded park toward the awning he saw fronted by a canvas sign that said Emerald Creek Rescue.

It was only a distance of maybe fifty yards between the two tents, but it took Luke forever to work his way through the crowd of people and dogs, especially those who wanted to stop and talk with him.

Since graduating from vet school and returning home to

Emerald Creek to practice, he had discovered it was very difficult to go anywhere quickly in this community, where people liked to visit anyway and especially liked to ask questions about their pets. Through his work, he was acquainted with most of the dogs in town and plenty of them apparently enjoyed visiting the farmers market with their humans.

He felt compelled to stop and greet all of them.

He and his siblings used to complain about their father taking forever whenever they ran errands around town, mostly because he always stopped to talk to everyone he met.

He could still hear Dan Gentry's calm words. *Good vets are an integral part of their communities. They should never be too busy to talk to people about their concerns for their pets.*

In the years since coming back to Emerald Creek, he had come to see how very right Dan had been, about everything.

Luke loved his job. He loved being that integral part of life here in this little Idaho community.

Yes, getting here had been tough, and there were times during vet school that he wanted to give up, especially when Sierra had been small and their lives had been so chaotic.

After Johanna died, he wanted to quit again. How could he be expected to care about a sneezing kitten when his daughter had just lost her mother?

Somehow he had managed to stick it out, to lose himself in helping others with their beloved animals. He would never regret it.

When he reached the ECAR booth, he found Madi chatting with a woman he didn't know while his daughter talked to a couple of girls around her age who were each holding a black kitten, among the hardest animals to rehome. He stood out of sight, enjoying the sight of both Madi and Sierra, each completely in her element.

"They're so cute," one of the girls exclaimed, holding her

freckled face to the kitten's. "I wish my mom wasn't allergic. I want one so bad!"

"So do I," the other one said. "Nobody's allergic at my house, but my dad says no more cats. We already have three. But they're not nearly as cute as this one. Maybe I should adopt him and then tell my dad later."

"I'm sorry," Sierra said firmly. "But since you're not eighteen yet, your parents have to agree to the adoption and sign papers in person or you can't take them home."

The dark-haired girl sighed. "Shoot. I guess I can't adopt him, then."

"You're still welcome to visit the animal sanctuary whenever you want, to hold the kittens and play with them. Everyone is welcome," Madi said, her voice warm.

"That's cool," the girl with freckles exclaimed.

"Maybe we can go on Monday," her friend said.

"Totally fine," Madi answered. "We're open to the public from 9 a.m. to 5 p.m. Check in at the office first."

Neither Sierra nor Madi noticed him as they took the kittens from the girls and returned them to cages.

Sierra was the first to spy him. "Hi, Dad," she said with a grin.

"Hi, kiddo. How are things going here?"

"Good so far," Madi answered for Sierra. "So far we've met with two families interested in adopting a dog and three who would like a cat. They've filled out our paperwork and I've scheduled home visits this week."

"All before 10 a.m.?"

She grinned with her half smile and Luke had to fight the overwhelming urge to kiss her right there in the middle of the farmers market, in front of his daughter and two other volunteers.

"It's an encouraging sign. I was hoping we could find homes

for ten animals and we're already halfway there. Assuming all the paperwork and the home visits check out."

"Nice. Well, in recognition of all that hard work, I brought some of your grandmother's muffins for you and your volunteers."

"Oh yum. I'm starving," Madi exclaimed. She scooped up a banana nut muffin and so did Sierra. The other two volunteers grabbed a blueberry muffin each, giving their thanks in return.

"How can I help?"

"Food is always a lifesaver," Madi said. "Other than that, I guess just be available if anyone has questions."

He was chatting with Ed Hyer and Ada Duncan when he spotted a familiar older woman approaching their stall with a determined expression.

As he expected, she moved straight in his direction. "Dr. Gentry. Hello. I thought I saw you earlier but you were several stalls away. By the time I had paid for my cucumbers, you were gone. I'm afraid I don't move very quickly these days."

"Hello, Mrs. Thompson. How are you?"

Miriam Thompson was eighty years old and had six cats and two bad-tempered dachshunds she pushed around the neighborhood in a baby stroller.

"I'm fine. But my little Booboo is under the weather again."

Booboo was her female dachshund, he knew. The dog didn't seem to like anyone, no matter how hard Luke tried to make friends. "What's happening with her?"

"She's not eating, and the other day, she bit me for no reason, right here, on my hand."

She thrust her arm, covered in age spots and blue veins, into his face. A bandage covered the spot between her index finger and her thumb.

"Oh dear. Did she draw blood?"

"A bit. Not much. But you know I'm on that blood thinner

medication, so it bled forever. I thought I was going to need a transfusion by the time it finally stopped."

"I'm sorry about your bite and about Booboo feeling under the weather. Why don't you call Monday morning and make an appointment? Tell Evelyn I'll find room in my schedule, even if it's packed."

"Can't you come over and take a look earlier than that? Your dad used to come to the house whenever I had a problem with one of my babies."

His father had lived down the street from Miriam and watched out for her as he did most of his neighbors, who often only wanted someone to pay attention to them.

Luke apparently shared that unfortunate habit. "My schedule is full today but maybe I could come by tomorrow morning. Would ten work?"

"Oh, splendidly. Thank you, my dear."

As she kissed his cheek, the scent of lavender and roses drifted from her, reminding him of his own grandmother.

With a satisfied smile, she toddled off.

"You are a soft touch, Dr. Gentry," Madi murmured after Miriam had wandered away with cane in one hand and her bag of cucumbers in the other.

He had to laugh. "Says the woman who runs the largest no-kill animal rescue for miles around."

"You mean the same no-kill animal rescue where you volunteer your services, free of charge?"

"Yes. That one."

Despite his embarrassment, he smiled. She was right. He was a soft touch. He often reduced his charges for some pet owners on a fixed income and wrote off other charges. He never refused to provide necessary care to any animal because of the owners' inability to pay.

"We're quite a pair, aren't we?" he said.

"Aren't we?" she murmured with her half smile that made him want to kiss her again.

He was about to comment when he spotted a well-dressed woman with perfectly applied makeup walking toward them on heels that really had no place in a grassy park. She was followed by a bearded man holding a large video camera.

A sense of foreboding butted into him like Barnabas did when he was annoyed.

"Heads up," he said, gesturing toward the approaching pair. "Looks like we might have some paparazzi."

She followed his gaze and he saw her eyes widen with nerves. "Maybe they're here to cover our adoption event."

"It's possible."

While he would have liked to believe that, something in the determined set of features on the woman told him she wasn't looking for a fluff piece about some dogs and cats finding new homes.

He walked out to try heading them off, but the woman targeted Madi.

"That's her," he heard the woman whisper to the camera operator. "It has to be."

The woman pushed her way into the small space. "Hi. You're Madison Howell, aren't you?"

Madi gazed at her, apparently at a loss for how to answer.

Luke quickly stepped in. "Are you interested in the pet adoption event for the Emerald Creek Animal Rescue?" he asked, though he was fairly certain he already knew the answer. "We've got some really great dogs and cats available."

The woman brushed back her dark curls with a manicured hand, the nails adorned with pale pink tips. "No. I'm Ashleigh Beaujolais with Nine News," she said, as if he should know exactly who she was.

She turned to Madison, giving her a wide smile with teeth that gleamed in the summer sun. "We're working on a story about your sister's book, *Ghost Lake*, and reexamining the events that happened near here fifteen years ago. We would love to talk with you. Do you have a minute?"

"No," Madi said bluntly.

Ashleigh Beaujolais looked nonplussed at her outright refusal. Her lush lips pursed in confusion and she exchanged looks with her cameraman.

"Okay. If now isn't a good time, we could schedule something else. What about this afternoon, whenever you're done here?"

"No," Madi said, her voice firm. "I don't have time now and I won't have time later."

"You're a very important part of the story, Ms. Howell. We would love to get your perspective. I mean, not many people can talk about what it's like to have a starring role in what's been called the biggest book of the summer."

Madi didn't raise her voice, but her refusal was clear and unequivocal. "I am not interested in talking to you, Ms. Beaujolais. About the so-called book of the summer or about anything else. Excuse me."

She turned away from the reporter to focus instead on a woman and a small boy who were looking at the puppies playing in an enclosure on the grass.

She even took a few steps in that direction but the reporter followed closely behind. Ashleigh Beaujolais did not strike Luke as the kind of woman who would give up at the first sign of difficulty. Unfortunately.

"Are you aware there are rumors that several celebrities are considering *Ghost Lake* as featured titles for their book clubs?" she pressed.

Now Madi turned to face her, eyes wide. "What celebrities? What book clubs?"

"I'm not at liberty to say," Ashleigh said, her voice coy. "But that certainly wouldn't hurt your sister's book sales, would it? You must be happy about that."

Madi's jaw clenched. "You're talking to the wrong person. You should find my sister. She's working at a stall near the courthouse."

Ashleigh made a face. "You don't think we started there? She refused to talk to us until we submit a formal interview request through her publisher. I don't suppose you could help us cut through the red tape, could you?"

Madi frowned. "I meant what I said. I don't have time for this. I'm interested in helping rescued animals, not in talking about events that happened years ago. Excuse me. I need to go grab some more water for them."

She picked up the two gallon containers and hurried away, doing her best, he could tell, not to limp.

Luke saw the reporter let out an annoyed breath and start to take off after her. He gave her a stony look and shook his head. She opened her red-painted mouth, then closed it again in frustration and went to confer with her camera operator.

After making sure the volunteers had things under control in the stall, he went after Madi, who had gone to a potable water spigot near the restrooms.

"I said I don't want to talk to you," she snapped, then whirled around, features furious. The hot expression faded when she spied Luke.

"Sorry. I thought you were that reporter. Is she gone?"

"Not yet. But I am pretty sure you made your point about not wanting to talk to her."

She sighed as she finished filling up one jug and moved the other one under the spigot. "I would have been happy to talk to her about the rescue, how we're trying to provide animals in need with a better life. But no. Why would anybody want to talk about that, the animals who need help *now*, when they can focus instead on something that happened years ago?

It's apparently much more interesting to talk about two girls stranded in the wilderness with a pack of deranged survivalists on their heels."

She set down the water container and swiped at her eyes. The sight of her frustrated tears moved him beyond measure.

"I hate that Ava has put me in this position. I would rather forget any of it ever happened and move on with life. Instead, I'm being forced to think about it every single day. I feel like it will never, ever end."

"I'm sorry."

She sighed. "What celebrities want to feature it in their book clubs, do you think?"

"I don't know that it matters. The point is that the story you don't want to think about has touched something in the public consciousness. I'm afraid you won't be able to avoid talking about it forever."

"Nobody can force me to do an interview." She studied him. "What about you? You and your family are part of this story, too. Why don't you have reporters knocking down your door?"

He decided not to mention that he and his family already had fielded media requests and were discussing how to handle them. As he had said to Madi, he knew they would eventually have to talk to someone. Interest was too high right now and it was better to take control of the narrative rather than letting others speak for them. He and his siblings and his mother were trying to figure out their best options.

He should have known Madi would be able to interpret his silence correctly. "You *have* had reporters knocking down your door."

"We've had a few phone calls. Not the same thing. We're considering how best to handle the media interest."

"Doesn't it bother you to have strangers like Ashleigh Beaujolais digging into your past?"

"Our part in the whole thing was very small."

"Small?" Her voice rose. "You saved our lives. You threw your body over mine when bullets started flying. Your father sacrificed his life for us. I wouldn't call that *small*. I can never repay you and your family for that. You saved us. I don't want to think about where we might be today if we hadn't stumbled onto your campsite."

He couldn't help it. He reached for her hand, tracing his thumb over her small, curled fingers.

"My dad might have helped rescue you and Ava from the dire situation you were in. But both of you are responsible for how you have survived and thrived since then."

Her gaze met his, eyes wide and unblinking.

"I believe that's a big part of the story that resonates with people. Your strength and integrity. Others might have withdrawn from the world. Become angry and bitter at all they had lost. Instead, you are the most generous, loving, giving person I have ever known."

Her fingers flexed in his and he curled his own bigger hand over hers and brought her hand to his mouth. "I respect you for not wanting to live in the past, Madi. But I hope you can also acknowledge how that past has shaped you, forged you. It's given you a strength of will the rest of the world can't help but admire."

28

The last page turns, but the story of our survival is far from over.

—*Ghost Lake* by Ava Howell Brooks

Madison

LUKE'S WORDS SEEMED TO WRAP AROUND HER, WARM and sweet and somehow...healing.

She gazed at him, quite sure all the tenderness she had been fighting for him was clear in her eyes.

He looked down at her, then with a sigh, as if surrendering to the inevitable, he leaned down and kissed her.

Oh. She had been dreaming of this for weeks, since the last time he had kissed her. It was even better than she remembered. He tasted of blueberries and sugar and she wanted to taste every inch of his mouth.

She forgot where they were. The crowded park, the busy market. She forgot that both of them were supposed to be helping at the adoption event.

All that mattered was this, right now, being here in his arms, his mouth sliding over hers, tasting and exploring with a tenderness that took her breath away.

She was in love with Luke Gentry.

The truth of it seemed to wash over her as if someone had dumped the two gallons of water on her head.

She loved him. She had probably loved him since that afternoon he had risked his life for hers.

Even after he married someone else, had a child, lost his wife, some part of Madi's heart had always belonged to Luke. What had begun years ago as friendship—with a healthy dose of hero worship mixed in—had shifted over the years to something else.

What was she supposed to do now? She had absolutely no experience with being in love. All she could think about was tightening her hold around his neck and not letting go.

"Hey, Dad, are you back here? Somebody has a question about the puppy who is deaf in one ear. Can you come talk to them...?"

The voice trailed off into a shocked silence and Madi wrenched her mouth away from Luke's to find Sierra staring at them, jaw sagging and her eyes huge.

Madi quickly stepped away, almost stumbling because of her stupid leg. He reached to catch her.

"It's not what it looks like," Madi said quickly, then regretted the words instantly. It was *exactly* what it looked like. She and Luke had been wrapped in an embrace, completely oblivious to the rest of the world.

"What is it, then?" Sierra shifted her bewildered gaze from one of them to the other.

"I... Your dad was just... The television reporter upset me and..."

"And you thought you somehow would feel better about a reporter trying to talk to you if you kissed my dad?"

She did feel better, actually. For that entirely too-brief moment, she had forgotten all about Ava's book and the reporter and the past.

How could she focus on any of that when she had only now faced the stunning truth that she was in love with one of her dearest friends?

"Is something going on with you two?" Sierra pressed, the beginning of something else entering her expression, something that looked like hurt. "Are you two…dating?"

Oh, this was so complicated. Far too tangled to explain to a thirteen-year-old girl in the middle of a crowded farmers market.

"Nothing is going on," Madi said quickly. She didn't dare look at Luke. What was he thinking?

"I'm not a child. I thought you, of all people, would never treat me like one, Madi. I asked you outright a few weeks ago if you thought my dad was dating someone and you looked right at me and lied."

"I didn't lie. We're not…dating."

"Only kissing?"

"That's enough," Luke said. "We can talk about this later, Sierra. Let's all just take a deep breath and return to the adoption event."

She gazed at her father, then whirled around and practically ran back to the animal rescue tent.

Madi couldn't look at Luke. She knew all her emotions would be clear in her expression. She often thought Ava completely lacked any sort of a poker face but she suspected hers wasn't any better. Instead, she reached to pick up the water jugs.

He reached out and pulled them from her. "Madi. We have to talk about this thing between us."

No. They didn't. Why couldn't they go back to the way things had always been between them? Easy and friendly and warm, without this chaotic morass of emotions that threatened to ruin everything?

"This isn't the time."

He sighed. "I know. I'm sorry about Sierra. I'll talk to her."

She didn't know how to answer that, so she simply turned and walked away.

After returning to the animal rescue tent, she tried to concentrate on the reason she was there, helping these animals find their perfect forever homes.

As she spoke with people—some serious, others only there to look at the cute puppies and kittens—a low drumbeat of anger throbbed through her. It was focused on only one person.

Ava.

If her sister had bothered to tell her a news crew was in town, Madi might have been prepared for the ambush.

She helped a young couple interested in adopting a kitten with the necessary paperwork, then finally turned to Ed Hyer, unable to quell the simmering frustration.

"Can you handle things here for a while?" she asked. "I need to go talk to my sister."

"Sure. No problem."

Without looking at Luke or any of the other volunteers working the event, Madi walked away, striding briskly toward her grandmother's stall.

She found Ava chatting with a couple she didn't recognize. One of them, Madi noticed through a burgeoning haze of fury, was holding a copy of *Ghost Lake*.

When she approached, Ava gave her a look she didn't immediately register. After a beat, she thought it almost looked like *relief*. Surely that couldn't be right, could it?

She didn't know her sister anymore. Not really. How could she presume to know what might be going through Ava's head?

"When you're done signing autographs with your fans," she said, her voice low and intense, "I need to talk to you."

"I'm not signing autographs," Ava protested. "We were only chatting."

"When you're finished chatting, then, I would appreciate if you could squeeze out a moment for your sister."

"Are you Madison?" One of the tourists lit up, eyes bright, and held her book out as if she wanted *Madi* to sign it.

Madi didn't realize she was glaring darkly at the woman until Ava stepped in, tugging her arm.

"Excuse me, won't you?" she murmured to the two women. She grabbed Madi's arm and dragged her away, probably before Madi could fully lose her temper.

Ava led her to the steps of the courthouse. "Okay. What's so important?"

"I didn't say anything was important. Annoying, yes. Important, no. A half hour ago, I was ambushed by a reporter from Nine News who wanted to know my thoughts about your stupid book."

Now it was Ava's turn to glare. "It's not a stupid book," she snapped. "That refrain of yours is getting really old. Other people don't seem to think it's as terrible as you do."

"You could have warned me. Why didn't you tell me a reporter was in town?"

"If I had known she was in town, I would have. I didn't know until she ambushed me, too. I told her I didn't have time to talk to her right now, and anyway, she should have cleared interview requests with my publicist."

"Your publicist," Madi echoed with a scoff. "Well, unfortunately, not all of us have a fancy publicist to vet our interview requests for us, do we? What am I supposed to do when the next reporter comes out of nowhere while I'm in the middle of something important?"

"Tell them to go to hell. You seem to have no problem telling me that in so many words, over and over again."

"And just look how well that has worked out for me. You're still here."

She saw the hurt flare in her sister's eyes, quick and jagged, before Ava blinked it away.

"Where exactly would you like me to go?" she asked, her

voice low. "Back to Portland? I can't do that right now. More to the point, I won't. I'm afraid you'll have to suffer my presence for another few weeks. After that, I'll be gone, though. You won't have to worry about me being around and ruining your perfect town."

Out of nowhere, Madi was hit by a sneaker wave of sorrow washing over her. She didn't want her sister to leave. How mixed-up was that?

She couldn't tell Ava. She would sound ridiculous, especially after she had just yelled at her sister for something completely out of her control.

"What am I supposed to do when the next reporter comes along?" she pressed.

Ava sighed. "You are under no obligation to speak with anyone. You can decide whether you want to give any interviews. I will talk to my publicity team. They can arrange interviews for you as well, if you'd like."

"I don't want to talk to anyone. I want everything to go back to the way it used to be, before the book came out."

"I'm afraid I left my time machine back at my Portland apartment."

"Go ahead. Make a joke. I don't find any of this particularly funny." Madi knew she was acting like a petulant child, behavior she hated, but she felt powerless to stop it.

"I don't, either," Ava answered quietly. "I'm sorry they bothered you. I'll see what I can do about keeping them away but I can't make any promises. I'm sorry."

If she were really sorry, Madi thought as she stalked back to the animal rescue tent, Ava wouldn't have written the book in the first place.

29

We were just teenagers when our father led us into the depths of the Coalition, promising a utopia forged in self-sufficiency and communal living. Little did we know that the idyllic vision masked a sinister reality. Life within the compound was a twisted dance of obedience, isolation and the constant fear of the charismatic leaders who wielded power like a weapon.

—*Ghost Lake* by Ava Howell Brooks

Ava

AS MADI TURNED AND WALKED AWAY, AVA TRIED TO breathe through the pain in her chest at the unbreachable distance between her and her sister.

Everything she did when it came to Madi was wrong. Misstep after blunder after miscalculation.

She thought they were making progress, especially after Madi helped her go into the mountains to speak with Cullen. For a while, her sister had seemed to warm a little more. Each time Ava visited the animal shelter, Madi would stop and talk to her about the baby, about their grandmother, about Gracie and Beau and the other animals at the shelter that Ava was coming to care about.

She had hoped they were slowly repairing their cracked relationship, bit by bit.

Now it felt as if all that progress was for nothing, as if a huge, jagged fissure had spread between them in an instant.

She wasn't sure which was worse, the ache in her heart or the steady, dull ache in her abdomen that had been bothering her since she awoke that morning.

She pressed a hand there. *Easy, little one,* she murmured in her head, which she knew intellectually made no sense. The baby didn't have ears yet to hear actual words, forget about reading her mind to catch all the unspoken sentiments.

Another cramp rippled across her abdomen and Ava inhaled sharply, grabbing for her ever-present water bottle.

Her grandmother was beside her instantly. "Are you all right, my dear?"

"I... Yes." The cramp subsided and she drank more from her water bottle. More than likely, she was simply dehydrated. She always forgot to drink enough during these Saturday markets.

"You should sit down while you have a minute. I can handle any customers."

"I'm fine," she insisted.

Her grandmother gave her a stern look that brooked no argument and Ava obediently subsided into one of the camp chairs.

She sat quietly, willing the last of her discomfort to ease, until Leona called her over to help with a problem charging a customer's debit card.

The rest of the market passed uneventfully, with no more reporters or angry sisters accosting her. Again, Leona sold out of all her baked goods, most of her vegetables and fruit and all but two of her bouquets.

They were back in her grandmother's kitchen, enjoying a sandwich and some lemonade while all three dogs flopped on the floor, when Leona set down her lemonade and gave Ava a long, solemn look.

"I think it's time you tell Madi the truth."

Ava set down her lemonade glass, pearled with condensation. "What truth? The baby? She knows all about that."

Madi seemed excited about Ava's pregnancy. She called the baby the Squiglet and talked about how she intended to be the fun aunt, even from long distance.

Their own relationship might be forever damaged because of *Ghost Lake*, but Ava held on to hope that at least they would be able to salvage something for the sake of her child.

"I'm not talking about the baby," her grandmother said, a thread of impatience in her voice. "I think you should tell her that you're the anonymous donor that helped her establish the animal rescue."

Shock slammed into her like an avalanche roaring off the mountain. "I'm... What?"

Leona gave her an impatient look. "Contrary to popular belief, I'm not stupid. I also don't believe in coincidences." She shrugged. "You happen to get what I can only assume was a fairly healthy advance from your publisher for a book none of us knew you were even writing, and a short time later, Madi suddenly receives an anonymous donation to the animal rescue foundation, one large enough to make all her dreams come true. I'm smart enough to put two and two together."

Ava inhaled sharply, trying to settle the panic that suddenly tasted like bile. "That's ridiculous."

"Is it?" Leona studied her with eyes that seemed to see entirely too much.

"Yes! I really don't know what you're talking about."

Leona sighed and reached for Ava's hand. "I'm talking about a woman who loves her sister, who has spent fifteen years trying to take care of her, even when that sister continually insists she doesn't need help from anyone. You should tell her."

Ava could feel her fingers tremble inside her grandmother's

hand. Her emotions, always close to the surface these days, spilled over.

She couldn't lie to her grandmother. What would be the point? Leona could always see right through her, anyway.

She gripped her grandmother's hand. "I can't tell her. And you can't, either. Promise me."

"Why?"

She squeezed those fingers that could ruthlessly yank weeds and deftly arrange flowers with the same inherent grace. "Madi already believes I think she's incompetent because of her traumatic brain injury. She will be furious if she finds out I was her angel investor. I'm sure she will take that as further proof that I don't believe she can do anything on her own."

"Not if you explain you did it out of love."

Ava was quite certain that nothing she said or did would convince her sister that her motives were anything but presumptive and dictatorial.

"Madi's dream of an animal rescue is the reason you agreed to publish the book, isn't it?"

She thought about denying it but knew there was no point.

"Not the only reason. But yes. A big part of it. I wanted to be able to help her. She's my baby sister. I love her and want her to be happy."

"You should tell her," Leona said again. "She deserves to know the truth. You might think you're protecting her. But which of you are you really protecting?"

Ava thought of all the harm she had caused by keeping secrets. She hadn't told Cullen the truth about everything that had happened to them at Ghost Lake. He was the man she loved and trusted more than any other in her life, yet she had kept that part of herself and her history separate. It was purely for self-protection, because she had feared that if he knew the truth, he wouldn't see her the same way. He would see her as damaged, scarred forever by all that had happened to her.

The same way she looked at Madi.

Ava scrubbed a hand over her face as the enormity of the realization sunk in. After Madi had been shot, Ava treated her as a victim. As she had watched her sister's long road to recovery, all those hours of physical therapy, occupational therapy, she had come to consider Madi someone who needed to be protected at all costs.

Of course their relationship had suffered in the years since. Because they weren't equals in her mind. She had survived and moved on while Madi would be forever scarred.

They were both victims.

Madi might have scars on the outside. The brace she wore on her leg, her hand that didn't work as she might want.

Ava's scars were all internal. She didn't trust. She didn't confide in others. She always protected part of herself to make sure she was never vulnerable again, as she had been at Ghost Lake.

"Tell her," Leona said now, her eyes determined and wise. Ava knew her grandmother was right, as usual.

If Ava ever wanted to have a mutually healthy relationship with her sister, she could not withhold the truth from her. Madi needed to know and Ava needed to be the one to tell her.

"All right. I will."

"Good. Promise me."

"Do I have to pinky swear, too?"

"No. A promise will suffice. I trust you."

"Fine. I promise I will tell Madi the truth."

"Today?"

She couldn't see any point in arguing. "Yes. Today."

"Good." Leona leaned back on her chair. "Now that's sorted, tell me why Cullen didn't make it to the farmers market today. I missed seeing him."

So did Ava. With every heartbeat, every breath.

She sighed. "He picked up a few supplies when he came down earlier in the week."

"I suppose that makes sense. It was good to see him, wasn't it?"

Beyond good. It had been wonderful. She had been shocked to return home from volunteering at the shelter to find Cullen coming out of the guest bathroom at Leona's house, hair wet from the shower and a smile on his handsome features.

She had been tempted to pull away the towel and drag him into her room. Since her grandmother was downstairs—and since they still had so many unresolved issues between them—Ava had refrained.

He said he had a free evening and decided to come down and take his wife out for dinner, if she was free.

She was completely available, that night or any other night he wanted. Her fatigue from the day had lifted as soon as she saw him and she had quickly changed clothes, hugged the dogs and Leona, and left with her husband's hand in hers.

They had gone to dinner at a favorite restaurant in Sun Valley and she had wondered if everyone inside the place could see how deliriously happy she was in her husband's company.

Before he drove away later that night, they had sat in the lush, sweet-smelling garden here, talking and laughing, their fingers touching, almost as if everything was back to normal between them.

It wasn't. She knew that. They still had a long way to go before they could regain all they had lost. But at least she had some hope that they were both on the right path together, moving in the same direction.

"He said he would try to come down tomorrow or Monday."

"If it's tomorrow, we're invited to dinner with Boyd and Tilly again. Cullen would be more than welcome to join us, if he wants. You know how Tilly is. The more the merrier. That's the way she likes things."

"We talked about maybe renting e-bikes and riding over to Hailey, then having a picnic lunch."

Her grandmother's features brightened. "That would be lovely, too. But are you sure you're up for a bike ride?"

"On an e-bike? Definitely. The motor does all the work for me."

"Maybe I should get me one of those things. What do you think?"

Ava wrapped her arms around her grandmother and kissed the top of her gray hair. "I think you would be even more of a terror than you are now. By all means, get an e-bike. In fact, all your friends should get them as well and you can start a biker gang."

Leona laughed hard at that mental picture. Fortunately, she was so amused, she dropped the subject of Ava talking to Madi about her gift to the animal rescue.

30

Madison and I share a silent understanding, a bond forged in
the crucible of shared trauma. We are survivors, two sisters
who found strength in each other when the world outside our
isolation seemed like a distant fantasy.

—*Ghost Lake* by Ava Howell Brooks

Madison

"OKAY. WHAT'S UP? THIS IS THE FIRST CHANCE WE'VE
had to hang out together in weeks and you've hardly said two
words all evening. If I didn't know better, I would think I'm
boring you. You haven't even asked me about Austin."

Madi looked up from the red-and-white container of Chinese takeout Nicole had brought home after her shift at the ER.

"I'm sorry." She set down her chopsticks, her appetite gone.
"You're not boring me at all. I'm just…lousy company. It's been
a really strange day."

"Why is that? Last I heard, you said you would be busy all
day at the farmers market with an animal-adoption event. I can't
imagine that part was too unusual. You've done them before."

"That part was fine. Good, actually. We found homes for all
the puppies and kittens as well as a couple of our older animals."

"Terrific. That means the shelter might be relatively quiet for all of five minutes."

"Maybe."

"So what made your day strange?"

She felt like a lousy friend, focusing only on herself. "Tell me about Austin first."

Nicole made a face. "I broke up with him last night. Hence the need for Chinese food and girl talk."

"What happened? I thought you liked him."

"I did at first, but he was becoming way too clingy. He was talking about moving here and finding a job for the winter, finishing his master's degree online. He even talked about us finding a condo together or something. After a month of dating!"

"Oh wow. That's fast."

"Right. And he suddenly became super possessive. Last night, I agreed to dance with a tourist from Virginia, a guy named Zach who is in the coast guard, and you would have thought I had made out with the guy right there on the dance floor. No thank you. Zach is in town for a week, so we're going to a concert in Sun Valley on Tuesday. Some bluegrass band. I don't know them but Zach says they're good."

"Sounds fun," she said.

"He might have a friend, if you want to come along. Or I know Ryan is still interested in you. I've seen him a few times at the Burning Tree and he always asks about you."

Her friend's dating life suddenly seemed exhausting, moving from new guy to new guy.

How could Madi say anything, though, when her love life had mirrored Nicki's exactly for the past few years?

Had she really been interested in any of those guys or had she only been going along with her friend?

Or had she only been waiting, biding her time until Luke was ready to move on after Johanna's death? Hoping on some subconscious level that when he was ready, he would finally turn to *her*?

"Tell me about your day," Nicki said. "What happened at the farmers market that left you so distracted?"

I was ambushed by a reporter pressing me to talk about things I would rather forget. I kissed your brother. Again. Your niece caught us and wasn't happy about it. I yelled at my sister. Is that enough?

She said none of those things, of course. "A hundred different things. Nothing specific. It was only one of those days where everything seemed twice as hard as it needed to be."

"I hate those kind of days. The other night in the ER, we got hit with one thing after another and absolutely anything that could go wrong did. In spades."

"I'm sorry my schedule has been so frenetic the past few weeks that you haven't even been able to come home and tell me all about it."

"Don't worry. I'm keeping a file of all the weirdest cases. Without any names or identifying factors, of course. I would never abuse my patients' privacy. Still, I figured one winter night, I can spill them all and totally gross you out."

She smiled, grateful beyond words for Nicole, who had been her dearest friend since they were fourteen years old.

"I spent seven years as a vet tech. My gross stories will beat your gross stories any day."

"We should have a contest."

"I can't wait," she said.

Nicki grinned and set down her chopsticks. "Hey, I know we talked about heading out tonight and finding some live music somewhere. I'll be honest, I'm not really in the mood."

"I get it. You might run into Austin."

"There's that. But I was thinking how nice it would be to stay in. We could get in our jammies, pop some popcorn and stream a good movie."

Madi felt so much relief, she wanted to hug Nicki. The idea

of hitting the bar scene seemed pointless and exhausting, especially when she knew she would have zero interest in dancing with anyone except Luke.

"That is the best idea I've heard all week," she declared, already heading for her bedroom.

She had just slipped into a loose T-shirt and her favorite sleep pants, pink with little black doggy paw prints all over them, when the doorbell rang.

Mo and Mabel both barked and hurried to stand sentry beside the door. Nicki, who had been busy putting away the leftover Chinese food and had yet to change into her pajamas, reached the door first.

Since she had already taken off her bra, Madi had no intention of going out in her pajamas until she heard Nicki's greeting to their visitor.

"Ava. Hi. This is a surprise. We were about to watch a movie. Why don't you stay and join us?"

Madi winced, all her good feelings toward her friend disappearing in a rush.

Why did Nicki have to go and say that? What if Ava took her up on the invitation and decided to stay?

That would be the last thing Madi would find relaxing at the end of the day, forced to spend even more time with her sister right now.

In fairness to her roommate, Madi knew why Nicole had issued the invitation. Since Madi and her sister had gone up into the mountains together a few weeks earlier, they had been getting along, if on a superficial level. Nicki must have assumed everything was cool between them after Ava started working at the animal rescue with her.

It was Madi's own fault for not telling her friend about the fight she and her sister had that day at the market.

She held her breath and was deeply relieved when she heard Ava refuse the invitation.

"No. Thank you. I just… I need to speak with my sister, then I'll get out of your way so you can watch your movie."

"Sure. No problem. Come in. Can I get you something to drink?"

Nicki didn't know Ava was pregnant, Madi remembered, as her sister was keeping the information under wraps for now.

"I could use a glass of ice water," Ava said as Madi walked into the living room.

Ava looked upset by something. Madi wasn't sure what gave her that impression. Maybe something in her pallor or the way she was kneading her hands together.

"I can get you some water," Madi said. She headed into the kitchen and filled a glass with ice and water, then returned with it to the living room.

"Here you go," she said, handing over the glass. She heard the coolness in her voice, the tightness.

"Thank you," Ava murmured. She grasped it, sipping it gratefully as if Madi had handed her a healing elixir.

"Please. Sit," Nicki offered.

After a pause, Ava perched on the front edge of the soft easy chair that was usually the dogs' favorite as it gave them a good vantage point out the window.

Predictably, Mabel jumped up beside her and snuggled in and Ava reached down automatically to pet the dog.

"I'll get out of your way," Nicki offered.

"You don't have to," Madi said quickly. "Stay."

Something told her that both she and Ava needed a buffer between them right now.

After a pause, Nicki slid onto the sofa beside Madi.

Ava curled her fingers into Mabel's fur and seemed content to pet the dog and sip at her water.

She obviously had a good reason to come and Madi wanted to tell her to get on with it, but she forced herself to wait patiently until Ava was ready to speak.

"I don't know where to start. I...didn't want to have this conversation at all but Grandma persuaded me it would be better if I am...up front with you."

Madi was aware of an odd sense of foreboding she couldn't have explained. "About what?"

Ava looked miserable. "About the reason I agreed to a contract to publish *Ghost Lake*. I didn't really want to. I know you don't believe me, but I never intended to go public with the story at all. I wrote it as part of my...my therapy and then decided to use it as my master's thesis."

She hadn't realized that part, or that Ava had felt she needed therapy. Madi had gone through counseling as part of her rehabilitation but Ava always insisted she was fine.

"I never submitted it to a publisher."

"Who did?" Nicki asked, looking intrigued. "Your husband?"

Nicki didn't know Ava and Cullen were estranged, as Madi hadn't breached her sister's confidence by sharing that. Ava shook her head. "No. My faculty advisor did, in kind of a roundabout way. A friend of a friend of hers was an editor at a New York publishing house. My faculty advisor was moved by it and sent it to the editor, who liked it enough to offer me a book contract. It really came out of the blue. They...made it very difficult to refuse but I did."

"You refused?" Nicki asked.

Ava nodded. "I wasn't ready. I didn't feel I could publish the book without talking to your mom and Luke. Or to Madi."

That was when Ava had first told her she had written her memoir for her master's thesis, Madi remembered. She had asked Madi if she would mind if she published it.

Madi had foolishly assumed it would only be seen by a few academic types. It was also around the same time she had learned Eugene Pruitt was donating his farm to the Emerald

Creek Animal Rescue Foundation and she had been desperately trying to obtain grants to cover operating expenses.

"Through a couple of other contacts of my advisor, I ended
up obtaining an agent. In a very short period of time, a matter
of weeks, the book went to auction. The original editor won
the bid. Their terms were so favorable I... I couldn't say no."

"It's not that hard," Madi said. "It's only one little syllable."

Ava sighed. "I'll admit, I had some selfish reasons for signing a contract. Cullen and I had been talking about buying a
house one day before we started a family. We were saving for
it, but he's an associate professor of paleontology and I teach
middle school English. Portland is a really expensive place to
live and we're not exactly rolling in dough. The contract would
provide a nice down payment on a really nice starter home in
a good neighborhood."

"Not a big house in a fancy neighborhood?" Madi asked. "I
thought you said it was a good deal."

"It was." Ava pursed her lips. "But I only saved a third of
the advance for a down payment. The rest I...chose to donate
to a good cause."

Nicki whistled from her spot on the sofa. "Wow. That was
generous of you."

Madi stared at her sister, the words tumbling around in her
head.

Donate.

Good cause.

Grandma persuaded me...up front.

She saw Ava twisting her hands together in her lap and all
the separate puzzle pieces seemed to float through the ether to
gel together in one stunning picture.

"You're our angel d-donor."

Ava gazed at her, jaw slack, but she didn't bother to deny it.

The gift had been so thrilling, as generous as it had been
unexpected. Delivered by an attorney for a person who wished

to remain anonymous, the donation had given the foundation enough operating funds to keep going for at least two years. With the other grants and from selling off part of the land Eugene Pruitt had left, they could push that to three years.

It had been enough for her to quit her job, to put the finishing touches on the facilities, to expand their outreach efforts.

All because of Ava.

She didn't know what to think, what to feel.

"Why didn't you tell me?"

"I made an anonymous donation because I wanted to stay anonymous. I didn't want you to know. If Grandma hadn't insisted that keeping it secret was a mistake, I'm not sure I would have told you at all. I am telling you only because I am afraid that if you find out on your own at some future point, it might damage our relationship more."

Madi wasn't sure it was possible for their relationship to feel any more fractured.

Emotions seemed to wash over her in waves. She thought of her bitter anger toward her sister since the book came out, the harsh words she had thrown at Ava about being greedy and self-serving. How was she supposed to respond now, knowing that Ava had ultimately agreed to publish the book so that Madi could start the animal rescue?

She had acted like a petulant brat when she should have been grateful at the enormity of the gift from her sister.

"You should have talked to me first," she muttered, not knowing what else to say.

"Would you have taken the money from me if you had known where it came from?"

She didn't have a clear answer to that. Madi wanted to think she could stand on her own and eventually fund the rescue through grants and fundraising. But she couldn't deny that Ava's generosity had pushed up their timeline to open by at least a year.

They were helping animals in need, something they wouldn't have been able to do without Ava. That day alone they had found new homes for more than a dozen animals. They had provided a home to others, like Barnabas and Sabra, who likely would have been put down otherwise.

Because of the donation, she had been able to build the barn, to hire her full-time assistant to handle the office work and even give herself enough of a salary to enable her to leave the vet clinic.

None of that would have been possible without Ava's gift.

She was deeply grateful. Of course she was grateful. So why did some part of her still simmer with indignation?

"We can't know whether or not I would have taken the money from you, can we? You didn't give me a choice."

"I'm sorry you see it that way," Ava said, her tone stiff. "I thought it would be easier this way, if I simply donated anonymously. No strings attached."

"Nothing comes without strings."

Because she now knew the truth, she felt suffocated by obligatory gratitude. It would take time for her to figure out how to process the enormity of her sister's gift.

"Why did you do this?"

"I knew how important the creation of an animal sanctuary is to you. You've talked about it for years. You used to talk about it even when we were girls. Do you remember?"

Yes. She remembered. Through all those dark days at the camp, they would talk about their hopes and their dreams. Those dreams had sustained them. She had wanted to be a veterinarian who rescued animals.

Ava, bookish and quiet, had wanted to be a writer. She dreamed of using her words to change the world somehow.

"I wish you had told me."

"I'm telling you now. You can be angry with me, resentful, whatever you want, but it's done. I can't take it back and

I wouldn't if I could. I love seeing what you're doing with the animal rescue. You're making a difference to these animals. Mom would have been so proud of you."

She paused and rose, her features pale and her hands trembling slightly. "*I'm* proud of you. I love you, Madi. Whatever you think about what I've done, please don't ever doubt that. I love you and I'm proud to be your sister."

Madi struggled for a response but the words didn't come. She only felt hollow, carved out by shock and shame at how she had treated her sister when Ava didn't deserve it.

"Good night," Ava said. She made it as far as the door when she suddenly cried out, clutching at her abdomen, then collapsed to the floor.

31

In this moment, survival becomes our singular focus, a primal instinct that drives us to endure against the odds.

—*Ghost Lake* by Ava Howell Brooks

Ava

SHE WAS LOSING THE BABY.

She didn't need to look to know that she was bleeding. She could feel the wetness between her legs and the cramps that rippled through her.

All day, she had been achy, her back sore and cramps hitting her at random moments. She had ignored them, never once imagining those might have been early indications she was miscarrying.

No. She fought the wail building inside her. *No. Please, God. No.*

"What's wrong?" Nicole Gentry was at her side immediately. The ER nurse's voice was calm but concerned.

Ava couldn't answer. She could feel the tears leaking down her face as all her hopes and dreams were dying inside her.

She must have managed some sound. An instant later, Madi was at her side, crouching on the floor next to her.

"What's wrong, Ava? Is it the baby?"

"I… I think so." It was all she could say as shock and pain and grief roared in her chest.

"You're pregnant?" Nicole looked shocked. "How far along?"

"Eight…eight weeks."

"Have you been cramping?"

She nodded, pressing her hand against her abdomen. "All day. I thought… I thought maybe I had a stomach thing going on."

Another cramp hit her hard, so intense she doubled over with a keening cry.

"Easy. Let's get you into the bathroom. Madi, can you help?"

Her sister, who had been so angry with her, now appeared stricken. She reached her curled fingers down and helped lift Ava off the carpet. With Nicole on her other side, Ava managed to make it to the bathroom.

She didn't want an audience, even her sister and one of their closest friends. "I'm okay from here," she said to the other two women.

"Are you sure?" Nicole frowned.

Ava nodded. "Yes. Please. I… I'll let you know if I need you."

"There are pads under the sink if you need something," Nicole said gently, squeezing her arm.

Madi hovered outside the door, her mouth twisted with fear and sorrow. Ava couldn't deal with it right now. She couldn't even handle her own raw grief and didn't have space to take on anyone else's.

She closed the bathroom door and stood for several moments, breathing through the physical pain and the deep emotional loss.

Finally, she looked and the thick clots of rusty blood staining her underwear, much more intense than any mild spotting, confirmed her suspicions.

She was losing the baby.

Bereft, shattered, she rocked back and forth, arms wrapped around her abdomen as if she could hold on to the pregnancy by force of will alone.

She let out a sob and then another one.

She thought the worst moment of her life had been when her sixteen-year-old self had been married off to a man older than her father. When he had kissed her, sloppy and wet, and touched her with his fat, horrible hands.

She had been wrong. This was so much worse.

That had been over in a few moments. This pain she knew would linger forever.

She had only known about the baby for a few weeks but its existence had been a shining light of hope in a cold, harsh world.

Cullen. She had to tell Cullen.

She sobbed again, burying her face in her hands.

She didn't hear the bathroom door open and was only vaguely aware when her sister entered, when Madi knelt on the cold tile of the bathroom and wrapped her arms around her.

Her brave, amazing sister held her, rocked her for a long time as Ava rested her head against Madi's shoulder and wept, huge, wrenching sobs that seemed to well up from the depths of her soul.

Later, when she had cleaned up as best she could and changed into a fresh, soft nightgown provided by Nicki, Ava clutched at the small comfort her sister had offered so generously, holding it to her heart.

"You can stay here tonight," Madi said when they both emerged from the bathroom. "You'll sleep in my room. I'll call Grandma and let her know what's going on."

She nodded, feeling listless, wrung out.

"Ava, I'm so sorry."

"It's not your fault."

"I shouldn't have…yelled at you."

She shook her head forcefully. "This isn't your fault, Madi. Don't think that. It… I think it started last night."

She pressed trembling fingers to her mouth to hold back the sob there. "I had some spotting and my back has been hurting since then. And today, I've been crampy on and off all day."

"I've had patients describe it as the worst menstrual cramps of their lives." Nicole's eyes were drenched with compassion.

"Yes. That's what it feels like." She looked at the other woman. "Do you think I need to go to the ER?"

Nicole squeezed her arm. "Not unless you bleed heavily for several hours and it won't stop."

"Is there a way to reach Cullen?" Madi asked.

Ava closed her eyes, fighting sobs all over again as she felt keenly how her husband would grieve this loss as well. "No. They have a satellite phone, but he said it stopped working and they have to get another one. He's supposed to be coming down tomorrow. I will…will wait to tell him then."

She wiped at her eyes with the tissue Madi provided. The joy they both had felt about the pregnancy had been a tensile thread knotting her together with Cullen in the midst of their painful separation. Now that thread had been cut, how would her marriage possibly survive?

She didn't know which hurt worse. The aching cramps in her womb or the fearful, anxious pain in her heart.

32

I embrace the uncertainty of the future with open arms, knowing that the power to shape our destiny lies within us.

—*Ghost Lake* by Ava Howell Brooks

Madison

AFTER MORE THAN AN HOUR OF WEEPING ON AND OFF, Ava fell into an exhausted sleep on Madi's bed, curled into a fetal position with her hands still clutched tightly around her abdomen.

Feeling helpless and filled with sorrow, Madi watched the last rays of the sun, striped by the window blinds, play over her sister's lovely features, now ravaged by grief.

She found it grossly unfair that Ava had to suffer one more loss, after everything she had already endured.

She wanted Ava to know only joy and light and love.

With the natural instinct dogs seemed to have, compelling them to provide comfort when needed, Mabel was curled up in the small of Ava's back, offering heat and comfort.

When the elderly schnauzer mix had jumped onto the bed as Ava had been crying, Madi had moved to take her off, intending to push her out of the room and close the door to keep her away.

Ava, her sister who feared dogs because of that long-ago vicious attack at Ghost Lake, had shaken her head and held a hand out to the dog.

"Let her stay," she had rasped out.

So now Mabel was snuggled against Ava, sleeping soundly.

Satisfied the dog would watch over her sister, Madi made her way to the living room, where she found Nicki reading, of all things, a copy of *Ghost Lake*.

Instead of the baffled fury that usually came over her whenever she spotted someone reading the book, Madi only felt a twinge of annoyance.

Nicki set aside the book and moved to make room on the sofa so that Madi could sit down next to her.

"How is she doing?" she asked.

"Asleep," Madi answered. "Finally. Poor thing."

"Miscarriages can be so rough. She's going to need a lot of love and support. Pregnancy loss is tough at any stage. Breaks my heart every single time we have someone come into the ER."

"I feel like I should be doing something else to help her."

"There isn't much you can do, except to let her know she's loved. And also to reinforce that a miscarriage does not indicate any failure on her part. There was probably nothing she could have done. An estimated fifteen to twenty percent of pregnancies end in a miscarriage, usually because the fetus has some chromosomal anomaly making survival unlikely."

Madi made a small sound in her throat and Nicole reached out and squeezed her fingers. "I know. Statistics don't mean anything when a woman finds herself among that number. All that matters to Ava is that she will never have the chance to hold the child she was coming to love."

"I need to call my grandma. She needs to at least know Ava will be staying here tonight, so she doesn't worry."

Though afraid she would cry through the whole call, she still somehow managed to find Leona, the first name in her favorite phone contacts, and initiate a call. Her grandmother answered on the second ring.

Madi took a deep breath and relayed the information with as much calmness as she could muster.

She heard one low, sighing sob before her grandmother fell silent. "I would offer to come get her," Leona finally said, "but I think she might be better off there with you. She needs you."

"She needs her husband," Madi countered.

"Yes. But since he's up in the mountains for now, you are the next best thing. Give her my love and tell her I'm so sorry."

After she hung up from her grandmother, Madi stared down at her phone for several moments, then stood up.

"I have to go up to Ghost Lake so I can tell Cullen. He needs to know. He needs to be here with his wife. He wouldn't want her to go through this on her own."

Nicki stared. "Are you serious? It's dark. You can't go up there by yourself!"

"I have the side-by-side. It has headlights. I can be there and back in a few hours. He should be here when she wakes up."

"You can't, Madi. It's not safe."

She was really tired of people telling her what she could and couldn't do. "I'll be fine. It's a well-maintained fire road, until the last few miles."

"You can't do this on your own. I'll go with you."

Madi shook her head. "I don't want Ava to wake up alone. That's the last thing she needs."

"Then, you stay here. I'll go up to Ghost Lake."

"You've never been to the dinosaur camp. You don't know where to go."

"I can follow a map. You can give me directions."

Madi shook her head. "I should be the one to tell him. He's my brother-in-law. This kind of news is better coming from family than from someone he hardly knows, no matter how wonderful you are."

With her mind already spinning with what she might need to take with her, Madi started heading for the door.

"Take Luke with you, then," her friend said quickly. "He knows the way and he can drive his own UTV. It's newer and faster than yours."

Nicki reached for her phone and started texting before Madi could figure out a way to stop her.

She tried, anyway. "That's not necessary. Don't text him. Really. I can do it."

The words were hardly out of her mouth before her phone rang. She looked at the caller ID and somehow wasn't at all surprised to find it was Luke.

"What did you say to him?" she demanded of Nicki.

Her friend shrugged. "I sent him an SOS and said you needed help."

Oh. How was she supposed to resist a man who responded instantly when he thought he might be needed?

Warmth settled on her shoulders as she answered.

"What's going on?" Luke asked, his tone urgent and worried. "Is it one of the animals?"

"Hi. No. Sorry about that. Nic jumped the gun a bit in sending for the cavalry. It's not one of the animals. It's Ava."

She wasn't sure what to tell him, as this was Ava's pain and loss to share with those she wanted to know. Luke would not betray the confidence, she knew, and she had to tell him something to explain why she needed his help. She *did* need his help, she acknowledged. Having him along made the prospect of driving up to Ghost Lake in the dark much less intimidating.

"Ava is miscarrying the baby."

"Oh no."

At the genuine sorrow in his voice, tears burned behind her eyelids once more.

"Yeah. It sucks. Right now, we have no way to reach Cullen. Ava wants to wait to tell him until he comes down out of the mountains tomorrow or Monday, but I feel like he needs to know now. He should be here, helping her through this. I want to go up to his camp to tell him and bring him back down, but Nicki doesn't want me to go by myself."

"I'll be there in ten minutes."

He said the words without any hesitation and hung up before she could even respond.

This was what every woman should have, she thought. A man who would drop everything to be there when she needed him.

"Is he coming?" Nicki asked when Madi slid the phone back into the pocket of her jeans.

"He's on his way."

"Oh good."

As she gathered warm clothes, a blanket, a water bottle and headlamp, Madi thought about Luke and what a good man he was.

Of course she loved him. She'd never really had much of a choice.

He had risked his own life to save hers fifteen years ago. Since then, he had been a steady source of support and encouragement. Even when he had been away at vet school, married with a child, Luke would always send her a card or call her on important days like her birthday or the anniversary of their rescue to connect and make sure she was okay.

Her entire adult life, she had compared every other man to him, she realized now. All those summer guys and ski bums. No wonder she had wanted to date only casually and never let her heart become too involved.

Part of it had always belonged to Luke.

Before he arrived, she went back into her bedroom to check on Ava. Mabel looked up through the dim light, her tail wagging, then snuggled against Ava's back once more. Her sister was asleep, eyes closed, but tears still trickled slowly down her cheeks, as if even in sleep, she couldn't escape the pain of loss.

Oh, Ava.

Madi made sure the blanket was tucked around her sister, then retreated back to the hallway as she heard Nic open the front door. When she walked into the living room, Luke immediately crossed the room and enfolded her in his arms.

He was warm and strong and wonderful. She closed her eyes and leaned into him, feeling anchored for the first time all evening.

"I'm so sorry, Madi. Poor Ava. How is she?"

"Sleeping, for now. I hope she stays that way until we get back."

"I'm ready to go when you are."

"I'm ready." She gestured to her travel backpack, which he picked up and slung over one shoulder, already heading for the door.

"Thanks, Nic," she said, hugging her friend.

"I've got Ava. Don't worry. I'm here for her."

She nodded and hurried out into the pale blue twilight, where Luke's truck and trailer waited in the circular driveway. He helped her into the passenger seat and then climbed in and pulled away from the house.

"Is it reckless to head up into the mountains at this time of the night?" she asked.

"We'll be fine. The UTV has headlights."

She was suddenly fiercely glad his sister had reached out to Luke. This would have felt like an impossible journey without him.

"What did you tell Sierra?"

"Not much," he admitted. "I assumed Ava might want her

privacy protected, so I only told her there was an emergency at the shelter here. No details."

"Thank you for that. I'm sure Ava will be grateful. Did you take Sierra to your mom's house?"

"No. I wanted to, but she reminded me she's thirteen and insisted she would be fine by herself. The security system at the house is armed, plus she's got two big dogs to protect her. She also has her cell phone with Mom's number and Nicki's number."

Sierra still seemed like a young girl to Madi, but she had to remind herself she was a teenager now, only a year younger than Madi had been when she and Ava had escaped through the darkness, into the wilderness.

She wanted to ask him if Sierra was still upset about what had happened earlier, about that kiss that seemed as if it had happened a lifetime ago, but she bit back the question. It seemed wrong to even think about that kiss when her sister had suffered an unbearable loss.

She looked out at the passing trees and the black mountains looming in the distance, as a few raindrops began to spatter against the window.

"Oh no," she exclaimed.

"With any luck, it won't last long."

"Even a quick rain will make the trail muddy and harder to navigate."

He glanced at her briefly before turning his attention back to the road. "Do you want to turn around?"

She considered briefly, then shook her head. "Cullen needs to know about the baby. Ava should have her husband with her. What's a little mud?"

His mouth lifted into a smile. "Right. What's a little mud?"

He reached a hand down and his strong fingers folded around her smaller curled ones and they rode that way through the night as the headlights sliced through the darkness and the wipers beat away the rain.

33

Days blur into nights, and our strength is tested in ways we never imagined.

—*Ghost Lake* by Ava Howell Brooks

Luke

THE TRUST MADISON HOWELL HAD IN HIM WAS AS remarkable as it was humbling.

Luke drove toward the Sawtooths, more aware with every passing mile of her hand curled inside his. He could no longer avoid the overwhelming truth.

For the second time in his life, he was in love and the reality of it scared the hell out of him.

He had loved Johanna and had grieved the loss of her for four long years. He had told himself he would never let himself be vulnerable to that kind of loss and pain again.

But when his sister had texted him, saying only that Madi needed his help, he was fairly certain he had stopped breathing for a full minute while he waited for her to answer his call.

In that moment, he had accepted the truth that had been hovering at the edge of his subconscious for months now, nudging at him to wake up and pay attention.

This thing between them was not a passing, somewhat inconvenient attraction.

He was in love with Madison Rae Howell.

As the truth soaked through him like that rain outside soaking into the ground, he knew that he had been in love with her for a long time but hadn't wanted to see it.

Maybe he hadn't been *ready* before now to admit it to himself that the affection and friendship he had for her since that day fifteen summers ago had gradually begun to shift and grow into something else. Something *more*.

Madi was strong and courageous and amazing. She was the only one who couldn't seem to see that in herself.

He squeezed her fingers now and she gave him a small, uncertain smile.

How did she feel about him? He wasn't completely sure. She kissed him with a tenderness and passion that took his breath away. But her pattern was dating a different guy every few months. Maybe he was only the flavor of the summer for her.

No. He was suddenly sure this thing between them was bigger than that.

He wanted to tell her how important she had become to him, but he knew this wasn't the time. Right now, her focus had to be on her sister and Ava's heartbreaking loss.

Still, he didn't release her hand and was grateful that she seemed to find comfort and support from his touch.

"I have to tell you something," she said, her voice low. "I found out s-some shocking information tonight."

"Oh?"

She nodded. "Ava is the angel donor for the animal rescue."

"I suspected as much."

Much to his regret, she pulled her hand away, and he could feel her gaze boring into him as he turned onto the dirt road that would eventually lead up to the dinosaur camp.

"Why didn't you tell me?" she asked, her tone accusatory.

He sighed. "I said I *suspected*. I didn't know for certain. I figured if she was behind the gift, she had her reasons for donating anonymously. I had to respect those."

"I wish you had said something. Maybe if I had even considered it a possibility, I wouldn't have acted like such a jerk to her."

"What could I have said? I didn't know anything for sure. I might have been wrong."

She sighed, bouncing as the truck went over a rut on the dirt road. "She said she finally agreed to the publishing contract mainly for the animal rescue, because the amount they were offering her for a contract would allow her to help make it a reality."

"Wow. That's great."

She nodded. "She also agreed to the contract so she and Cullen would have enough for a down payment on a house in order to start their family. Poor Ava."

Her voice broke on her sister's name and Luke reached for her hand again.

She sniffled. "I hate remembering how awful I've been to her this summer. All my snide comments about the book. Blaming her for invading my privacy. Telling her she ruined my life. I don't believe she even *wanted* to publish the book. She mostly did it for me, so I could have the start-up funds we needed."

"She loves you. The two of you have an unbreakable bond, forged through all you have survived together."

She swiped at her eyes with the sleeve of her hoodie. "I keep saying I want to forget the past, to focus on my life now and what's ahead. But it's always there."

"Read Ava's book, Madi. I think you'll find it moving. Transformative, even."

He wasn't sure she believed him but she at least seemed to be considering the suggestion this time, where before she would have rolled her eyes.

They couldn't take his truck all the way, because for much of the distance, the trail was too narrow for more than a small off-road vehicle. He drove as far as he could, until he had no choice but to pull off into a small clearing and park the pickup.

The rain wasn't heavy but it was steady, with a chill wind that knuckled under his slicker. He didn't like the idea of Madi out in that cold. He gestured back to the pickup. "Why don't you stay here in the truck and wait where it's dry and warm? You'll freeze on the side-by-side. I can go up the rest of the way by myself."

Madi shook her head. "No. I feel like I need to tell him. I'm his sister-in-law. I told Nicki the same thing."

He set his jaw at her stubbornness. "You can still be the one to give him the sad news. I won't say anything. I'll tell him there's an emergency with Ava and you will explain what's going on back here at the truck."

She reached for his hand, her teeth already chattering. "I'm grateful for your concern for my safety and comfort, Luke. Believe me, I am. But I need to do this."

He sighed, expecting nothing less. "Fine. Let's hurry, then."

She climbed into the passenger seat wearing a coat and a rain slicker, with a blanket that she tucked over her legs.

His side-by-side had a roof and front windshield, which cut the worst of the mud and rain from coming in and soaking them. It did not have side windows, though, and the wet wind still managed to blow through as they made their way up farther into the backcountry.

It took all his concentration to drive on the narrow, slick trail. He drove slowly, about half as fast as he would have liked, with his headlights illuminating only about twenty feet ahead of them in the inky darkness.

At least he had a heater, which he turned on high for Madi.

Finally, they reached the toughest part of the trail, the steep climb up to the dinosaur camp. He revved it, the tires spitting muck and gravel, and then he saw the lights and wall tents of Cullen's camp.

A dog barked at them menacingly and approached, followed by a man holding a lantern.

"What the hell are you doing, coming up here in these conditions?" he yelled. "This is a private research camp. You could be arrested for trespassing!"

In that instant, as he drew nearer, Luke recognized the man as her brother-in-law. The man spotted Madi at the same moment.

"Madi? What's going on? What's wrong? Is it Ava?"

Madi looked tortured as she fumbled to open the door of the side-by-side. She hurried toward him with a sob and wrapped her arms around her brother-in-law.

"Yes. It's Ava. She needs you, Cullen. She's losing the baby. I'm so, so sorry."

Cullen sagged against the vehicle, mud and all, looking suddenly shattered in the light of his lantern.

"What? When?"

"Now. Tonight. She's been having cramps since last night, I guess, but they hit her hard this evening and she started bleeding, too. My roommate, Nicki, is an ER nurse and she confirmed that's what's going on. But I think Ava already knew. She's so sad, Cullen."

Luke hadn't felt this helpless since Johanna had first been hospitalized with COVID and he hadn't even been allowed to be with her at the end.

"We can take you back down to her," he said, his voice low. "Madi felt like it was important for you to know as soon as possible."

"Is she…is she okay?" His voice sounded rough, thick.

Madi shook her head. "Not really. She's devastated. She already loved the baby so much."

Cullen released a breath that sounded like a sob. "Oh man.

Poor Ava. My poor Ava. Give me ten minutes to grab a few things and tell my research partner what's going on."

"Of course," Luke said. "We'll wait. Do what you need to do."

Cullen nodded and reached a hand blindly for the dog, who came at once, nudging the man's hand with his head as if urging him to hurry.

34

Every breath is a struggle, each inhale laden with the musty scent of fear and uncertainty. The silence is broken only by the distant howl of the wind, a haunting reminder of the vast wilderness that surrounds this hidden enclave of madness.

—*Ghost Lake* by Ava Howell Brooks

Madison

THEY DROVE DOWN THE MOUNTAIN MOSTLY IN SILENCE, with only the occasional comment about the slick conditions.

Madi sat in the back seat of the side-by-side while Cullen was in front with Luke. Whenever the moon would emerge from the clouds, she could see his features in profile. They looked carved out of stone, as forbidding as the peaks around them, but every so often, she would see the utter devastation in his eyes and her heart would break all over again.

Finally, after what felt like forever, they reached the pickup truck. Luke started the truck for her and Madi again slid into the back seat of his crew cab as he and Cullen loaded the side-by-side onto the trailer. The atmosphere was warmer here inside the truck but no less fraught with emotion.

When they reached the farmhouse, three interminable hours

after they set off, she unlocked the front door. Nicki must have gone to bed as the living room was dark.

"Ava is in my bedroom," she told Cullen, pointing to the door.

He stood outside the room, his hand on the knob, then seemed to square his shoulders before he opened it and slipped through.

Luke had walked them up to the house, she suspected because he didn't feel right about simply dropping them off and driving away.

Now he waited on the porch, petting Mo, who had walked out when Madi opened the door.

She walked back outside to the quiet night. After the rain, the air smelled fresh and lovely.

He straightened up when she came outside.

"Thank you for everything. I probably could have made it up to the camp by myself but I'm so grateful I didn't have to."

She didn't think through the wisdom of it, she only acted on impulse, moving toward him and wrapping her arms around his waist.

He exhaled as if he had been waiting for exactly this and pulled her close. They stood that way for a long time while crickets chirped and an owl hooted somewhere in the nearby trees.

Her heart seemed to overflow with love for this man, who had been willing to drop everything and come running when she needed help.

When he lowered his head and kissed her, it seemed inevitable. The kiss was slow and gentle, less about passion, after their difficult evening, and more about tenderness.

His gentle touch just about shattered her emotions.

She loved him. It seemed absurd that she hadn't realized it a long time ago. The words almost spilled out but she held them back, afraid of ruining everything.

He was the first to step away and a shiver rippled through her at the loss of his heat, though the evening wasn't particularly cold now that the rain had stopped.

"You need to get some rest."

"I'm not sure I'll be able to sleep," she admitted. "My mind is whirling a hundred miles an hour."

He smiled. "I know a good book you could read."

She couldn't help her rough laugh. "Enough already. What are you, Ava's publicist or something?"

"No. I don't think she needs me to hand sell her book. It seems to be doing fine on its own. It really is a beautiful book. It might give you a different perspective about Ava. And maybe about yourself."

"I'll think about it," she said, which she considered a huge concession. "You'd better get home to Sierra."

"You're right." He kissed her forehead again. "I'll check in with you tomorrow. Good night."

"Good night, Luke. And thank you again."

He kissed her one more time, with that same aching tenderness, then turned and hurried down the steps.

After a moment, Madi went inside the house, Mo on her heels. Mabel was nowhere in sight and she assumed she was either with Nicki or had stayed to comfort Ava.

It occurred to Madi for the first time that she couldn't sleep in her own bed since Ava and Cullen were there. She found clean pajamas in the laundry room and changed into them after she quickly showered off the mud and grime from the ride, then headed for their tiny guest room.

On the way, she spied Nicki's copy of *Ghost Lake* on the side table in the living room. Impulsively, she picked it up and carried it to the narrow bed in the guest room. She would read for a while, she decided, which was probably all she could manage before she fell asleep.

Hours later, right before sunrise, she closed the book, mentally and physically exhausted.

Tears dripped down her cheeks for her brilliant, beautiful, brave sister, who had somehow managed to condense all of the fear and trauma into a story that, far from feeling exploitative or sad, resonated with humor, with compassion and with hope.

35

As we stand on the precipice of a new beginning, the mountains behind us hold the echoes of our struggle, and the horizon ahead beckons with the promise of a life unshackled from the dark chapters of our past.

—*Ghost Lake* by Ava Howell Brooks

Ava

SHE DREAMED SHE WAS LOST IN THE MOUNTAINS again—cold, wet, hungry, afraid. Hiding from anyone they saw because they had no idea whom they could trust, if they indeed could rely on anyone.

It was a familiar dream she had entirely too often, when she relived the crushing fear of being responsible for her younger sister. The odds of them both surviving were slim at best. Ava hated those odds and she was determined that Madi, at least, would make it safely to their grandmother, no matter what she had to do to make it happen.

This time felt different somehow. Madi wasn't there. Instead, Ava carried a small bundle in her arms.

Her baby. She had to keep her baby safe from the cold, from

the rushing waters, from the mountain lions and the dogs and the horrible, ruthless men with guns.

She couldn't let anything happen to her baby. She stumbled, fell, got up again, running through thistles and scrub oak and sagebrush that snagged at her clothes and ripped at her skin.

And then she was falling again, arms spiraling at a cliff's edge as she went down and the bundle in her arms soared away, beyond her reach.

She cried out and the sound woke her. For a moment, she lay in a bed that felt unfamiliar, her heart pounding wildly. Her face felt wet with tears, and as consciousness gradually returned, she remembered.

It hadn't all been a dream. She had lost the baby. She sobbed out and in her hazy half-asleep state, she thought she felt arms around her.

"Easy, darling. Easy. I've got you."

And somehow her husband was there, holding her, calming her.

She knew it was impossible. Cullen was in the mountains. But in her dreams, the man in the bed beside her smelled like Cullen and the arms around her felt like his.

With Cullen, she was safe. No matter what happened, he would keep the darkness away. He always did.

She closed her eyes and sagged into him, letting sleep claim her again.

When she awoke hours later, Ava lay in her sister's bed, watching the pale dawn light come through the blinds. The heavy ache in her chest reminded her with clarity of the stark, unavoidable truth.

Her baby was gone.

Her eyes felt gritty and sore, as if she had been crying all night long. She didn't want to get up. She wanted to stay here, pull the blankets over her head and pretend none of it had happened.

Would Cullen come down from the mountain that day? She didn't want to tell him, to say the words that would extinguish that bright light that had flared in his expression the past few times she had seen him, when he would return to town to spend time with her and they would talk about the baby.

She closed her eyes again. Only then, as consciousness fully returned, did she realize she wasn't alone in the bed. She knew Madi's little schnauzer mix had cuddled with her before she fell asleep but this presence felt much bigger.

She felt an instant's fear before the familiar, beloved smell of soap scented with sandalwood, black pepper and leather pushed through.

She opened her eyes, shifted her gaze and found her husband lying beside her, his arms cradling her and his eyes open.

"Ava. My darling Ava," he murmured, his voice hoarse. "I'm so sorry."

"You're…you're here. How are you here?" She couldn't seem to make the puzzle pieces fit in her head and wondered if she was still dreaming. What else could explain her husband in bed beside her, bearded now and sun-weathered from long hours spent at the dig, but so dearly familiar.

"Madi and your friend Luke Gentry drove up in the middle of the night in a rainstorm to get me."

"Oh." The exclamation escaped on a sigh and then she turned to face him. Cullen pulled her into his embrace and she pressed her face into the curve of his neck.

Cullen was her safe space. From the day they met, she had found strength and comfort and peace in his arms. He loved her. Why had she ever believed that his love couldn't be strong enough to endure if he truly knew all the pieces of her?

"I'm so sorry about the baby. Are you okay?"

She shook her head, unable to meet his gaze. "It hurts," she admitted on a whisper. "I'm not sure I can bear it."

She didn't mean physically. The cramping had stopped some-time in the night. Now she only felt...empty inside.

"I wish I could take this pain for you."

She didn't know how to tell him that his presence was eas-ing it, going a long way to helping her not feel so alone.

She couldn't lose this. Them. She needed him too much. Yes, being completely vulnerable with him, sharing the complete truth about everything, was terrifying. The idea of spending even another night without him was far, far worse.

"I'm sorry about everything," she said softly. "So sorry. I'm sorry about our baby. I'm sorry for keeping so much from you all this time. I'm sorry I wasn't strong enough to tell you, that I let fear rule my choices."

"Oh, Ava. It was never about you not being strong enough. I wondered what I had done or said to make you feel you couldn't trust me with the truth about all that you went through."

She had hurt him. That was the core of everything, why he had needed to put distance between them. He had hurt, learn-ing there were parts of her she had never shared with him.

"I'm sorry," she murmured again.

"Don't." He pressed a soft kiss to her forehead, his arms tightening around her. "I love you, Ava. No matter what. I can't bear being without you. These weeks have been hell. Can't we simply move forward from here?"

She listened to his heartbeat, strong and comforting. "Yes. Oh please, Cullen. I love you."

He tucked her head against his shoulder and they stayed that way for a long time.

While the pain of loss was still there and probably always would be, on the fringes of her subconscious, Ava caught a tiny sliver of bright hope, like a rare and precious mountain blue-bird flitting across an alpine meadow.

36

With the weight of the past lifted, we face the future unbur-
dened, ready to embrace the limitless possibilities that await
two sisters who refused to be defined by the chains that once
bound them.

—*Ghost Lake* by Ava Howell Brooks

Madison

WHEN SHE AWOKE, SUN WAS STREAMING THROUGH
the lacy curtains of the guest room. Mo, who had slept on the
floor beside her, now stood by the guest room bed, nudging
her hand and urging her to wake up so she could let him outside into the yard.

Madi was so tired, she wanted to stay here all day, but knew
she couldn't. She had things to do at the animal rescue and her
own dogs needed care.

The house was quiet. Nicki had left for work, she saw by
the empty coffee mug in the kitchen sink.

She let Mo outside and was trying to figure out how to
sneak into her bedroom to get Mabel when the door opened
and Ava walked out behind the smaller dog.

They gazed at each other, then Mabel broke the silence by trotting over to Madi, whose hand was still on the door.

She opened it for her and Mabel scampered out to find her buddy, Mo.

"Hi," Madi said, then fell silent, not knowing what else to say.

"Hi."

Ava mustered a smile, which broke Madi's heart all over again. She remembered the beautiful words her sister had written and especially how Ava had described *her*.

Not as weak, damaged. Someone to be protected.

But as a warrior who had given Ava strength when she needed it.

"Cullen says you went up to Ghost Lake in the middle of a rainstorm to bring him back down. Thank you. I didn't know how much I needed him here until I woke up and found him."

"I'm glad it helped. I couldn't think of anything else to do."

"Do you remember what Mom always used to say? When you don't know what to do, just do the next right thing."

Madi felt a pang of loss for their wise mother, who had held them all together.

"Bringing Cullen here," Ava went on. "That was the next right thing. He was exactly what I needed so that we can... can start the grieving process together."

Madi moved to her sister and hugged her, thinking Ava felt fragile in her arms. She wasn't, though. She was fierce and strong and amazing.

"Where is he? He didn't go back, did he?"

"No. He's in the shower right now. He's going to drive me in my car to Grandma's house and we'll stay there together for a couple of days. When I'm feeling a little better, after I've seen my doctor here, I thought I would go up to the dinosaur camp with him for a few weeks."

She stared. "To Ghost Lake? Really?"

Ava shrugged. "It's only a place, right? Someone I love told me that. Once, some terrible things happened there. Despite that, it's still a beautiful place. I decided I need some happy memories to replace the dark ones."

"I read the book last night." She hadn't intended to blurt the words out like that but now they hovered between them.

Ava stared. "You... When?"

"After Luke brought us back here. I couldn't sleep. My mind was whirling too fast from everything, so I picked up Nicki's copy. And then I couldn't stop reading."

Ava looked nervous, suddenly. She swallowed and looked down at her hands. Madi touched her arm.

"It's a beautiful book, Ava. Everyone is right. You've written a gripping, compelling story about the terrible things that happened to us. It should have been awful, reliving it all again but...it wasn't. I laughed a dozen times. And cried more than a few. I'm so proud of you, Ava."

Her sister looked stunned at the praise, and Madi felt guilty all over again for being so negative and whiny all summer about her sister's book.

"Thank you for writing it—and not only because the Emerald Creek Animal Rescue was the biggest beneficiary. It's a story that needed to be told. And it needed to be told by you."

Ava gazed at her for a long moment, then sniffled and gave a half laugh at the same time. "I thought I didn't have any more tears left."

"If you really want a good cry, I've got this great book you should read," Madi said.

Ava gave a watery smile, resting her head on Madi's shoulder until the dogs yelped at the door to be let in for their breakfast.

Madi knew their relationship wouldn't heal overnight, but she still felt as if a huge deadweight had been lifted away from her heart.

She had her sister back. Together, the two of them had endured things that would have broken others. Despite it all, they had emerged stronger than ever.

Ava had suffered a terrible loss but Madi knew she would get through it. She had Cullen and Leona and Madi to help her.

After Ava and Cullen left, Madi was sorely tempted to climb back into the guest room bed in the quiet house, cuddle Mo and Mabel against her, and sleep the rest of the day away.

Unfortunately, the shelter animals needed care, regardless of her shortsighted decision to read all night long. She couldn't take the day off simply because she felt like it.

She showered again and dressed in her usual uniform of jeans and a T-shirt with the animal-rescue logo on it, put on her leg brace, then her boots and headed out to the barn. While other volunteers were scheduled to feed the animals, Madi had planned to clean out a couple of the stalls today. Not the most enjoyable of activities, but at least the exercise would keep her awake.

Maybe.

She opened the door to the office and greeted a couple of the newer volunteers, Jennifer Quinn and Olivia Morales.

"How's everything today?"

"Quiet so far. Everyone seems pretty happy."

"That's good. Have the dogs had their exercise?"

"Not yet. The first two are about to head out."

She wouldn't mind a good walk. She decided to grab a couple of the dogs and walk them along with whatever volunteer was on the schedule that day.

She was about to go into the dog area when the door opened and Rocky, their Siberian husky, and his Aussie shepherd pal, Zeus, pranced out…followed immediately by Sierra Gentry, holding their leashes.

Madi jolted, her face heating instantly. All she could think about was the awkwardness of their last meeting, when Sierra had caught her and Luke in an embrace at the farmers market.

"Oh. Hi. I didn't realize you were on the volunteer schedule today."

Sierra shrugged and seemed to focus on anything but Madi.

"I'm not. I wasn't doing anything this morning and was feeling sorry for myself since Mariko and Yuki went on a family vacation to Colorado. I figured I would come and help out for a while. Walking the dogs is always a good chance to clear your head."

"True enough. Funny, I was about to do the same thing."

"We can wait and you can grab a couple of the dogs and come with us, if you want." Sierra made the offer tentatively.

Sensing it wasn't an easy suggestion for her to make, Madi agreed immediately. "Sure," she said. "Give me a few minutes."

She decided to take Lulu, a mixed-breed boxer, and Rosie, a bulldog. Both were well-behaved and enjoyed interacting with the other dogs.

Soon she and Sierra set off around the building toward the trail that ran through the farm's twenty acres, moving slowly to let the dogs sniff each other and every clump of grass.

Madi knew that the sensory stimulation of a walk was as important to dogs as the exercise.

"I also came to the shelter today because, um, I was also hoping to have the chance to talk to you," Sierra said.

"Oh?"

The girl sighed. "I'm sorry I was a jerk yesterday. It's just… some days I really miss my mom a lot, you know? It's weird to think about my dad kissing anyone else but her. It was extra weird to see him kissing *you*."

Madi really didn't want to have this conversation when she felt hungover and gritty-eyed from her sleepless night.

"Why is that?" she managed.

"Because you're our Madi. Aunt Nicki's best friend. You've

always been, I don't know, kind of like another aunt to me, right? I never thought about you and my dad together."

Madi gripped the dogs' leashes. "We're not together," she said quickly.

Sierra gave a scoff and an eye roll at the same time. "Oh please. I saw you yesterday. There was more chemistry between you than Elizabeth and Mr. Darcy in that *Pride & Prejudice* show we watched together. You like him, don't you?"

"Colin Firth? Yes. Very much. What's not to like?"

Sierra made a face. "Not Mr. Darcy. My dad. You like my dad."

Like was such a bland word. Her feelings ran leagues deeper than that. She loved him with all her heart, for a hundred different reasons.

"Yes. I do. Your dad is a pretty wonderful guy." She decided to be honest with his daughter. "That still doesn't mean we're together. We have…kissed a time or two. But that's all."

Madi stopped near the goat pasture. "Really? Because last night, he told me I would have to get used to seeing the two of you kissing because he intended to do a lot more of it."

Madi stopped on the trail, her face suddenly on fire. "Did he?"

"Sierra."

At the chiding voice behind them, Madi turned to find Luke standing behind them, holding his vet bag, obviously on his way to or from treating one of the animals.

Why hadn't Sierra or the other volunteers mentioned Luke was here? He likely had been checking on Barney's injury.

She should have noticed his truck when she walked over, but she supposed she had still been in a daze when she walked to the shelter barn from the farmhouse, distracted by worry for her sister and still trying to wake up.

Now he was there, looking big and gorgeous and…rather mortified.

"What?" Sierra asked. "That's what you said, isn't it?"

He let out a breath, not looking at Madi. "Okay, yes. But

do you remember what else I said? I added that my intentions of kissing her were dependent on whether Madi wanted me to in return."

His daughter didn't even bother to roll her eyes this time, though her expression conveyed the same thing. "Again. I saw you both yesterday, remember? Believe me, she wanted you to kiss her."

Madi risked a glance at Luke, whose face still looked suspiciously pink. She could relate since hers now felt hot.

"Anyway," Sierra went on blithely, "the point is I'm sorry I acted like a brat yesterday. It won't happen again, I promise. I was just shocked. I told Dad this morning that I thought about it a lot last night while he was gone and decided that if he is going to kiss anyone, it should be you. You guys are basically perfect for each other. All my friends agreed when I told them."

"Um. Okay." Madi didn't know what else to say, fairly horrified that she and Luke had been the subject of discussion among Sierra's friends.

Sierra gave them both a mischievous grin. "How about I take the dogs to the exercise yard instead of a walk?"

Without waiting for an answer, she grabbed the leashes of the other two dogs from Madi and headed back in the other direction, toward the fenced area where the dogs could play and run.

Luke's thirteen-year-old daughter had effectively maneuvered the situation so they could be alone together. Madi had a feeling that had not been accidental.

He raked a hand through his hair, making it stand up in an adorable way that gave Madi a wild urge to smooth it down again.

"Sorry about that," he murmured. "She's thirteen. Apparently she's at a stage in life when she thinks everything should be like a scene out of a romantic novel."

"I'm not sure age has anything to do with it. I'm twenty-nine. I tend to agree with her."

He smiled at that. After looking around to make sure their only audience was the goats, he stepped forward and reached for her hands.

"I meant everything I said to Sierra yesterday. I would like to do much more of the kissing with you. Along with other things."

She was suddenly acutely aware of her curled hand, the brace on her leg, the mouth that didn't straighten completely.

"You know I'm not...perfect."

He squeezed her hands in both of his. "You might think that. I certainly don't. To me, you are *exactly* perfect. You're brave, smart, funny."

He paused, his gaze locked with hers. "You are also the woman I happen to love."

She stared at him as the words seemed to wrap around them both, twisting and curling them together into a delicious tangle.

"You don't need to look so shocked. It can't be that much of a surprise to you, can it?"

"Yes. Yes. It can."

Her words suddenly felt slippery as trout in a stream, flashing silver in the sunlight before disappearing. She couldn't seem to catch a single one.

His tender smile warmed her, healed places inside she didn't know were still scarred.

"I love you, Madi Howell. I don't know how or when it happened. Only that loving you feels perfect, too."

He brushed his mouth against hers with aching gentleness and she wrapped her arms around his neck, wanting to be nowhere else on earth than here, surrounded by the animals she loved and in the arms of the man she had been waiting for since she was fourteen years old.

"Tell me Sierra was right. That you wanted me to kiss you yesterday. That you want me to kiss you today."

"T-today and tom-morrow and next week and next month. And every single day after that."

Forever.

He smiled against her mouth. "Fine by me."

He had said the words and she felt she needed to say them in return, not out of any sense of obligation but because she wanted to.

"I love you, Luke. I've loved you for a long time. Maybe since the day you saved my life on the mountain. I didn't re-alize it until this summer."

What would his father think about them being together? She wondered as Luke kissed her again. Something told her Dan Gentry would be happy for them, thrilled that they eventually had found each other after all the pain and loss and sadness.

The thought of loss reminded her again of Ava and she felt momentary guilt for the joy bubbling through her with the healing, life-giving force of a mountain spring.

How could she be so happy in this moment when she should be grief-stricken for her sister's loss?

She was. She ached for Ava.

At the same time, since that summer fifteen years ago, she had learned that life was a jumbled, chaotic, beautiful mess of good and bad, sadness and light.

When these moments of sheer joy came along, those who had fought their way through the darkness only appreciated them more for the gift they were.

Luke kissed her, his mouth warm and tender on hers. Madi leaned into him, her heart overflowing. One of the goats bleated, Sabra brayed in response and a couple of dogs barked in the distance.

Madi surrendered to his kiss, grateful beyond words for her chaotic, exquisite life and the rare and precious joy she had miraculously found after weathering the storm.

Epilogue

Madison

ON A BEAUTIFUL AUGUST AFTERNOON, SIXTEEN YEARS after the summer that changed her life, Madi married her best friend in the small stone chapel in Emerald Creek.

The groom cried. So did the groom's mother, his daughter, his sister and the bride's grandmother.

Oh, and so did the matron of honor—the bride's sister— as well as the bride's six-week-old niece, Ava's newborn baby girl...until her father finally took her out.

Madi didn't cry. She was too filled with an incandescent joy that seemed to blaze through her as she said her vows to the most amazing man she had ever known.

Later, at the reception that followed in her grandmother's lush garden, she sat on a bench, holding Ava's tiny daughter, Sophia Beth Brooks.

"I don't want her to spit up on you in that beautiful dress," Ava fretted.

"I wouldn't care," Madi assured her sister, cradling the precious miracle more closely to her chest. "It's only a dress. Anyway, I think I've already got dog hair all over it from the pictures we took earlier with Sierra and all the fur babies."

Her fourteen-year-old stepdaughter, who had loved planning every detail of the wedding, for which she felt personally responsible, had insisted they needed a picture together with the three of them as well as Madi's two dogs and the two that Luke and Sierra were bringing into the marriage.

"They're all part of our blended family now, right?" Sierra had said with a grin. "Anyway, it will be adorable, since the animals brought you and Dad together and you both love them. We'll definitely post it on the socials for both the vet clinic and the animal rescue, but I also think we should have a print framed and hang it over the mantel at the new house."

Wanting a fresh start, Luke had sold the house he had purchased with Johanna, and together, he and Madi had purchased land next to the animal sanctuary. They were building their own house, a beautiful log home with windows that overlooked the mountains and acreage they eventually could use to expand the animal rescue.

"I don't need to ask if you're happy," Ava said now. "You're lustrous, Madi. I've never seen a more radiant bride."

"I didn't know I could ever be this happy. Why didn't anyone tell me?"

Ava smiled and Madi didn't miss the look she sent through the crowd, unerringly finding her own husband. "Believe it or not, when you pick the right person, it only gets better."

Madi reached for her sister's hand, moved by her sister's happiness. Ava deserved this joy and more.

More than a year after publication, *Ghost Lake* was still showing up on bestseller lists, this time in paperback form. She imagined when the movie came out the following summer, it would only generate more sales for her sister.

Ava had slowly managed to come to terms with her unexpected success. She quit her teaching job at the end of the school year, right before she had Sophia. To Madi's joy, her sister and her husband and baby had moved to Emerald Creek for the summer while he worked at the dinosaur dig again. Madi knew that in between caring for her newborn as well as their two rescue dogs, Beau and Gracie, Ava was writing another book.

She wouldn't share much about it yet, except to say it was fiction this time and would have suspense, danger and a healthy dose of romance, naturally.

Luke came over then, in search of his new wife.

"Here you are. I should have known you would be holding the baby."

"Either that or playing with a dog somewhere," Ava said with a smile. "Here, let me take her back. You two should go dance. What's the point of booking the Rusty Spurs to play at your wedding if you can't enjoy it? You can hold your niece anytime. How often do you get to dance with your brand-new husband on your wedding day?"

"Good point."

After kissing the baby's forehead that smelled of innocence and dreams, warm milk and whispered lullabies, Madi handed her back to Ava.

Luke pulled her to her feet and straight into his arms, where he kissed her with that stunning tenderness that still took her breath away.

As he led her out to the dance floor amid the laughter and the lively notes of the band, Madi savored the magical summer night, surrounded by all those they both loved, in this garden aglow with fairy lights and small lanterns hanging in the trees.

As she gazed into her husband's eyes, Madi knew their story would endure far beyond this dance under the stars.

★ ★ ★ ★ ★